dark orbit

dark orbit

Carolyn Ives Gilman

A Tom Doherty Associates Book

New York

This is a work of fiction. All of the characters, organizations, and events portrayed in this novel are either products of the author's imagination or are used fictitiously.

DARK ORBIT

Designed by Mary A. Wirth

A Tor Book
Published by Tom Doherty Associates, LLC
175 Fifth Avenue
New York, NY 10010

www.tor-forge.com

Tor® is a registered trademark of Tom Doherty Associates, LLC.

The Library of Congress Cataloging-in-Publication Data is available upon request.

ISBN 978-0-7653-3629-3 (hardcover)
ISBN 978-1-4668-2769-1 (e-book)

Tor books may be purchased for educational, business, or promotional use.
For information on bulk purchases, please contact the Macmillan Corporate and
Premium Sales Department at 1-800-221-7945, extension 5442, or write to
specialmarkets@macmillan.com.

First Edition: July 2015

Printed in the United States of America

0 9 8 7 6 5 4 3 2 1

dark orbit

chapter one

In the course of Saraswati Callicot's vagabond career, she had been disassembled and brought back to life so many times, the idea of self-knowledge had become a bit of a joke. The question was, *which* self should she aspire to know? The one she had left behind on the planet of Andaman nine years (and one subjective second) ago? Or the ones whose molecules she had left elsewhere, strewn across the Twenty Planets in a zigzag as detoured as her life? Since she was now comprised of an entirely different set of atoms than she had been a breath ago, could she really claim to be the same person?

"Welcome to Capella Two," said the technician. It was her cue to clear out of the translation chamber so he could assemble another migrant waiting in the queue. Too weary to think of a cheeky retort, she slid off the metal slab where she had been reconstituted and followed a sign into a waiting room of truly stunning banality. A medtech gave her a drink that tasted vaguely of mango, to restore her fluid balance, then left her to wait until they could be certain she was not about to have some actionable medical complication. The upholstery on the chairs was worn and splitting, the tile floor was so scuffed it had lost any color, the shuffle of travelers in and out was constant.

Traveling by lightbeam was not hard; arriving was the problem. She still had to steel herself against that feeling of having dropped into a bewildering future, jerked out of the continuity of time, out of step with everyone else. Even with endless experience, she still felt like an anachronism until she accounted for the years everyone else had lived, and that she had spent as a beam of clarified light.

It had been five years in her subjective time since she had left Capella Two. She struggled to calculate how many years in elapsed time. Twenty-three, she decided. Not a terribly long absence. But Capella Two was so addicted to change, so avid for every novelty and innovation, that twenty-three years here could be like a hundred on another planet. She supposed this was home, as much as any place was, since she was a graduate of UIC, and that would always give her an automatic entry card. But Capella did not arouse any patriotic loyalties or emotional attachments in her. Being Capellan was not so much an ethnicity as an attitude. You could carry it anywhere.

A technician who looked far too young to trust came by with a handheld monitor to measure Sara's heartbeat, brain function, and immune status, then gave her a vaccination update and waved her on. Down the hall she joined a line of new arrivals being processed through immigration. In line ahead of her, a teenage girl with skin dyed crimson and silver stared at her a few moments, then turned to whisper to her indigo companion. Sara recognized the evidence that she was a walking fashion antique. She would have to buy new clothes. Again.

When she reached the head of the line, the immigration agent gestured her to look in an eyepiece, where she was treated to a startling view of her own retina. "Magister Callicot?" the young agent said politely, studying the display on his terminal. Sara admitted it, though she never used the title. "UIC," he went on in a friendly tone. "Class of—Wow." His eyes widened at the date. He looked like he had barely been born when she had last left Capella Two.

"You'll need to pick up an identity chit at the security kiosk in the concourse," he told her.

"Identity chit?"

"Your security clearance," he explained. "It's got your arrest record, outstanding warrants, restraining orders, that sort of thing. Don't worry, all of yours are old as the hills."

She didn't know whether to feel reassured or insulted. After picking up her backpack, which had come through the low-resolution receiver, she stopped in a bathroom just to make sure that the lightbeam translator had put her back together right. She looked reassuringly similar to the old Saraswati—rangy, big-jointed body that had seen its share of misadventures; black hair in a braid down her back; long, lean face with deep parentheses on either side of her mouth and river deltas of wrinkles fanning out from her eyes. She had always considered her face a kind of practical joke on her. It was a reckless, generous, kind, unlucky face.

Sara had grown up in a Balavati family, which meant she had been taught to reject all articles of faith except disrespect for authority, the lodestone of her life. But it was hard to survive serial resurrection without entertaining thoughts of the perpetual cycle of birth, suffering, death, and rebirth. Nothing is constant but change, her Buddhist ancestors might have said. She understood it in her reduplicated bones.

The concourse was new—a bright mall bristling with surveillance cameras. The security kiosk was open but Sara ignored it on principle, since it seemed to represent authority. She stopped to withdraw some cash from an old account, but passed up the information vendors, relying on her old knowledge of how to get around Paratuic. As she neared the glass doors, the way was lined with protection franchises renting out weapons and electronic alarm devices, each claiming to answer calls faster and cheaper than the next booth.

Outside, the daylight had the familiar orange tone lent by the presence of the gas giant Gomb in the sky, but otherwise the landscape was strange. Sara stood staring at the distant gray mountains—the rim wall of an ancient crater, she realized. She was not in Paratuic.

"Looking for a security convoy?" a man in a uniform asked.

"What city is this?" Sara said.

The man's face took on that uniquely Capellan smile that meant *I'll help you for a price*. Nothing was free on Capella Two, least of all information. Sara paid the man, and he said, "You're in Onowac. They moved the waystation here twelve years ago. Been gone a while?"

"Yeah." With a sinking feeling, Sara realized she would have to buy some hotel information. "Listen, is there a Waster enclave nearby?"

The man looked silently helpful. More money changed hands. At least it was preferable to paying a corporation. "Sure. Join convoy three. They'll get you there safe."

At a price, no doubt. Sara waved away the offer to carry her backpack, and set out toward the convoy lines.

Convoy three turned out to be an overworked and sagging armored bus. The driver demanded Sara's identity chit, but was content with a few bills instead. Sara stared out the grimy window as the bus passed the razor-wire perimeter of the waystation into the city. The architecture of mercantilism had changed. Gone were the plate-glass windows showing off wares for sale, replaced by brick-faced stores with large-screen video displays to attract shoppers. As the bus waited at an intersection, Sara watched the larger-than-life image of a model undulate through a magically changing set of clothes and skin colors.

Sara got off the bus at an intersection where the driver claimed four hotels were located, though it took her several minutes to realize that their only street-level manifestations were registration machines behind sliding security doors. As she approached one of them, the slot on the wall lit up helpfully, INSERT IDENTITY CHIT. There seemed to be no way of speaking with a human being. It probably cost extra anyway.

The jostle of passersby had paused, leaving a conspicuous space around her. She looked up to see two alarmingly large men in nondescript business suits approaching her purposefully. She faced them, backpack to the wall. Their pockets had embroidered logos for WAC, one of the giant infocompanies.

"Saraswati Callicot?" the larger of the two said.

"Who wants to know?" Old Capellan habits came back fast.

"We're here to escort you to WAC headquarters," the man said.

"Why?"

"Delegate Gossup's orders."

Delegate Gossup. The title meant that Sara's old faculty advisor was on his way to becoming one of the most powerful men on Capella Two. "How did you know where to find me?" she asked.

The big man gave her a pitying look. "We work for WAC, ma'am."

That was the other side of an information economy: absolutely anything about you was for sale, at the right price.

The silent security man took her backpack, and the talkative one gave her a WAC logo badge with an embedded tracer chip. "Wear this. In case we get separated."

"What's all this security paranoia about?" Sara asked.

"Crime. Terrorism. They've been pretty bad."

"Have they thought about restricting weapons?" she asked mischievously. "It works on other planets."

The man didn't find it funny. "That would drive the security industry out of business," he said coldly. "Follow me."

Sara followed, dropping the WAC badge into an inside pocket. She was damned if she was going to walk around looking like a product.

They headed for the nearest public wayport. She had expected them to try to impress her by leading her in through the opulent WAC headquarters lobby, but what they did was even more impressive. While one security man stood by to discourage ordinary travelers from approaching, the other fitted a chip into the wayport controls, overriding its destination programming. There was a brief frisson of transubstantiation, and Sara stepped out into the private administration floor of WAC. It was a world of wood paneling and silence, all footsteps swallowed by the deep wine-colored carpet that seemed to silently reproach her Andaman mudboots. The security man led her down a discreet back hall to a door with inlaid malachite designs, and knocked. Then, without so much as a moment in a waiting room, Sara stepped in.

The office was restrained and elegant, decorated in geometric black and gray, with bonsai in recessed niches under grow-lights. One wall held the best window simulation Sara had ever seen, tuned to a picture of Capella Two itself, as if from high in a tower, looking out on a pinkish sunset cityscape. The man who rose from behind the black enamel desk matched the room: tall, impeccably cultured, serenely Vind. The carnelian caste-stone in his forehead was the only decoration he wore, if it was a decoration. His close-cropped hair had gone entirely silver, a sight that gave Sara a shock of surprise. He had always seemed immortal, unchanging, one of the few stable points in a flowing universe.

Banter—that was what she needed to counter the subtle intimidation of this setting. "Are you sure I should be here, Magister?" she said. "This place oozes oligarchy."

Delegate Gossup did not smile—that would have disturbed the

surface of his calm detachment. But he said, "Sara, welcome. It is refreshing as always to see you. And your timing is impeccable."

"Well, I'm glad something's impeccable about me," she said. The room was trying its best to make her feel scruffy.

"You are genuine as always," Gossup said, searching her face with a gaze like deep, still water. "That is a rare commodity here. Rare and valuable."

"I ought to open a franchise," Sara said.

Gossup gestured her to a seat on the settee. "Can I offer you a drink?"

Knowing who was paying, Sara tried to think of the most rarefied luxury she could imagine. "Single-malt whiskey," she said. "Neat."

The Vind's eyebrow went up a millimeter, but he activated the terminal in the coffee table and placed the order. A glass instantly substantiated in a niche next to her. Sara sank into the cushion facing the window. She saw now that little silvery fish were swimming in among the buildings of the city, and a giant jellyfish was rising into the sky. It looked perfectly natural.

"So, you're on the Magisterium now?" she said, emboldened by the golden glowing liquid slipping down her throat.

"For the past fourteen years. I was recently elected to the steering committee." There was no joy in his voice. It was no wonder he looked tired and aged.

"But you're still working for WAC?"

"Not at the moment. Today, I am acting on behalf of a . . . third party. WAC is providing some resources."

"And doing it very well," Sara said, stretching out her legs, savoring the comfort her well-used body felt. She had just noticed the almost subliminal sound effect of wind in pine needles. It made the room seem more spacious than it was. "Are you going to tell me who this mysterious third party is, or do you want me to guess?"

Gossup hesitated, caught off guard by such directness. In her place, another ethnic Vind would have probed subtly for half an hour, while he parried, without either of them coming to the point. "That depends," he said, "on whether you are going to accept the job I am going to offer you."

So that was what this was about. But the news only sharpened her curiosity: he could have offered her a job in a far less dramatic way.

With a show of weariness, she said, "What a trial to be so employable. I was actually hoping for some downtime."

"I take it you have not been in touch with the university yet."

There was something in his delicate manner that made her take notice. "No, why?"

"There was an unfortunate difficulty with the data you sent back from Andaman."

This time she did sit up. "What sort of difficulty?"

"Some of the ethnobotanical data you collected proved to have a high value for the pharmaceutical industry."

"No shit," she said, pleased. Visions of royalties danced in her head, perhaps lucrative ones.

"Unfortunately, there were certain interest groups on Andaman who claimed the information had been . . . improperly appropriated. They brought a cultural patrimony suit in the Court of a Thousand Peoples."

"That's ridiculous!" Sara said, stung at this slur to her professionalism. "I followed every protocol."

"Unfortunately, the paperwork was . . . not quite in order."

She had been meaning to take care of that as soon as she arrived home. It was not really out of order, just in a transitional state of creative chaos. But she had not expected the information to be truly valuable; that raised the bar on dotting i's and crossing t's. Sara downed the rest of her drink in a fiery gulp and set the glass down with deliberate care. "When does the case go to trial?"

"It was settled six years ago."

"Without my testimony?"

Gossup nodded. "It couldn't wait. WAC and the university lost a great deal of money. They had to return all the information you collected."

Five years of work, gone. Wasted. Even the time limit for appeals had expired. She wanted to protest, but knew it would be useless. It was the theme of her life: dreams snatched away just as they seemed attainable. She laid her head back against the cushiony leather and stared at the ceiling.

"Under the circumstances," Gossup said delicately, "WAC and the university are not eager to renew your contract."

"No, I guess not," Sara said dully.

"That is why I thought you might be receptive to another opportunity."

In fact, she could scarcely refuse, no matter how unsavory the job. She brought her gaze down from the ceiling to his face, and their eyes met for a long few seconds. Was he acting as her benefactor, or as an opportunist seizing advantage of the situation? She wanted to challenge him, to strike out at someone. But even so, she was the first to look away.

"Would you like another drink?" he asked politely.

"Yes," Sara said, against her better judgment. One always needed one's wits when dealing with Gossup, especially if negotiations were in order. But what the hell, she thought, I have nothing to negotiate with.

"Is it illegal, or just immoral?" she said.

"What?"

"The job you want me to do." Why else would he turn to a down-at-luck Balavati?

"Neither," he said smoothly. "In fact, I believe you may find it stimulating."

Bending over the coffee table terminal, Gossup activated a security shield. The background sound suddenly cut off. Sara felt static electricity on her hands and neck, and a prickle of alertness inside, despite the whiskey.

The words he said next changed everything. "It is not widely known yet, but we have recently received a communication from one of the questships."

It was something that only happened once a generation, if that. Centuries ago, the ancestors of humankind had sent out a fleet of robot questships in search of habitable planets to receive the seeds of the human diaspora. The origins of the grand scheme had been lost in the demise of Capella One; no one knew how many ships there were, or where they had gone. They crossed the desert of space in mute hibernation, communicating only when they had found something. It had been over a hundred years since a questship had woken from its slumber and called home, and everyone had begun to accept that there were none left to hear from.

"A new planet?" Sara asked. "A habitable one?"

"Yes," Gossup said.

"Inhabited?" For that was the great mystery: often the planets the questships found already supported human communities. Somehow, a first diaspora had taken place in a time so remote as to be lost to knowledge.

"We are uncertain as yet," Gossup said. "If the planet is inhabited, then it is at such a primitive stage that evidence of it cannot be detected from orbit. But we are inclined to be skeptical."

After soaring, Sara's hopes sank back. To be a member of a First Contact team would have been the reward of a lifetime.

"But the planetary system has other attributes that make it extremely interesting. You may recall from your elementary physics that some ninety-six percent of the universe is comprised of something we cannot detect."

"Dark matter—or was it dark energy?"

"Both. We can only observe their effects on the four percent of the universe we *can* see, but we know virtually nothing of their na-

ture. 'Dark matter' is a misnomer; it is probably not matter. It interacts with nothing we can see, except on the largest scale. You cannot
shine any light on it, because it interacts with no form of energy we
know. You cannot build a detector, because it does not collide with
normal particles. It casts no shadow on our world. Gravity is the only
reason we know it exists, for we can detect its cumulative warping
effect on the shape of space. But that tells us nothing of its nature.

"It seems that this new planet is embedded in a region of space
that contains an odd concentration of dark matter. We know this
because the light from a distant galaxy is very slightly bent, or lensed,
in passing through the space around this otherwise unremarkable
star. And also because the questship seems to have encountered
something on its approach—a gravitational anomaly which gave it
a good deal of trouble. We are still analyzing the data to reconstruct
the circumstances."

"But the ship is still functioning?"

"Oh yes. Its internal diagnostics indicate that it is quite intact.
A lucky thing, because as you might expect, the physicists are very
eager to get out there and begin their research."

Yes, Sara could imagine that. They would go, even though the
lightbeam receiver on the ship was centuries old, the ship itself in
questionable condition, the space around it full of anomalies. There
would be no shortage of volunteers. It was the mysterious power of
this driving will to *know*.

Knowledge is our wealth, our honor, our sacrament, Sara thought.
It drives us to give up family, home, and place in time for its sake.
Would we also sacrifice our lives, like ancient martyrs longing to
see the face of God? Is knowledge that sacred to us?

"Would you go, if you had the chance?" Gossup asked, and then
Sara knew the answer.

"Yes," she said.

"It is fifty-eight light-years away," he said.

Farther than any other discovered planet. A 116-year round trip to be deducted from her life. Exile—but exile on a new planet. "I'll still go," she said. "If you need an exoethnologist. But if there is no native population . . ."

There was a secretive look on his face, and she knew that was not what he wanted her for. "All right," she said, impatient with his Vind indirection, "what is it?"

"Epco won the contract and is assembling an expedition now—"

"*Epco?* You're recruiting for an Epco expedition? Is that the third party you're working for?" The rivalry between the two great info-companies, WAC and Epco, was legendary, and Gossup had always been on the WAC side. Come to think of it, they were sitting in the heart of WAC headquarters now. No wonder he had activated the security screen.

"No," he said. "The third party is . . ." He paused, searching for the right words. "Myself. I have a personal favor to ask."

Being able to do a personal favor for a member of the Magisterium was not a bad position to be in, not bad at all. Sara waited, afraid to ruin it with an incautious word.

"I have a young relative who is to be on the expedition team. She has been through a bad time recently, and I would like someone to be there to look after her, and keep me informed as to her well-being. Her name is Thora Lassiter." He glanced at Sara to see if she had any reaction to the name, but it rang no bells.

"What did she do?" Sara said.

"I beg your pardon?"

"Well, a Vind of the ruling caste—one of the Ral lineage, no less—being sent to the far edges of the universe . . . I'd say you were trying to get rid of her."

For a moment he looked like he was going to deny it, but then thought better of it. "She was an emissary to Orem when she suffered a health crisis, a mental breakdown. The place where she was posted was too primitive to diagnose her correctly; when she heard voices, they imagined she was receiving revelations from a god. In such isolation, she came to believe it, too. There was a mystical sect that embraced her as a prophet, creating a religious revival and a volatile political situation. You can find out the details if you are curious. Suffice it to say, there was turmoil and backlash, and we had to evacuate her in such a way as to convince the Oreman faithful that she was dead. Since then, she has undergone reconstructive treatment and is quite cured. But now we are in negotiations with the new Oreman regime, and her story complicates the diplomacy considerably. Altogether, it is safer and simpler to have her out of the picture."

"Wow." When Vind elites got in trouble, they *really* got in trouble. Sara already liked this renegade. She wondered if the woman herself had had any choice in the way the situation had been handled. Probably not; Vinds of that status were created to serve. Still, why didn't they just ship her back to their home planet of Vindahar? Sending her fifty-eight years into the future seemed a rather permanent way to get rid of a temporary problem. Almost like a punishment. Or a cover-up.

Sara wanted to know more, but she was not going to learn more by asking. It was extraordinary that Gossup had told her this much, and was willing to put her in a position to learn the rest, as he must know she would try to do. Any glimpse into the closely guarded world of Vind power politics was too enticing for a Balavati to pass up. Not to mention that scandalous information about a powerful family could be sold for a lot of money. Enough to finance a retirement.

Sara looked at her patron's face, silhouetted against the rosy ersatz sky. Could she betray him? She had always considered herself cheerfully amoral, culturally relative to the bone. Conscience needed to adapt; morality was contextual. Yet she had never had a temptation that really mattered. She had never owned information that could transform her from a gypsy outsider into a player, a person who could reach the levers of true power.

"Do you trust me?" she asked.

He considered carefully before answering. "I trust you to act in the way I think you will."

"And what's that?"

"If I told you, it would affect the outcome."

He was deep water under a glassy surface: an intricate mind, complexities turned in upon themselves. Perhaps betrayal was already part of his plan.

"All right," she said. "So what's my cover story?"

It turned out that her contract would be with the Magisterium, though only she and the director of the expedition would know that. Her secret reports would be sent by instantaneous transmission directly to Gossup; but in the meantime there would actually be some useful work for her. "Epco wants an independent observer to assess the internal dynamics of the research team," Gossup told her.

Hugely amused, Sara said, "I get to study the interactions of a bunch of scientists locked up together on a questship?"

"I thought it might interest you."

It was a topic she had some experience with. Exoteric science was her specialty. She had studied all sorts of scientific traditions— all but her own. "It's as good as a pass into the locker room."

With a warning glance, Gossup said, "Epco needs useful managerial analysis."

"I'll bone up on some management theory," Sara promised, but her grin belied her show of sincerity.

They settled on a handsome price for Sara's services, and Gossup gave her the name of the Epco recruiter who would accept her application without question. From now on, she would appear to be an Epco employee.

When Sara rose to leave, Gossup asked, "Where are you staying?"

She remembered the world outside then. It was easy to forget in here, cradled by wealth. "I don't know," she said. "The hotels seem to be requiring résumés these days."

"My secretary will get you a room," Gossup said. "Just give him your identity chit." Sara shrugged quizzically and held up her hands. Gossup shook his head with professorial impatience. "Sara, you can't go around arbitrarily disobeying rules. Some of them are for your own good."

"I didn't realize the planet had adopted universal surveillance."

"It's the price we pay for a free society. Here, give me your thumbprint and I'll get you a chit."

Hopelessly caught, Sara pressed her thumb against the scanpad.

Before long the security man returned, carrying her new chit and her backpack—probably well searched by now, Sara thought. As she was about to step out the malachite door, a tug of reluctance made her pause and glance back, her hand on the ebony doorjamb. It was then that it struck her: the interview had been stage-managed with a feather touch to manipulate her. All her life, Sara's declared persona had been as an iconoclast, a disputatious romantic, a brave enemy of elitism. She had studied the exercise of power in order to expose its flaws and inner contradictions, those channels by which to subvert it. And yet, in the end, access to the inner sanctum appealed to her immensely. It wasn't just the power; she savored the aesthetics, the refinement, taste, and civility. She enjoyed being in this patrician world—not *of* it, mind, not taken in—but as participant observer. And Gossup had known she would jump to seize the slightest thread of access to it. Every detail of this interview said so.

Sellout, she thought to herself. But it was without youthful rancor. Her patron was watching. "What is it, Sara?" he asked.

"I was thinking that I dwell in moral ambiguity."

"A fairer house than prose," Gossup replied obscurely.

"Maybe for you it is."

"I have not asked you to do anything compromising."

"It's not what I'm doing," Sara said. "It's knowing why I'm doing it."

chapter two

from the audio diary of thora lassiter:

Iris, they have called it: the rainbow planet.

It is an enigma clothed in light.

As we orbit over the night side, the world below is dark and featureless—none of the spider-web nets of illumination that humans throw across the faces of other planets. Then, as the ship sweeps toward dawn, the pageant of day on Iris begins. Random, rainbow glints appear out of the darkness, growing in number. As the sun rises, the continent ignites into a shimmering mass of light. It is like looking at a world encrusted in gems, glistening so bright you can see no coasts, no mountains, just an endless play of reflection. Dazzled, I watch it till my eyes water. When I look away, rainbows play across my vision, clothing the drab bulkheads in color.

Iris, my lovely, quicksilver planet, you hide who you are under a cloak of light. Just as I veil myself in false serenity.

Parts of me feel oddly alive, for someone they took such pains to kill. The curators packed my brain like a fragile trinket in a cotton batting of calm. To prevent my hearing those disembodied voices, they muffled everything—colors, pain, beauty. For weeks I floated a foot above the world, never touching down in the dirt of existence. I could observe, but not experience. Nothing was acute. But now I can feel a tingling inside, like limbs deprived of blood, waking. Underneath the blanket of calm, sharp things are clashing. I now think I have become a patchwork of dead and alive, a chimeric woman.

Perhaps something changed during the years that I flashed across the parsecs encrypted in a lightbeam. For the barest moment after I arrived here, a memory hung unformed, smokelike, in my mind—as if, somehow, I had been aware. In quiet moments, that memory still comes back to me, and I feel filled again with brightness. Light flows in pure currents through my body, until I shine, an illuminatus, a life-form made of photons. They tell me it is impossible, that I had no brain, and therefore could not think. And yet, all I am was in that lightbeam, every mistake and memory. I was still a human being, though reduced to pure signal. How could anyone be certain I didn't have a soul?

Light is supposed to illuminate, but on Iris it conceals. On the ship, we use light to carry all our information, but on the planet, light is a random babble. Up here, we trust it to encode our bodies in its clarified beams. Trapped in optic fibers, it is our docile servant, but down below us it rebels, it riddles with us, uncapturable. I want to escape into it.

▶   ▶   ▶

Sara was practically the last one to arrive aboard the questship. When she sat up on the slab in the translation chamber, she found that she was in zero-G, and would have pitched headfirst into the room but for the webbing. A strong, dry hand grasped her wrist and brought her back down to the slab.

The doctor—for that was what he was—handed her a squeeze-bulb full of electrolyte solution, and when she had drunk it he quickly performed a variety of simple neurological tests. Reflexes, coordination, sensation in the extremities. Gradually, Sara's body was coming back to her, connecting piece by piece.

Done, the doctor pocketed his instruments. He had blue eyes and a lean face under a trim gray beard. He looked like a man of quick intellect, ironic, competent. Sara liked him immediately.

"Welcome to the new century, Magister Callicot," he said. "Happy fifty-eight birthdays." He had a dry way of speaking, as if mocking his own words.

"Did you have to remind me?" Sara said.

He held out a hand. "David Gennaday," he introduced himself. "You're my last arrival today. Do you want to rest, or shall I show you the good ship *Escher*?"

It would have been Plantlike to act as if a mere lightbeam journey merited rest, so Sara said, "Sure, give me the tour."

The doctor launched across the room toward a hatch in what seemed like the ceiling when they started toward it, and like the floor when they arrived. Sara came to rest a yard from the spot she had aimed at, thrown off by the rotation of the ship. The polymer composite bulkhead she landed on was pitted as if by the bombardment of centuries.

"This must be one of the early questships," she said. "It seems old."

"Yes," he said. "They've had a devil of a time getting it running. We're pushing the endurance limits of the technology. It's a credit to the workmanship of the ancestors that the old fossil could be waked at all."

Sara had been aboard questships before, preserved as historic sites. They were all spindle shaped, like long accretions of crystals clumped around a central axis, but inside, each one was different. As the doctor led the way downward and outward from the hub, Sara began to understand why he had called this ship the *Escher*.

"The architect must have been demented," David said over his shoulder, "or he wanted to drive *us* that way."

The ancient designer had taken playful advantage of the fact that in the spin-gravity created by the ship's rotation, *down* was always the outside of the ship, which formed a 360-degree arc. Instead of tactfully hiding that disconcerting fact for the comfort of the inhabitants, the builders had left open atriums and skylights where you could catch seemingly impossible vistas of other residents walking on walls or drinking coffee at tables affixed to the ceilings. Not content with that, they had deliberately created rooms turned sideways, so that you walked on the wall with the ceiling lights to your right and the carpeting on your left; or they had distorted spaces to play havoc with perspective. As David and Sara walked along one corridor, the ceiling and walls suddenly converged, forcing them to exit through a door into another corridor that was slightly tilted from vertical.

So far, there was none of the individuality an inhabited ship acquires: no wall murals or friendly clutter of bulletin boards, no cartoons on the doors, no smell of personality. That would come soon, Sara thought. From the increasingly firm contact of her feet against the floor, she guessed that they had come close to the craft's perimeter, but it was difficult to tell, since no corridor was on any particular level.

The refectory was always the social center of a ship, and so David led the way there. "There are some people here you know— or at least, they know you," he said.

That didn't surprise Sara; in fact, she had expected it. The people qualified and willing to go on long-distance missions formed a strange sodality out of time, a troupe of intellectual hunters and gatherers. Outsiders derisively called them Wasters, and they called the rest of the human race Plants. For a Waster, time seemed like a mere convention—an arbitrary way of sorting events into a sequence, no more. Their lives consisted of fragments snatched from other people's histories, separated by long gaps of travel. Over and over, they outlived all they knew. Their homes were torn down between visits, their siblings became their elders, they would meet and strike up friendships with the descendants of people they had known. At every stop, they plunged into new trends, new attitudes, new inventions. They saw governments change, companies rise and fail. Each time they leaped off into the void it was an exercise in faith—faith that the equipment would still be operating to receive them at the other end, that people would still remember, that people would be there at all.

Sara had known Wasters who had tried to give it up. They became weary with the constant feeling of being out of synch, of having no cultural referents (or the wrong ones), of being strangers. They wanted to rest in one place for a while. But even that was hard. What did a Waster have to say to people who had never seen by the light of another star, who had existed in a single sequential time frame? To Plants, their own time, their own place, was of universal importance. Sara sometimes thought that planetary gravity warped the imagination, bent perspective till the horizon was uncomfortably close, and everyone had a uniform myopia. And so the Wasters would set off again, searching for places without horizons.

For others, time passed. For a Waster, it was always just *now*.

The door into the refectory was through a small closet, and positioned three feet above the floor. Someone had temporarily placed a stepstool below it, and there was a line of people waiting to get in and out. "We had a devil of a time finding it at all," David said.

Once inside, Sara paused, scanning to see who was there. People were scattered around the room in clumps at round tables. She had barely had time to take it in when she heard a menacing growl from a table by the back wall, and saw a familiar form rising from his chair—and rising, and rising, till he unfolded to his full seven-foot height.

"Touli!" she called out, waving.

With a forbidding glower, he started across the room toward her, attracting alarmed stares from other tables. Black as carbon soot, with a crown of hair matted into a solid mass atop his head, he still wore the orthodox *gbinja*'s tubular garment. He had put it on at puberty and would never remove it while he lived. It looked in better condition than Sara remembered it—but then, she had once had the duty, compelled by pure rebellion among her peers, of taking Touli aside and persuading him to bathe, *gbinja* robe or not. They had been pals ever since.

"So. You are still alive, heathen," he roared like heavy machinery. The Worwha Shana believed all races but themselves were on a swift path to eternal damnation. But Touli didn't hold it against anyone.

"I think you're older than me now," Sara said with some surprise. He had been barely out of graduate school when she had known him before—only seven years ago, in her life.

"You travel too much," he said.

"It keeps me young."

"It gets you in trouble."

So he must have heard about the Andaman debacle. She tried to put a devil-may-care face on. "Well, I'm temporarily out of trouble now and ready for more, if you are."

He bellowed—laughter, though not immediately recognizable as such. "You forgot—I *am* trouble," he said.

Sara and David followed him back to his table, where Ashok Chittagong was waiting, sipping his usual brew of poisonously strong green tea.

"Ashok!" Sara said, taking the chair beside him. "Thank God I'm not going to be the only discipline problem on board."

Like Sara, Ashok was Balavati. He looked the part: dark, brooding eyebrows, and a mustache and beard that framed his mouth squarely, like ancient images of the devil. Everyone knew that Balavatis were rebels who loved to undermine all hierarchy, and Ashok fit the description: he was fascinated with authority and all its susceptibilities. What people didn't know was that, to undermine hierarchy in truly creative ways, you have to understand it extremely well. The exercise of power was something Ashok absolutely rejected for himself, but analyzing it in others filled him with evil glee. His dilemma, of course, was that to study authority, he had to leave it strictly alone.

Sara had often told Ashok that he should have been an exoethnologist, but of course he rejected sensible advice. His training was in an arcane branch of particle engineering. He was the operator of the paired-particle communicator—the PPC, or pepci, as Wasters called it. It was their means of instantaneous communication with home base on Capella Two.

"So fill me in," Sara said. "What have you two been up to? Ashok, you look like you're at a wake."

Glumly, he said, "We didn't capture the first batch of paired particles for the pepci."

Pepci technology had not existed when the questships had been launched, so the equipment was always one of the first things sent out by lightbeam. The entangled particles that made the communicator work had to travel like lightbeams, through space, to be captured in a magnetic bottle on this end.

"They sent more than one packet, didn't they?" Sara asked.

"They were supposed to," Ashok said. "They were supposed to send more every two weeks for six months."

Of course, no one could phone home and ask, until they had the particles. Without a functioning pepci, they were isolated by a fifty-eight-year time lag. It was then that Sara realized, deep down, that she had never been so far from home.

To shake off the odd feeling, she said, "Oh, stop worrying, Ashok. Are you really in a hurry to find out that your grandchildren are older than you are?"

"Thanks, Sara. You're always such a comfort."

Touli was scratching his beard with a sound like steel wool on a rusty file. "I've been telling him, it might not be his equipment at fault. This is a strange part of space we're in."

"You people are just full of cheerful suggestions," Ashok said. "What you mean is, it might be a problem we can't do anything about."

"What are you talking about?" Sara asked.

Touli's specialty was gravity mapping, which normally put him in the geology department, but not this time. "We've been deploying a network of space-based gravitometers," he said. "The gravity map of this system is incredibly complex, but the gravity wells don't all match the distribution of matter."

"Is that because of the dark matter?"

Touli inclined his head in ponderous agreement, but only said, "Presumably. The physicists expected the dark matter to be clumped around the central star. No one thought it would be in linear streaks and pinwheels."

"That's bizarre," Sara said.

"You have no idea. We have cosmologists who are going to need counseling. Anyway, Ashok's particles could have been deflected by a close approach to a gravity hole we can't see."

Which gave Sara the uncomfortable thought that the same thing could have happened to her lightbeam. She didn't know if that were possible, and didn't really want to know.

"Did you show her the planet yet?" Touli asked David.

The doctor shook his head. "Saving the weirdest for last."

"You mean it gets weirder than this ship?" Sara asked jokingly.

All three of them nodded. Touli said, "Iris is tiny, just an overgrown moon, but its average gravity is the same as Capella's. On top of that, the gravity's not evenly distributed; there are heavy spots and light spots, and they don't match the terrain that the radars show. I'm not talking about the usual small variations in gravity caused by planetary mass; you would be able to *feel* these differences. It's as if there is a dark-matter planet that occupies the same space as the visible-matter planet, or some sort of dark-matter *structure*. We'll need to get down to the planet to know more."

And that was not where the strangeness ended, Sara found out as they continued to talk. Electric currents skittering over the planet's surface at first had made the physicists think they had been wrong in supposing it to be uninhabited, but the pulses were too random for power lines—more like weak horizontal lightning. The planet had no magnetic field strong enough to shield life from the solar wind, but strong local fields were scattered over the surface, polarities randomly oriented. Even mapping, usually the easiest part of a survey, had proved difficult. Iris, it seemed, was an escape-artist planet, resisting attempts to harness her in explanation.

Inevitably, the conversation exhausted the peculiarities of Iris and came around to Sara. Ashok said, "Don't take this wrong, Sara, but what the hell are you doing here? There is no native population, so why did they send an exoethnologist?"

Sara said, "Well, don't take this wrong, Ashok, but I'm studying *you*."

Touli guffawed, a truly frightening sound.

"I'm serious," Sara went on. "Epco is trying out some sort of new management strategy, and wants to know how well it works."

She had half expected the reaction she got, an eruption of cynical laughter.

"Trans-Methodism," Ashok intoned, mock evangelical. "Brothers and sisters, I have seen the light, and I say to you, throw off your blinders and embrace the new vision."

Sara said, "What are you talking about?"

It was David who answered. "See the Three Horsemen over there?" His eyes flicked at another table where three people sat stiffly, each one obviously unhappy with the identity of the others. "Those are our heads of science. We're not going to be discipline based, but method based. Our departments are Descriptive Sciences, System Sciences, Intuitive Sciences, and Corroborative Sciences."

"Corroborative?" Sara said.

"The people who are trying to combine scientific method with already-formed systems of thought, mostly about the creation of the universe. What a happy department that's going to be. They've lumped the animists in with the orthodox monotheists and the Gnostics. They're headed by that elderly gent who looks like he just swallowed a beetle and can't cough it up."

"You can't blame him," Ashok put in. "His belief system teaches that God is watching him every second, literally. Can you imagine the invasion of privacy?"

"Descriptive and System Sciences are both reason based, at least." David nodded at the man and woman in starchy lab coats, glaring at each other. "Each just believes the other is fundamentally misled. Descriptive is all the analytical scientists who classify and reduce to parts. System is the inductive reasoners who model relationships, patterns, and interaction of wholes."

"And—what was it?—Intuitive?"

"Some Vind too mystical even for Vindahar. We haven't seen much of her."

"Why do you think they organized it this way?" Sara probed.

It was Ashok who answered, this time mimicking a motivational speaker. "We've got a chance in a lifetime to rise above the narrow intellectual imperialism of the past. This is a cutting-edge, innovative plan to form trans-methodal teams to produce new thought-modes."

"What kind of word is 'methodal'?" David asked.

"A buzzword," Ashok answered, this time himself.

"Methodal. Sounds like a drug."

"That's what buzzwords are. Tranquilizers."

"Thought suppressants, you mean."

Sara wasn't nearly as scornful as her friends. Her specialty was the study of non-Capellan scientific methodologies. On one planet she had visited, they explored the nature of a thing by swallowing a sample and letting it pass through their bodies. Another culture composed songs from statistical data, with different harmonies implying different conclusions. She was rigorously nonjudgmental about it all. Now, she simply said, "Science used to be so simple when we were all empiricists."

David said, "Well, if we can't get everyone down to the planet pretty soon, my main medical problem may be homicide."

Sara looked around the room, thinking it was going to be interesting to be a fly on the weirdly tilted walls of this ship. The body language in the refectory was all self-consciousness and unease. Everyone was trying to figure out how the team skeleton would fit together. It was fluid so far; no one was locked in a role, and everyone was uneasy with it. They were assessing each other, measuring, trying out hierarchies and alliances in their minds. Who would be dominant and who subordinate? Where would the clique lines form? They were like the surface of a lake on the verge of freezing.

Just then a striking newcomer entered. He was tall, thin, ebony skinned, and held himself with a lofty hauteur—a prince in an Epco security uniform. As he assessed the room with narrowed eyes, half a dozen conversations faltered and the temperature seemed to drop.

"Our head of security," David whispered. "Dagan Atlabatlow."

"He's from Orem," Sara observed.

"No, he's not," the doctor said, frowning. "I've seen his file. He's Capellan."

"Maybe this generation," Sara said. She had been doing some rather recent research on Orem. "His family is probably Otlala. He'd have a tattoo on his upper arm."

From the doctor's expression, she knew he had seen the tattoo. "What does it show?" she asked.

"A knife impaling a snake. The snake is writhing back to bite the blade. Quite lurid."

"Quite aristocratic. That clan was known for its war leaders. They were nearly wiped out a century ago. His family must be refugees." She watched Atlabatlow say something into a lapel mike, then cross the room and sit alone at a table, straight as a steel ruler. She was trying to figure out whether his presence had any relevance to her other assignment, the secret one. "I wonder what he's doing working guard duty for Epco."

"Feeling it's beneath him, that's for sure," the doctor said. "But maybe that's normal. I don't know much about Oremen."

"They believe the closest relationship in life is between predator and prey."

David's left eyebrow went up. "What nice people."

A small, dark-haired woman in a monosex business suit entered the room, glanced at Atlabatlow, then followed his gaze to their table.

"The eye of Epco is upon us," Ashok said. "My friends, it's been nice knowing you."

"Who is it?" Sara whispered as the woman started across the room toward them.

"The Director's flunky, Penny Sutton."

When Sutton came up, it became clear that Sara was the one she had come for. She held out a hand without smiling. "Magister Callicot," she said gravely. "We have been awaiting your arrival. If you have time, the Director would like to see you. Now."

A little mystified, Sara rose and nodded to her friends. "It's heartwarming to see how you've all bonded, guys," she said. "See you later."

She followed her guide, wondering what the woman's real title was—Flunky was probably not it—as she traced a winding path down a ramp, around a hairpin turn, and through a hall where the walls were slightly akimbo. At last they came to a stop outside a massive door finished to look like it was clad in copper. Sutton pressed her thumb to a scanpad, and a latch clunked open. She opened the door for Sara to enter.

Inside was a carpeted antechamber that Sara recognized instantly as an imitation of the rooms of power on Capella Two. To someone who had not seen those rooms, it might have sufficed. But Sara instantly spotted telltale differences—a seam in the carpet, wood-grain laminate on the walls, and worst of all, in the recessed niche where an enigmatic artwork should have gone, a motivational poster showing an eagle rising with prey in its talons. This was not power, just ostentation. It said something to her that the Director had used scarce resources for office décor.

A pretty receptionist in a tight sweater sat alone behind a curved desk. She and Sutton seemed to communicate with a silent eye signal. The receptionist pressed a button on a console, said something inaudible to it, then rose and keyed a code into a pad next to another door. When the door opened, she showed Sara through, asking if she wanted anything to drink. Sara declined, and was left alone.

It was another waiting room. The only other door had no handle, so Sara did not try it. There was a fifty-eight-year-old Epco annual report on the side table, and a silver bowl of mints. She waited just long enough to make her wonder if she had been forgotten. Then the knobless door clicked open and Director Nelson Gavere entered.

He was a handsome man with expertly styled gray hair, a strong chin, and too-white teeth, wearing an expensively tailored suit. He shook Sara's hand with both of his, gazing solicitously into her eyes. "Magister Callicot," he said, "I hope you had a good trip here to the *Epco Explorer*. Please, come into my office. Did Leandra offer you a drink? Good, good."

The window simulation in his office showed Epco headquarters on Capella Two. He gestured her to a chair facing it, so that when they both sat, his head was framed by the administration tower.

"I want to make sure we get started on a good footing," he said, leaning forward so that Sara was afraid for an instant he would pat her knee. "I know the nature of your assignment, and I want you to know, I support it wholeheartedly."

"Thank you," Sara said, not sure what else to say.

"This is a showcase project. We have an opportunity to demonstrate how new management methodologies can achieve breakthroughs that our shareholders will profit from for decades. I expect great things from this expedition."

Sara realized that he was talking about her public assignment from Epco, not her private one from Gossup. He thought it was *him* she had been sent to observe. No wonder he was so ingratiating.

"I'm excited about the expedition myself," she said.

"Can I ask about the rubrics you will use to conduct your evaluations?" he asked.

"Oh, well, you know, we have customized metrics for assessing multiplatform work flows," Sara improvised.

He nodded as if he understood perfectly, and her opinion of him dropped. He said, "Well, if there is anything my office can do to assist you, be sure to let us know. My door is always open."

Sara hadn't seen an open door yet, but decided not to mention that. Instead, she said, "I haven't had a chance to view the planet. Where is the observation deck?"

"Sutton will show you," he said. "She's quite a sight, Iris."

He ushered Sara through to the first antechamber and told Leandra to summon Sutton. Then he shook Sara's hand with the other hand on her shoulder, and disappeared back into his office.

When Sutton appeared from another door, Sara said, "Really, all I need is directions—"

"No, he wants me to show you," Sutton said firmly, as if obeying to the letter were a matter of dogma. As they left through the brazen doors, Sara tried to make some aimless conversation, but Sutton answered only in monosyllables, so she gave up.

The observation deck was a bubble that projected out from the bow of the ship, turning so as to stay stationary with respect to the outside world as the ship spun behind it. Because it lay on the ship's axis, there was no gravity. By the time Sara passed through the circular hatch, leaving Sutton behind, she was already queasy from the transition back into weightlessness. Then she had to pull up short at the acrophobic sensation the room gave her. The curved floor, walls, and ceiling were all transparent. It gave Sara the impression of being suspended in open space. She closed her eyes and pressed her back to the door to regain her equilibrium.

When she opened them again, she realized that she was not alone. A figure was outlined against the stars, floating weightless in lotus position. The woman had turned to study Sara with dark, unblinking eyes set in seamless, golden skin. A river of straight black hair streamed back toward the clasp at her neck, interrupted by a streak of white at the temple, like rapids where black water stumbles and foams over a hidden rock. The caste-stone in her forehead gazed at Sara, still as the axis of a whirling world.

There was no doubt in Sara's mind that this was the person she was supposed to spy on. But at the moment she was concentrating on not introducing herself by vomiting.

"Hello," she managed to say.

"It helps if you look first at the stars," the Vind advised calmly.

Sara tried it, and found it did help anchor her. She still didn't let go of the door handle. "This is embarrassing," she said. "I'm supposed to be the sophisticated Waster who's seen everything and can't be impressed. Fact is, I've never spent much time in space."

"You'll get used to it," the other woman said.

"Sorry to barge in," Sara said. "I'm Saraswati Callicot."

"Thora Lassiter," said the Vind, confirming Sara's expectation. "You got here just in time."

"In time for what?"

"Sunrise," Thora said, turning back to the window.

The ship's bow was pointed at the planet. They had been on the night side, where Iris was only a dark circle against the stars. Now, a bright arc appeared, the outline of the planet's limb against the night sky. Seconds later, the sun edged over the horizon, a blinding-bright jewel set on a tiara. Irresistibly drawn, Sara let go of the door and floated forward, quelling the feeling that she was going to fall. Thora stared out fearlessly, completely absorbed.

As they orbited into day, the planet below became a shimmering mass of tinsel. The surface was a sea of reflections stirred by the wind. Sara had never seen anything like it.

"It's beautiful," she said, mystified. "But what makes it sparkle?"

Thora looked back, her face sidelit by Irislight. "Organic crystals," she said. "The dominant form of plant life."

"But—"

"It's a non-Terran biota." She turned back to the planet, a look of utter love shining through her mask of detachment. "Every other live planet we've been to was terraformed in the First Diaspora. Not Iris. This is independent evolution—a real alien ecosystem."

Trust Ashok and Touli not to mention this little detail, Sara thought. They were physicists; biology was a sideshow to them. As she absorbed the news, Sara frowned in puzzlement. "I thought the planet was habitable. How could it have an Earthlike atmosphere without Earth organisms?"

"We don't know yet," Thora said. "It's one reason we need to get down there soon."

Below them, prismatic gleams danced across the land. Out of the shifting mass of reflections, patterns formed, then dissipated. A thread of river appeared, a silver whiplash in the glitter; then it snaked sideways, and was gone.

"Did you see that?" Sara asked. "What makes those patterns?"

"We're not sure. Most likely, they're like parts in the planet's hair, that disappear when the wind blows a different way."

Sara had to look away from the planet. It had gotten too dazzling; little pinpricks of light danced before her eyes. She watched the light playing on her companion's face. "Are you a biologist?" she asked.

Thora tore her eyes away from the planet with an effort. "No," she said. "I have trained as a Sensualist."

"A sensualist, eh?" Sara grinned broadly. "Good, so am I."

"You are thinking of the ordinary meaning of the word," Thora said gravely.

"Sensualism's not ordinary to me. I practice it very seriously," Sara said.

"Sensualism is a philosophy of sensory perception," Thora explained. "Its basic tenet is that the human sensorium is capable of observing a greater range of phenomena than we normally realize. It's devoted to discovering new techniques of observation."

This hadn't been part of her briefing, but it was ringing a bell in Sara's mind. "From the planet Gammadis, isn't it?" she said.

A spark of animation lit Thora's face, for a moment. "You've heard of it? Its modern founder was a Gammadian philosopher named Prosper Tellegen, but it's much older—it goes back to Plato, really."

"So you're a philosopher?"

"A noncognitive researcher."

"Are there others in your department?"

"I don't know. Probably not."

Everyone else on board was linking up in social structures, but this woman must have been walking around in an envelope of oblivion. Sara wondered what the curators had really done to her. The woman's gaze was unnervingly direct and fixed; Sara felt like a specimen, or a bug about to be whacked.

"Have you traveled much?" she asked, to deflect the scrutiny from herself.

Thora didn't look away. "Never this far."

"The long journeys are hard," Sara said. "For a while, you go through a period of mourning for the world you left behind."

"Yes, I suppose that must be true," Thora said.

"But after a while, the Wasters become your family. You detach from sequential time and join the gypsies who live like stones skipping across the surface of history."

"Yes."

Thora's eyes hadn't moved, but her mind seemed to be elsewhere, studying something Sara could not see. It was odd; from the files, Sara had expected someone more unorthodox and strong-willed, not this serene sleepwalker. Another wave of nausea threatened her poise. Since it was hard anyway to keep up a conversation with someone who had mentally left the room, Sara held out a hand and said, "Well, I've got to go find my berth. See you around."

"Yes," Thora said, shaking her hand.

Sara glanced back when she reached the hatch, but Thora was only a black silhouette against the dazzling planet. She was staring outward again at the light.

from the audio diary of thora lassiter:

I know the Magisterium must have sent someone here to spy on me. They are angry and guilty, a dangerous combination. Angry because I disgraced them, guilty because they cured me against my will. I have not spotted the spy yet, though I have my suspicions. But then, suspicion is my nature.

In the Vind language we have only a single word for both "strength" and "weakness"—nkida. But in the union of two opposite meanings, a new one is born, for nkida can also be translated as "power source." A person's most abiding flaws are also the driving forces of her personality. A practitioner of the mind-body disciplines of apathi will seek to develop those flaws, draw strength from them, and explore their nature.

My cousin Bdiwa Ral had known me only two weeks when she looked at me and said, "I know what your first nkida is: inability to trust. That is what you must cultivate."

She was right, of course, though I argued for a long time that it was simply a rational response to the world. I thought then that she was criticizing me for lack of trust, but no—it was my nkida, a thing I could never overcome, and should not want to. Unacknowledged, it could destroy me. Developed, it might still destroy me—but it could also lead to focused, disciplined power over myself and the world around me.

To others, my nkida manifests as aloofness when I am not in control of it, judiciousness and even mysterious authority when I am. But to me it means a life sentence of isolation. All my life I have observed people forming communities wherever they are thrown together, as if it were part of their nature. It is a skill even children possess, but not me. My shipmates here have been forming bonds and groupings, on what bases I am not sure. Today, an artless Balavati woman spoke to me of friendship and family. I envied her ability to offer spontaneous friendship to a perfect stranger, and felt suspicious of her motives for doing so. This was my nkida out of control. She was so perfectly unreflective that you could see straight through her, and there was nothing hidden inside. I longed to be like her, even as she left in discouragement.

I think friendship may be nothing but the ability to trust someone enough to put your happiness in their hands. If my discipline stays strong, it is a feeling I will never know. But if ever I do, then I will lose my power, and become like all the other content, unmindful people, ordinary and undriven.

I need to record this now, while it is still fresh in my mind. Eyewitness accounts are unreliable, because the senses are unreliable, but *memory plays havoc even with the shards of truth that come through to us untouched. So, before memory has distorted everything, let me set this night's events down.*

It started with a dream. I stood in an empty white corridor, in a part of the questship I had never seen. The ship was larger than any of us had realized; it stretched for miles into space. Behind me lay the familiar, inhabited part we had begun to make our home, a tiny human outpost in the immense structure we had not yet discovered. Ahead, everything looked sterile, scoured clean. It was perfectly silent. Not even my footsteps made any sound, and when I knocked on a wall as an experiment, I felt the impact on my knuckles but heard nothing. Vacuum, I decided. The air had all escaped from this part of the ship. I would have to be careful not to fall through any holes into space.

Moving forward, I passed empty, branching corridors. It was a perfect maze, acres of it—but what was its purpose? Doors began to appear, but all were locked. One of the doors was cold to the touch, and something was moving around behind it. I felt dread at the knowledge that I was going to open it. I did not want to, but it was the logic of the dream. As I touched the door the lights in the corridor failed, plunging me into gray dimness. The door fell open, but I could not see what lay inside. All I knew was that something had found me. I turned to flee, but now I had to grope my way forward, torturously slow, unable to see. I strained on, propelled by panic, desperate to find my way to the parts of the ship I knew.

A sickening ripple passed through my body, and I woke. The bed under me was shuddering. But was it me that had jerked, or the ship? "Lights!" I ordered, and they immediately came on, showing me the inside of my tiny berth. It looked oddly distorted, just as it had before.

With the dream still vivid in my mind, I listened to the soft breathing of the ventilation. When I had fallen asleep only a little while before, the man in the berth next to mine had been talking and mov-

ing around, as he often did. I did not know his name or position, just his nighttime habits, which at first had disturbed me. But I had studied my own reactions and now the sounds he made were familiar enough to be soothing. He was silent now. I got up and pulled on a robe, then opened the door.

The berths are arranged in pods of five, all opening onto a shared relaxation area. When I first arrived aboard I chose a berth in a deserted pod, but it had gradually filled up around me. When I stepped out, the lights were already on in the common room but no one was there—an odd thing, since the lights are activated by motion sensors. I looked at the door next to mine, and felt an uncomfortable fullness in my throat. A dark pool was seeping under the door, staining the carpet. I knelt beside it, but could not tell what it was, so I touched it. On the tip of my finger, it was red.

I quickly crossed the room to the on-ship comlink. "Security," I said, and it connected me. "I think you had better send someone down here." My voice was weirdly calm in my own ears. "There may have been an accident."

Then I faced a choice: to open the door or not? The dream was still thick in my head, clogging my usual responses. I had no desire to see what lay beyond the door. But what if I could be of some help? So, unwillingly, I crossed the room and tried the door handle. To my relief, it was locked. I knocked, but there was no response.

The first to arrive was Dagan Atlabatlow, the Oreman head of security. He took in the situation at a glance and radioed for backup. Then he used a security pass to override the door lock. When he opened the door, a sluggish pool of blood that had been backed up against the door flowed out. Inside, the body crumpled on the floor was wearing a security uniform. Its head was missing.

As the pod filled, first with security, then with medical personnel, I took a seat on the other side of the common room and focused on my dova, my center of gravity, hanging like a plumb bob inside me. It is one of the first exercises they taught me on Vindahar. It turns a person's face into an impenetrable, blank sheet. When a security man sat down to take my statement, he frowned and commented, "You don't seem very upset." I gazed at him till he looked away.

In truth, I felt a distance from the event, the stance of witness rather than participant. Perhaps it was the medical treatments, or the fact that I feel sure I have seen such a thing before, though I cannot call to mind exactly where. I watched Atlabatlow direct the investigation with the hungry intensity of a stalking panther. He never raised his voice, but everyone who came within the field of his concentration instinctively mimicked him. He almost had the look of a man in love—and in a sense, so he was, for whoever had committed this brutal act was now his prey.

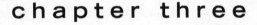

chapter three

News of the murder spread through the ship at the speed of rumor, casting sinister shadows everywhere. In the first terrifying hours after the discovery, people gathered spontaneously in the refectory to talk in intense little groups. But the comfort of being together was offset by the knowledge that the murderer could only be someone still on board.

Two grisly facts stoked the panic and claustrophobia: the pointless violence of the act, and the missing head.

"Sheared clean off, as if with a cleaver," the doctor told Sara in an undertone when she pumped him for information. "Even a particle weapon would have left some trace."

"So you think someone's got a trophy?" Sara asked.

"Let's just say I'm being careful when I open closet doors."

You could always trust David for some gallows humor. From him, Sara also learned the other puzzling aspects of the incident: how the door had been locked from the inside, that the only fingerprints on the door had been the victim's and Thora Lassiter's, and the absence of any sign of a struggle. "He probably never even knew what hit him," David said.

"Who was he?" Sara asked. So far, no one she asked had known the victim.

"One of the security guards," the doctor said. "Nothing in his record to make him stand out. So far, we haven't found a past history with anyone on board, other than his boss."

"It makes you wonder if he was chosen randomly." Sara voiced the fear that was spreading like contagion through the halls.

"Or whether the assassin got the wrong room," David said with a significant look.

That had occurred to Sara, as well. It seemed curious that the attack had taken place in a berth next to the only person aboard with the connections to make her a political target. It made Sara's curiosity flare all the brighter: what had Thora Lassiter done, and who had she done it to?

"It seems crazy," she mused.

"What?"

"That anyone would bring a grudge fifty-eight light-years to settle."

"People can be strange that way."

Sara noticed several things about the staff reaction to the crime. First of all, everyone got a little sentimental. The day after the incident, Director Gavere called a convocation of the entire staff in the lecture hall, the only room large enough to hold everyone. He did well, since his speech was full of conventional compassion. Listening, Sara realized that everyone had needed a homily infusion. Familiar words deflected the panic and confusion, making the situation seem more normal. Due to the number of belief systems aboard,

Epco could not sponsor any overtly religious memorials for the dead man, but the Director's secular sermon satisfied all but the most hard-bitten rationalists.

The second reaction was that the faculty became unusually tolerant of authority. Ordinarily, scientists and security formed a combustible mix, but now guards visibly patrolling the halls in their gray-and-maroon uniforms were accepted as a reassurance, not a provocation. Nor did anyone object when an announcement went out that there would be a search of the entire ship, personal quarters not exempted.

But though every nook and cranny was supposedly inspected, neither murder weapon nor head was found. As the days passed without progress in the investigation, amateur theories metastasized underground.

"What can be so hard about finding the culprit?" Magister Sarcodan asked as several of them sat talking over bags of beer. He was head of Descriptive Sciences; he had a black beard and a booming voice that made it easy for him to win arguments with sheer volume. In a bar he could be genial company, but his alpha male behavior gave Sara an unbecoming urge to disagree with him even when she was on his side.

"After all, there's a limited pool of suspects," he continued, "and they have all our personnel files."

"Yeah, you'd think they'd do a database search for all the psychopathic killers," Sara said.

The magister didn't acknowledge the sarcasm. "The number of people who had motive, means, and opportunity can't be that large. Why not just eliminate all the ones who were accounted for at the time of the killing? All it takes is some deductive reasoning."

"I'm sure they will appreciate your explaining it to them," said Sandhya Prem in her inconspicuous way. Sara had learned to respect her. She was head of System Sciences, a woman who cultivated a mousy image to hide extraordinary intelligence. Right now, her limp brown hair was pinned back with a paper clip. Her sharp humor was mouselike too, darting out from dark corners. As a rule, you only saw it out of the corner of your eye.

"Some people are saying the security guard wasn't the real target," Sara let drop, to see where it would take the conversation.

"Oh right, our Vind celebrity," Sarcodan said. "Well, if anyone is out to get her, it would be that Oreman they've got in charge of security. The whole affair gave his planet a black eye."

"He's from Capella," Sara said.

"Well, even so."

"I was traveling while that episode went down," Sara said. "What happened?"

But the magisters knew even less than Gossup had told her. The public version was that a radical Oreman sect had taken Thora hostage, and Capellan authorities had been forced to extricate her. There had been hints that she was brainwashed to collaborate with her captors, but nothing about a mental breakdown.

The ship's tension would have continued to fester unresolved, except for two pieces of good news that came almost simultaneously. Ashok and his technicians finally managed to capture a packet of paired particles to get the pepci working, and the planetary shuttle was declared fit for duty. Instantly, everyone's attention was refocused on a mission to the planet.

Ordinarily, First Contact missions were long, slow, and meticulously planned to avoid introducing the native population to culturally inappropriate technology or information. But Iris's uninhabited state simplified matters immensely. It would be possible to ferry an exploring expedition down with all its equipment at once.

Word spread that a meeting of the department heads had been called to plan the first foray to the planet, so Sara tested the Director's promises by sending a memo asking to observe the meeting. To her delight, permission was granted.

They met in a trapezoidal room with a window simulation set

to show the Epco logo. The Director went around solicitously shaking everyone's hand, then took his seat at the head of the table. At his right side sat Dagan Atlabatlow, an ebony carving in uniform; at his left sat Penny Sutton. She had on a headnet that was recording her visual and aural perceptions of the meeting for the record. The others at the table were the four department heads. Sara sat beside Thora Lassiter and received a serenely opaque greeting.

"I have asked Colonel Atlabatlow to draw up a plan for establishing a base of operations on the planet," the Director announced. "Colonel?"

The Oreman rose and pressed a button transmitting a document to the screens recessed in the table in front of each of them. Sara leaned forward to see her copy. It was a fantastically detailed threat assessment. As she looked at it, her impression of Atlabatlow gelled suddenly: he was one of those second-generation immigrants who claw their way up by conforming—a militantly by-the-rules man. She glanced at Thora to see her reaction, and found her watching the man rather than the document.

He proceeded to talk them stiffly through each major area of potential danger—toxins, microbes, radiation, fauna, and of course the unknown. Conspicuously missing was the danger from each other.

"This is the action sequence to be followed. Only four of our human assets will ferry the shuttle down to the planet—two pilots, a security professional, and a lightbeam technician. This is partly to maximize cargo capacity, and partly to reduce risk exposure. The shuttle's manifest will include a lightbeam receiver mechanism suitable for subsequent transport of personnel. Once on the planet, the security agent will conduct safety assessments. When his review indicates an acceptable level of risk, an additional six investigators and three security personnel will go down via lightbeam to commence their studies of the planet, using the shuttle as a base."

"Six!" Sarcodan said, dumbfounded.

"It is the maximum number whose safety we can assure, initially," the colonel said. "It provides one slot for each department, plus two to be chosen by the Director."

"How long will 'initially' last?" Sarcodan demanded.

"That will depend on what we encounter."

"I want a number. A day? A week?"

"I cannot make a commitment."

Sarcodan turned to the Director. "This plan is paranoid."

"It's the plan we're following," Gavere said. His tone was meant to shut down discussion, but Sarcodan did not pick up the signal.

"We came here to do research—"

"Safety is Epco's number one priority."

Sarcodan subsided, smoldering.

They then turned to a discussion of the research proposals that the scientists had brought. Prem's staff were going to create a computer model of the planet's ecology and run it back in time to see how it had evolved. They needed to start by gathering data on the ecosystem and its adaptations, if any, to the dark matter clusters. Sarcodan's scientists had zeroed in on several "anomaly islands" in the gravitational patterns that they wanted to investigate with sensors and monitors. They had picked out a landing site close to one of the anomalies.

Sri Paul Niyama was representing Corroborative Science in place of its department head, who was observing one of his days of ritual isolation. Paul was a willowy young man with a gentle, self-effacing air and a youthful face under bobbed black hair. He gave off a heady aroma of earnestness. "We wish to search for some aspect of consciousness on Iris," he said. "If we find no conscious organisms, it would be strong evidence for the centrality of human beings in the universe, as many creation theories predict."

Last, the Director called on Thora to present her proposal. Hesitating a moment, she said, "I can't give you a proposal, because I don't know what I will discover until I discover it."

After a moment of silence, Sarcodan said, "Well, we can certainly use the extra opening in the roster."

"No, I wish to go down to the planet," Thora said.

"What for?" Sarcodan pressed.

"I want to supplement your efforts with other modes of observation. You will be investigating with your own techniques—with instruments, and classification, and rational analysis. My only experimental device is consciousness itself. I want to use myself as a sensor—to observe, record, and accept without hurrying to conclude. I am hoping to reach insights that objectivism can conceal."

"Doesn't this belong in the Corroborative Sciences Department?" Prem said. "I don't see the distinction."

"The corroborative scientists are defending beliefs," Thora said. "Sensualism is not a belief; it's a method."

"Not a scientific one," Sarcodan said.

Thora didn't react defensively. "I'm not criticizing your methods. You learn vital things by abstracting yourselves from the world, and viewing it from without. The hypothesis I am testing is that the human mind is sensitive to a wider spectrum than we suspect. It senses things we have never categorized or named, things we have never studied, whose origin we are unsure of, and whose meanings we don't know."

Sarcodan turned to the Director. "Prem's right. There is already a department for religion. We don't need two."

"Did I mention religion?" For the first time, Sara heard in Thora's voice an edge of steel.

"That's where you're going, isn't it?" Sarcodan said. "You want to meditate on the unknowable. Well, science denies there is anything that can't be known. Only religion revels in mystery, in order to reserve a place for God."

"It is unscientific, wouldn't you say, to deny that there are things we don't know?"

"We're not going to learn them by—what is it you want?—merging with the planet's emanations?"

"All right, all right," the Director interrupted. "This has been a good theoretical discussion, but we have to move on." He looked impatient, as if at trivia. "I think Epco would want us to be tolerant of a variety of cultural traditions, wouldn't you say?" He was looking at Sara, as if trying to guess the right answer.

"Oh absolutely," Sara said. "Epco's all about tolerance." She hoped lightning wouldn't strike her.

Sarcodan was looking as if he suspected she and Thora were in cahoots.

"Well then," the Director said, relieved, "it's decided. Magister Lassiter will go as planned. Anything else?"

The scientists started haggling over which departments would get the remaining two slots. The Director cut off the discussion. "I will be making those assignments," he said. "Magister Callicot will also be on the team, as observer. And Mr. Gibb will record the expedition for transmission back to Capella."

Sara instantly saw the logic of his choices: the person with political connections, and a publicist. It made crystal clear the role science would be playing. Ordinarily, it would have galled her as much as it clearly did the scientists, but she was enjoying the novel feeling of being one of those rewarded because of politics rather than deserts.

"There is one last order of business," Director Gavere announced. "As you know, the paired-particle communicator will soon be operational, and we will have real-time contact with Capella Two. We will be instituting some temporary procedures for the staff to follow. Penny?"

Sutton transmitted a policy memo to everyone's screen. "You will each be responsible for communicating this policy to your staffs, and explaining it to them. Essentially, all communications with Capella must be submitted in advance, and will be transmitted as time becomes available. Only department heads will be allowed real-time conversations with headquarters. Until further notice, we are asking everyone to omit references to the recent . . . *incident.* This is to avoid compromising the investigation. Your cooperation will be appreciated."

There was a shocked silence for several seconds. Then Prem said, "This is not going to be popular."

"We understand that," Sutton said, "and we would not insist if the security situation did not call for it."

"How can keeping the crime secret benefit the investigation?"

"I did not say it would benefit the investigation. I said it would avoid compromising it."

By preventing Epco headquarters from getting concerned about it, of course, Sara thought.

When the meeting was over, Prem and Sarcodan met in a hallway huddle out of sight of administrative eyes. Sara would have joined them, but for the suspicious glance Sarcodan flashed at her and Thora.

"I guess we are *vermin du jour,*" Sara said to Thora.

"They are uncomfortable with Sensualism," Thora observed, unruffled. "I am used to it. Did you notice how quickly he got to God? There are people for whom whole categories of knowledge are off-limits because they can't be objectively explored, so the objectivist can't imagine any possible explanation but a religious one."

"Maybe a god scared him when he was a child," Sara said irreverently. "Now he's phobic about them."

"It doesn't matter," Thora said. "As soon as we are on the planet, everyone will forget all this."

That nightshift, Sara suborned Ashok Chittagong into a conspiracy. It was, of course, easy.

The PPC room lay in one of the technical sections of the ship, close to the ventilation and heating systems, and remote from the habitations. At the off-hour when she had arranged to meet Ashok, only a skeleton staff was on duty in this isolated section, and the empty corridors were dimly lit to save energy. She realized how edgy recent events had made her when she heard whispery footsteps down a darkened side hall, and whirled around, fists clenched. She thought she glimpsed some movement in the shadows, but the more she stared the less sure she became.

"I think we've got rats," she said to Ashok when she joined him in the tiny, warm control room crammed with equipment.

"I could have told you that," he said.

"I don't mean the human variety."

"Oh."

He had gotten the PPC operational earlier that day, and a steady stream of news had been coming through ever since, much of it personal messages going straight into the mailboxes of the staff. Tomorrow, people all over the ship would be waking up to find parents dead, children married, homes sold in their absence—Wasters went through it again and again.

"What can I do for you?" Ashok asked.

"I need to send a private message the Director's office can't find out about."

"Hmm." Ashok stroked his beard, looking like a casino gambler. For a moment Sara worried that he was thinking about the ethical problem, but it turned out to be the technical problem his attention was on. "I'll have to falsify the time codes, or fake a little breakdown. Do you have the message ready?"

"No. Can I compose it here?"

"Sure. You realize we can only send text so far, right? Until we get a few more packets of particles, this is only a step above smoke signals."

"Okay." Sara sat down at a console to compose her message to Gossup, including the news Director Gavere had explicitly forbidden them to pass on. In the meantime, Ashok was busily falsifying the communication log.

When Ashok told her to press the Send key, she obeyed, wondering if Gossup would even be alive at the other end, and whether her assignment would have died with him.

"I assume that if there's an answer, you'll want that hidden, too?" Ashok said.

"Right. I'll wait a little to see." If he was dead, she would probably get an automated response.

As they waited, the room buzzed quietly, and imaginary prickles chased across Sara's skin at the thought of the powerful electromagnetic fields around them.

"Where are the paired particles actually kept?" she asked to fill the silence.

Ashok laughed. "That's a question that'll start a fistfight at a physicists' conference. The magnetic bottle is just beyond that wall— but whether the particles are there, who knows?"

She understood what he meant. The physicists spoke as if they had created two entangled particles, born and split in the same instant, that continued to influence one another across whatever distance separated them. But in fact, it might be that they had only separated two aspects of the same particle, existing simultaneously in two spots, and resonating back and forth. To detect the particles directly would destroy the effect by freezing them into existence in one spot. Until then, they had only potential existence in both spots. In this unresolved state it was possible to use them to communicate by observing their indirect effects on the magnetic field around them. But the magnetic bottle was like Pandora's box—a thing they were forbidden to peek in for fear it would make their particles real.

Sara gazed at the wall beyond which she imagined the paired particles trapped. In some unknowable way, the space inside the magnetic bottle *was* on Capella Two, because the particles' longing to be whole was so strong it could collapse distance itself. It was one of the tragic drawbacks of being human that the longings of people could never have that kind of power.

"Hang on!" Ashok exclaimed, taking his feet off the table as his monitor lit up with the seal of the Magisterium. "Someone wants to talk to you."

"Right now? In real time?"

"Yeah, you'd better sit over here."

Sara moved to the other console and hit a key to indicate that she was there.

It was Gossup himself, still alive, though his letterhead indicated he was now executive delegate of the Magisterium. The words appeared one by one. "I was very pleased to hear from you, Sara, though your message has caused me some concern." It was disconcerting to think that he was writing at this instant, fifty-eight years since she had last spoken to him.

"Can you offer me any advice?" she typed back.

"I fear that an act I intended as conciliatory has been seized upon as an opportunity for mischief," he said, uninformatively. "The incident you refer to may even have been intended as a message to me."

"Who would wait all this time to send a message?" Sara asked.

"We are dealing with people whose time frame is in the centuries."

"WHO?" Sara banged at her keys.

"Have you observed any symptoms of relapse in our mutual friend?"

"No. Answer my question."

"I will be in touch. It might be best if you did not mention my name to anyone there. Please be careful, Sara."

The Magisterium seal appeared again, signaling the end of the conversation. "Damn!" Sara exclaimed.

"Well, well," Ashok said. He was leaning against a stack of electronics, arms crossed. Sara realized he had been reading over her shoulder. "Studying management theory, my ass. I should have known you were up to something underhanded."

"Except I really suck at it," Sara said. "You're not supposed to know."

"That little conversation took almost seventy seconds. You realize how hard it's going to be to hide that?"

"You're a prince, Ashok. I know you'll find a way."

"You want to tell me why I'm risking my job?"

"I can't. I'm sorry. To tell the truth, I'm not even sure."

"This is the disadvantage of getting mixed up with Vinds."

"It's not just the Vinds. It's getting mixed up with power."

"Same thing, isn't it?" Ashok said dourly.

from the audio diary of thora lassiter:

Is discovery impossible, or only implausible? That is what I wonder.

We wait here, circling above our heart's desire, caught in a paradox: to discover something new, we must understand it, yet the very act of understanding changes the thing we observe.

To perceive, describe, explain: these are the essence of discovery. "I do not know" does not constitute learning. And yet, what happens when we encounter something so genuinely outside our previous experience that we have no mental categories for it, and the only truthful statement is "I do not know"? Why, we liken it to something we do know, however bad the analogy. We apply to it rules that lie within our experience. We resist incomprehension as reflexively as we recoil from pain.

Only gradually, if all goes right, does the new information start to soften our mental walls, so that we can begin to perceive what we have encountered. But often by that time it is too late: we have so misconstrued the unknown that our learning is flawed forever. What was truly new is now just a subcategory of the old. Perhaps it is the only way

we can learn, an anatomical limitation. We are organisms evolved to
destroy unfamiliarity by the act of understanding it.

I think of my companions, the argonauts of Iris, and wonder how
their expectations will affect the planet. Our first impressions will shape
our second ones, and those will shape the expectations of whoever
comes after, till the planet is remade in our image forever. Are we the
proper people to remake Iris? Do we carry with us desires like viruses
that will infect the planet, and kill off the fragile truth?

None of us has the qualifications to be first to witness a new world.
But who does? It is not a skill you can learn, for who could teach it?
All I know is, we are embarked on a mission of invention, and what
we find will say as much about us as it does about Iris.

► ► ►

On the day when the shuttle was launched, all activity on the questship came to a temporary halt, as people gathered around monitors
to watch. A great deal depended on one cranky old machine that
had spent a few centuries in mothballs, since if the shuttle were lost
there was no other simple way to get the lightbeam receiver onto
the planet.

On the feed from the copilot's headset, they watched the shuttle dip into the atmosphere. Sound came back, bringing the sense
of velocity entirely missing in space. Soon the elemental roar of air
on the hull drowned out all but the dry, crackly exchanges of the
flight crew. Outside the window, the sky gradually brightened to a
startling aquamarine above the sparkling land. Suddenly the horizon tilted, as the craft banked to approach the landing site. Jets
roared, landing gear clunked into place, and with a thump, the shuttle landed on alien soil.

All across the questship, cheers went up and people who had been
suspicious and cold now slapped each other on the back and shook
hands.

It would take several orbits of the questship for the shuttle's crew to test the lightbeam receiver and deploy some robots to perform safety checks outside. Even so, the six members of the first expeditionary team were impatiently assembling their gear. When Sara arrived with her rucksack in the corridor outside the lightbeam translator, she met Touli with two big field detectors, one under each arm. Descriptive Science had elected to send him down to set up a grid of sensors to study their gravitational anomaly.

"Sure you have enough of those?" Sara asked as he set the machines down by the door to the lightbeam translator. Descriptive had already filled half the cargo bay of the shuttle with equipment.

He sighed heavily. "Everyone in the department wants to measure something different. It's going to take me a week to set it all up."

Sara, by contrast, was traveling light: a headnet and recorder, a change of clothes, and equipment for camping in primitive surroundings. She wore plain, durable coveralls with many pockets.

The scientists were assembled in the corridor and waiting for the go-ahead when Mr. Gibb, the publicist, showed up in a state-of-the-art headset helmet with the controls clipped to his belt. He was already recording his experiences, and gave a low narration as he drew near. "The exploring party is all here, waiting to step into the unknown. What is on their minds? Let's see." He surveyed them, then zeroed in on Thora Lassiter. "Emissary Lassiter," he said, fixing her with the glassy gaze that came over people who were recording their perceptions. It was as if they felt transformed into machinery, and had no more social graces than a camera. "How does it make you feel to be going into danger again?"

"Oh, piss off, Gibb," Sara intervened. "That is so tasteless."

Defensively, he said, "But people are interested in the personal stuff." He had curly brown hair and an eager, puppy-dog face. Disliking him seemed a little like wanting to pull the arms off a stuffed bear. Sara was ashamed at how easy it was.

"Well, pester someone else," she said.

"But Emissary Lassiter"—he turned to her with a winning smile—"you're the perfect focus for this piece. You've got name recognition back home, a dramatic past, and my god you look like some sort of Hindu goddess . . ."

In a booming voice, Touli said, "Stop emitting pheromones, there."

"Oh, for pete's sake," Gibb grumbled, and went off to document his own reactions.

When the all-clear came, the anticipation was quiet but electric. The three security guards went through first. When Sara's turn came, it all seemed oddly routine. She lay down on the slab, as she had a thousand times before, and the next moment she was on a new planet.

The shuttle was hot and crowded inside because the guards weren't letting anyone out till the whole group was assembled. Atlabatlow was there, having decided to command the security detail himself. His face was intent as a cat's, quiet but poised to spring.

When everyone had arrived, Atlabatlow turned to the air lock. It held only two at a time, and he motioned one of his guards to come with him, leaving another posted to make sure no one else exited without permission. The scientists waited in various stages of impatience, irritation, and boredom till the guards had had time to circle the craft and verify its safety. The lapel radio of the inside guard sputtered with some coded message, and he opened the inner door. "Two at a time," he said.

Sara had somehow ended up at the front of the line, along with Touli, so they were the first pair through. The outside air rushed in with a tangy, sour smell, and Sara sneezed. Touli wrinkled his nose. "This place stinks," he said fastidiously.

"Get used to it," Sara said. She was feeling elated and eager. A whole new world was before them, a story just beginning.

The landscape outside was blindingly bright. Squinting and fumbling for her sunshades, Sara saw that the shuttle had landed on a level plain of grasslike plants, their blades reflective as polished metal. In contrast to the land, the sky above seemed dark. It did no good to shade her eyes with her hand, because the brilliance was all from below. A warm breeze gusted across the prairie toward them, making the grass bend and dance till she had to close her dazzled eyes. Even the sound it made was strange—a harmonic whistling rather than the normal rustle.

The shuttle steps were already lowered, so Sara and Touli descended onto the soil of Iris. Sara knelt to look at the grass—the first human scientist, she thought with a thrill, to see a non-Terran life-form. The stalks grew almost knee-high, the ground underneath covered by a mossy green mat that looked and smelled distinctly Terran. Sara took a broad blade of grass in her hand. The top of it was like polished chrome, but the underside was rough and dull. As she ran it across her finger, a bright slit of blood appeared on her thumb. The blade edge was sharp as a razor. She put her thumb in her mouth and reached into one of her pockets for a bandage.

Atlabatlow appeared from around the end of the shuttle, where he had been scanning the horizon for threats. The legs of his pants were shredded from the knee down, his shiny black boots showing through. "This is wicked grass," Sara said.

"Yes," he agreed. "We need to use caution." He sat on the steps to tuck the remains of his pants into his boots.

The second pair of explorers came through the air lock, and Sara called to them, "Tell everyone to bring sun goggles. And tuck your pants into your boots; the grass out here is like knives."

For the next hour the scientists laughed and joked like children as they took samples and recordings, any differences forgotten in the sheer wonder of it all. Mr. Gibb wandered around, recording scenes of excitement and delight.

It took them only minutes to solve one mystery, that of the oxygen-rich atmosphere. "It *has* been terraformed," said Hua Ming, the ecologist from System Sciences, holding up a leaf that was unmistakably clover. "There are two systems of life here—one Terran and one alien—coexisting and independent. Somehow, the Terran life-forms must have taken an ecological niche that the native biota could adapt to. Oh, this is going to be fun to model."

And yet, Iris quickly proved that she could not be taken at face value. They found that the grass was thick with tubrous plants whose only aboveground manifestation was a three-inch spike as strong as metal, and pointing straight up. It was only by sheer luck that no one had impaled a foot on one of them, for they were easily able to pierce a boot sole. After this discovery, no one needed any reminder to be cautious.

Sara had noticed a slight ticking sound near the shuttle, but thought nothing of it till one of the guards gave a curse of pain and plucked something out of his neck. They all gathered round to look. It was an insect of sorts—a silver body shaped like a straight pin sharpened on both ends, with netlike wings. It had embedded itself a quarter inch deep in the man's skin. Ming put it in a sample box. Now that they knew what to look for, it was easy to see a cloud of them high in the air around the shuttle, glinting in the sun.

"They don't seem drawn by us," Touli observed. "It's the ship they're interested in. Our body chemistry must not appeal to them."

"Lucky for us," Sara said.

"Keep your goggles on," Atlabatlow warned. "Even if they're not after us, they can obviously hit us."

All this time Sara had been keeping an eye on Thora Lassiter, who had the look of a sleepwalker in paradise. Twice she had wandered away into the grass, and Atlabatlow had intercepted her, like a herding dog jittery to be out of control. Now Sara spotted her wandering away again, and set out to corral her.

When Sara came up, Thora was standing still as an ivory figurine of a woman, gazing out into the prairie, her dark goggles pushed up on her forehead.

"How can you stand to look at it?" Sara said.

Thora slid her goggles down guiltily, as if caught doing something forbidden. "It's the light," she said. "I could bathe in it all day."

"You're giving Security fits, you know."

Thora glanced over her shoulder to where Atlabatlow was standing, watching them. Her expression was complicated, and Sara felt sure there was some insight into the woman's past hidden here. In a low voice Sara asked, "Does he bother you?"

"No more than . . . I just . . ." Her voice trailed off. Then she shook her head. "It doesn't matter. Here we are on a new planet— none of us has any past here. We can all start over from scratch."

If only that were true, Sara thought. We packed our past in our baggage. We always do.

It was getting close to noon, and the sealike brilliance all around was becoming wearing, but no one wanted to gather in the shadow of the shuttle for fear of the pinflies. So when Touli rumbled something about scouting the anomaly island, everyone wanted to go.

The shuttle had landed as close to the odd gravitational feature as the pilots had dared, but it was still a mile or two away. Touli aligned the map on the screen of his navigational slate to the topography around them, and pointed west. Sara squinted into the distance. On the horizon was something irregular that would have looked like a low hill, if it had not been brighter than the surrounding plain.

They returned to the shuttle to rest their eyes and prepare for the short journey. By consensus they decided to help Touli by bringing along some of the more portable of the sensing devices he would have to set up.

"You all have locator beacons on your belts," Atlabatlow instructed them. "Please set them to transmit. If you get separated, we will be able to locate you. Please do not proceed ahead of the security personnel."

They set out in single file across the prairie, Atlabatlow first, parting the grass carefully with a walking stick to locate spikeplants and a kind of low ground cactus with metallic needles that they had also discovered in the grass. There was little conversation except for the occasional warning or exclamation when a pinfly pierced someone's coveralls. Behind her, Sara could hear Mr. Gibb narrating notes to himself. "The explorers are setting out to penetrate a virgin planet and lay her secrets bare. Iris, veiled in mystery, and so on and so forth."

It was slow going. Their eyes were, necessarily, on the ground ahead, and so they heard the anomaly shortly before seeing it.

Over the whistling of the wind on the grass, there was a faint, musical undertone, not unlike wind chimes. By now the boundary of the area was plain to see ahead, and they came to a halt, perplexed.

Sara could make not the slightest sense of what she was looking at. One moment it looked like a vertical lake surface; the next, like a mass of angular fissures, cracks in the day. For a moment she felt she was looking *down*, over the edge of a precipice, and put a foot forward to break her fall, only to find that the ground was still horizontal, though she was swaying, disoriented.

"What the *hell*?" she breathed.

Thora, beside her, was gazing in entranced fascination. "It's something our senses are not evolved to perceive," she said.

Surprisingly, it was Mr. Gibb who figured it out. "Oh, I get it," he said suddenly. "It's a forest."

"What?" Sara could see no organic shape at all in it—at least, not as humans defined organic.

"The leaves are all the little reflections," he explained. "The trunks are the vertical surfaces, like faceted mirrors. Some of them have these reflective fronds and streamers instead of leaves. That's why it's so hard to see the trunks."

With a mental effort, Sara could begin to see what he meant. It was like looking at a visual paradox, and making herself see the two faces instead of the vase.

"That is very clever," Thora said softly, "and very wrong."

Wrong or not, the shimmering wall of reflections now resolved into a kind of cubist origami scene that at least made a sort of weird sense. The music was coming from inside.

"Chime trees," Sri Paul said. He had his pocket recorder in hand, and now set it to play a Chorister campania. When the first chord of the bell concerto rang out, it was instantly echoed back from the forest. An arpeggio followed, mimicked a split second later in liquid chimes. Paul paused the recording, and the forest music returned to the more complex harmonies of its previous state. "Record it and play it back," Ming suggested. Paul did, and the music from the trees jangled joyfully in reply.

"You must be setting off some sort of sympathetic vibration," Touli said.

"Mirror images," Thora mused, almost to herself.

Cautiously, they approached the edge of the forest. Close up, Sara had to make yet another mental effort to see the trees. Their bases looked like clumps of transparent crystal, rock sugar on a stick. Around them hung the "leaves"—long, dangling prism-shaped things, transparent as glass, that rang as they struck each other when stirred by the wind.

The chime-leaves formed a thick curtain at the forest edge, reaching almost to the ground. They cast rainbow shadows as they shifted and turned. A spectrum chased across Atlabatlow's intent face as he reached out with his cane to touch one of the largest leaves, nearly as tall as he. But instead of making contact with the surface, his cane passed through the leaf, and the end emerged on the other side, at a sixty-degree angle from the way it had gone in. Slowly he drew it out, and they gathered around to inspect it. It looked perfectly whole, unaffected.

"It's got to be some sort of optical illusion," Touli said. Then, before anyone could react, he stepped forward and reached out to touch the leaf himself. His hand passed through the mirrorlike surface and protruded on the other side, twisted backward at an impossible, broken angle. It looked so horrible that several people gasped. But he withdrew his arm whole, looking at it curiously and wiggling his fingers.

"Please be more cautious in future," Atlabatlow said gravely. "We do not have a doctor with us."

"What did it feel like?" Thora asked intently.

"Like passing through a surface, like water," Touli rumbled thoughtfully. "I don't think it is an optical illusion after all."

The chime-leaf had rotated in the wind, and Atlabatlow now reached out with his cane to spin it back. The instant it contacted the leaf edge the stick fell apart in two pieces, cut as cleanly as with a silent buzz saw.

Everyone looked at Touli, glad he had not tried that experiment.

"I think this would be a good place to set up some monitors," Touli said.

The party spent most of the next hour assembling a solar power array, aiming the satellite dish to send data direct to the ship, and plugging everything in. While the others worked, Thora and Sara strolled northward along the forest edge as far as they could while staying in sight of the base camp. They found that the boundary was uneven, and in places the grassland penetrated quite far into the forest in chains of clearings connected by alleys of grass. Sara was just glancing back to see if they could get away with exploring one when their radios both sputtered to life with a request from Atlabatlow to return to the base camp.

When they reported what they had found, Touli wanted to take some monitors to set up as far within the forest as they could safely reach, while the others wanted to stay and pursue their own studies. So Touli, Thora, Sara, and Atlabatlow each slung some equipment on their backs and set out, promising to return within the hour. As they skirted the edge of the forest, Touli tried to map its irregular contours. He kept shaking and tapping his navigational slate, and finally asked to borrow Sara's. "Mine keeps freezing," he said.

Soon they came to one of the inlets where the prairie penetrated the woods, and followed it inward. Once they were surrounded by trees, the sound changed timbre, and deep gonging vibrations kept the air alive all around them. Beyond the edge growth, the chime-leaves became larger, like huge dangling doorways. The explorers followed a twisting path of grass that split and re-formed in S-curves, like a braided waterway, deep into the forest.

Touli, who had been trying to keep track of their position, finally shook his head and gave back Sara's nav slate. "Now this one has stopped working," he said. "There must be some sort of interference."

Hearing this, Atlabatlow immediately tried his radio link with the guard they had left at base camp. When he spoke, his own greeting came from the speaker, transmitted back to him in overlapping waves. "A radio echo," Touli observed. "That's different."

"We had better set up the equipment and withdraw," Atlabatlow said. "We are cut off from base."

But for the others, curiosity exceeded caution. "I'd like to find as large a clearing as I can," Touli said, "to minimize interference from the trees. It looks like there's a bigger opening just ahead."

And yet, the larger clearing he needed kept receding, mirage-like, in front of them. Always it looked as if the forest opened up just beyond the next curve; always it proved to be an illusion. At last they had to give up and admit they would not find the perfect place. They heaped the equipment they had been carrying on the ground and began assembling it.

It was late afternoon and the sun's light was slanting when they had their mechanical observers up and running. Touli tested the satellite link; the focused beam heading straight into the sky suffered only a slight degradation from the surrounding trees. Sara straightened up from the solar collector she had been helping with and scanned the clearing. "Which way did we get in here?" she asked. Ordinarily she had good directional sense, but the change in lighting had made the forest look different.

Atlabatlow and Touli each pointed in a different direction. "That way," they said simultaneously.

Sara laughed at them. "Our wilderness scouting skills a little rusty, are they?"

Atlabatlow did not seem nearly so amused. "Wait here," he said, and set off toward the forest opening he had indicated. Suspecting that the security chief would find it hard to admit if he were wrong, Sara went to check out the one Touli preferred.

The path was lined with low, spiny plants whose leaves were like serrated sabers. Sara had no memory of having passed them, but she continued on a few more paces to make sure. Ahead, there was a movement through the trees. She glimpsed a khaki jumpsuit and black boots, and realized it was Atlabatlow. The two paths evidently ran parallel, and probably converged. She called out to attract his attention, but her voice came back to her, echoing from every direction, and he did not notice. She sped up to overtake him, but he was moving fast. Again she called out; again he ignored her.

The sound of footsteps to her right made her glance in that direction, and she saw a person in a khaki jumpsuit following her. Thinking it was Thora, she stopped. Her companion stopped as well. Only then did she realize she had been following her own reflection.

She was standing in a grove of trees with trunks like mirrored, many-sided columns that jutted up into the curtain of tinkling chime-leaves overhead. Everywhere she looked were reflections of reflections, infinitely repeated, creating endless corridors that did not exist. She saw herself—far away, close up, approaching, receding, her own back in front of her. Completely disoriented, she turned around to find the way back, but the only thing in the grove was herself, and herself, and herself.

She heard a step to her left and whirled around to see that she was surrounded by a host of towering black Worwhas. Touli caught her elbow, and she clutched at him, relieved to have located a patch of solid, tactile reality.

"I was following my own image, like some sort of damned solipsist," she said, trying to laugh.

"So what's new?" Touli muttered like a distant explosion.

"I guess this isn't the way back," she said.

"I guess not," he agreed.

They turned to retrace their steps, Touli leading, but again the path misled them into a cul-de-sac. Laughing a little anxiously at themselves, they tried again, and this time managed to stumble on the clearing where they had left the monitors.

Atlabatlow was there, pacing impatiently. "I told you to wait here," he said.

"That's the thing about Balavatis," Touli said good-naturedly. "Give them a rule and they think it's their duty to disobey."

"That could be a dangerous trait in a place like this." Atlabatlow looked around. "Where is Emissary Lassiter?"

"She was here a minute ago," Touli said.

They called out, but as before, their voices came back from a thousand directions. There was no response. With a mutual glance, they began to search the clearing's edge, peering into the now-shadowy forest, inspecting the ground for any hint of which direction she might have gone—footprint or broken branch or torn cloth. There was nothing.

Atlabatlow became very cold and focused. Without a word, he went over to the satellite dish, unplugged the monitor they had spent so long setting up, and plugged his radio into it. It took him several tries, but at last his radio crackled with a startled response from the ship.

"I need a fix on Lassiter," he said.

The reply took several seconds, and then it was so full of static

Sara could understand nothing. Atlabatlow seemed to make it out, though. "Can you locate us?"

This time Sara heard the radio give coordinates for herself, Touli, and Atlabatlow, then for the others at base camp.

"That's it?" Atlabatlow demanded. The radio sputtered in response. "All right," he said, and unplugged the radio, returning it to his belt. He glanced at the sun, which was barely skimming the tops of the trees by now. "We need to get back to the shuttle," he said.

"We can't leave her here," Sara said.

"She isn't here."

"That's absurd! How could she not be?"

The glance Atlabatlow threw at her was so full of fury and venom that it took her breath away. "You tell me."

In the silence that followed, the chiming of the trees sounded discordant and sinister. There was no other sound—not a pinfly's flight, not a breath.

It was impossible, but Thora Lassiter had vanished as if she had never been.

chapter four

They slunk back on board the questship, all five of the remaining "nonessential personnel," banished from the planet. Iris was officially off-limits until Thora Lassiter was found, or her disappearance explained. Only Atlabatlow remained below with his guards, the pilots, and the lightbeam technician, to conduct the search and rescue mission. In orbit above, half a hundred research projects froze in mid-plan, and as many unhappy scientists faced indefinite imprisonment on a ship where no one trusted each other. The members of the exploring party were as welcome back as viruses.

Sara returned with her suspicions blazing. During the long trudge back to the shuttle she had had time to think: in fact, neither she nor Touli had been last to see Thora. Atlabatlow had been closest to her at the time of her disappearance, and they had found him standing in the spot where she was last seen. Moreover, he was the only one among them with any reason to wish her ill. So he had motive, opportunity—but means? That was where Sara's thinking stuck fast.

During that long walk, the colonel shadowed her so closely that she could not pull Touli aside to talk in private. Only once did Atlabatlow leave them, when he went into the shuttle to report to the Director, and emerged shortly after to order them all back to the ship. In the face of his icy authority, Sara's suspicions flared even brighter, and for a reckless moment she thought of confronting him. But a glance at the guards flanking him, and at the worried and flustered group of witnesses, made her think better of that plan. So, with a show of false obedience she sensed he did not believe for an instant, she went to the lightbeam translator, determined to flank him the instant his scrutiny was turned elsewhere.

To her frustration, they had instituted quarantine procedures on the ship. When she arrived in the translation chamber she was greeted by a moonsuited technician who gave her a plastic garment to seal herself in, then ushered her into a room where she was forced to wait until all the explorers had assembled, looking like deep-sea divers in the low gravity. They were then fumigated and herded down to the clinic for medical checks.

Sara volunteered to go in first to see the doctor. She found that the news was all over the ship.

"How the hell could you just *lose* her?" David said when he had conducted his initial checkup through the plastic. "It seems downright careless."

"She lost herself," Sara said, unwilling to share her suspicions just yet. "She was always wandering off, daydreaming."

"Hmm." David frowned.

"What is it?"

"Lie down and let me scan you," he said.

The scanner gaped like an open mouth, ready to swallow Sara

whole. Inside, concentric circles of emitters were ranked like teeth, ready to bite down. She tried not to think of the invisible forces probing all the secret malfunctions inside her.

When she emerged, the doctor was sitting across the room studying a holographic image. "Hmm," he said.

"What's wrong?"

"With you? You're pigheaded, Callicot."

"Your scan shows that, does it?"

"I wish. I could declare half the staff disabled." He turned around, pocketing his light pen. "Well, there's no Irisian cooties that I can find. You can take off the suit."

With relief she peeled it off; it had long since gotten sweaty and unpleasant. "All right, David, now you have to tell me what you meant by 'hmm.'"

"Meant? When?"

"When I mentioned Thora wandering away."

"Oh." He hesitated, looking down at his crossed arms.

"Listen," Sara said, "I know about her . . . medical condition."

The doctor speared her with a look. "How?"

"She told me."

He looked skeptical, so she barged on. "What I'm wondering is, does Atlabatlow know?"

David shook his head. "Not that I . . ." He stopped. "Come to think of it, he had access to the files, for the murder investigation. I suppose he could have looked it up."

Oh, what a handy murder it had turned out to be for the head of security. It had gained him information, authority, and cooperation he never would have had without it. Sara could hardly believe what she was thinking. An anxious sense of failure was tugging at her gut.

"Thanks, David," she said. "Could you do me a favor, and check out Touli next?"

She waited outside the clinic till Touli loomed through the doorway. "I've got to talk to you," she said.

Her berth was close to the clinic, so she led the way there. It was barely big enough for two under normal circumstances, and Touli had to fold himself like an army knife to fit in. Sara sat on her desk to give him room.

Quickly, she explained her suspicions. He listened, shaking his head with the ponderous speed of a wrecking ball, as he realized where she was heading.

"Listen," Sara said, "if Atlabatlow finds Thora alive I'll eat my words, and my pride too, if you like. But I'm willing to bet he won't. Sure, he'll make it look like there's been a search, just like he made the murder investigation look convincing. But somehow it'll come up empty, or find only her body. In the meantime, we can't afford to wait. Touli, you and I were the only witnesses; if I'm right he's going to try to pin it on us."

"What do you propose to do about it?" Touli said.

"We've got to find out what really happened."

Ashok met them this time in the communications center, a circular room slightly more spacious than the pepci control room, but just as lined with equipment. Through this hub were routed the internal ship communications, the links with the planet, and messages to and from the satellites they had launched. Ordinarily, there was a staff of four, but at this hour everything was running on automatic.

Sara had jokingly offered Ashok a bribe—his choice of chocolate or beer—but the real inducement was the opportunity to subvert authority. As he opened the door for them he said, "We've got an hour before Security checks this area."

"We've got to work fast, then," Sara said.

They shoved three chairs around the terminal that accessed the archive. Ashok sat at the keyboard, dramatically flexing his fingers before inputting a passcode. "That can't be traced to you, can it?" Sara asked.

He gave her a look of wounded pride. "Give me some credit."

They went first to the log from the locator beacons they had all been wearing on the planet. Speeding through the display, they watched themselves, represented in colored lights, leave the shuttle, arrive at the forest edge, then split apart. Sara pointed to the four beacons that represented herself, Touli, Atlabatlow, and Thora, and said, "Follow those."

When they entered the forest, the signal from the beacons degraded significantly. The lights kept winking out, then popping back on in a slightly different place, looking jittery and unstable. Mapped against a topographical display, their route staggered like a drunkard's path, much more circuitous than it had seemed at the time. Even so, they penetrated a significant distance into the forest before coming to a halt, the beacons still twinkling from interference. Then, as Ashok slowed the display, they watched Atlabatlow depart from the group, then Sara, then Touli. Atlabatlow turned and began retracing his steps toward the clearing. Then a shudder ran across the screen. Thora's light disappeared first, then Atlabatlow's, then Sara's and Touli's. Six seconds later, three of them reappeared; the fourth did not.

"Damn!" Sara whispered. "There was interference right at the critical moment."

"Run it again slowly," Touli said. "Can you get more detail?"

Ashok set the display to maximum resolution and focused on Thora's beacon. When Touli left, she stayed motionless for a while; then, just as Atlabatlow returned, she moved quickly in the opposite direction, and vanished. A split second later, Atlabatlow's beacon winked out as well.

"She started moving before he reached her," Touli said.

"She might have seen something that alarmed her," Sara speculated. "But whatever happened, it went down in those seconds of darkness."

Thwarted, they sat back, silent.

"Is that it?" Ashok asked.

"Oh no," Sara said. "We were all wearing headnets."

Ashok gave her a sidelong glance. "Those files are proprietary, you know."

"Thanks for the copyright notice," she said. Of course she knew. Everyone held the rights to their own experiences; it was one of the most sacred tenets of Capellan law, not to mention ethics.

"Just tell the judge I warned you," Ashok said, and turned back to his terminal to break into the protected caches.

Touli shifted uncomfortably. "My Gbinjadan always warned me about you Balavatis," he said. "And I thought he was prejudiced."

"Look, I doubt copyright infringement is uppermost on Thora Lassiter's mind right now," Sara said. "We're doing this for her sake."

It took Ashok several minutes to thwart the locks on Thora's files, and then he found another barrier. "Not only proprietary, but classified," he said. "It's already been flagged and protected by someone in Security. But not very cleverly."

Sara was glad she had insisted on doing this tonight. Once Atlabatlow came back, she doubted there would be much chance of finding the trail of evidence. She glanced at the clock. "Half an hour left," she said.

"Don't rush me," Ashok answered.

At last he succeeded in gaining access to Thora's files. Sara had located some spare headnets for them to view the recording, and now she offered them to Touli and Ashok. Touli declined with a wave of his hand. "I can't violate her privacy like this, regardless of why." Sara shrugged and offered the net to Ashok. He accepted it.

Sara spread the metallic beadwork mesh on her own hair and plugged it into the terminal. When Thora had worn an identical one on the planet, it had recorded the neural activities of her visual and aural cortexes, and it would now induce identical patterns in Sara's brain, reproducing the same visual and auditory impressions.

Ashok asked Touli to lower the lights so they could see Thora's experiences without interference from their own.

He started the recording close to the end, when she was already inside the forest. "Holy shit," Sara said when she saw what Thora had seen, "is she blind?"

"It's probably bad signal," Ashok said. "The headnets were broadcasting to a booster relay on the shuttle, just like the beacons. Whatever was interfering with one degraded the other as well. The recording on her own device would be better, if we ever find it."

Ashok skipped forward through the routine moments of setting up Touli's monitor. Sara watched herself through Thora's eyes, trying not to think what a horsey face she had. At last Sara straightened up, pushed back a strand of hair, and asked, "Which way did we get in here?"

The familiar events unfolded. Atlabatlow left, then Sara. Touli spent some time fiddling with his mechanisms, then finally grumbled something about irresponsible Balavatis, and headed off to haul Sara back in.

As soon as she was alone in the grove, Thora drank in the dazzling display of the forest. In the setting sunlight the canopy was a fabric of colored gems: amber, azure, ruby. As the forest filled her visual field, Sara felt again a stab of disorientation. The world looked like a child had taken a scissors to it, cutting out portions of the scene and scrambling them, triangles and trapezoids overlapping. In places, the scene was superimposed upon itself, half of it upside down or reversed. A patrician-looking woman in khakis appeared, standing in the forest, and Sara stared back at Thora's reflection. Then it broke apart like a shattering window.

Suddenly, the ground filled the scene as Thora pitched forward onto her knees as if struck from behind, giving a surprised gasp. A brief sight of her clutching a handful of the razor-edged grass flashed by, then the scene was jumbled motion for a second. Thora screamed for Sara and Touli. Then, darkness. The recording ended.

When Sara let out her breath and opened her eyes, she felt mentally bruised. Touli was watching her, frowning. Ashok punched the keyboard. "She didn't see what hit her," Sara said. "But she called out our names, Touli."

"Just ours?" he asked.

"Right."

They sat silent for a few seconds. Sara was thinking that she might have just relived the last moments of a murder victim's life.

The next step would take strong nerves as well. "We've got to look at Atlabatlow's," she said.

Ashok didn't look at her, but shook his head. "You can't argue he would give his consent."

"Not if he's a murderer, he wouldn't. And if he is, the instant he gets back on board, that file will be gone. If it's not already. This may be our only chance."

"Well, let me see if I can find it," Ashok said, and set to work.

It took much longer this time, and Sara began to wish they had some coffee, since she had had no more than a restless catnap since going down to the planet that morning. The security patrol passed by, shining a flashlight into the communication center, but they had already evacuated into an adjoining office, and the guard had no idea that the automatically running terminal was in fact trying encryption keys to break into his boss's private files.

At last the terminal warbled and Ashok ambled over to see what was on his line. When he read the screen, he sat down, his drowsy air gone. "We got lucky," he said. "We're in."

"Is the recording there?" Sara hung over his shoulder.

"Hang on. Yes, it looks like no one's been in here since it was autofiled. I guess he doesn't let his ham-handed subordinates into his private cache."

"Would you, if you had something to hide?" Sara said.

Again Ashok and Sara put on their headnets, Touli lowered the lights, and the show began.

This time it did feel like a personal invasion, as if she were infiltrating Atlabatlow's skull, looking through his eyes without permission. Sara strove to distance herself from what she/he was seeing, as if it were only a moving image. The quality of the recording was much higher than Thora's. They saw Sara ask about the way back, and heard the colonel tell them to wait as he started off to scout the path. He encountered nothing remarkable before turning around. As he came back there was a jerk, as if he had momentarily stumbled, and then he entered the clearing. It was empty except for the equipment. Not a sign of Thora.

"He never saw her," Ashok said.

"Just a second," Sara said. "Run it back. I want to see that bit where the picture skips. Do it slow this time."

When they played it at a crawl, it was clear to see that there was a discontinuity in the recording, a splice where the picture jumped between one second and the next. "Isn't that what it would look like if he had turned off his headnet and turned it on again?" Sara asked.

"It could be that," Ashok said thoughtfully. "It could also be from the interference."

"I don't know why I thought he would have recorded a crime. He's way too smart for that. Of course he would have shut off the headnet, and then retraced his steps to create a false record."

"But Sara, there's not enough time," Ashok argued. "This glitch happens at the same point where his beacon disappears. Then there's no record of anyone's location for about six seconds. That's not enough time to kill someone, dispose of the body, and return to the starting point."

Sara's thoughts felt like glue. She felt sure she could work it out, if she could just sit down with the data for a while. But as she was drawing breath to continue, the terminal screen went black, except for a single blinking cursor. Ashok swore.

"What's wrong?"

"We were detected. He must have had a break-in tracer. He'll know which terminal we used."

"I think it's time to cut and run," Touli said calmly.

As they retreated down a hall that led to the maintenance areas, they heard booted footsteps coming to a halt behind them at the door to the communication center. There was a low conversation, then the sound of the door opening. While the guards searched the room, the three culprits escaped.

Sara lay on the bed in her darkened berth, listening to Thora's quiet voice on her earphones.

She had stopped by Thora's berth on her way back, forcing herself to keep going in the precious hours before the Security bureaucracy organized itself to clamp down. So far, Thora was officially only lost; there was no criminal investigation, so her door was not yet sealed. Using old skills, Sara had hotwired the door lock and gotten in. The berth, unlike her own, was immaculate, regimentally ordered, everything in place. It had taken her several minutes of searching to conclude that there was nothing of any interest there. Then, just as she was about to leave, she found the box of recording chips, identified only by date. Without stopping to play any of them, she pocketed the box and left.

It turned out that Thora Lassiter had been a compulsive diarist. Every day, sometimes twice or three times a day, she had dictated entries into a little handheld recorder. At first, Sara had been elated at the discovery. But now, after listening for over an hour, perplexity had set in. Thora was as much of an enigma as ever.

The woman rarely spoke about the ship, or events of the day, or other people, the types of things that filled Sara's life. Instead, the audio diary was internally focused. Dreams, musings, memories, and speculations filled Thora's journal. She was torturously self-aware, always critiquing herself, analyzing her own motives. The slightest event led to endless echoes of self-examination: why did I act so? why did I think of acting another way? did I want some other outcome, or am I content? if I had acted otherwise, what would that have reflected about me? was there some better way I could have acted? what do I mean by "better?"—and on and on, to a paralysis of introspection. It was a miracle that the woman could stir from bed, Sara thought.

It was entirely foreign to Sara's own method of living. Her mind had never struck her as a terribly promising research topic. It was an uncomplicated affair, motivated mainly by the twin desires to escape boredom and not to get caught doing the things that prevented boredom. She preferred to barrel forward through her day, collecting new experiences, regardless of their impact on her character. Living as Thora did, in a world of her own thoughts, would have been like prison.

Impatient to find something useful, Sara decided to search for keywords. The first she tried was "Atlabatlow." There was only one hit, a rather striking entry on the night of the murder. *He almost had the look of a man in love,* Thora had said. The idea boggled Sara's imagination.

Because his name turned up nothing else, Sara searched next for "Orem." This word turned up several entries. She settled back to listen.

from the audio diary of thora lassiter:

I had thought my memories of Orem were gone forever, erased by those clever mentationists who treated me. But since arriving here, puzzling pieces of them have started coming back, especially at night. They are disturbing, because they make it impossible for me to pretend that I wasn't truly ill.

This is one memory:

A child is approaching down the long gallery, dwarfed by the towering vault. Strips of dusty sunlight paint the limestone floor, shaped by the line of tall, narrow windows on the west. As the child passes through them, she is alternately bright and dark, gilded then tarnished all the way up the hall.

My companion ignores her approach. "We have always thought of you Capellans as childlike, impulsive people," *she says.* "You seem to indulge every whim, every craving, as if you had never outgrown your infancy. You even traffic in entertaining fables, as if we were children to be lulled asleep."

"We traffic only in things there is some demand for," *I say.*

"That troubles me. I do not like the reflection of ourselves I see in the mirror you hold up to us. I have come to realize you are predators in your way, but you prey not on what is noble in us, but what is base."

The child is close enough to hear us, but still Kithmother Laocata does not acknowledge her presence. She is nine or ten, dressed in an intricately patterned dolman and sandals. Her straight black hair shines lustrous when the sun touches it. She is carrying a plate of dried fruit.

I stay silent, not certain where Laocata is leading. There is a thriving black market in Capellan entertainment on Orem. My original mission was to make it an open market, so that the legitimate copyright holders would profit. But the mission changed as we found how faulty our knowledge of Orem was. We had assumed that in a strictly male-dominant society like this, our dealings would be with the pack leaders. It took us several months to discover our mistake. In fact, the men of power here despise commerce and money as women's work, and only spoke to us because they thought our talk of trade was a screen for our real interest in arms and alliance. War and politics are the male sphere. Once we realized this, I became our chief negotiator. At last we are talking to the right people, and things are beginning to move. But I have been deceived by Orem before this.

"But you," *she says,* "have changed my mind about Capellans.

There is a core of discipline in you. Perhaps your licentious indulgences do not weaken you, as they do to us. Perhaps you even get strength from them."

She is fishing for information, but I don't know what she wants. "No two Capellans are alike," I say. "We all come from different planets, different cultures."

At last she turns to look at the child. She has come to a halt at the base of the three steps that lead up to the platform where Laocata brought me to see the frescoes. The whole thing seems oddly staged. "Well, Kirwa, offer our guest some refreshment."

The girl seems to gather her strength to mount the steps, and when she stands before me she sways as if the effort makes her lightheaded. She holds out the plate, and I take a fruit, having learned never to refuse food, no matter how unwanted.

"How long has it been since you ate?" the old woman asks the child.

"Three days, Kithmother," she says.

"You have touched nothing?"

"Only some fruit juice at sundown."

"Good girl. Are you ready for your wedding tomorrow?"

The child's eyes fill with tears and she looks down. The tray in her hands trembles a little, but she manages to say, "Yes, Kithmother."

My heart goes out to her, she is so obviously terrified. It is not my place to pass judgment on their culture. All the same, I cannot restrain myself from saying quietly, "Isn't she a little young?"

Laocata's tone is indifferent. "She is lucky anyone will take her. She has no family, no fortune. All she has to recommend her is youth."

And that only recommends her to a child predator. I remind myself there is nothing I can do. Even to think it is against my instructions.

From behind my left ear, a voice speaks then. It is a gusty voice, like wind, and stirs my hair. It says, "I am here."

I turn to see who has spoken, and realize that one of the frescoes is burning. It is a circle of fire, of a pure white color, and odd as the *sight is, I have the conviction it is deeply meaningful. Certainty fills me then, and I turn to the child, Kirwa. "Don't worry," I say. "You are protected."*

I have no idea why I said it. A moment later, I do not believe it is true. But she is gazing at me with such hope, I cannot take it back. I look at Laocata. She has a puzzled expression that tells me she has neither heard the voice nor seen the fire. She dismisses Kirwa then. I watch the child withdraw, back through the columns of light.

"How did you know?" Laocata asks.

"Know what?"

"That she is an abindo *child."*

That means her parents were locked in a violent, predator-prey relationship outside their marriages. I started out thinking the forbidden abindo *relationships were aberrations, but now I think they are more common than anyone admits. "What does that mean for her?" I ask cautiously.*

"It means she will be prone to the madness herself someday," Laocata says. "Her husband is a fool to take her. Either he feels invulnerable, or he is hoping to taste madness himself. If so, he is deluded. Only men with the self-control of great kithfathers prevail in abindo.*" She looks at me, eyes like black marbles. "That girl's father failed the test. The child is the living evidence."*

Why is she telling me this? I am growing uncomfortable under her piercing gaze. She says, "You see, we do not need to import your weaknesses. We have weaknesses of our own. But even they are strengths."

There is something challenging about her expression, as if daring me to say more. But I have already said too much, so I am silent.

▶   ▶   ▶

Late the next morning, Sara went down to the clinic for a bracing dose of news and commentary from Doctor David. Gossip was the only real sport aboard the *Escher*, and many were highly skilled at

it, but David was a championship-level competitor. He always seemed
to know what was going on. She found him in his office, looking
jaded and satirical.

"What's up?" she asked.

He said, "Oh, insurrection, rebellion, turmoil. The usual."

"About the ban on travel to the planet?"

"Oh no, that's yesterday. I take it you haven't seen the latest di-
rective from Lord Nelson."

Sara hadn't checked her mail that morning, so David handed
her a copy. It was a memo to all department heads, demanding reports summarizing their scientific discoveries so far. All new discoveries were to be listed on a cover sheet in bullet-point format in clear,
nontechnical language. Each report was to conclude with a section
summarizing how the expedition would improve the lives of ordinary Capellans. The reports were due by the end of the day to
Mr. Gibb in Public Relations.

"Our admiral is a little rusty on the concepts of peer review and
replication of results," David said drily. "Not to mention the research
process."

"He's getting pressure from home because of all the bad news
we're generating," Sara said, handing the memo back. "It's a diversion to distract his bosses."

"You know that. I know that. The scientists thought they were
here for the sake of knowledge. They're all walking around like cats
petted backwards, hissing about violations of professional standards."

Sara could understand their point. The kind of public announcement that would make Nelson Gavere look good would make the
scientists laughingstocks with their peers back home. He needed
product; they needed prestige.

"The person he ought to be putting pressure on is Dagan Atlabatlow," Sara said. "A dramatic rescue would solve his problem."

"Well, it doesn't look like that's going to happen," David said.

"What's the story there?"

David's tone became more grave. "They've been using the shuttle to fly over the search area, doing infrared mapping. So far, no luck."

"Infrared kind of assumes she's alive," Sara said.

"That's been the assumption up to now. The colonel came back to the ship by lightbeam a couple of hours ago to report to the Director. It looks like they're going to change strategies."

Sara was about to ask another question when there was a knock on the door and David's assistant, Bakai, looked in timidly. "There's a security guard out here looking for Magister Callicot," she said.

Sara got up, trying to look nonchalant. "Well, duty calls," she said.

"Is that what they're calling him now," David muttered.

When the guard showed her into Colonel Atlabatlow's office, she found it unrevealing—spartan and professional, with no hints of personality. No pictures of faraway family, no diplomas on the wall, no files open on the desk. The man himself was freshly shaved, wearing a crisp new uniform, but he looked haggard, as if he had not slept for two days. He gestured Sara to a seat facing him across his desk. The guard who had fetched her stayed in the room, standing against the wall behind her.

"I must warn you that this conversation is being recorded," Atlabatlow said.

"I have no objection," Sara said. Two could take advantage of that.

"Please state your name and title."

Sara did.

"Were you a member of the party that was present when Emissary Lassiter disappeared?"

"You know I was. You were, too."

His eyes on her narrowed for a moment, but his voice remained neutral. "Please describe in your own words what happened."

Sara recounted the events, cautious not to elaborate with facts she had learned the night before. Atlabatlow listened carefully, utterly still. Sara found herself wishing he had some nervous tic to make him seem human. Whoever had manufactured him had left out the verisimilitude.

When she finished, he leaned back a millimeter, but his gaze never left her face. She tried meeting his eyes, but found she couldn't win at that game.

"Did you know Emissary Lassiter before arriving here?" he asked.

"No," she said, wondering what the question revealed about his investigation.

"You were quite friendly with her. Why was that?"

"Because I'm a nice person," Sara said. "She looked left out, kind of lonely, like she didn't fit in. So I tried to befriend her."

"Was that because of her reputation?"

"No. I was traveling from Andaman to Capella when all the mess about Orem happened. I didn't hear about it till I got here."

"Did she confide anything to you about fears or suspicions she may have had?"

"No. Not even when I asked her."

He watched her intently. "What did you ask her?"

"I asked her about you. Whether you made her uncomfortable."

Finally, she got a reaction. He made not a sound, but it was as if a furnace door had opened. The desk between them suddenly seemed too narrow.

"Why did you ask her that?" he said in a tone as smooth as a cat's purr.

Good riposte. It was impossible to bring up his planet of origin without seeming ethnically prejudiced. So she feinted. "You're not exactly the warm and fuzzy type. You make a lot of people uncomfortable. Sorry to be frank."

"Don't worry about it." He studied her for a long time without speaking. She wondered if he was considering whether to escalate this duello. His next question answered her.

"Before you left Capella, did you receive any instructions regarding Emissary Lassiter?"

She realized she was going to have to lie on the record. Had he known that? "No," she said.

"What is your relationship to Executive Delegate Gossup?"

He *did* know something about her role here—how, she could not fathom. "He was my graduate advisor at UIC," Sara said. "He keeps in touch with a lot of former students. In fact, I gave him a visit just before coming here. Why?"

"Your contract," he said. "Is it with Epco?"

"Who I'm working for is a matter of record. What I want to know is, who are *you* working for?"

She said it impulsively, and as soon as it was out of her mouth she half regretted it, since it precluded subtlety forever. But it was on tape now; there was no going back.

He cut off the interview quickly after that. She was grateful to leave. The room had gotten altogether too small and too hot.

After leaving the security offices, Sara went looking for Touli, to compare notes. He was easy to locate—all she had to do was go to the Descriptive Sciences section and listen. When she heard a laugh like an earthquake, she homed in on it, and soon found him in a cluttered back office with Magister Sarcodan and Emile Begoya, a theoretical physicist.

Sarcodan was in his usual state of simmering dissatisfaction. As she came to the door he cut off what he was saying till he saw it was only her, then continued. "We'd get carte blanche to deploy our equipment if we could just announce a new use for toilet paper," he said. "As it is, we could have found how to surf on gravity waves, and we couldn't get permission to study it. Unless it looked like a tourist attraction."

"Come on in, Sara," said Touli. "We're trying to figure out how to get back down to the planet."

Sara found a chair in a corner and pulled it up to the worktable, whose erasable surface was covered with sketches, equations, and doodles. "What's the rush?" she said.

Sarcodan answered. "The rush is, we think we may have a genuine discovery on our hands, only we can't confirm it or argue it's going to improve the lives of ordinary Capellans." He said "ordinary Capellans" in a tone only an overeducated person could use.

Ignoring his tone, Sara said, "What discovery?"

Both Sarcodan and Touli looked at Emile Begoya. Emile was a brilliant little man, perfectly at ease with an equation, who seemed perpetually baffled by the actions of vertebrates. "Well," he said to Sara, "are you familiar with the theory of gravity?"

"Sure. Things fall down," Sara said. "Or did you mean something more complicated?"

"No, no," said Begoya, flustered, "I had the theory of fractional dimensions in mind."

"You'd better explain it," Touli said.

Begoya blinked rapidly, but continued: "Well, there has been a theory for a long time that space has a fractal structure at the smallest scale. At the scale where space becomes grainy rather than continuous, there are openings into cavities that have fractional dimensions, and which may open on the other side into other whole dimensions. The graininess of space is not evenly distributed; it's clumped. Gravity occurs where space is more complex—there is simply more *of* it, which makes it curve. This attracts matter, making it look as if the matter were creating the gravity well, when it's actually a property of the space itself."

"Cool," Sara said. "But what does this have to do with us?"

"Well, as you know, there seems to be more gravity than the

observable matter accounts for, so we talk about dark matter to explain it."

"Like here, for example," Touli put in.

Begoya nodded. "According to this theory, there is no such thing as dark matter—just complex space."

"Get to the forest," Touli prompted.

"Right," said Begoya. "Well, the first thing is, it's not a forest. It's an area of complex topology that has many characteristics of fractal space."

"Oh, of course," said Sara, ironically hitting her temple as if to kick-start her brain. "Why didn't I see that?"

Undeterred, Begoya went on, "The exciting thing is, it's not on a sub-quantum scale. It's on a macro scale—something we never dreamed to be possible. It's as if something has folded our four-dimensional space into shapes that intersect a fifth dimension. Imagine you were a two-dimensional being living on a sheet of tinfoil, and something crinkled it up in the third dimension. The result would seem very complex to you, but only because you couldn't see the true simplicity of the shape in the higher dimension."

"So we were in a spot of five-dimensional crinkle?" Sara said.

"Absolutely," Begoya said happily. "You kept on seeing reflections, true? Or at least that is what you took them for. In fact, space was curving around through the fifth dimension, as if light were making a U-turn, and showing you yourself. It wasn't a reflection you saw. It was yourself."

Sara felt as if her brain were going to explode. "This is way beyond weird," she said. "I can't fit this into my head."

"What we need to do now," continued Begoya, "is to map the dimensional folds, in order to find out what the shape really is, five-dimensionally speaking. We need more data, more sensors, more measurements. We need lasers, radar, sonar, whatever we can point at this anomaly."

Sara saw Sarcodan's problem. The chances of conveying the excitement of fractal space to Mr. Gibb seemed vanishingly slim. But there was another possibility. "What would happen to a person who walked into a patch of crinkled space?" she asked.

Begoya blinked at her in bemusement. "We have no idea. Of course, on the quantum scale, particles go through all the time, which is why tunneling works, and instantaneous communication like the PPC. But on the macro scale? We've never observed such a thing."

Touli saw what Sara was thinking. "If someone walked into a space fold, there's no telling where she might end up. We couldn't send in a search party after her, in case they got crinkled."

"But mapping the folds might help trace where they lead," Sara said. "You could argue that your research was part of the rescue mission."

Sarcodan was still glowering. "We shouldn't have to come up with excuses for doing what we were sent here to do."

People who stood on principle were a mystery to Sara. "But the fact is, you *do* have to, so why not do it skillfully? Manipulate the system, Sarcodan. And who knows? You might find Thora and be a hero."

"It's worth a try," said Touli.

The discovery that changed everything they thought they knew about Iris came not from any of the scientists, but from Security.

Sara was in her berth, listening to more of Thora's diary, when the emergency message alert on her terminal sounded. She sat up, dragging off the earphones, and answered. She was surprised to see David's assistant, Bakai, on the screen. She had a voice that made Sara think of pink, soft things, which in fact Bakai was.

"David asked me to call you," she said in a breathless rush. "He's heading up to the lightbeam receiver. There's been an accident on the planet, someone injured. The party's coming back right now."

"Who is it?" Sara asked, unable to think of any reason why she was being notified. "Did they find Thora?"

"No. David wanted you there because you're the only exoethnologist on staff." She paused, looking utterly at a loss. "Sara, it's a native."

chapter five

I am in darkness. Not the dark of space, shot through with starlight. Absolute dark, so thick it almost has weight and texture.

I need to create a record in case I am ever found, or this recording device survives me. I need to talk to keep the panic from taking over. It will help me distance myself from my situation. I am not really here; I am simply an intelligence observing.

So, what do I perceive? I am sitting on a cold, hard surface, very smooth, like glass or polished stone. From the echoes I can tell that I am in a large space, a great chamber with hard walls. Far away, I can hear a slight trickle of water. The air is cold and humid, and smells subterranean. If it were not for the regularity of the surfaces around me, I would conclude that I was in a cave. To my right is a wall of columns, cubic and smooth. To my left is a drop-off, an edge beyond which I have not ventured.

How I got here is harder to describe. My memories seem unreliable, based on sensory perceptions that make no sense. But they are all I have to go on, so let me try to be as objective as possible.

I was with Sara, Touli, and Atlabatlow in the forest—no, I should not call it that. Truthfully, I was never able to see the phenomenon as a forest. From the way the others spoke, I realized that it was a metaphor they found helpful, in order to make sense of the incomprehensible, but on repetition it began to assume a reality of its own, obscuring the true nature of what they were seeing. Everything became a "tree" or a "plant," regardless of how unlike trees and plants they were. The explanatory convention replaced the reality.

When I looked at the anomaly, I saw not leaves, but edges in the air, like shattered glass or crushed tinfoil. I saw fissures and angles that intersected in ways that violated the rules of dimensionality, as a Klein bottle or a Möbius strip does. Most of the time it was a geometric jumble that my mind strained to make sense of. It was exhausting to see.

At any rate, we had finished setting up the monitor equipment when we simultaneously became concerned about finding our way back. Atlabatlow left us to verify which way was correct. Sara, who evidently disagreed with him, went to scout a different path. Touli worked on his monitors for a short time, then set out to find Sara and bring her back, leaving me alone in the clearing.

Frankly, I was glad of the solitude, because it gave me a chance to truly study the place. At first I simply listened. The wind-chime music that came from the anomaly had changed since we had scouted its edge. Here, deep inside, it seemed less random. For a moment I thought I picked up the shadow of a melody, sweet as childhood. It was the water-pipes playing in my cousin Bdiwa Ral's formal garden on Vindahar.

But of course, it was not. I took my goggles off to better see the phenomenon, but it was like trying to make sense of a scene in a kaleidoscope. I saw myself reflected a thousand ways: receding and approaching at the same time, magnified and diminished, shattered on a lattice of mirrors. I was seized by disorientation at the topological absurdities I was witnessing, and put out a hand before me, no longer able to distinguish near from far, or surface from space.

Suddenly, I felt that I was standing on the edge of a precipice, gazing down into immense depths. The ground was no longer level, but tilting underneath me. The shifting screens parted till I saw an azure hole gaping below me. What had been near enough to touch was now so far it would take days of travel to reach it. I fell to my knees, clutching the ground to keep from falling into that well. But the ground had grown too steep, and I had no handhold to keep from pitching forward.

"Sara! Touli!" I screamed, but the gonging chimes echoed my voice, obliterating the meaning from the sound.

Then I was in free fall, with nothing to stop me.

The moment of falling was a mere blink, but in it I felt the presence of a great structure around me—a cathedral of alcoves, infinitely complex. Every micrometer dot held echoing chambers, all connected to one another. Revelation rushed into me; this structure explained everything. For an instant that could have lasted a century, I was filled with joy; I was connected, the circuit was complete. And then my mind pulled back, an instinctive flinch. Suddenly terrified, I recoiled into my own self, my own solidity, and I dropped out of that wondrous place into darkness, into this paltry, limited existence.

At first, the memory was so overwhelming that I sat and wept. I felt empty, like a cinder that had once known God. It was so moving that it was some time before I noticed that I could no longer see.

I thought it was my eyes that had ceased to work. The panic that flooded me then was almost incapacitating: my heart was whamming against my ribs, my hands shook. I called out for Sara and Touli again, and the echoes came back, telling me I was no longer in the same place.

I forced myself then to focus on my dova, *hanging like a plumb bob inside me. Flow smoothly, like a river, I recited to myself. All control is ultimately self-control. No matter what has happened, I have a place where proportion, duty, and serenity prevail.*

Once my mind was no longer blundering around in fear, I commanded it to examine my situation. Amid all the useful equipment I had brought in my pockets, there was no such thing as a flashlight. Setting out into the blinding brilliance of Iris, light had seemed like the last thing I would need. Moreover, I could think of no way to generate any. I had the batteries in my recorder, but no bulb or filament, and no fire-generating tools. There was not even an indicator light on the recorder.

I began to explore my surroundings with my hands. When I discovered the glazed surfaces that surrounded me, the thought came that perhaps I had passed out, and had been transported back to the ship, because it seemed so manifestly man-made. So I called out again, but the echoes convinced me that I was not on the ship. There is no space this large on the ship, unless the whole thing were gutted, and even then it would not have this feeling of . . . solidity.

So I must be in a cave, surrounded by some sort of natural crystalline formation. If this is so, then my locator beacon will be of no use, since its signal cannot reach through rock. Rescue seems unlikely, then. I am on my own. Somehow, I must find my way out.

I am resting now. My muscles are exhausted but still quivering with the tension of trying to move through this hellish blackness, and I am bruised and scraped from banging into rocks. I cannot move normally, for fear of plunging off some precipice or catching my ankle between tumbled boulders—for I have encountered both. At times I have had to feel my way forward on hands and knees, nearly reduced to tears with frustration. And the worst part is knowing that I may simply be moving aimlessly, or becoming more trapped than I was already.

My first instinct was to return back the way I had come. I tried, and failed, to find any chute or slope down which I might have fallen. In fact, I could not even find a path off the narrow ledge on which I was trapped, with columnar cliffs on one side and a precipice on the other. When I decided the only way off was over the drop, I scoured the ledge for pebbles, but everything was smooth and sheer. At last I searched my pockets for something to sacrifice, and chose my pen, since the likelihood of my taking notes here seems remote. From the sound when it fell, I determined that it was a shallow drop, but when I lowered myself over the edge I found that I was a poor judge of heights in the dark, for my feet could not touch ground, so I had to let go and trust.

The drop could not have been more than a few feet, though it felt much longer. At the base of the cliff were tumbled blocks of smooth material that reminded me of enormous ice cubes. Making my way through this talus slope was dangerous and exhausting, and I moved at a crawl. At last I came to a more level spot where I could walk on a slippery stone textured with ripples. I edged forward until my foot landed in water, and I knelt to find myself at the edge of a cold, invisible puddle. Here there were some pebbles, so I tossed one out. In this way, I determined that I was at the shore of a silent underground lake.

This at least gave me some orientation. Water, I reasoned, must come from somewhere, and go somewhere. If it had carved this cavern in the first place, then perhaps it would lead me to its outlet. The sound of trickling water that had been present since I first arrived was clearer now; I could discern its direction. So I made for it, following the edge of the lake.

My way was soon blocked by a rock wall that ran out into the lake. I felt along it, searching for a broken section where I could clamber up. But when I tried, I knocked my head painfully against a solid overhang. The thought of the tons of rock over me, waiting to fall and crush me at the slightest shift, made my muscles so weak and trembling that I was forced to climb back down to the level spot near the lake.

My world has contracted to what I can feel in front of me; I have no way of grasping the overall shape of the chamber or plotting a sensible route through it. But I have to do something, so I have decided to go along the lakeshore in the other direction. The only evidence that I have made progress is that the sound of falling water has grown fainter. This makes me uneasy, since it is the only landmark I have. Ahead lies only undifferentiated silence.

I must have been here for hours, perhaps as much as a day. Hours of exhausting effort, and I have no evidence that I have even left the chamber in which I started. There is no way to know; I have become so thoroughly disoriented, I could not find my way back if I wanted to. The futility of my efforts weighs on my spirits. I cannot allow that. If I let myself think of how trapped I am, how hopeless it is to find my way to daylight, then it is all over. I must remain calm, and not expend energy in panic.

Hunger is beginning to trouble me. I have a meal bar in my pocket, but I do not want to use it, since it may have to sustain me for a long time. On the other hand, why put off the inevitable? But I must not think like that.

Several times I have seen phantom lights floating ahead of me and made toward them, only to realize that they were just photisms generated by my straining, light-starved brain. This darkness is so oppressive, I want to rip it to shreds, to revenge myself on it. It presses in on all sides, suffocating and impenetrable. Sometimes I find it difficult to breathe, the darkness is so thick. Nothing could keep me prisoner more effectively. I am perfectly free to move, to escape, and yet completely unable to act. No sadist could have invented a more infuriating captivity.

I have to acknowledge that I may not escape. This is not despair speaking; it is anger. To die this way seems so random, so trivial. I have been robbed of meaning before being robbed of life. To die in darkness, alone—for what purpose was I ever alive? It is as if I emerged from darkness into delusion, then sank back into darkness forever.

If only I knew which direction leads to the surface.

The events that have happened since I last recorded an entry are so extraordinary that they have completely altered everything I thought I knew about Iris.

I cannot tell how long I blundered around, blindly seeking some way out with no more than my hands to feel my way. I finally gave in and ate half the meal bar in my pocket, drank from my canteen, and sat down on hard rock to doze off to sleep.

I was awakened by the sound of someone singing. She was still far away, but in the utter silence of the cavern the sound was sweet beyond describing. I leaped to my feet, painfully aware of hope. I could see no sign of light, but I called out for help as loudly as I could. The singing stopped for a moment, and I was seized with fear that she would pass me by, so I cried, "Over here! Help! I'm here!"

Impatiently I waited while the sounds indicated that someone was approaching. Still I could see no light. From time to time I called out to let her know my position, but got no reply. At last a tapping noise became audible, and I cried out again, "Over here!"

"Who doth cry so?" a voice said in antiquated Universal. It was not Sara, nor anyone else I recognized from the ship. In fact, it was a young girl's voice. She was either traveling entirely without light, or my eyes had failed.

"It's Thora," I replied.

She was silent a moment, then said, "Who's that?"

"Who are you?" I said.

"It's Moth," she said. Then, more formally, "Moth-Das Torobe."

"You're not from the ship, then," I said.

"Ship?" she repeated in utter puzzlement.

We had all been told that Iris was uninhabited. Either the reports had been wrong, or I was no longer on Iris.

"Where am I?" I said. "I can't see a thing."

"Thou'rt off the path," she said. "Wait there, I'll come to thee."

She approached with the same tapping sound I had heard before. I realized she must be carrying a stick, like a blind person. Other than that, she moved quite silently. I was startled when she touched me on the cheek, but the feel of another human was so welcome that I quickly grasped her hand. It felt reassuringly familiar and ordinary—a little sweaty and sticky, small, fitting into my hand like a casting into its mold. "Moth," I said, "I am glad to meet you." I have never said a truer thing.

"How came thou here?" she asked.

"I don't know," I said. "I was outside, on the surface, exploring a spatial phenomenon, when there was some sort of gravity shift, and I fell, and then I was here."

"Oh," she said, as if this explanation were the most incomprehensible thing she had ever heard. Then, "Who beminded thee?"

"I don't know what you mean."

She tried another tack. "What habitude are thou from?"

Searching for an explanation she would understand, I said, "We call our ship the Escher. We have come from far, far away to visit you. We want to be your friends."

"Oh," she said brightly. "Thou'rt one of the newcomers!"

"You knew of us?" I asked, thinking they must have seen the shuttle land.

"Oh, aye," she said. "Such a knot as thou hast made is not an easy thing to hide. But we could not visit, as thou knew us not."

She was speaking Universal, but I could not make much sense of what she was saying. I said, "We didn't know you were here. Now that we do, we will be better neighbors." What a botched First Contact this will be, I thought. Epco is not going to be pleased. I would have to take care to minimize the damage. "Can you lead me out of here?" I asked.

"To Torobe, you mean?" she said a little uncertainly.

"Is that your village?"

"Aye."

"Yes, take me to Torobe. Please."

To my horror, she let go of my hand and started off through the darkness.

"Moth!" I cried out, panic-stricken. "Don't leave me!"

"I'm right here," she said from a few steps away, puzzlement in her voice.

I took a step toward her, then another, groping the air with my hand.

"What is amiss with thy feet?" she exclaimed.

"Nothing," I said. "It's my eyes. I can't see."

She grasped my arm again, then ran her hand from my waist down my pants leg to my feet. When she reached my boots she gave a little cry of horror. "Thy feet. They are deformed."

"No, no, those are just my boots," I said. "They come off."

"Thy feet come off?" she exclaimed.

"No, just the boots." To reassure her, I sat down and took off one boot, and showed her the foot underneath. She touched it gingerly.

"Well then, leave them off," she said.

"I can't. I would hurt my feet."

"But how can I lead thee to Torobe if thou cannot walk?"

"I can walk," I said. "I just can't see. You need to hold my arm, and lead me."

"Very well," she said in a tolerant tone, as to a cripple or an idiot.

I took her arm; she shifted the stick to the other hand and set out confidently, tapping the path ahead. Before we had gone five steps we came to an uneven patch, and I stumbled. "You need to tell me if there is a step," I said.

"If thou would but take the casings from thy feet, thou could tell for thyself," she suggested.

"No, I couldn't," I said. "I would just stub my toe."

She led me back the way I had so laboriously come, toward the sound of trickling water, walking at an even, unhurried pace. Somehow, she found a path through the pitch-dark chamber full of boulders, and we soon left the sound of water behind.

"Moth," I asked, "why do you use the stick?"

"To see the path," she said, slowing down. "It is not well marked here."

"So you are using the stick to see?"

"Aye, that's what I said."

"Can you see with your eyes?"

She laughed as if I had asked whether she could see with her shoulder blade. "Can thou?"

"Not now," I said. "Where there is light, I can."

"Well, that must be a comfort to thee," she said tolerantly.

So she was blind. Her seeming competence in this environment was born of familiarity.

"Is that why they send you into the cave?" I asked.

She came to a halt. "What frothy questions thou doth ask. Now be quiet, or I shall lose the way."

So I held my tongue and concentrated on not stumbling. We had been walking perhaps half an hour or more when I began to hear ahead a rushing sound, as of water falling. A breeze touched my face, bringing a complex of smells—sulfur, as of hot springs, and cooking food. I strained to see light ahead, but all remained inky.

Presently I heard a tinkling sound, as of wind chimes, nearby. Moth stopped to put away her stick. "We may go by cord now," she said, letting go of my hand.

"What do you mean?" I said.

She took my hand and placed it on a line that had been strung between posts along the side of the path, approximately waist-high. When I touched it the chimes sounded, and I realized they were hung at intervals from the cord.

"Just follow me," Moth said, and started off again.

"Stop!" I cried out. "Moth, I can't tell where you are. Let me hold your hand."

"By my troth," she said, "dost thou have someone to lead thee about Escher?"

"I don't need anyone to lead me about," I said. "There, I can see."

"Aye, so thou hast said," she replied.

The path led uphill, punctuated with steps and rough spots that Moth seemed to navigate without difficulty. Soon, out of the darkness ahead, an old man's voice called out, "Winden-Wan Torobe! Who doth tread so heavy?"

"Moth-Das!" Moth called out. "I have found a wender lost in the cold lands, and brought her back. Tell the others."

We reached the top of a slope and began to descend. Now the sounds of trickling water and chimes were all around us, and soon we began to pass other people. I could hear hammering not far away, and a whir that sounded like a potter's wheel. At one point I could have sworn we passed a coop of chickens. In fact, I was surrounded by all the sounds and activities of a normal preindustrial village—but all without a particle of light.

No wonder we failed to detect the inhabitants of Iris. They live inside caves, hidden deep in the ground.

Moth kept greeting people along the way, and telling her remarkable news, so that soon people began to come out to verify the rumors. As we progressed toward what was evidently the center of the village, a crowd of giggling children surrounded us, grasping my hands, exclaiming at my boots, feeling me all over. The adults at least announced their names before thrusting their hands in my face and stroking my hair and shoulders. They examined everything about me with their hands, feeling my hair and the caste stone on my forehead, probing into my pockets. I soon felt handled all over. The manner of their greeting convinced me that Moth was no aberration—all of these people were blind.

A tremor of silence passed through the crowd, followed by whispered warnings: "Anath-Not is coming!"

I whispered to Moth, "Is this someone in charge?"

"Well, she thinks so," Moth said flippantly.

The authoritative voice of an elderly woman came from beyond the crowd. "Moth-Das! Hast thou beminded this person?"

"Nay, upon my honor!" Moth said indignantly. "I found her a-wandering in the cold lands. She is helpless as a cripple. She must wear hard shells on her feet, and cannot move a step without being led. She says she is wiser in her own land."

The crowd had parted, and now Anath-Not's voice came from directly in front of me. "Anath-Not Torobe," she said, and out of the dark two hands touched my cheeks, cradling my face.

Moth nudged me. "Greet her, Thora."

Copying Anath-Not's actions, I said, "Thora Lassiter, of Capella." I groped to find her face, though it felt uncomfortably personal. She had the soft, loose skin of old age.

"What brings thee to Torobe?" the old woman asked.

"I came by accident," I said. "If Moth had not found me, I would have perished. I owe her my life. I hope someday I can repay her, and all of you."

"Are thou a trader?"

From this, I realized there must be other villages, and exchange between them. "No," I said. "Perhaps in future there may be trade between your people and mine. But I came to learn about your planet first."

There was a slight pause, as if I had said something nonsensical. But she continued, "Where do thy people dwell?"

Moth interrupted excitedly. "She is from the new habitude, Anath."

Severely, the old woman demanded, "Did this young jackanapes bemind thee?"

"No," I stammered. "That is, I don't know. I don't understand the question."

"We have those about us who bemind all manner of riffraff."

This barb was apparently aimed at Moth, because she protested indignantly, "Not I!"

"Please don't blame her," I said. "I will cause you no trouble, I promise." I could not help thinking how untrue that would be. "All I want now is to find my friends, and return to my home."

"Nay, bide with us awhile," Moth said, taking my hand.

"Hold thy tongue, Moth-Das," Anath said. "This is above thy ken. If Thora wishes to leave, then she shall."

Hesitantly, I said, "I will need some help. Some guidance."

"I told you, she is helpless as a babe," Moth said.

"What mean thou by guidance?" Anath said.

"I need someone to lead me out of here, to the surface, where I left my friends."

There was a short silence, then some puzzled murmurs from the crowd. "What surface is that?" said Anath.

Was it possible they had never been outside? "The surface of the planet," I said. "Outside the cave. The open. The outdoors." None of these words seemed to elicit the comprehension I was striving for.

"What is she prating of?" Anath said impatiently.

"I told you she's no wender," Moth said.

Fearing they would dismiss me as a lunatic, I said, "Our language is a little different from yours. I don't know all the words you use. But I do need to get back to my home. I can't do it unless someone comes with me, to show me the way."

There were subtle stirrings in the listening crowd. Without being able to see facial expressions, I could not interpret their reaction.

"Is Songta there?" Anath demanded.

"Aye, Anath," said an older woman's voice.

"We need to converse. Give us some privacy."

I expected everyone to move away then, but instead they all started to hum. The sound drowned out the voices of the two older women as they spoke quietly to one another.

"Cease!" Anath ordered, and silence was restored. "We have decided to wait till Dagget-Min returns. Thora Lassiter Capella, thou must wait awhile. Someone will show thee hospitality."

"Me! Let me!" Moth cried, seizing hold of my elbow possessively. "She is my stranger. I found her. Let me take her home."

"Moth-Das, know thy place," Songta said sternly. "This concerns the weal of all Torobe, not just thee."

"I have no wish to offend," I said, "but Moth has been a good friend to me. She saved me when I could not save myself."

"As you please," Songta said, though her tone sounded reluctant.

Moth was tugging at my arm to get me away. Apologizing again, I followed her. We left the crowd behind except for a few children who dogged us till we came to a set of stone steps with a little rivulet running beside them. "There are seven steps to climb," Moth informed me.

At the top, she let go of my hand and called out in a breathless rush, "Hanna! I have brought a visitor. I found her in the cold lands, wandering lost. The others tried to steal her, but she came with me instead, because I saved her life."

"What idle chatter is this?" another voice said out of the darkness. It was the calm, tolerant voice of a youngish woman.

"Come and greet her, and thou will see she is no fancy," said Moth.

Moth came bounding to my side like a puppy, leading someone else. "Thora Lassiter," I announced, having learned the etiquette of Torobe. When I put out my hands to feel her face, I found that she was carrying a baby in a sling across her chest.

"Hanna-Das," she said, greeting me.

"Are you Moth's mother?"

Hanna laughed gaily. "Nay, I am not guilty of that. We are sisters."

"My apologies," I said, embarrassed.

"Come sit thee down, and let me fetch some quencher," Hanna said. Without prompting, she took my hand and led me over to a low table, which she showed me by touching my hand to it. Pillows were strewn all around it, so I settled down on one. The floor was covered by some sort of woven mat. Although I had no impression of having passed a door, we were evidently in a house now. Behind me I could hear a rustling sound.

There was a creak of hinges, and presently Hanna came back to the table and poured liquid three times. She set something before me, and I groped for it. It was a pottery vessel, full of something cool. I carefully smelled it before tasting; it had a fruity flavor with a tinge of mint.

"Thank you," I said. Sitting down made me realize how hungry and exhausted I was, but more than either food or rest, I longed for some light. The fact of plant-based food and drink showed they had connections with the outside, though they obviously called it something else. "Where does this come from?" I asked my hostess.

Hanna paused. "This?"

I would have to learn to be more specific. She had no way of knowing if I were speaking of the cup, the drink, or the table. "The drink," I said.

She described for me how to squeeze fruit for the juice, then add water and herbs.

"Where do you get the fruit?" I asked.

"Oh, a wender came by of late," she said. "I bought it."

"Do wenders bring all your food?"

"No, we keep guinea pigs, in the hutch behind you, and chickens. Others raise fish and crabs, or crickets and grubs for feed. Moth is good at finding shrimps, eels, and lichens. But grains and such we buy from the wenders."

"How do you cook your food?" It had occurred to me that there were no fires visible.

"Why, the usual way," she said, humoring me like an idiot. "In a cookpit."

"Can I see your cookpit?"

"I know not," she said, puzzled.

"No, I mean, could you show it to me?" If I could locate some fire, I might be able to fashion a torch.

She clearly thought me demented, but rose and said, "Over here." I rose as well, but almost immediately collided with a piece of furniture.

"Thou must lead her, Hanna," Moth said. "She is purblind."

Hanna came back and took my hand. She led me into what must have been the kitchen. Stooping down, she placed my hand on a surface that was smooth and warm to the touch. "This is the drypit," she said, then switched my hand to another surface. "This is the wetpit."

The smooth surfaces were covers, with handles in the middle. I moved the drypit cover aside, and heat blasted out against my face, together with a delicious smell of cooking food. There was, however, no light.

"Where does the heat come from?" I said.

"From the ground," Hanna answered.

It was apparently some sort of geothermal vent. This would explain the slight smell of sulfur that permeated the air of Torobe. It also would explain why the village was here. They had a self-contained energy source.

I investigated the wetpit and found that it was a boiling hot spring. It was an ingenious and convenient setup. But it got me no closer to seeing.

The smell of the food had made me aware of my hunger. "That smells delicious," I said.

"Well then, let us eat some," Hanna said immediately. She started making thumping noises in the dark; I heard the clash of pottery bowls and the clunk of a ladle. She handed me a spoon and a warm bowl full of something. Moth took my elbow and led me back to the table. For a moment I hesitated, not knowing what was in the bowl, but my hunger overcame my scruples, and I dug in. It proved to be a delicious stew, meat with corn meal. This meant that somewhere on Iris, someone was raising maize.

After the meal, Hanna showed me their bathroom—merely a chamber pot with a seat for a toilet, but a lovely hot spring basin for bathing. The warm water bubbled in from below, and continuously ran over the edge into a channel that carried it off somewhere. My bedroom, which she showed me next, was a pillow-lined alcove separated from the rest of the house with a bead curtain. Nearby, a little waterfall played. After the cave, it seemed idyllic.

The meal, the safety, the comfort had made me stuporously tired. I apologized to Hanna and told her I needed to sleep. "I hope we can talk more in the morning," I said.

There was a puzzled silence, and for a moment I thought I had violated some custom. Then Hanna said curiously, "Morning?"

The ordinariness of the house had made me forget that there would be no morning. They lived in a world without the renewal of day, without even time markers—an eternal Now.

"After I've slept," I said.

"Oh. Good dreams to you."

I dreamed of Orem.

A hot wind touched my face, scented with cooking odors, diesel fumes, and sewage. I was in one of the narrow back streets, sand-colored stucco buildings rising on either side. It was twilight, the only time of day when the women of Orem ventured onto the streets, and there was not an adult man to be seen. "Come quickly," Ashana said at my side—though it was hard to tell it was her, so wrapped she was in brightly printed shawls: one over her head, one around her shoulders, a third around her waist, despite the residual heat that radiated off the walls around us. I gripped my own shawl under my chin and followed her through the jostle of textile lumps under which women were buried. The light was fading fast, and soon the moon would be up; then it would not be safe for any woman to be caught outside the walls of a compound.

Ashana seemed to know the part of the city we were in, though I had always avoided it for its reputation as the haunt of prostitutes and thieves. The half-crumbling buildings seemed full to bursting. Lumpy, well-swathed women leaned out windows to empty garbage cans onto the street, shout for their children, or conduct shrill arguments. I dodged a pile of well-baked rubbish, glad that I had worn shoes, not sandals. At last Ashana led me down three steps to a rickety, urine-stained door. I could not imagine where she was taking me.

Inside, a beaded crone took our money, and we dumped our shawls on the floor where mounds of them were already piled. "Don't worry, this is a place no man ever sets foot," Ashana reassured me as if I were unused to men seeing me undisguised by yards of cloth. She shook out her sweaty hair, and I followed suit. The ceiling was so low I had to stoop, and the gas lamps cast a smoky light, but the scent of burning sage told me we were in a shrine. The wooden door into the next room squeaked on its hinges. We passed through and joined the end of a line of women shuffling forward around the perimeter of the clay-walled room. In the center, women crouched in praying position. The air was full of whispered devotions. On Orem, it was uncommon to see such a mingling of ages and social classes as in this group, united only by their femininity.

As we inched forward, I saw that we were waiting for a chance to peer through a peephole into some sort of cupboard whose contents were hidden behind carved wooden doors. The sight seemed to move the women ahead of us profoundly. One broke into tears; another's legs gave way beneath her and she had to be helped away. "It is the power of Witassa, the Shameless One, that fills them," Ashana said to my bewildered look. "You will see."

When my turn came, I pressed my eyes to the hole and saw into an alcove lighted with dozens of candles. An ancient wooden sculpture stood there: a woman with arms upraised in wild triumph, holding a snake in one hand and in the other a drymen, a ceremonial bronze ax with a crescent-shaped blade. She was clothed, but sensu-

*ality radiated from the image. Her breasts were swelling globes that
seemed to press against the flimsy fabric of concealment, her skirt clung
tight around voluptuous hips and thighs. The idol was viciously hacked
by what looked like ax marks, and there had been no effort to repair
it. The scars of wanton violence were shocking, but in her defiant pose,
the goddess seemed to rise above them.*

*Ashana and I joined the women on hands and knees before the
hidden altar. For a while I knelt silent, trying to work out my reactions. Then I moved my head close to hers and whispered, "Why is
she kept behind the doors?"*

"Her power would be too great, if she were not secret."

"Why are only women allowed to see her?"

*"Men go crazy with terror at sight of her. Did you not see the ax
marks? They have tried to destroy her, but she cannot be destroyed.
Those are the marks of helpless male fear." She spoke with a fierce
pride I had never expected from her. Ashana had seemed the model
of docile obedience.*

"Do men know that women worship her?"

"Of course. They try to stop us."

*The women were here for a glimpse of raw power such as they might
never know. It was intoxicating to them, in their circumscribed
lives.*

"Why is she called the Shameless One?" I asked.

*Ashana turned her head to look directly at me. "Figure it out your-
self."*

*Shame was the primary method of social control on Orem, I
thought. A woman without shame was a woman without restrictions.
One whose innate power could exert itself—at terrible risk.*

*Too great a risk. These women would all go home to their com-
pounds swathed in shawls, never daring to emulate their goddess. I
felt my fists clench, and looked down at them. They were oozing with
blood, but I felt unsurprised at the sight, as if I had expected it. An
urgent prickling sensation passed through me, and I became aware*

*that someone was kneeling behind me, so close I could feel the warmth
of her body. She wanted to speak, had to speak, and so I listened.*

*"It is our power," she said. I could feel it then, surging through me,
currents of sexual magnetism refusing to be concealed. "We are the
hunters, they are the hunted," she said. Her voice was the sound of a
once-placid river in flood. All around me the air was filled with shrill
ululations, and I was transported by the sound. Then the river receded,
and I found that I was standing with my hands raised. I looked at
them, and they were no longer bloody. The women were turned,
gazing at me in astonishment, and I was seized by fear that I had
spoken. I sank back down.*

"Did I say something?" I asked Ashana, shaken.

*"No," she said. "Witassa spoke through you." She glanced at me
sideways, her eyes appraising. "She picks some to be her voice."*

"Why me?" I said.

"Perhaps you have less to lose than the rest of us."

*"Get me out of here," I said. I was suddenly terrified that some-
thing so primitive, so preverbal, could have happened to me—me, a
practitioner of apathi, despite all of my training, all of my control.
Or because of it.*

*When I woke, I lay for a while in the grip of the dream. The emotions
were raw and fresh. Did it truly happen to me, or was it a fabrication
of my overstressed mind? I opened my eyes, and after the bright,
visual dream, the unchanging blackness of the cave left me feeling
stifled and oppressed.*

*At first, I was completely disoriented. I remembered where I was,
but had no sense of my body's relationship to the space around me.
Was I lying in the same direction I had laid down the night before,
or had I shifted 90 degrees, or even 180? My uncertainty about something that had always been instantly knowable filled me with panic.
Frantically I groped around, trying to find something to anchor me.*

My hand brushed the bead curtain, making it clack loudly. I then tried self-consciously to still it, fearing I would wake someone else with my thrashing, and have to explain.

I forced myself to examine my fear. It was almost a reflex, a physical reaction of the deep, primitive brain. My senses longed for light the way a starved person longs for food. Do not people in sensory deprivation start to hallucinate and grow paranoid? And yet, the inhabitants of Torobe function perfectly well. If they can do it, surely so can I. I am an emissary of the Capellan Magisterium.

For a while I sat listening. The soothing rush of the little waterfall near my bed provided a kind of white noise that drowned out most other sounds, giving my room a kind of acoustical privacy. Perhaps that was what it was for. As I kept listening, I could hear chickens rustling and squawking nearby in a quiet, conversational way. Someone was moving around, so I rose and groped my way past the bead curtain. Having removed my boots the night before, I now discovered that the floor was intricately textured under my bare feet. When I came to the edge of the woven floor mat I stopped, knowing there was furniture ahead. "Hanna? Moth?" I said.

"Here, Thora." It was Hanna's voice. She was moving around in the kitchen, just as she had been the night before. Or was it days before? I felt a time-disorientation to match my previous space-disorientation. I had no idea how much time had passed.

"How long did I sleep?" I asked.

Hanna did not answer at once, and I realized I had posed another senseless question. "Longer than my babe," she said from close by. She pressed a mug into my hand, and I found that this time it was full of something hot, an infusion like tea.

"Were thy slumbers peaceable?" she asked pleasantly.

"No," I said. "I had a strange dream."

"Ah." She took my other hand and placed it on a piece of furniture. "There lies the settle," she said. I think I managed to sit down without spilling any of my drink, though I could not be sure.

"Do you wish to tell your dream?" she asked formally.

"No." I was embarrassed by it, and it would mean nothing to her anyway. But there was something troubling that the dream had brought back to mind, though I could not tell why. "I want to ask you about something that happened to me, just before I found myself here." I then described, as precisely as I could, the strange moments before I found myself in the cave.

She was silent a while after I finished, and I finally laughed nervously. "You probably think I'm mad."

"Nay," she said. "I think thou hast touched the Ground."

Thinking back, I had fallen to my knees, and probably did touch the ground. "What does that matter?" I said.

"Not the ground," she said, slapping the floor to show what she meant. "The Ground. All answers lie there, they say, but not plain for the taking. On this side, all we see of it seems like riddle and delusion; on the other side, all is clear."

I could not tell whether she was repeating a folk belief, or describing something real. "How can I get back there—touch it again?"

"Thou can never find thy way deliberate," she said. "Thou cannot seek it, only allow it to come. It is a great gift. There are places where the world is thin between us and it, but those places must be within thee, as well. To reach across, a person must reach inside. Allow happenstance to happen."

"Have you ever . . . touched the Ground?"

"Aye," she said, and her tone was a little bitter. "It gave me no comfort. Sometimes it seems the least worthy find what they seek there, and those who long for solace are barred. I speak not of thee."

"No offense taken," I said.

I was puzzled, but very intrigued, by this information. I now must consider the possibility that these blind people are perceiving something about their environment that we cannot. Perhaps they have evolved a new sense, something that allows them to survive and even flourish in this inhospitable place, despite their handicap. It may be *that they are sensing something real, but explaining it in the language of fable, as other traditional peoples explain things they cannot fully understand.*

I am now determined that as soon as I can escape this cave, I will come back—this time with a light—to study the people of Torobe. I am tantalized by the thought that they can lead me to something I have been seeking for a very long time.

chapter six

"A *native*?" Sara said. "A *human* native?" Her head was too crowded with questions for anything else to make its way out.

On the screen of her terminal, Bakai said nervously, "Yes, a human. That's absolutely all I know. They're bringing it up here to treat its injuries. You'll have to ask David for the rest."

There were not supposed to be any natives. No scans had found fields or villages; there were no plumes of cooking smoke or infrared traces of human body heat. The expedition would have been designed entirely differently if there had been. Linguists, anthropologists, and diplomats would be on board. Not just a single exoethnologist with other assignments.

When Sara emerged into the hall, she saw that the rumor had already gotten out. Little knots of people were gathered in the hall, talking. They looked expectantly at Sara, hoping for news, but she passed them with only a shrug, heading for the lightbeam wayport.

The room outside the translation chamber was now transformed into a decontamination area. David was already there, floating weightlessly, with a wheeled stretcher. A security guard posted at the door tried to prevent Sara from entering. "This is a quarantine area," he said. "No entry."

"David!" Sara called out past the guard's broad shoulder.

"Let her in," David said. "I'll need her."

She floated forward, trying not to collide with the doctor in the excitement.

"Have they arrived yet?" she asked.

"No, they're on the way."

"How bad is the native's injury?"

"Stun gun," the doctor said, disgusted.

"Oh dear God," Sara groaned. The first indigene they met, they stunned and kidnapped. This was going to get things off to a good start.

Bakai arrived with an armful of isolation suits. She shoved one in Sara's direction. Sara took it, but hesitated to put it on. "You know the rules, Callicot," David said, breaking out his own suit.

"This alien is already traumatized," Sara said. "We've injured him, then dragged him into space; now you want us to greet him wrapped in plastic?"

"It's for your own good," he said implacably.

Reluctantly, she pulled on the suit. Before she could seal it, she felt a touch on her arm, and looked up, startled. Atlabatlow had arrived and had floated up behind her, ominous in a black uniform. His hand was icy cold. So was his voice. "Magister Callicot, I must ask you to leave."

Sara fought back an unprofessional urge to raise her voice. "This is a First Contact situation, Colonel. I am the only one on this ship trained for this. In fact, I must ask *you* to leave."

There was an almost imperceptible lift of his chin and lowering of his lids that gave him an expression of raptorlike predation.

There was a commotion at the door as Penny Sutton arrived and pushed her way in past Atlabatlow's guard. Ignoring Sara and David, she turned to the colonel. "Fill me in," she ordered.

His tone of slight aristocratic condescension was so subtle Sara doubted that Sutton even heard it. "We are attempting to set up a quarantine, as the Director ordered," Atlabatlow said. "I am trying to clear the area of nonessential personnel."

Sara didn't wait for an invitation to speak up. "The First Contact would go more smoothly if there were no weapons, soldiers, or other signs of aggression. Security has already done enough damage."

Atlabatlow said, "The alien presents an unknown danger. It would be reckless to expose the scientific personnel."

Sutton's eyes shifted from one to the other of them. That they were enemies was plain now: Sutton saw it, David saw it, even Bakai saw it. Sutton hesitated, then said, "I need to speak to the Director."

"There are established protocols for a First Contact," Sara argued. "If we violate them, there will be hell to pay. There is nothing to decide here. We need to follow the guidelines—or at least, get back to them now that they have been thoroughly trashed."

Sutton looked at Atlabatlow, then back to Sara, and said, "Both of you stay. But Colonel, have your guard wait outside the door. And Colonel . . ." Her voice grew hard. "The Director is going to want an explanation of how this happened."

Stiffly he said, "You will have a report as soon as I am able to question my men."

"Good. Let me know when you have more information." She turned away to the door, gesturing the guard to come with her.

In the ceiling above them, the hatch into the translation chamber slid aside. Bakai shoved an isolation suit at Atlabatlow, and Sara heard him pulling it on. She was watching the ceiling.

First through the hatch was one of Atlabatlow's guards, looking poised for combat inside his isolation suit. He scanned the room, saw his commander, then signaled someone else beyond the hatch. Together they guided a small, limp form through the opening. David guided the stretcher into position, and they gently strapped the unconscious alien onto it.

Sara pushed forward to see. It was a girl just on the cusp of adolescence. She wore a woven gray shirt and short pants over rangy, barefoot legs that the rest of her body hadn't quite grown into. Her limp hands had blunt, dirty fingernails. Her face was impossible not to smile at—pudgy cheeks and little snub nose decorated with freckles, framed by dark ringlets of hair that looked carelessly neglected now. In a few years that hair would be her greatest beauty—that and the long, dark eyelashes that were now motionless against her cheeks.

The doctor bent over her, testing vital signs. Sara looked at the guard. "What happened?"

The guard glanced at Atlabatlow, and apparently got a nod to tell the story. He addressed his commander, his voice muffled by the isolation suit.

"We were continuing our IR grid search over the forest when we got a return indicating a human presence. We immediately landed in a nearby clearing and formed a perimeter circle, when—there she was, right in front of us. No one saw her come out of the forest. Private Ktar was so startled he fired. After that, we didn't know how badly she was hurt, so we elected to evacuate her for medical treatment. There was no one with her."

"Did she say anything?" Sara asked.

"No. It all happened too fast."

"How much do you think she saw?"

"No idea."

David completed his initial medical check, and straightened up. "We'd better get her down to the clinic. She's going to come to pretty soon."

He raised the sides of the stretcher's isolation tent and sealed the girl inside. To Atlabatlow he said, "Tell your guards to clear the halls between here and the clinic." The colonel spoke into his radio, then nodded for the doctor to proceed.

All the way down the illogically angled halls to the clinic, Sara could feel eyes on them from the intersecting corridors, curiosity hanging like static electricity in the air. This was what everyone had come for—contact with the alien. But no one had expected it to come in the form of an ordinary little girl.

At the clinic, David motioned Sara and Atlabatlow to wait outside the double-seal doors of the biohazard suite. "I want to run some quick tests while she's still out," the doctor said.

"I need to be there when she wakes," Sara said.

"Don't worry, I'll call you."

Ill at ease, she watched the stretcher disappear with Bakai and the doctor through the decontamination lock into the next room. Atlabatlow posted himself just inside the clinic's outer door, arms crossed. Voices came from the hall beyond it, but no one tried to enter.

Sara was thinking feverishly about how to conduct a First Contact with a captive, injured alien. She was in a situation that few exoethnologists could ever hope to encounter—dissertations would probably be written about it someday—but she had only minutes to map out a course of action. At last she stripped off her isolation suit. Until they could decipher the language, gesture was going to be the best method of communication, and the girl needed to know they were human, not beings with skins of plastic. Besides, if any biohazards were on Iris, Sara had already been exposed.

The door sucked open, and the doctor reappeared alone, his plastic suit unzipped. "Not yet," he said to Sara's expectant look. "They really gave her a dose."

"Will she be all right?"

"I don't know why not. She'll have some tourist-attraction bruises, but nothing's broken. She's young and healthy."

Beyond the double doors there was a muffled shriek, and a thump. For an instant David and Sara froze, staring at each other; then he dived for the door. But the red light was on, meaning the lock was cycling, and it refused to open. They waited, on edge, till it completed the cycle and Bakai tumbled breathlessly out. Her plump, pretty face was full of fear.

"She attacked me," she blurted.

David made a move as if to rush into the next room; Sara put a restraining hand on his arm. "Attacked you? How?"

"I didn't even know she was awake," Bakai said, stumbling a little in her nervousness. "I was passing the bedside when she lunged at my face."

Sara looked at David. He said, "I gave her a mild stimulant before I left, to help her over the effects of the stun. I've never heard of it making a patient violent."

"She's probably scared out of her wits. David, prepare a sedative, but don't use it unless absolutely necessary. I want to try communicating."

The two of them stepped into the air lock together. There was a window in the inner door, and as the chamber cycled, they pressed forward to look. The native was crouched in the far corner, feeling the walls. Her hands ran back and forth over the smooth ceramoplast surface with an air of intense concentration.

At last Sara signaled David to open the door. The girl did not turn to face them, but her body stiffened, listening.

Sara spoke gently, knowing her tone was all that would come through. "We won't do you any harm."

The native took her hands from the wall and rose from her crouching position. She had the awkward posture of someone not quite grown into her lanky body. Her eyes were closed. She wavered a moment, as if debating whether to bolt for an escape. Sara was about to speak again, in a soothing tone, but the native spoke first.

"Why hast thou beminded me?"

Sara was too surprised to answer. The girl spoke perfect, though antiquated, Universal.

Though she understood the words, Sara couldn't make sense of her question. "What do you mean?"

"Do I know thee?"

"No. My name is Sara Callicot. Don't be afraid, you can open your eyes. Are you feeling all right?"

"Aye." As soon as she said it, the girl swayed dizzily. Then she drew herself up with the dignity of an ambassador and said, "I am Moth-Das Torobe."

"I am honored to meet you," Sara said. "Do you want to sit down?" She gestured at a chair, but the girl's eyes were still closed, and she didn't react. Something crucial occurred to Sara then. "Are we recording this?" she asked. David pointed up to a security camera on the wall and nodded.

With the linguistic problem so unexpectedly resolved, Sara had to abruptly discard most of the plans she had scrabbled together. "I apologize for the way you were brought here, Moth-Das," she said. "It was an accident."

Moth seemed to be listening for something. "What manner of place is this?" she asked.

"It's a place we call a questship," Sara explained. "We have come from very far away to visit your people and be your friends. This is our home."

"You are Thora's people!" Moth exclaimed.

At first Sara was speechless with surprise. Then she said, "You have met Thora?"

"Aye," Moth said. Then, proudly: "I succored her."

Sara felt a surge of relief that she hadn't utterly failed her assignment. "We are grateful," she said. "We have been looking for her. Is she all right?"

Moth hesitated. "Nay, helpless as a babe. She cannot walk, but must needs be led."

That did not sound good. "Where is she?"

"In Torobe, with my sister Hanna."

"We would like to fetch her back. Can you show us the way to Torobe?"

"Now?" Moth asked uncertainly.

"No, when you are ready."

"Oh aye, of course." Then, recollecting something, "But first I must ask the elders. They are already wroth with me for bringing Thora back."

"We don't want to do anything without the consent of the elders."

Ordinarily, a First Contact group spent months doing long-range observations so they knew something of the culture before revealing their presence. That chance was already gone, but Moth offered a new opportunity. In Sara's mind, the urgency of getting the girl back to her family—and Thora back to medical treatment—warred with the need to extract as much information as she could beforehand. She crossed the room to where Moth still stood with her eyes closed. "You can open your eyes," she said.

Moth obeyed, but her dark eyes were fixed and staring. "Why?" she said.

Sara realized the problem then. She asked, "Moth, can you see?"

"See what?"

"Me."

Moth hesitated. "The good dame who came by erewhile was discomfited when I did greet her."

"How do your people greet one another?"

Without a word of warning, Moth reached out for Sara's face. Instinctively, Sara pulled back. The girl cried out contritely, "Alas, I have offended thee."

"I was startled, Moth, that is all," Sara said. "I didn't know what you were doing. Please, greet me."

A new thought must have struck Moth, for she asked in a small voice, "Are thou human?"

"Yes," Sara said.

Now she seemed positively reluctant, so Sara took Moth's right hand and placed it on her cheek. Slowly the girl explored Sara's face with her fingers.

Sara looked back at David. He shrugged, looking as surprised as Sara felt. "Her pupils reacted normally," he said. "There was nothing to suggest . . ."

"Moth, are you . . . unlike the others in your village?" Sara was wondering if Moth were an outcast for her disability, but was trying not to ask a leading question.

Moth's expression didn't change, but her voice took on a new tone of frustration. "I want to be a wender. 'Tis not an unworthy part to be a wender. What would we do without them, survive on snails and crayfish?"

This was not the answer Sara had expected, so she tried again. "Do they think you can't be a wender because you cannot see?"

Part sulky and part defiant, Moth said, "Nay, they want me *not* to see. They want me like unto them, cooped up in Torobe, never venturing past their noses."

"I understand that. But do they use their eyes in ways you cannot?"

"Nay, what mean you?"

Sara said, "It may be that we newcomers have another sense than your people have. Sight."

Moth was silent, though she looked alert. At last she said, "Does it give thee great power, this sight?"

The question surprised Sara, but she said, "I suppose it does, in a way."

"Can thou give it to me?"

Sara looked at David. He shrugged. She said, "I don't know. We'd have to find out . . . learn more about you, and your people."

"Oh, please! I will do aught thou command."

Sara couldn't help smiling. The girl was clearly thinking mythically. Here she had been spirited away to another world by incomprehensible powers—no wonder she thought the beings she met had magic gifts she might earn by performing some task. But wasn't it true, in a way? If the people of Iris were blind, sight would seem like magic to them. It struck Sara that this might be one of the most ethically daunting First Contacts any Capellan expedition had faced. And they were totally unprepared for it.

Moth was sagging back against the wall, and Sara came to her senses. "Where are my manners? We need to offer you food, and drink, and rest. We need to welcome you to our village." She took Moth's hand in hers, and squeezed it. It was small, damp, and a little sticky.

"Welcome to *Escher*, Moth," she said.

On the screen, five isolation-suited figures urgently wheeled a sealed gurney down the hall. The music was low and pounding; the recording was slightly speeded up to make them walk faster. "No one knew what mysteries they would find," a deep-voiced male narrator said. "But the Epco explorers could never have guessed the strangeness of the discovery waiting for them."

The scene shifted to Moth's face, a little grainy from the security camera. She said, "What manner of place is this?"

The music had fallen expectantly silent. "Moth, can you see?"

"Nay, what mean you?"

"It may be that we newcomers have another sense than your people have. Sight."

"Can thou give it to me?"

A cut to a scene of the sun rising over the planet, a swelling chord of music as the light spread. The narrator said, "This would be the Epco mission of mercy: to bring light to a planet of the blind."

The Epco logo glowed with a slogan, CREATING NEW FRONTIERS.

Groans of protest went up all around the table. "Get that man something useful to do," Magister Sarcodan said.

"You've got to have an angle," Mr. Gibb said defensively. "It's not dramatic otherwise. If people knew how boring you scientists really were—"

"This crap undermines our professional credibility," Sarcodan said. He turned to Sara. "Don't give him permission to use your image."

"Our images are all Epco's property," Sara said. "It's in our contracts."

There was a startled silence around the conference table. Apparently no one had read the commercial-use addenda.

"You mean we're really actors in an Epco advertisement?" Magister Prem said.

"If they'd wanted actors, they would have sent me attractive ones," Mr. Gibb grumbled in an undertone.

"All right." Director Gavere closed down the discussion. He was clearly nettled that his attempt to unite them all in support of Epco had instead bonded them in opposition to Mr. Gibb. "Our mission is the overriding purpose here. The potential of a medical market in optical implants is the first good news we've generated for Epco so far. It might help underwrite some of your more . . . esoteric interests."

Sara had come to this meeting thinking that it had been called to discuss how the discovery of natives on Iris had altered the mission. She was astonished to find that she was virtually the only one concerned. All the other scientists were still competing to persuade the Director to allow them back down to the planet.

Sandhya Prem stood to introduce Hua Ming, the botanist, who had come to make a presentation advocating his studies of the native ecosystem. "Magister Hua has made extraordinary progress, considering the short time he had on the planet," she said.

As the botanist showed picture after picture of Irisian plants, Sara gathered that she had missed a raging controversy among the biologists about taxonomy. She concluded that Ming's viewpoint had prevailed when he showed a picture of a plant like a globe on a stalk, crowned by a ring of sharp spikes. "This is the type specimen of the first new species discovered on Iris," he announced. "We have named it a brickle, species name *Brickellia*."

Nelson Gavere, who had been stifling a yawn, sat forward. "So this is new, never before discovered?"

"Yes," Ming said, pleased at the reaction. He then showed a slide of a seemingly identical plant. "This is *Impedomia*. The difference, you see, is that there are five spikes instead of seven."

Everyone was silent. Hua Ming was about to continue when Sara spoke up. "What's the significance of having five spikes?"

Ming stared at her a second, then explained, "It's the difference between two otherwise identical plants."

"But why is it so meaningful?" Sara pressed.

"Because it puts them in different species."

"But you just made up those species."

"No, I didn't. The plants are different, can't you see?"

"Couldn't there just be five-spiked brickles and seven-spiked brickles?"

"No, because the five-spiked ones are impedomia."

Sara gave up, and Hua Ming continued on with his pictures of brickle meadows. Sara found herself mentally sorting out the species in his pictures. It was satisfying, because the comprehension-defying mix of Irisian plants was now composed of known things, brickles and impedomia. Known things about which nothing was known but their names—still, it gave her a sense of mastery.

Director Gavere was looking pointedly at his watch, so Penny Sutton spoke up. "Thank you, Magister Hua, that was very informative. Are there any other matters to bring up?"

Sarcodan said, "When can we get back down to the planet?"

Penny turned to Atlabatlow, who was sitting sphinxlike, arms crossed. "I cannot authorize that yet," he said.

Sarcodan started to argue, and so Sara waved her hands to get everyone's attention. "I'm really sorry to have to break this to you," she said, "but the discovery of natives on Iris changes our whole legal situation. In Capellan law, the natives have copyright on all the knowledge generated from their planet. Until they give us informed consent, we can't take any more information. If we do, they could sue Epco to get it back, and all our work would be for nothing."

The scientists were staring at her in shades of disbelief and outrage. Clearly, none of them was familiar with First Contact protocols. How could they be? A lifetime had passed since the last First Contact. "Even information we discover ourselves?" Hua Ming asked.

"Even that," Sara said. "It's proprietary, until we have permission."

"Well then, how do we get permission?" Sarcodan said briskly.

"We'll have to negotiate a deal."

"How quickly can you do that?"

Sara rolled her eyes. "We've got to establish trust and friendship. Our having kidnapped one of their children hasn't gotten things off to a very good start."

Atlabatlow's attention was focused on her like a laser weapon. "We can return her as soon as the doctor gives clearance. The less she learns about us, the better."

"You think Moth is a *threat*?" Sara said.

"The first thing out of her mouth was a lie," he said. "My men have searched the entire area where they found her, and there is no village within walking distance, even for a sighted man, much less a blind girl. She clearly has unknown abilities that allow her to survive in a hostile environment, despite her handicap. Her first question on hearing of our sight was whether it gives us power. And her people are currently holding one of our expedition members. I think that is all significant."

His paranoid revision of events left Sara breathless. She scarcely knew where to start. "They're not holding Thora; they rescued her."

"So the native says. I still think it is fortunate we have a hostage to exchange."

Sara was speechless.

"Well, if we're going to exchange her, let's do it quickly," said Sarcodan. "Get together whatever beads and trinkets they want for their informed consent, so we can get back to work." Then, seeing Sara's horrified expression, he said, "It's a joke. Don't be so humorless."

Sri Paul spoke up in his gentle, earnest voice. "My department is deeply concerned about the natives, and our impact on them. We do not wish to see the natural concord of their world disturbed by our greed and our technology. We think they ought to be protected, since their simplicity may be the salve our souls need."

Once again, Sara barely knew what delusion to address first. There was no evidence that the natives were simple, or in concord. She finally settled for saying, "This is why First Contacts are so complicated. We have to balance all these concerns, and the wishes of the natives themselves. It takes time, everyone."

"Well," said Director Gavere, "I am sure Epco chose the person most capable of carrying it out, and we are very glad to have you. You'll have my support, whatever you decide. Just move it along as fast as you can."

After the meeting, Sara paused in an empty hallway, overwhelmed by the enormity of the trouble she was in. Whatever went wrong, it was going to be blamed on her. And this mission was guaranteed to go wrong.

The truth was, it was already too late for Sri Paul's concerns. First Contacts were like particle physics: the act of observing changed the thing observed. The explorers' first step—revealing themselves— forever altered the people they had come to study.

Sara had no ideological qualms about changing other cultures— that was inevitable, and no people wanted to be frozen like flies in amber. Sara had always thought of herself as a prospector, but not for crude resources like minerals or water, which were untransportable anyway. Exoethnologists were after cultural resources—new knowledge and new ideas, the ultimate source of all profit. They took advantage of the fact that, in both biology and culture, isolation created diversity. In a closed information system, divergence took place, and the more different the system became, the more valuable it was. But when the isolation was broken, cultures were like thermodynamic systems—uniformity quickly resulted. There was always a short window of opportunity to document and save the precious information before it was hopelessly contaminated by adaptation. Biologists' window of opportunity was longer. Culture could change with blinding rapidity.

Iris was more isolated, more different, than any planet yet discovered, and its cultural treasures might be incalculable. Yet Sara would have to resign herself to seeing them lost before her eyes, simply for lack of resources to record it all.

As she approached the clinic, where Moth had spent the night sleeping off the effects of the stun gun, Sara passed two guards dressed in maroon-and-gray Epco uniforms. The first one stared through her as if she were not there. She tested the atmosphere by greeting the second one civilly; he scowled and nodded with a chopping motion of his chin. There was a pugnacious taint in the air.

When she entered the clinic, she found Moth enthroned in an examination chair, wearing a helmet that was scanning her brain activity. "Moth, you gave consent for this, didn't you?" she exclaimed in alarm.

"Oh, aye!" Moth said brightly. "'Tis right curious."

"Please give me some credit, Callicot," David said.

"Sorry, I've been talking to ethical Neanderthals."

Moth's brain activity was displayed in bright colors in a three-dimensional vitrine. "See anything interesting?" David said.

"Not my field," Sara admitted.

David rotated the image so the back of Moth's brain was displayed. "The visual cortex," he said. "In our brains, it's what processes visual information."

It was lit up like a patchwork quilt. "Does that mean it's active?" Sara said.

"Yes, she's doing something with that part of her brain; who knows what."

"Have you checked out her eyes?"

"Yes. I'm no ophthalmologist, but I can't see anything wrong, and neither can my diagnostic devices. You can help me by watching this display. Tell me if it changes." He took a light pen and shone it in Moth's eyes, moving it slowly back and forth. "Moth, tell me if you see anything," he said.

She didn't answer, but Sara saw a change in the display of her visual cortex. There was a pattern of activity as if something were moving back and forth across the surface of her brain.

"I'll be damned," David said when Sara pointed it out.

"Is that the image of the light pen, projected on her brain?" Sara asked.

"Yes. The input from the retina goes by optic nerve to the thalamus, and then it gets mapped onto the visual cortex, just like a screen. That's how a headset works. It records the patterns of one person's visual cortex, and then replicates them in another person's, by exciting the neurons in the same patterns. Our brains then interpret it as sight."

"How could the input be getting to her visual cortex, but she still can't see?"

"It must be a processing problem. The raw visual input goes through a lot of editing and interpretation before we become aware of it. I expect you don't notice that the image of the world is inverted on your visual cortex, just like a pinhole camera. And you don't notice that there's a big blind spot in your visual field where the optic nerve attaches to the retina. Or that your eyes actually move in saccades about four times a second. Our brains edit all that out. We just don't see it."

"So you think maybe her brain is editing out too much?"

"Could be. It could also be something like attentional blindness. To see something, you have to be aware of it. When people are paying attention to something else, their brains edit out distractions right in front of them."

Sara turned to Moth, who was listening. "Moth, look again and tell us if you notice anything."

David moved the light back and forth in front of her. For a while she didn't react. At last she said, in a puzzled voice, "Dost thou mean the blotches?"

"Maybe. What do the blotches look—seem—like?"

"Like vapors, unrealities. They come only when I'm not trying to think. They are like unto noise that meaneth naught."

"All right, concentrate on the blotches, and describe them."

"Nay, they go awry if I concentrate."

"Then just relax. See if you can notice anything."

For a long time nothing happened. Sara had just about given up when she noticed that Moth's hand was moving back and forth in time with David's. She gripped David's shoulder and pointed. "You're seeing it, Moth!" she exclaimed.

"Nay. Nay, I'm not," the girl protested.

"You were moving your hand!"

"Oh. 'Twas but a rhythm I thought I heard."

Sara and David looked at each other. "That is fascinating," David said. "She was seeing it, but her brain interpreted it as auditory input, not visual."

An idea came to Sara. "David, you said the headset recorded the patterns of the visual cortex. If we recorded hers, couldn't one of us experience what she is seeing?"

David looked disturbed. "That's an ethically slippery idea, Callicot. There is no way she could give informed consent."

"Oh. Right." Sara felt embarrassed at her lapse.

"Sorry. I don't mean to be a prig," David said.

"No, you're right. We've got to watch each other's backs."

She realized now that while David had been absorbed in the experiment, his whole demeanor had changed. He was one of the most urbane men she had ever met outside a city, but his sarcastic wit hid a weariness of spirit. That had vanished when an idea had captured him, and he had become like a boy. Now that he was self-conscious again, it came back. She wondered briefly why he had come on this expedition.

Moth, who had been waiting patiently while they discussed her, finally interrupted. "Well, what say you? Am I worthy of sight?"

"Oh, you're worthy, Moth," Sara said, squeezing her arm. "We just can't figure out why you can't see now. There's nothing preventing you. It's like you never learned."

"But I could learn now?" she said eagerly.

Sara looked at David. "I don't know," he said. "It sure would be interesting to try."

"Someday, maybe," Sara said, remembering her own obligations. "First, we have to get you back to Torobe, Moth."

"Why?" she said, disappointed.

"Your family will be worried about you."

"Nay, not them. Hanna knows I go a-wending. I would stay here and receive thy teachings."

There was nothing Sara wanted more than to have some time to learn about Moth's culture before diving into it. "Well, maybe just a little while," she said.

She appropriated a suite of empty rooms next to the clinic for Moth and herself to move into. "It's meant for chronic patients," David told her, "but the two of you are as chronic as I've got now."

"Perfect! An Irisian embassy," Sara said.

And so she started calling it the Embassy. Four bedrooms opened onto a combined dining and lounge area. To Sara, it looked gray and sterile, but when Moth entered, it was transformed from drab to miraculous.

Sara watched Moth explore her new domain. She moved hesitantly at first, but as her confidence grew she adopted a gliding gait that made every gesture a dance. The kitchen fixtures, those marvels of Capellan technology, held no interest for her; it was the walls that drew her attention. She ran her hands across them, following them all around the perimeter of the room, then around the doorway into the next room. "They go on and on!" she marveled.

"Don't your houses have walls?" Sara asked.

"Nay, not like unto this. At home, the world is all of a piece. Thy world is all divided up into bits." Sympathetically, she added, "Dost thou not know how to be rid of them?"

"The walls? We don't want to be rid of them. They give us privacy. Without them, we'd be all heaped in together."

"Would that be an ill shift?"

"We would have to look at . . . hear every word everyone else was saying," Sara said.

Moth frowned a little, troubled by some thought. Sara asked, "What is it?"

"Dost thou not wish to be with thy husband, Sara?"

"What, you mean David? He's not my husband."

"Why not? He seems a goodly man."

"He's very goodly. But we are colleagues, that is all."

If the walls had been amazing, the bathroom was a source of endless delight. Moth loved the cool texture of the ceramic, and startled herself into a gale of giggles by turning on the spigot. Since she was conspicuously grubby, Sara suggested an adventure with the bathtub. Without the slightest hesitation, Moth stripped off her clothes, and Sara surreptitiously bagged them to send to the lab for analysis. She explained the various dispensers of soaps and shampoos, and left

Moth to her discoveries. Half an hour later, the girl emerged into the common room, glowingly clean and perfectly naked. Sara headed her off into one of the bedrooms, and said, "When you come out where others might see you, you must always wear clothes."

"Why?" she said.

"Because it's our custom not to look at each other naked."

"Oh. Are the workings of thy eyes harmful?"

"No, nothing like that. It just offends people."

Moth seemed mystified, but Sara didn't want to get into a discussion of nudity mores just then. She dug out a stretch suit with an Epco logo for the girl to wear. But when she tried to offer slippers, Moth refused. "How should my feet know where they are, if I wrap them in casings?" she argued.

"But what do you do on the plan—in your home? The grass is like razors there."

"Only the mad go into the grass," Moth said.

She was surprisingly dexterous at avoiding obstacles. When Sara saw her avoid a door she had been about to smack into, she asked how Moth had known it was there.

"I felt it on my face," she said.

"What did it feel like?"

"A stillness."

Later, when Sara mentioned this talent to David, he theorized that she might have some sort of echolocation sense. But when they tested her, they found that her obstacle-detector only worked on massive objects that came near her face. She was still quite capable of tripping over a low table. Sara was actually disappointed when David did some research and found the phenomenon had once been well documented, and called "facial seeing."

Moth's hearing turned out to be only marginally more acute than a sighted person's. She could hear a slightly larger range of frequencies, and distinguish smaller variations in frequency, but the differences were not significant.

"Her hearing *seems* more acute than mine," Sara told David on the second day. "She sometimes calls a sound to my attention that I didn't hear."

"It may be a matter of skill, not ability," David suggested. "She *notices* more. She can make more sense of what she hears than we do, because her attention's not divided."

What Moth could not learn was navigation. Even in the small complex of rooms that comprised the Embassy and the clinic, she was continually lost.

"A murrain on thy walls!" she exclaimed. "Why dost thou bear with them?"

"What is your village like?" Sara probed.

"In Torobe, all is texture and detail," she said. "In thy cavern, all ways are alike. Thy floors do not talk to my feet, and there are no songs in the paths. Thy habitude is ugly." She stopped herself, and was about to apologize, but Sara laughed.

"Yes, compared with your planet, our habitude is very ugly." But she knew they meant different things, because all her own concepts of beauty were visual. There was a fundamental wall at the very core of their experience. Sara could never know what Moth meant by a simple word like "ugly."

"How did thy people find this place?" Moth asked.

"We didn't find it, we built it." Seeing Moth's speechless amazement, she added, "Or rather, our ancestors built it, and sent it away to journey out here. When it found your planet, it called us and we came out to live in it." Even in her own ears, this explanation sounded bizarre.

"You are very clever folk," Moth said thoughtfully.

It was two days before Sara had a chance to take a break. When she finally strolled down the hallway away from the Embassy, she was startled to come upon a security checkpoint staffed by a beefy guard of ambiguous sexual identity, named Sal, who looked strong enough to snap Sara's neck. "Name?" she demanded as Sara came up, though she surely knew it already.

"What is going on here?" Sara said. Beyond the checkpoint, two uniformed guards were installing a surveillance camera trained on the hallway.

"Just give your name," Sal advised, consulting a checklist.

"No. I demand to see your boss."

Sal spoke into her radio, and Atlabatlow arrived so promptly that Sara wondered if he had been lurking nearby in hope of a confrontation.

"This is sheer intimidation," Sara said hotly.

"We are taking necessary precautions," he said in a voice that would have stopped glaciers in their tracks.

"Precautions against what? A little blind girl? Does she really scare you so badly?"

The taunt only tightened his control. "We have no idea what abilities she may have. Everything we learn about her makes that clear. Her visual cortex is doing something unknown, her attentional blindness means she is concentrating on something we can't imagine."

"You've been watching us?" Sara said, feeling her privacy violated.

"You should have expected that," he said.

"I didn't know I was under surveillance. I thought we had rights. The right to consent."

"You didn't hesitate to propose invading someone else's mind by headset."

Stung, Sara said, "But I didn't do it!"

"Didn't you?"

He was staring as if to burn her to cinders on the spot. She realized he wasn't talking about Moth; he was talking about his own headnet recordings. He had found out that she too had dabbled in surveillance.

She returned to the Embassy to think. Moth was with David,

performing more tests, so the rooms were empty. In the silence, Sara felt watched. She placed a voice call to Ashok.

"Ashok, come here, I need you."

There was a pause before he answered cautiously, "What for?"

"I'll tell you when you get here."

He came about ten minutes later. "You realize you have gorillas in your hallway?" he said when she let him in.

"Yes. That paranoid spook's got a vendetta against me," she said.

"I know."

"Has he gotten to you?"

"Oh, yes." Ashok managed to look nonchalant, but he was clearly angry. "If we had another pepci technician, I think I'd be on my way back home. But he couldn't prove anything."

"He's probably listening now."

"I've begun to assume that at all times. Hello, Colonel."

"Can you help me out?"

He understood. "Of course. Let me just fetch a little equipment."

He returned with a satchel full of handmade bug detectors. "I told your handlers it was a scientific experiment," he said, stroking his Mephistopheles beard.

Sara watched in admiration as he scanned the room. "Your hidden talents amaze me, Ashok."

"Someday I'll tell you about my time in the Balavati underground," he said, climbing on a chair and raising a ceiling panel.

"*What* Balavati underground?" Sara said skeptically.

"We don't reveal it to people who collaborate with our oppressors," he said, his voice muffled by the ceiling.

"As if you could bear to keep any resistance secret."

"Aha!" He emerged with a small device trailing antenna wires.

By the time he was through, there was a little pile of microphones and spycams on the table. Looking at them, Sara felt her skin crawl. "That does it," she said. "I'm moving to Torobe."

But when she brought up this plan, she met an unexpected

obstacle: Moth. "*Escher* is full of wonders," the girl said. "Methinks I would stay and earn my sight."

"But Moth, we're worried about our friend Thora. We want to make sure she's all right."

"I will lead thee to her," Moth bargained, "if thou will but teach me to see."

"How on earth are we supposed to teach someone to see?" Sara asked.

Ashok, Touli, David, and Sara had found a private retreat: the observation bubble where Sara had first met Thora. The room was flooded with Irislight. The three men were floating next to the windows, like daredevils above a three-hundred-mile precipice. Sara kept a solid wall at her back as an anchor.

They all broke the seals on their beer bags and drew long draughts through straws. "Ah," said Ashok, "pretty good, for beer reconstituted from a lightbeam."

"If the wayport couldn't handle beer, I'd worry about all of us," Sara said.

"You mean you *don't?*" Touli muttered.

There was an easy companionship among them, a camaraderie Sara savored. This was the perfect relationship—not too close, not too far.

She returned to the problem that was puzzling her. "It's not like any of us ever learned to see. We just did it."

"Actually, we *did* have to learn, as infants," David said. "Babies do it in the first few months of life, when they're still laying down neural circuitry. Whether Moth can do it now, who knows? At least she's young and motivated."

"But even if we can teach her, *should* we?"

"Why not?" Touli rumbled, basso profundo. "Wouldn't you want to learn, if it was you?"

"This from a man who's devoted his life to inventing machines that sense things we can't. Of course *you* would."

Ashok stirred restlessly. "But even when Touli's machines bring back data, we've still got to interpret them through senses that evolved to detect things with a bearing on our survival. Anything that doesn't threaten us or improve our chances to reproduce, we can't sense."

"Not even that," David said. "Can you tell me what your liver is doing right now? Your liver is essential to your survival, and you still can't sense it."

"You're making me feel inadequate," Sara said.

"We're all inadequate," David answered. "Just think: the light from the outside world is mapped onto the retina, then further mapped onto the visual cortex, then broken apart and analyzed in other areas of the brain. At every step there's a loss of information. In the end, what we are aware of is not the outside world per se, but the image of the world projected onto our brains. Plato was anatomically right; we do see shadows on a wall."

Three hundred miles below, the pageant of light that was day on Iris was building to its climax. The continent, as far as the eye could see, was a bed of tinsel stirred by the wind. The boundaries of a phantom mountain range had emerged in the northern hemisphere. It was an optical illusion that would be gone by the next orbit. Visual light had proved useless in mapping Iris.

Touli stretched out his legs like a graven colossus, looking at the planet. "The Corroborationists are beginning to say that Iris is actually a metaphor placed here for our benefit, and the proper mode of understanding it is not analysis, but allegory. A planet of illusions, where gemstones grow from trees, and all you see is your own reflection."

"Oh, who the hell are we kidding?" Ashok said. "We're all Corroborationists. We've all come here to confirm our preconceptions. Some of us want to confirm that analytical thinking is best. Others want to confirm theories about how life evolves. But you know what?

We're all going to be right. Because Iris is going to be exactly what we each came here to find."

"I don't know," Sara said, "I think Iris might have some surprises for us."

"But will we be able to see them? When you lot were down on the planet, every one of you called those things you encountered 'trees.' They didn't look like trees, they didn't sound like trees, they obviously *weren't* trees. But because you called them that, everyone who comes after us is going to shrug and say, 'Oh, that's just a tree.' We've undiscovered them."

They all watched the blinding crescendo of colors below. David said, "It doesn't seem fair. All this beauty in a planet, and the only sentient life-form can't even see it. What kind of preconception does that support?"

"That the universe is deeply ironic," Touli said.

chapter seven

I am exhausted. All day long I have been disoriented, unable to re-lax, straining to make sense of this cursed, lightless place. If only I could sneak a look from time to time, just to get my bearings, it would make all the difference. I suppose this is what babies must experience all the time: having to construct a world out of a bombardment of new sensations. But my brain is not as supple as theirs. I long for the familiar.

Sitting here in my bedroom in Hanna's house, my heart is still pounding too fast. I can feel the weight of dark pressing down on me, making it hard to breathe, as if I were trapped in a small space. I am trapped—in the small space of my mind, with nothing but invisibilities outside.

It seems to be night here—no, I need to stop thinking in terms of day and night, because I have no idea how much time has actually passed. It is a sleeptime, and the village has gone quiet. I have no tangible evidence it has not vanished around me. For all I know, Torobe and all the world could have ceased to exist beyond the mat I am sitting on, the recorder I am holding. Reality has shrunk to what I can touch.

But why should that be? Why did I trust my eyes so implicitly before? Eyes can be deceived, too. On Orem I saw things that did not exist. I find I am thinking of Orem too much. Perhaps it is the strength of the emotions I have been feeling, breaking down the barriers the curators built around my memories. Perhaps that was why I felt such dreamy detachment when they declared me cured—because emotions open windows they didn't want me looking through.

I need to concentrate on something else. I need to record the events of this day—this wake cycle. I have learned a great deal, but I am no closer to finding a way out.

That was the first subject I raised with Hanna after breakfast. She only said, "We must bide awhile till Dagget-Min or another wender of probity returns."

"No one else can help me?"

"Not to get to thy home."

I tried to explain that I didn't need them to lead me home, just to the outside where my tracking signal would work. But I soon ran into the same linguistic barrier I had encountered before. I didn't know what they called the land outside the cavern, and all my guesses were wrong. For a moment I suspected that they were deliberately concealing it, but that is probably just my nkida.

"I can show thee round Torobe," Hanna offered, to mollify me.

I quickly agreed, and stood to set off. She said, "Nay, let us stay till the weather is better."

"Weather?" I said blankly.

"Aye, listen," she said.

I did. "I can't hear anything but the waterfall."

"That's it. There is no world out there."

I had no idea how to take this. "You're not serious, are you?"

She laughed. "'Tis still and dead. Not fit to be going far. Best to wait till there is a direction in the world."

I learned what she meant a little while later, when a wind began to stir—first just a gentle gust, then a steady, damp breeze smelling of rock. It woke a thousand wind chimes all around us, and I remembered the cords strung with chimes along the paths. From one direction came a clacking noise, from another a rustle of fabric. With the wind, Torobe became a soundscape with dimension and direction. There was now near and far, upwind and downwind.

"We have a saying, that the wind is gracious, for it bringeth the world out of silence," Hanna said. "Each time it comes is like a new little creation, when all things form out of the void. When the wind speaketh, its language is the world."

I stood a while with my eyes closed, listening to the creation of the world around me.

Then my Capellan senses came back. The wind must be driven by atmospheric conditions on the outside, I thought. It might be a significant clue. "Does the wind always come from the same direction?" I asked.

"Nay," said Hanna. "There is the hotbreath and coldbreath, and the fragrant easebreath. There is the uneasy fretwind and the bowler blow. We have many winds to amuse us."

"What direction does the easebreath come from?"

"Why, from the easebreath direction."

I soon deduced that the winds are the natives' orientation mechanism. They have no north, south, east, or west; instead, they have a three-way directional system of easebreath, hotbreath, and coldbreath. I think she called the easebreath fragrant because it smells of foliage, *and therefore comes from outside. It is a clue, but not a useful one at the moment.*

As she was getting the baby ready to go out, I heard another clue—a chittering sound in the air far above. When I asked Hanna about it she said, "Birds."

I think they are actually bats. We must not be far from the outside. Bats need to forage for insects by night. "Where do the birds go?" I asked.

"Wherever they please." There was amusement in Hanna's voice.

"Has anyone ever followed them?"

"Nay, we have not wings."

I apologized for my crazy questions. "I am just trying to find my way home," I said.

"And you would fly thither like a bird?"

"If I could."

I was pulling on my boots when Hanna said, "Nay, leave off thy clompers."

I hesitated, but since I had been going around in bare feet I had noticed that the floor of Hanna's home was textured in patches: here a rubbly surface, there a grooved one. I asked her if it were meaningful. "Oh, aye," she said, as if suddenly realizing why I was so blind.

Now that I had a patient teacher to lead me, it turned out that I was surrounded by coded markers. Absolutely everything in Torobe has meaning. The textures on the floor signal thresholds, edges, and steps. The paths are lined with water channels to give them aural definition, and to signal stairs, slopes, and turns.

Demonstrating, Hanna said, "The furrows tell thy feet that steps are ahead. Then the cascade doth tell when they start."

"Isn't it dangerous to have a stairway in the path? Don't people fall?"

"Well, if they are drunk or not paying attention, all manner of ill may befall. They must listen to their feet."

Hanna led me into the heart of town. She would have walked with a measured, methodical gait, but I held her back, moving like a timid old lady, afraid of unseen hazards. As we passed people's homes, Hanna explained that the chimes on the cords lining the pathways were also coded; each resident had a particular set of notes, so that she always knew where she was. Doorways were marked with rattling curtains of something like seedpods. Even people were defined by the jingling jewelry they wore on ankles, wrists, and hems. If I stood still and paid attention to all the clues, I could almost form a mental map of the village around me. For me, it took an effort; doubtless Hanna does it automatically.

When I understood how deliberate and orderly everything was, I said in awe, "Did your people build all this?" As soon as the words left my mouth I was ashamed at the condescension in them. Why should I doubt that people without sight could manage such sophisticated engineering and construction? They are competent and self-sufficient here, while I am the disabled one. I had to think that in worlds where there are still blind people, the main obstacle they face is coping with a landscape not designed for them. What would an influx of sighted immigrants do to this culture, so perfectly adapted to their circumstances? Would we not overwhelm them with our haste, disorder, and acoustical pollution?

Fortunately, Hanna heard no paternalism in my tone, only admiration. As we passed into the heart of the village, other people we met called out their own names in greeting, and Hanna replied with hers. It seemed to be the equivalent of midday.

She finally turned aside into a home that stood a little back from the path. "I have an errand here," she explained, "with Rugli the sound carver."

"Sound carver?" I said.

"Listen and thou shalt hear."

She shook a clacker by the door, and a man's voice called out vigorously, "In the workshop!" Hanna led me forward through the blackness into an area that was a perfect cacophony of whirring, jingling,

hooting, ratcheting, sighing, crackling sounds. "Is't not wondrous?"
Hanna said at my side. "'Tis like being in a world of shapes unknown."

I could not imagine what she meant.

Rugli came to greet us, and Hanna explained who I was. "Welcome, stranger," he said, feeling my face curiously. I touched his, and got an impression of apple cheeks and a short frizz of hair and beard. "Comest thou to trade?" he asked.

"No—not yet."

"Well, if thy people love music, I fashion it," he said. "Instruments, chimes, reeds, knockers, and whimsies."

The sounds around us were evidently being produced by the wind blowing on an assortment of devices—the whimsies, I had to assume. We had interrupted Rugli in the midst of cutting some wind chimes. "Where do you get the materials?" I asked.

"The chime leaves?" he said.

I thought of the chime trees outside and said eagerly, "Yes!"

"Rugli is a master songwender," Hanna said. "He hath taught Moth a bit."

"Nay, she took to it natural," Rugli said.

"But the leaves," I persisted. "How do you get them?"

"Do your people lack leaves?" Rugli said slyly. "I can sell you some."

He deflected every question so deftly, I finally realized I was impolitely asking for proprietary knowledge, like a trade secret. A Capellan would have acted the same as he.

He did explain how he cut a chime, first scoring then breaking it like glass, drilling a hole, and carefully tuning it by sanding the edges with a treadle-driven wheel. At the end he demonstrated his wares by striking a series of chimes that all sounded the same note.

"You must have perfect pitch," I said.

He understood at once what I meant. "Aye, 'twould be a tedious job without it, like speaking without knowing the words."

When his demonstration was over, Hanna said in a low voice, "I have brought thy smudge."

"Ah, let us go in."

I now learned what Hanna does for a living. She is an aromatist—a craftswoman specializing in perfumes, incense, potpourris, and other scented things. From the quiet way they spoke, I gathered that it is not an entirely respectable profession. Later, when I asked her about it, she said, "Scents are dangerous things. They can bring back memories, or change a mood. Some folk act unwisely under the influence of a scent, or fall in love. Scents can even cure or kill. A scent-vendor must be very careful."

So she is like a pharmacist, or perhaps a witch.

"Where do you get the raw materials?" I asked. But I got only that all-purpose reply, "From the wenders."

By now, I was finding the economy of Torobe quite puzzling. They seem to have access to foods, wood, cloth, and many other products that can only come from outside. Yet I haven't discovered what they produce for export. Nor can I understand with whom they are trading— "other habitudes" is all Hanna will say. They must be settlements that entirely escaped all our orbiting sensors. I will have to wait for the return of the wenders to have my questions answered.

As we were leaving Rugli's house, a woman who passed us in the street said to Hanna, "Songta is seeking thee."

In a tone of strained patience, Hanna said, "What doth she want?"

"The Three wish to treat with the stranger."

My interview with the authorities, I assumed. "Who are the Three?" I asked Hanna.

"The old ladies—Songta, Rinka, and Anath."

"Are they in charge?"

"Only when we let them be. I will go with thee."

She led me a circuitous way I could not hope to retrace, till we came to another doorway. Hanna shook the rattle, and when a voice called out, we passed through into an enclosed space. The sounds from outside were muffled, and our voices dampened, as if we were in a tent or shelter. A soft carpet cushioned my steps, and a fragrant scent *hung in the air. Hanna prompted me to say my name, and we were greeted by Anath-Not and Rinka-Doon. "Sit thee down, visitor," Rinka said in a thin, birdlike voice. I groped for a chair, but all I could find were pillows, so I sat on one of them.*

"Is it mannerly to greet a guest with aromatics?" Hanna asked softly.

"'Twas Songta's wish," Rinka replied.

"I dare say."

Unable to see their faces, I could not interpret this exchange. I realized I was almost as handicapped in a social situation as in a physical one, because so many of my cues were visual. It made me feel uncomfortably vulnerable.

Songta-Min soon joined us. She did not seem too pleased to find Hanna there, but stopped short of asking her to leave. They passed around a plate of savories, and offered me a drink, which I declined. I was preparing to exchange small talk, but instead the old ladies proceeded one by one to give long, formal recitals of their life histories. Anath went first, giving me a picture of an uneventful, domestic life punctuated with achievements like sewing thirty-seven coats, installing drains in the family home, and the births of three children, each by a different husband. Never had she ventured away from Torobe, not even as far as another village. As the others proceeded, the stories grew repetitive. I listened over and over to the same quotidian events, listed in unrelenting detail, and my mind began to wander.

When the last one finished there was a long silence. At last Songta said, "And where do thy people hail from, Thora Lassiter? Camest thou by songpath or tanglepath?"

"I . . . my people come from many places," I said. "We call our homes the Twenty Planets. We came here by a vessel that is now floating above your sky. We didn't know you were here, but now we want to meet you, and learn from you. I need to return to my people and tell them the good news."

Another long silence followed as they attempted to process this explanation. At length Songta said, "What do thy people have to trade?"

"Knowledge," I said. "We want to share ours, and purchase some of yours in return."

This seemed to elicit interest; I heard them whisper to each other. "What sort of knowledge?" Songta asked, her voice sharper.

"Many sorts. It depends on what you need."

"There hath been a rumor of a new knot in the tangle. Can thou tell us aught of it?"

"I don't understand what you mean," I said. "If I did, I might be able to help."

Once again, there was a long pause. At last, Anath-Not said impatiently, "Leave off thy craft, Songta. We have to ask Thora of the riffles. We have been sore plagued of late."

They seemed to be waiting for me to say something, so I stammered, "We can cure many diseases."

"Nay, riffles," Anath said, as if repeating the word more loudly would make me understand. "The forerunner of the fold rain."

I shook my head, then remembered they couldn't see me. "I'm sorry," I said.

"We seek to know if thy people are wise enough to dispel the conundrum," Songta said.

No, I wanted to say. If you only knew us you wouldn't ask. But I had no idea what she really meant. "Whatever your problem is, we will be glad to help, once we understand."

"Thou art very close," Songta said.

"Nay, Songta," Rinka said gently, "perhaps she is but ignorant. Her people may know naught."

They were on the verge of dismissing me as useless, leaving me with no bargaining power to effect my escape. I decided to change strategy. "Elders," I said, as if they were forcing it out of me, "I am not our expert in these matters, but on the Escher we have an eminent riffleologist who is famous for dispelling conundrums. I just don't know if you have any knowledge valuable enough to trade for." Forgive me for the lie, whoever listens to this, and understand that I was desperate.

"Can thy people tie knots anew?" Songta asked.

"Yes. We do it all the time."

"Then why dost thou need our aid to journey home?"

Improvising madly, I said, "The paradoxes here are too thick for my objectifier to work."

Hanna spoke up for the first time. "Perhaps she is testing us."

Even better; that idea would give them incentive to prove what they could do. I said nothing, either to confirm or deny.

"An artful bargainer," Songta said.

"Prove to me what you can do, and we will open trade negotiations," I said with just a trace of hauteur.

The old women whispered to one another. I waited till they reached a conclusion. Then Songta said, "There are no wenders here at present. Dagget-Min will return anon, and he will answer thy needs."

So at the end I was back where I began, waiting for a wender to come.

I think Hanna could tell I was frustrated as she led me home through the lightless paths of Torobe. "The Three used up a long time," she observed.

"Yes."

"They had all heard each other's testimonies before, of course, but were waiting to hear yours. And then . . ."

I said, "Was I supposed to tell my life story?"

"That was what they thought. Did you not mark how suspicious they became? They thought you were trying to hide something."

"I'm sorry, I didn't realize." I tried to imagine what I might have said. My life would have been incomprehensible to these people. "It would have bored you," I said.

She laughed. "Then a good thing it was you did not tell it. I was quite bored enough."

Hesitantly, I said, "What did you mean at the beginning, about the aromatics?"

"They had boiled unguents to put thee off guard. It is very like

Songta. She would be the only one tying knots in all Torobe. She wanted to get thee well tangled, so she could pull thy cord." From her tone, I could tell there was no love lost between her and Songta.

When we reached Hanna's home it was empty. "Where is Moth?" I asked.

"Oh, off on her own. I cannot keep her still anymore."

There was something I had been wondering about, but wasn't sure how to ask politely. "Pardon me if I am being ignorant, Hanna, but where is the father of your baby?"

A tone of deep sadness came to Hanna's voice. "He is wending. He would have given it up to bide with me, but he is Songta's son and she would not hear of it."

So Songta is Hanna's mother-in-law. That explains the tension. "Is wending something young men are expected to do?" I asked.

"Aye," she said regretfully. "It is the manly thing. They are supposed to provide for us."

I realized I had met no young men so far in Torobe. It is a village of old people, women, and children. "It is hard on you to have to raise a child alone," I said.

"Aye," she said, and now her voice was a little bitter. "But it is the ancient way. We like not change in Torobe."

I have no idea how much time has passed. In Torobe there are only two intervals of duration, shorttime and longtime. A longtime is any interval that exceeds expectation—the years since a house was built, or the hours since a person was supposed to have returned home. Absolute intervals like hours, days, and years have completely disappeared from their language. Not a person in Torobe knows how old he or she is in any but a relative sense. I have never heard of a culture so lacking a sense of time. I suppose it is because the rest of us live inside celestial clocks, where cycles of sun and stars make time seem natural. At first I tried to keep track of my sleep cycles, but it became pointless when I *realized the perpetual night has disturbed my circadian rhythms. I feel like a prisoner unable even to mark the days of my sentence on the wall. The people around me can't understand why I care. Time passes differently for them, not as a stream but as a lake in which they float. It does not flow with purpose, but extends all around them, undifferentiated.*

My sense of space has also changed. The world now exists in concentric spheres around me. Closest—and most real—is the circle of touch. Outside that is the circle of hearing. I find I am mentally mapping this place not as a floor plan, but as a dome with pie-shaped sectors, each containing textures, smells, and echoes. A sharp echo morphs into a hard texture up close. An air movement is an open space or passage. I can even sense something large and nearby as a stillness on my face.

I make it sound like I am adjusting. That isn't true. I crave light with a deep hunger. I want to feast my eyes on the sky, or a grassy lawn, or human faces. I want to stoke my mind with so much beauty that it will fill me up and last as long as darkness does. Sometimes I think I see light—a floating blob of incandescence, or a spray of twinkles. But then I turn to look, and it disappears. Photisms, I suppose— my brain, starved for stimulation, producing illusory light from within.

Always before, my mind was a refuge. Now it is a prison—a black box of consciousness. I want to claw through the barrier, and let in the world outside me. I want someone to laugh and admit it has all been a practical joke. I am not really trapped here.

At times, I am oppressed by a sense of the unreality of everything around me. I cannot trust that anything is truly there, unless I can touch it. It is particularly disturbing when I am with people; their disembodied voices surround me, floating here and there, now before, now behind. I imagine them as flies dancing around my head. Then someone touches me, and their body materializes as if from nowhere, an abrupt transition from abstract to concrete.

Even my own solidity seems to be dissolving sometimes, as if I were becoming no more than a free-floating consciousness without an edge. Several times, when Hanna or her friends have fallen into storytelling, they have related tales of people who become disembodied spirits. These stories of body-loss make me more anxious than ever. I wonder if the Torobes are also troubled by a sense of their own unreality.

One sleeptime, I had a dream. I was in a questship, traveling through space. There was a cockpit, like an antique aircar, and I could look out the windows in all directions. The pilot told me we were traveling at a tremendous speed, but when I looked out, it seemed as if we had come to a dead halt out in the middle of space. There were no stars around us, no galaxies, just blackness. Then I looked out the back window and saw behind us a ball of dim light. It was our universe, all the galaxies clustered there in a delicate little dustball sphere. As I watched, it grew smaller and smaller behind us. I said, "Why are we leaving? We've got to turn back! We're going too far—too far away!"

When I woke, I groped for a lamp, then felt panic. There was no longer any light to reassure me that I was awake. I was trapped with my nightmare, unable to break free. I slapped my hands hard against the floor till the pain assured me that I was really here. Then, to quiet myself, I tried to imagine my body bathed in light until I could relax a little.

The next waketime I was plagued by a tension headache. Hanna's baby was also restless and wailing. Finally, at her wits' end, she thrust him into my hands and said, "You mind him." The sudden sensation of holding that wriggling little being was so vivid that I was shocked out of my self-pity. He was so alive, so loud, so unexpectedly heavy. After that, I volunteered willingly to care for him because he seemed so much more real than I am. Still, I have come to feel a sharp pity for him, just learning to explore a world that is only half a world.

There is very little else to occupy my mind in the monotonous rhythms of life in Torobe. To stave off depression, I have been trying to think of the teachings of Sensualism and how they might apply to my situation. The core principle is that our senses receive a far broader spectrum of messages than the narrow range we are taught to pay attention to. Our brains still receive many of those messages, but they are shunted into the subliminal and subconscious, and surface only as intuitions, emotions, premonitions, dreams, and visions. If we study those experiences not as illusions but as cues to other modes of apprehension, it might give us access to layers of reality we barely suspect, since the evidence for them is drowned out by the noise of ordinary perception.

Here, I have had a sense subtracted from my life—sight, the sense we rely on most, that occupies the greatest area of our brains. Could I see this as an opportunity to discover what lies beneath? Could I study the perceptions that vision normally hides from us? Easy to say, hard to do. I have to think about this.

The event I have been waiting for finally arrived: Dagget-Min returned from wending.

There was great excitement all through Torobe. It was an event, like a stone thrown into the still pool of their existence. I went visiting with Hanna, and listened to endless speculation about Dagget's news, the goods he brought, his effect on power relations in Torobe. He is Songta's husband, but in contrast to Songta, people speak of him with reverence, loyalty, and love.

When I finally met the man, he defied all my expectations. I had pictured him as worldly and well traveled, bargaining his way from village to village, crafty enough to outwit me. What I found instead was a gentle, enigmatic man of few words. He is a thinker rather than a doer, and his role in Torobe is more that of priest than peddler. Where I had expected practical help from him, I soon realized his people were expecting spiritual guidance. My first conversation with him completely altered my idea of what this "wending" is. He spoke as if he had been off on a vision quest.

The people present were the same as during my previous interview—

Hanna and the Three, with the addition of Dagget. We met in the same place, but Dagget was smoking what smelled like a pipe, so the air was filled with the sweet tobacco. The darkness, the smoke, and Dagget's quiet voice coming from somewhere in front of me created a mood of reverie in my mind. He spoke of what he had encountered in his wending, but it was not a conventional traveler's tale. Much of it was incomprehensible.

"When I entered the Ground, I could hear a new chord at once, all dissonant and jangling. Some power is playing the strings, but not as we do—it is reckless, unharmonic, full of undertones that gave me unease. I followed a cord to a great vibrant knot. Within the knot lies a place that feels like boxes within boxes, complex and secret. Beings dwell there; I could feel the wind of their passing to and fro, but they knew me not, so they could not bemind me or fill my bag. I was sore troubled, so I went on to Gorachin to think of what it meant. Then I went to Stoll to seek counsel of the wise. They could give me none."

Everyone was silent after this, and there seemed to be an air of dread in the room. At last Anath-Not said, "Thora Lassiter, is this knot thy people's doing?"

I had no idea what to answer. I have studied many descriptions of mystical experiences, and Dagget's tale reminded me of those, if you subtract the visual component of a vision. It is a topic of vital interest to any Sensualist, because true mystics and adepts are skilled at perceiving what the rest of us cannot, the information from subconscious sensory input, but they are often unable or unwilling to share their experiences. I wanted to probe further. So I said, "It is possible. I would need to know more."

No one volunteered any information, so I said, "Dagget-Min, you said you entered the ground. We must use different words. Do you mean you went into the cave?"

For several heartbeats he drew on his pipe, and I feared that I had revealed some monumental ignorance. But at last he said, "Aye, I went to the still place."

"Why did you do that?"

He was slow answering again, and I feared I had put him off. But he finally said, "Because the Ground is closer there than in other places."

This time I heard the way he said "Ground," and remembered that Hanna had also used the word in a specialized way. I said, "We use a different word than 'Ground.' Can you describe it so I will know what it is?"

He shifted on his pillow and tapped his pipe against something. When he answered, his words had the ring of some ancient religious teaching. "The Ground is the place of creation. All things await existence there, yet it is empty. The source of all is nothing."

"And it is a place you can sense?"

"It is around us now, at all times. It is everywhere. But it is easier to ken at the still place."

I thought of the holy spots that exist on all planets, places where oracles dwell and prophets go to sit vigil in hopes of revelation. Some Sensualists have theorized they represent a natural phenomenon accessible only to the senses of those attuned—a thin spot, perhaps, in the fabric of reality, through which information leaks. "Could you show me the still place?" I asked.

"I could," he said slowly, "but it would be better if thou could find it thyself."

This answer made me doubt it was a physical place, and not a state of mind. "How do you get there?" I asked.

"Tell her not," Songta interrupted sharply. "It is hidden, and we know not why she seeks it."

"I don't disrespect your wisdom," I said. "I am asking because . . ."

I had spent months hiding what I really wanted to understand—hiding it from the Magisterium and from my colleagues on the quest-ship, out of fear I would be sedated and sent back to the curatory. But I had an instinct that Dagget would understand. I said, "For a long time I have dimly sensed something beyond the surface of our reality.

I think I came in contact with it recently—in fact, I am sure. But it was a terrible, frightening experience. There was no one to guide me, and my people thought I had gone mad. Since then, I have been cut off, as if I had gone deaf."

He considered my words a long time, and when he spoke his voice was thoughtful. "Wending is a perilous thing. Many a cordwender suffers harm, or never returns. It is best to seek instruction only from the wise."

"Do you think I am too old and too . . . damaged to learn?"

"You may have come farther than you know," he said quietly. "It sometimes creeps up on a person unawares. It soaks into thee instead of showering down. For some it is trumpets; for others, just a sigh."

"I want to believe that," I said. I wanted to touch him, because I felt in the presence of a profound wisdom—but not a remote or fearsome wisdom; rather, a caring and human one. As if reading my mind, he laid both his hands on the top of my head. The warmth on my hair was vivid, like a rain of light I could not see.

Anath's voice penetrated my benediction. "If Dagget helps thee, will thou stop the dissonance?" Somehow, the question sounded irrelevant, and I smiled.

"I don't know what is causing your problem," I said, "but if my people are doing something wrong, I will make them stop."

"I thought thou was eager to be off home," Songta said.

"Perhaps," said Dagget, "this is her way home."

His words resonated with me. Perhaps he offered me the way to my real home, the one I have been seeking all along.

I have just had the strangest experience of my life. I am baffled how to describe it; there is no language that suffices. Language is too sequential, too limited. But I will have to try, because I need to document this. It will be mostly metaphor, I am afraid.

A shorttime after my interview with Dagget, word spread through

Torobe that there was to be a concert. The news was greeted with quiet anticipation. Hanna was busy preparing, because in Torobe scents are an important component of a concert. "They draw the cordwork close," she explained.

Concerts are held in a place called the Echo Sculpture, but Hanna could not tell me much about it. "It is a place of surpassing beauty," was all she could say. Since my ideas of beauty are entirely visual, this left me none the wiser.

When the time came, we left the baby with a minder, and I helped Hanna carry a pack of bottled philtres and distillations to the gathering place. Concertgoers were already waiting at the entrance, so Hanna left me in the care of her friends while she passed inside to prepare the space. I have noticed that a group of Torobes is more quiet than a comparable group of Capellans. There was no hubbub of multiple conversations going on simultaneously; they passed the time speaking sequentially with everyone listening. I suppose it is to avoid an auditory overload.

A bell sounded, and the crowd fell silent. A woman took my hand and we all started moving toward the passage leading to the Echo Sculpture. As we entered, my first impression was of overpowering fragrance, making it almost difficult to breathe. My second impression was how the walls whispered and resonated around us. Even though the barefoot audience moved quite silently, every swish of cloth, every susurration of movement was amplified by the echoing chamber.

When all had entered, the music started. The first sound was a single note plucked on a string—but the cavern sang it back from a dozen directions, amplified into an orchestral richness. The woman leading me tightened her grip on my hand in excitement. The echoes had barely died when a second tone came from a flute stationed somewhere across the room, and soon we were bathing in a lush shower of flute-notes, multiplied a hundredfold.

I would have been happy just to stand and listen as the notes began to overlap and form a complex, three-dimensional canon. But a second person took my other hand and they began to lead me on into adjoining chambers, each with its own sonic signature, so that the music sounded different depending on where you stood. The pungent fumes were making me feel a little dizzy and detached from my body. As the music became more and more complex, I could no longer tell where it was coming from, and disorientation took over. The people around me were moving rhythmically in a kind of dancing motion. Whirled along with them, I gave up trying to tell where my feet were, and what was close or far.

I must tell the rest in a sequence, though in my memory it all happened simultaneously, in an endless second. As I found myself enveloped in music, a revelation struck me like a blow: I could hear the shape of the cavern around me from its echoes. It was as if I were processing sound waves as I do light, my brain assembling them into a pattern. Every shape sang to me its nature—in one chamber I heard the rounded cauliflower cavities of the walls; in another, sharp crystalline cubes; stone pillars fluted like fabric; soft sandy mounds. It was profoundly emotional to suddenly understand what I had been missing, as if I had been deaf all my life. It was akin to seeing again. But there was one thing missing: myself.

I had lost all perception of how I fit into my surroundings. No longer was I in a particular location. Internal and external sensations merged, as if I had no edge, or a changing edge. I was a conscious space that filled the chamber around me. I remember thinking I could pass through a ring like a silk scarf and resume my old shape on the other side. It was strange but elating, and in the moment it felt deeply meaningful.

What makes one space me and another not-me? It was an absurd question.

Something was tugging at the edge of my mind, like a memory I could not quite bring into consciousness, from deep in my childhood. For a moment I could smell the beloved water-gardens of my cousin Bdiwa Ral, and feel a strong hand engulfing mine. I felt my father's *presence very close, an almost tactile sensation. He was thinking of me, drawing me to him, but I did not want to be the person he imagined me to be, so I pulled away, as I have so often done in life. It gave me a familiar pang of separation.*

A long time had passed, and none at all. What brought me back was the realization that I had lost all sense of scale. I was in a space like the inside of a geode, all crusted with crystals—yet I could not tell if the crystals were the size of a salt grain and very close, or as massive as a building and far away. For some reason, this filled me with terror. I needed to know how large I was—something I had always known without the slightest doubt—and nothing around me gave a clue. The terror sent me recoiling back into my body with a painful snap, like a rubber band resuming its shape.

The music had stopped and the cavern around me was empty. I thought they had all gone home and left me. On hands and knees I crawled over the stone floor, not knowing where I was heading, till I caught a familiar scent on a current of air. It was not one of the perfumes, but a wholesome smell of cooking food. I got up, waving my hands before me, and edged toward the smell till I heard a person moving a pot lid. "Who is it?" I asked, forgetting the Torobe protocol of saying my name.

"It is Hanna," she said.

"Hanna! Thank God you are still here."

"Are you hungry?" she asked.

I realized I was. "Why are you cooking here?"

"Why should I not? This is my kitchen."

It took me several seconds to realize she was in earnest; I was back in her house. I grappled with another wave of disorientation before realizing I must have passed out in the Echo Sculpture, and they had carried me back. "How long was I out?" I said.

"Not long." She handed me a steaming bowl of grain, and went to check on the baby. I sat struggling with my confusion, trying to assemble my memories before they all vanished like a dream.

When Hanna returned, she asked, "Dost thou wish to speak of it?"

I did, badly. I felt an urgent need to describe what I had experienced, to communicate how important it had been, but words were pitifully inadequate. My first instinct was to explain in analogies, but they were all culturally bounded and meant little to her. Then I thought I ought to strip out all but the sensory experiences, and realized that also was inadequate, because the emotional component was so fundamental; in fact, I think the emotions were a kind of sensory information—my wordless limbic system speaking directly to my cortex.

After several abortive attempts, I gave up. "I have no idea what happened," I said.

"Thou must speak to Dagget-Min," she said.

I did speak to him soon after. But he would not tell me what I had experienced. "What did it seem like to you?" he said.

"It felt like I was halfway between existence and nonexistence," I said.

"Nay," he replied, "thou was touching the layer of all existence."

"But I didn't exist there," I said, then immediately contradicted myself. "No, I must have existed, since someone must have been having those sensory experiences. Is it possible to be pure consciousness?"

"Nay," he said. "Awareness is unbounded, undifferentiated, and is present in all things. It doth not distinguish between 'I' and all else, because it dwelleth in everything. Consciousness is a manifestation of awareness that is bounded and particular. It is concentrated in a single place and time, and is limited to a single point of view. Consciousness continually reacheth out toward awareness, to join it, but it cannot without giving up what it is. The grain of salt cannot experience the brine without dissolving."

He spoke in such a matter-of-fact tone that I realized he was teaching me practical knowledge, though my culture saw it as the most recondite philosophy. He was simply giving me the benefit of his *experience, not a speculation. Dagget-Min is a person who has cultivated a skill through practice—the skill of sensing something we only guess at.*

What is it, this Awareness, this Ground? He says he cannot tell me; I can only find out for myself. But I am not sure I can pay the price of remaining here in sensory starvation much longer. Every time I wake to darkness it becomes more intolerable. I think I am close to an important discovery, perhaps more important than anything I have ever learned—yet if I could escape tomorrow, I would.

chapter eight

To Sara's dismay, the scientific faculty embraced the idea of teaching Moth to see. With the planet under embargo, an experiment on Moth promised the next best opportunity for some interesting data. The only faction opposed was Sri Paul's group of Corroborationists, who worried that meddling with the natives' blindness might infect them with objectivism.

Sara's misgivings were more about the invasiveness of the cultural interference. But when the issue reached Director Gavere's office, none of these concerns turned out to be relevant. There, the argument was entirely between publicity and security.

Mr. Gibb loved the idea. In fact, he already had a script in mind. "Epco gives a child the miracle of sight," he said, framing his hands to conjure up the inspiring scene. "The material will be golden."

Until Epco's rivals get ahold of it, Sara thought. Then the script would be, "Is she just a human guinea pig?"

Atlabatlow's script was predictably paranoid. "Our sight is the only strategic advantage we have over the natives at the moment," he argued. "While they still don't know our powers, it is also an advantage in hostage negotiation. It would be foolish to reveal our hand."

Sara had been wavering, but Atlabatlow's opposition made up her mind: whatever he was against, she was for. With her decision made, she left her trump card unplayed: she could have recommended referring the matter to the lawyers at Epco headquarters, and that would have killed it. In her experience, lawyers never wanted scientists to do anything.

In the end, Director Gavere approved the experiment if, and only if, Moth would sign a waiver of copyright. It was up to Sara to explain to her the legal rights and potential profits she was giving up.

Once again full of qualms, Sara went to talk to David. "Don't worry," he said cheerfully. "It won't work anyway."

"What won't work?"

"Teaching her to see." He gestured Sara into his office. His worktable was heaped with notes and diagrams; he had clearly been researching the subject. Settling in his chair, he said, "From what I can tell, Moth's problem isn't in her eyes; it's in her brain. That's where the biggest part of the job of seeing is done. People aren't born with the neural connections for sight ready-made; they are laid down over the first few years of life, in response to visual stimuli. For some reason, Moth never formed those connections in infancy. Even if the visual centers of her brain are still intact, she will almost certainly be agnosic: able to see, but unable to make any sense of it."

Sara was surprised at the disappointment she felt. Consciously, she had been full of professional reservations. Now, she became aware that part of her had been hoping it would work. She had spent a lifetime trying to learn other people's worlds and ways; just once she had wanted to give her world to someone else. She said, "So your advice is not to do it?"

"I didn't say that."

"You think it won't work, but you want to try anyway?"

"What can I say? We might learn something. Besides, there's always the chance I'm wrong. Moth is young, her brain is still malleable, and she's motivated to learn new skills. We'll never know if we don't try."

When Sara presented the waiver to Moth and tried to explain what copyright was, she found that Moth was following a script of her own.

"I know 'tis part of the test, that you will try to dissuade me," she said. "It is my part to be steadfast. I will do whate'er thou require." She was sitting cross-legged on the sofa in the Embassy, munching on a bag of snacks and looking quite unlike the heroic persona in her imagination. Her unruly black hair was bunched up in a clip behind her head, but tendrils were escaping in every direction. Sara was on the edge of laughing when she felt a terrible misgiving about the situation.

Moth noticed her silence, and said, "Sara? Have I not guessed aright?"

Sara sat down to face her. "Moth, this is an important decision. It's not likely to work. But if it does . . ."

If it did, they would be able to show her a sunrise, and a candle burning, and frost. She would discover the sky, and the stars, and space itself. She would be remade in the image of her teachers.

"Sara?" Moth said uncertainly. "What is it?"

Sara took her hands and gripped them tight. "This may change you, Moth. Not just you—it may change all of Torobe."

"Well, that's a mercy!" the girl exclaimed. "Torobe is dead and dull. They think no big thoughts, dream no dreams. What lies there for me?"

"Your home. Your family. Your past. Someday, you'll want that."

"Nay, I want to be different. I want to be like thee."

Sara felt the terrible burden of her illusions. "No, you don't."

"I do. If I pass thy test, and learn to use thy powers with wisdom, then perchance I will be free to go off and be a Waster, like thee."

Sara knew she had to put a stop to this. And yet . . .

"What ill may come of it?" Moth said. "If I cannot learn to see, then I am no worse off. But if I do, much good may follow."

Sara wanted to believe that it was Moth's decision, made freely and in full understanding of the consequences. That was what she was bound to obey.

"If you truly think you understand, and have made your decision without any pressure from us, then you need to press your finger to this scanpad," she said.

Bravely, Moth held out a greasy finger. Sara read her the waiver and asked the obligatory questions, and Moth affirmed her agreement.

The next day, the experiment began.

Moth had spent a lifetime disregarding visual stimuli the way Sara disregarded floaters or tinnitus, and now the girl would need to pay close attention to a hitherto meaningless distraction. Sara coached her until her face was set with concentration as she tried to maintain focus on the "blotches."

Sara, David, Bakai, and Mr. Gibb were the only ones in the room with Moth, though others were watching the transmissions from Gibb's headset. David started out by showing her the simplest visual stimulus he had been able to think of, a placard that was half white, half black.

"Do you see this pattern?" David said.

"Aye, I think so."

"Half of it is what we call white, and half is black. If you can see the difference, touch the dividing line."

Moth only looked perplexed. "How?" she asked.

It was Bakai who intuited her problem. She came over and picked up Moth's hand, holding it before her face. "This is your hand," she said.

Moth looked at it in surprise, then tried moving it to and fro, smiling in amusement as the image of her hand responded.

"Now touch the line between light and dark," David prompted.

Her finger hovered in space, at a point midway between herself and the placard.

"No," said David, "touch the placard."

She had no concept of depth. Sara took her hand and guided it forward till it touched the chart. Then Moth moved her finger to the dividing line between white and black. Her movements reminded Sara of a child playing with a servo mechanism. The image before her was not really her hand. It was merely something that she could trigger into moving as she moved.

David's other placards held parallel lines, converging lines, and other geometric shapes designed to test her visual acuity. Moth caught on quickly how to follow an outline with her finger. The last placard was in bright color, and she stared at it, concentrating.

"'Tis . . . beautiful," she said.

"Just wait, Moth," Sara said. "We'll show you things a thousand times more beautiful."

When the tests ended, Moth closed her eyes to rest, but still was dissatisfied. "What use are these games?" she asked.

"Be patient," David said. "We had to test how much you could see. You'll have to practice simple tasks before you can get to the complicated ones."

"I see nothing," Moth complained. "There be quaint figures, but I still cannot hear your thoughts, nor tell the future."

Laughing, Sara said, "Where did you get that idea?"

"I have observed thee many times," Moth said. "Thou will say, 'Such and such a person is coming,' and sure enough they do. Or 'Someone hath moved the table,' and when we come to it, it is moved. You live always a few steps ahead of now."

Sara and David exchanged a bemused glance. Moth had been misconstruing the evidence. But which of them would have done any better, asked to conceive of a sense they didn't have? "There's actually some logic to that," David said. "Moth needs to come into physical contact with something in order to know it, but sight brings us that information at a distance. You could say that sight collapses space, making distant things near. And so it collapses time, as well."

"You can also read minds," Moth said.

"What?" Sara protested.

"It is true, Sara. Oft hast thou marked what I was thinking, just by seeing me."

"That is because your face gave you away, Moth, not because I could read your mind."

"Pray, what is the difference?"

"Sight is a skill, Moth. It's like playing a musical instrument. When you get good at it, it will bring you information. But you're going to have to practice."

"Oh," she said, disappointed. "That's all?"

"Yes," Sara said. "That's all." She turned the swiveling chair Moth sat in to face her. "Moth, open your eyes. Can you see me?"

Moth looked uncertain, so Sara picked up the girl's hand, showed it to her, then held it to her own cheek.

"Doth this pattern symbolize thee?" Moth asked.

"Yes, in a way."

"Where doth it end?"

Sara was at a loss. David murmured, "She's having trouble separating foreground and background."

"Oh, I see!" Moth said. "Thou art the part that is changing."

Sara laughed. "Good enough."

Next they tried to lead her on an exploratory walk around the room, introducing her to chairs, walls, and people. Her steps were more timid and shaky than they had ever been. Finally she gave up and closed her eyes; then her tension subsided, and she moved normally back to the chair. "I beg thy forbearance," she said. "It is too distracting; I cannot tell where I am whilst minding the mirages."

Sara squeezed her hand encouragingly. "You did well, Moth. Don't worry, you will get used to it."

She had no idea how optimistic she was being.

In the days that followed, Sara became the teacher of a curriculum that she knew, but had never learned. There were no books or lecture notes to follow. How she had come to understand the concepts in the first few years of life, she didn't know. The course might have been called "Introductory Seeing."

What came to Moth from her eyes was an undifferentiated jumble of light, movement, and color. She could sense it, but not *make* sense of it. So Sara started out as with a language, teaching her nouns. She began by setting down a coffee cup on the table in front of Moth and saying, "Cup. Go ahead, feel it so you can relate its shape to the way it looks."

A few minutes later, after Moth had learned "door," "light," and "table," Sara said, "Now touch the cup."

Confused, Moth said, "I see no cup."

"Sure you do. It's on the table."

"Nay, 'tis not. The cup had a device to represent the handle."

Sara realized the problem. "You're just seeing it from a different angle now." She took Moth's hand and guided it to the cup, then turned it to reveal the handle.

"Why did thou make it change?" Moth protested.

"I didn't. You were just seeing a different side of it."

"Must I memorize all the ways it may appear?"

The question perplexed Sara, so she said to David, "Why do we recognize the cup even when the handle is hidden?"

"The different ways it appears are called object transforms," David said. "Somehow, we learn to integrate all the transforms into a unitary objecthood in our minds. I don't know how."

At that point, Sara decided she couldn't start with nouns. She first needed to teach Moth some underlying principles, a kind of visual grammar. "Okay, Moth, let's start over with how to tell where one object ends and another begins."

"Okay," Moth said. She was picking up some of their expressions.

So Sara taught Moth to look for contrasts, changes in color, and straight lines. But even this was far from the easy task Sara imagined. Color was the first thing to cause confusion. Moth insisted that the blue cup was a different color when viewed from the chair than it was from the door. Sara told her, "No, it's the same color, it's just the lighting that's different."

"So I must memorize many colors thou dost call blue?" Moth said in frustration.

Sara remembered her own frustration with Hua Ming's arbitrary botanical categories. Yet she had accepted the category of "blue" not as if it were imposed by humans, but as natural, self-evident.

Moth also had trouble telling which boundaries were the significant ones that defined the edges of objects. A simple chest of drawers had several dozen interior boundaries that, depending on the lighting, could look more significant than the ones at its edges. On the second day of lessons, Sara and Moth got into an argument about why the legs of a table, which were separated from the top by a very distinct boundary, ought to be classified as part of the table, instead of something different.

"Because they're attached!" Sara said in frustration.

"I cannot tell that," Moth said.

"Not from where you're standing. But if I move the table, the legs will come along. You know that."

She looked thoughtful. "So the table-symbol in the eyes is supposed to represent things about the real table?"

"No, the table in the eyes *is* the real table."

"How can that be? Doth the table send out thoughts about its nature that the eyes receive?"

That question led to a long explanation of electromagnetic radiation. At the end, Moth said, "So what the eyes see is the radiation bouncing off the furniture?"

"That's right."

"Not the furniture itself. So how can thou be sure the radiation is truthful?"

"Experience, Moth. Just trust me on this one, okay?"

But when Sara reported this conversation to David, he said, "You know, she has a point. Sight *is* a secondhand sort of sense. We can't be sure something isn't lost in translation."

Sara groaned. "Don't you get all epistemological on me, David!"

The next principle Sara had to teach was occlusion. It took several frustrating days before she realized that Moth did not understand that a close thing could hide objects that were farther away. Moth had already begun to figure it out before Sara realized the problem, but her interpretation was creative. As they stood looking into Sara's office one morning, she said, "Thy desk is very loud."

Since the desk was being no noisier than usual, Sara asked what she meant. "It doth drown out the chair and the cabinet," she said.

"No, it *hides* the chair and cabinet, because they are behind it." Moth looked quite puzzled, so Sara asked, "You only see part of the chair now, right?"

"Right."

"What would you do if you wanted to see more of it?"

Hesitantly, she said, "Wait for the desk to be quieter?"

"No, this is as quiet as it gets. Just walk forward."

This defied Moth's common sense. "How can my moving affect the desk?"

"When you change positions, it will no longer be in front of the chair. Try it."

She did, and was intrigued at the result. Sara said, "The scene is in layers, Moth. The desk is covering the chair and cabinet."

"Oh, I hear thee now," she said, then frowned. "But I did not move the desk."

"No, moving yourself accomplished the same thing, because you changed the angle at which you viewed the scene." But she knew as the words came out that Moth would have no intuitive grasp of angles, and it would be yet another thing to teach her.

This led to the next principle of seeing: parallax. Sara knew how the angle of separation between her two eyes allowed her brain to construct a three-dimensional picture, even though she was seldom conscious of it; but she had never thought about how much she learned from the parallax created when she herself moved. She had to teach Moth that when she moved, the objects in the foreground shifted position more radically than objects in the background. She could use this information, along with occlusion, to determine what was close and what was far off. But although the theory was easy for Moth to memorize, using it was far more difficult. Sara watched her practice, pacing across the room again and again, her face a study in intense concentration. The analysis of visual clues that sighted people did so automatically, she had to do with arduous, deliberate thought.

The topic of depth naturally led to another principle: perspective, or compression with distance. Moth noticed it herself, and complained that objects were never the same size twice. When Sara told her the key—that they were smaller when farther away and larger when close—she said, "Why?"

"Why what?"

"Why doth the chair shrink when I am not close?"

"It doesn't really shrink. It's an illusion."

Frowning, Moth said, "Thou knowest that, and yet believe thy eyes?"

"It's a useful illusion, not a deceptive one. We can tell whether we're likely to bump into things or not."

"So if a thing be small, I shall not bump into it?"

"Not necessarily. Things all have intrinsic sizes and apparent sizes, and the difference between the two reveals how far away they are."

"Why dost thou make things so hard?" she said in frustration.

"I'm sorry, Moth. I didn't invent the rules."

"Well," she said, resigned, "perhaps thou ought to show me everything's intrinsic size."

Sara hesitated. "That would be hard. With eyes, all you get is apparent sizes. You have to figure out intrinsic sizes by other means, like touch."

"What good is this seeing?" Moth exclaimed angrily. "All it gives thee is deception."

She had a stormy side to her personality, and a low tolerance for failure. Sara was also finding that she herself had less patience than she needed.

At last Sara devised a system of judging intrinsic size by viewing things at a standardized distance, the length of an outstretched arm. Even then Moth was skeptical, and Sara slowly realized it was because she did not have the kind of body image sighted people did. At an instinctive level she was unconvinced that her arm was always the same length.

"I think she would have found it easier to believe the chair really does shrink," Sara said to David. "She simply doesn't have the same concept of space we do. To us, space and everything in it is invariable. To her, it's as if things assume shape and size the moment she touches them; if she's not touching them they might as well not exist. No wonder she's having trouble."

It took only a week for Mr. Gibb to get discouraged at the slow pace of Moth's lessons. When he realized it was going to take a long time to get to the part where she tearfully thanked Epco for giving her sight, he told them to call if anything interesting happened, and decamped. Thereafter, Sara wore a headnet to record their sessions for the rest of the scientists.

Moth stuck with it doggedly even after her initial enthusiasm faded. They had been able to give her some novel sensations of color and movement. But her attempts to get beyond mere entertainment— to use sight as a tool—moved more slowly the further she got.

One day Sara got clearance from the Director to take Moth to the refectory, and insisted that she walk with her eyes open, focusing on the visual evidence. The girl moved with agonizing slowness, arms outstretched to fend off the looming shapes of posters, light fixtures, and carpeting. She flinched at stepping into a crevasse of shadow or barking her shin on a beam of light. After each step she had to pause to reassimilate the changed scene. They had barely gotten past the security station when she stopped, her eyes shut tight. "Nay, I cannot go on," she said. Her voice was not angry, but panicky. Her face was flushed and covered with sweat. "My head is like to explode."

Concerned, Sara put an arm around her shoulder, and could feel her trembling. She had pushed too far. Accepting defeat, Sara led her back to the Embassy, and left her to rest in a darkened room.

"A panic attack," David said. "It was sensory overload; her brain couldn't take it."

Sara felt terribly discouraged. "This isn't going to work, is it, David?"

He looked as if he wished disappointment were something he could medicate. "I told you it wouldn't work. You've got to be more detached, Callicot."

Sara didn't want to be detached. "Why should her brain be any less able to take it than ours?" she asked. "She's smart, and it wasn't a difficult or stimulating task."

David looked thoughtful. "Our brains have learned to extract pattern from a relentless, chaotic bombardment of stimuli. The main work in creating any pattern from noise is exclusion of irrelevant detail. So when you think about it, the brain's main function is *elimination* of stimuli: sorting the information from the noise. We do it so automatically that we're only aware of the data that form useful patterns, not the sea of irrelevant data around them. We couldn't make sense of the world if input wasn't radically simplified."

"So do you think Moth hasn't learned to sort out the irrelevant visual impulses?"

"That's almost certainly true. Walking down the hall doesn't overtax your brain because you see very little of what the eyes record, and notice even less. Think of it like a radio. All around you is a sea of radio signals you can't sense. Imagine I installed a receiver in your brain, but you couldn't tune it. It would pick up all frequencies at once, and you'd think radio was a completely useless invention. The only really useful receiver is the one that can exclude all but one channel at a time."

"But—" Sara stopped.

"Yes?"

"That implies there could be other frequencies—other messages— we're not receiving."

"Well, sure," David said.

"There could be whole categories of information—aspects of reality—that our brains are hiding from us, because knowing about them has no evolutionary advantage."

"Like invisible parts of the EM spectrum? Our cameras and instruments tell us about those."

Sara was pursuing a thought by now. "But cameras and instruments are just extensions of our senses, and designed to work like them. We can only design cameras to photograph things whose existence we can deduce. What about things our brains aren't wired to see?"

"Hold it right there, Callicot," he said, laughing. "It's too early in the day for a paradigm shift."

Moth's repeated failures eventually put her in a black mood. The drills and practices lost their novelty, and Sara could tell that she was on the verge of giving up.

"I can never remember all of this," Moth said. "It takes so much thinking. How do you have room in your minds for aught else?"

Sara wanted to find something to encourage her again, to convince her it was all worthwhile. So one day she said, "I have something to show you, Moth. Come along."

"Thou will not make me walk with mine eyes?" she said.

"No, I'll lead you."

At the security station they acquired an escort who followed them through the twisting, canted hallways to the forward end of the quest-ship. Sara ignored him. When they came to the stairway up to the observation bubble, she told Moth, "You're going to feel yourself get-ting lighter. Hang on to my hand."

When Moth's feet started lifting off from the steps, she looked alarmed. "Don't worry," Sara said.

"Is it not a riffle?" Moth asked nervously.

"It's just the way our ship is made. In this part you're weightless."

When they passed into the bubble, Sara positioned Moth where she could hang on to the door handle, then said, "Open your eyes."

It was nearly noon on the planet below. Moth was silent as Sara studied her face. She did not seem alarmed or acrophobic, so Sara turned to look at Iris, letting her eyes lose themselves in the dazzle.

"What is it?" Moth finally said.

"That is your planet," Sara said. "Your home."

"That is Torobe?"

"No, Torobe is below us, but it is so tiny you cannot see it. It is very, very far away."

Moth held out her arm, as if to verify Sara's claim of its distance. "Let go of the handle," Sara said, and guided her forward till she touched the windowpane. Moth felt its flat surface and said, "'Tis a wall."

"No, it's a window—something you can see through but not pass through."

From the expression on Moth's face, Sara could tell that this latest illusion was too much to bear. She looked like a person trapped in a nightmarish hall of mirrors, never able to believe anything she saw, never sure of what was real. Sara watched particles of light play across her face. Then her breath began to come in spurts, and Sara realized she was crying, tearlessly.

"I want to go home," she said.

Suddenly sorry for all she had done, Sara hugged Moth tight, stroking her quivering back. "Forgive me, Moth," she said. They had taxed her beyond endurance with deceptions. "We'll take you home, I promise."

They clung to each other, bathed in shifting Irislight.

The next day, Moth was gone.

When Sara first woke up to an empty suite, she assumed Moth was with David, so she used the time alone to catch up on her notes. But when she finally made it to the clinic, she found that neither David nor Bakai had seen Moth all morning. After a thorough search, Sara strolled down to the security station and asked if Moth had passed them. Sal, the guard on duty, shook her head, scowling. "No, why?"

"We seem to have misplaced her," Sara said lightly. "She's probably playing a joke on us."

As Sara was returning to the Embassy, she heard Sal reporting the news on her radio. Minutes later, Atlabatlow arrived with a team, radios crackling with reports.

The guards searched the Embassy while the colonel interrogated Sara with a demeanor a few degrees above absolute zero. When had she last seen Moth? Why hadn't she reported the absence right away? What had the girl said?

"She was frustrated yesterday, and a little homesick," Sara answered to the last question. "My guess is that she's hiding somewhere to get away from us. Teenage girls sometimes need to be alone."

Atlabatlow ordered her to stay where she was, then left to coordinate the search. Before long, the announcement system in the hallway gave off an alarm tone, and a man's voice boomed out, "Attention. This is a shipwide security alert. All personnel are ordered to stay in place until further notice. Anyone found outside assigned areas is subject to detention. This is an emergency."

Sara groaned. She could only imagine the panic and confusion spreading through the questship. People would be speculating on what had happened, whether their lives were in danger, whether someone else had died. There would be people caught in bathrooms and storage closets, afraid to come out. The halls would be patrolled by grim-faced security guards. And all because a blind girl had wandered off.

"This is ridiculous," she muttered to herself. Then, in case the guards had left a bug behind in the Embassy, she said loudly, "Did you hear that, Colonel? You're overreacting."

There was no response. She sat down to do paperwork, but it was hard to concentrate. Minutes passed, then hours. Weary with following instructions, Sara peered out the Embassy door into the hallway. The black-clad guard posted there turned swiftly; Sara thought she saw a weapon on his belt. "Return to your station," he ordered.

It was evening before the emergency order was lifted and people were allowed to use the hallways again. Sara was heading for the refectory when she was intercepted by a message on her pager, informing her that there was an emergency meeting in the Director's office. When she arrived, the department heads were all waiting in the antechamber. They pounced on Sara.

"This is the second person you've lost," Magister Sarcodan said.

"What was I supposed to do, put a leash on her? She's a guest, not a prisoner. You ought to ask our crack security team how she managed to walk right past them, since that's what she must have done."

As if on cue, the door into the Director's office opened. Just inside it stood Colonel Atlabatlow, stiff as a man of metal. Behind him, Director Gavere looked nervously off balance; a sprig of his hair was not properly shellacked down.

When they were all seated except for Atlabatlow, the Director cleared his throat and said, "I have called you all here to let you know of a change in the organizational structure of the expedition. In view of all the unexpected incidents, I have decided to put Colonel Atlabatlow in charge of all operations that are not strictly scientific. The first thing he will be in charge of is a complete shipwide search. You're going to have to warn your people that nothing is off-limits. We'll be searching cabins, offices, everything."

The silence was broken by Sarcodan's brass-cannon voice. "Does this mean that we will all be answering to . . . this man?" He couldn't even say Atlabatlow's name.

"Not in the design of your research and so on," Gavere said. "He will be handling all ship operations—supplies, logistics, transport and communications, office assignments, mechanical systems, and so on."

"So we don't answer to him unless we want to do something?" Sarcodan said sarcastically.

There was an outburst of argument around the table then. Overlapping voices jumbled together.

Sara watched Atlabatlow watching them, noting down each insubordination, each disloyalty, cataloging the untrustworthy ones, the actual enemies. They were academics, used to expressing their independence; they didn't know how his mind worked. His eyes came to her last, saw she was watching him, narrowed with . . . what? Not simple hostility. It had grown more complex than that. He dragged his eyes away.

Sarcodan was still leading the opposition. "Unless we're abandoning our mission, this is still more than a security operation," he said loudly. "If you want to step down, Director, why don't you give your responsibilities to someone with experience directing research?"

"I am not stepping down," Gavere said, weakly. Atlabatlow cast an imperious frown at him, and he said, more firmly, "I am fully in charge."

The colonel was operating the Director like a puppet, Sara thought. Atlabatlow was performing a coup without ever uttering a word.

The department heads were peppering the Director with questions about how to get authorization for various activities. Impatiently, he broke in, "This is not a discussion! I've told you the situation. Please inform your staffs about the administrative change and the search. That is all."

They still sat there, turbulent with dissention, and he had to say, "Go back to your jobs."

When Sara stepped into the clinic, Sarcodan, Prem, and David were waiting for her. As unlikely a cell of revolutionaries as was ever assembled.

For once, Sarcodan's voice was hushed. "The Magisterium needs to know what's going on, Callicot. You've got to contact them."

"I bet a cookie they already know," Sara said. "Atlabatlow's not stupid or suicidal. He would have gotten them to authorize this."

"Then they've only heard his side of the story, whatever that is. Tell them the truth."

"What makes you think they'd believe me over him?"

"Because you're working for them, right? You have a pipeline to them. None of the rest of us does."

So much for her cover story. There was no point pretending; she was useless at subterfuge. "I'm also Atlabatlow's number one suspect," she said. "He'll never let me talk to them alone." She looked around at their expectant faces, wondering how she had gotten elected ringleader. This wasn't even her battle. "Listen," she said, "let's wait till Moth decides to show up again. Then he'll look silly for having turned the ship upside down."

"If she is able to show up," Sandhya Prem said softly. "How do we know he didn't make her disappear in the first place?"

Sara was chilled by the thought. She had been sleeping in the next room; was it possible she hadn't noticed a stealth abduction? For once, her conspiracy detectors had failed her. "Do you really think he'd . . . ?"

"To seize power?" Sarcodan said. "What do you think?"

Moth's disappearance had allowed him to get an unruly crowd of scientists under his control, while simultaneously casting suspicion on the one person with Magisterium connections. If he was capable of it, he was more dangerous than she had reckoned with.

"All right," she said, "I'll try to get a message to the Magisterium."

The promise seemed to have an irrationally uplifting effect on their spirits. But Sara wasn't doing it for them; she was doing it for Moth.

"No way," Ashok answered when Sara messaged him to see if she could get a little private time with the pepci.

"Goon alert?" she messaged back.

"Around the clock," he replied.

She sat thinking. She needed to create a diversion, something to distract the guards long enough for Ashok to get out an SOS for her. It didn't need to communicate much; it just needed to draw attention. She was trying to compose a short message in her head when there was a knock on her door. One of Atlabatlow's gray-clad automatons was standing in the hall.

"You're needed in the pepci room," he said.

Ashok was a genius. How had he engineered this so fast? "What for?" she asked with a show of stupidity.

"Incoming call for you," he said.

She followed him down the hallways, feverishly trying to prepare her message as she walked.

When she arrived in the pepci room, she was flummoxed to find that it wasn't a ruse; there really *was* an incoming call for her, from Delegate Gossup. As she settled down before the terminal, she glanced at Ashok; his raised eyebrow told her he was innocent of manipulation.

"Could I have a little privacy?" she said, ostensibly to Ashok, but really to get rid of the guard. "This is Magisterium business."

Ashok's expression told her that true privacy was not an option, but he rose to leave and held the door open for the guard. Once alone, Sara turned to the screen and hit the Accept button.

They had improved the transmission quality enough that a visual image soon appeared on the screen. Gossup looked older, though not by the full fifty-eight years that had passed. If anything, his aura of equanimity had deepened. "Sara," he said, "it is good to see you."

"Magister," she said. "You don't look a day older."

"You are learning diplomacy."

"Me? You must be kidding."

"Yes," he admitted, "I am." His expression changed. "I apologize for interrupting you. I know from the reports that you are unexpectedly busy conducting a First Contact mission. You will be pleased to know that we are assembling a team of exoethnologists to back you up."

To arrive in half a century, she thought. How helpful.

"However, that is not why I called." He drew a breath, seemingly searching for the proper words. "You will think I have become a foolish old man, to heed a premonition—but I have become very concerned about Thora. Has there been any recent change in her status?"

Sara felt a twinge of guilt at how completely she had been neglecting her secret assignment. "We haven't learned anything new," she said. "She was rescued by the natives, and seemed safe enough with them. But we haven't launched a rescue expedition because our security chief has declared the planet off-limits. Why, is there something I should know?" The thought that they had learned something alarming about Atlabatlow's background leaped into her mind.

"No," he said. "It is just . . . Well, truth to tell, I had an unusually vivid dream about her last night. It seemed as if she were trying to contact me. I wondered if . . . there are accounts of such visitations from the recently deceased."

Sara tried to hide her astonishment at learning that her supremely logical mentor had a superstitious streak. Perhaps he *was* getting old. "I have no reason to think she is in any more danger than before," she said carefully, "but unless the security restrictions let up, I can't do a thing. You know we're under an enhanced security regime?"

"Yes," he said, confirming her supposition that Atlabatlow had cleared it. "It seemed prudent."

"I'm not so sure about that. This colonel has—"

"It must be difficult for the scientific faculty to accept. Please be patient. There are factors you do not know."

She waited for a moment, but when he didn't go on, she said, "Are you going to tell me?"

"No."

"Well, there may be factors *you* don't know."

"Almost certainly. I am sorry, Sara, but I must be going. This conversation has already been extremely expensive."

Worried that she hadn't yet gotten across her warning, Sara said, "Magister, you need to check into what's going on here."

Very carefully, he said, "Sara, there are limits to what I can do."

No, there weren't—not under normal circumstances. There must be something constraining him. Before she could formulate a probing question, he smiled benignly and said, "It has been pleasant talking to you, Sara. Do your best." Then his image was replaced by a blank screen.

She sat for a moment wondering what that conversation had really been about. Was there a hidden message she was supposed to have gotten in between the malarkey about dreams and premonitions?

She told the guard she didn't need an escort back, but he stubbornly stuck with her. They had barely left the communications room when Sara was stopped in mid-stride by a falling sensation in her stomach, similar to being in a too-fast elevator, though her feet were firm on the ground. Unexpectedly, she lurched against the wall. It was as if the hallway had rotated, and what had been the wall was now the floor. She tried to pick herself up, but a sickening sensation passed through her body, as if it were being stretched, then flapped like a piece of fabric being shaken, bones and all. She had a brief impression that the hallway had either become wider, or she had become smaller. As she strained to comprehend, everything snapped back to its original dimensions. The gravity changed again, and she fell onto what had started out as the floor.

The guard was on his knees, vomiting. He fumbled for his radio and an alarm started to sound. "What the hell?" he managed to say into the radio.

"Officer Lamar, please report," the speaker responded.

"What's going on?" he said. "Are we under attack?"

The voice on the other end sounded puzzled. "Everything is normal. Do you have a situation?"

"Yes," he said. "Send backup."

Sara checked herself for damage. She felt bruised and squeamish, but everything seemed to be functioning. She staggered onto her feet, bracing herself dizzily against the wall, not really trusting it to stay vertical. Two guards were approaching, and she had a strange impression that the corridor was longer than it had been a minute ago.

The new guards were skeptical at the story their colleague told, even though Sara backed him up. "You'd better check the pepci room," she told them. "I'll take Officer Lamar to the clinic."

The guard glared at her for this, but walked alongside her back to the clinic. The two of them had barely told the doctor their shared story of hallucinations and gravity shifts when Bakai came in with the bad news. "They're calling it a spatial anomaly," she said. "No one can explain it."

"Is the pepci all right?" Sara asked.

"The pepci is fine. This time, the trouble is with the wayport. They say the quantum imbricator is breached."

"What does that mean?"

"The quantum imbricator is what runs the lightbeam assembler," David said. "No assembler, no wayport."

So they could talk to Capella Two, but they couldn't go back. They were trapped, fifty-eight years from home.

chapter nine

Dagget-Min was reluctant to take me on as an apprentice. "Why does thou wish it?" he asked.

I didn't know what he wanted me to answer. "For a long time I have felt there was more to the universe than we normally see," I said. "I think I have touched something under the surface in the past. It's as if reality were a lake, and all we can see is the glare on the surface, not the depths below." As soon as these words left my mouth, I realized what a visual metaphor it was, and I searched for another way to say it. "Something is distracting us, preventing us from sensing all we are capable of."

"Aye," he said, "but why does thou wish it?"

I was unable to answer.

"Thou hath a knack," he admitted, "and this yearning of thine is a strength, for it may ease the toil. But it also may be a weakness."

"An nkida," I said.

"Eh?"

"Nkida. It is a word my people use for a weakness that is also a strength. We teach that those are the traits we must cultivate in ourselves, for they are our power."

"That is true," he said thoughtfully, "if one may do so with discipline."

"I can," I said.

"It is perilous to enter the flow," he said. "It taketh skill and self-mastery. Moral maturity."

"Let me prove myself to you," I said.

He said nothing else then, but when I asked if I could come back, he did not forbid me.

When I next came to see him, he said nothing, but handed me a long, light cane, slung a pack on his back, and took up a cane himself. "Follow me," he said.

"Where are we going?"

"Into the coldlands."

I was not yet confident of my ability to navigate with a cane, so I asked if I could hold on to his shoulder. It is remarkable how accustomed I have become to touching people here. Somehow, their invisibility makes it seem less intimate.

We left Torobe on a path that soon sloped downward. The smells of life fell away, and cool, dank cave air surrounded us. Our bare feet were silent on the rough stone walkway; the only sound was the tapping of Dagget's cane and the occasional drip of water. I began to feel apprehensive at how far behind we were leaving Torobe.

"I could never find my way back if you weren't with me," I said.

"A wender-wight must have mettle," he observed.

I kept my anxiety to myself after that, though I think my stiff and sweaty hand may have given me away.

We walked in silence a long time—hours, I think, perhaps most of the day. At one point we rested and ate some bread and bean spread on the shore of a silent, underground lake. I wondered if it were the same lake I had encountered on my way into Torobe. I was growing weary and hungry again when I noticed a change in the air—a wisp of warmth, together with a slight sulfurous smell that signaled geothermal activity ahead.

The volcanic fumes grew stronger, and with them a sense of dread. My exhaustion, my hunger, and the tainted air were making me lightheaded and unbalanced. Dagget's steady pace had slowed, and it became like walking in a dream—an immense time between the raising of my foot and its coming down. My breath was shallow and panting, laboring to get enough oxygen. I had the illusion that the floor had become springy, like rubber.

Ahead of us, I sensed a presence in the darkness—something cold and silent and malevolent. I wanted to stop, for every instinct was warning me of danger, but Dagget continued, so I had to push forward against my fear. Though I was barely moving, my heart was laboring to beat. It was like coming near a field of negative energy that wanted to suck away my life force.

"Do you ken that?" Dagget said in my ear. I could no longer tell where he was; he seemed all around me. I was not even sure he had spoken.

"Yes," I gasped.

"That is what to shun."

I nodded, unable to speak.

We retreated—though I had no sense of following a path now, only of two directions, toward danger and away from it. It took all my discipline not to flee in panic. We came to a patch of stillness, where the danger seemed to eddy around us like a whirlpool.

"Is thy body with thee?" Dagget asked.

At first I could not feel my extremities, and I was irrationally concerned that something might be missing. I felt for my toes and fingers. They were numb, but intact.

"Keep thy body in mind at all times," Dagget instructed me. "The body is our anchor to consequences."

"What was *that*?" I said.

"Just one of the perils," he said.

Whatever it was, my instincts had reacted strongly. That meant humans had evolved to sense it. We needed to avoid it. Had I belonged to another culture, I might have called it evil.

"The next peril is subtler," he said. "Before we attempt it, I must instruct thee."

I settled down to listen. My hands and feet were not sensing texture or weight properly, so I could not be sure it was rock underneath me.

"There is a flow in the Ground," Dagget said. "It is everywhere, and most places it is stable. In fact, that is all we are: a stable pattern in the flow. That is all anything is—rocks, water, air. Down deep, in the fundament, all things are like unto a stream where the water changeth ever, but the stream remains."

"But you can alter a stream," I said.

"Aye, you can. Shut off the flow, and the shape disappears. Disturb it, and the shape changeth. What we just went nigh was a turbulence. There, all things cease, or so we think."

I was not eager to test that hypothesis. "Are we safe now?" I asked.

"No," he said. "This is the still place, and here the test is different, for it giveth all we long for. Here, the Ground is close by, and those who are skilled or bred up to it may sense it and enter the flow. The danger is that thou will forget who thou are and lose thyself in bliss. Does thou remember what I told thee about consciousness?"

I did, because I had repeated it into my recorder. "Consciousness is bounded and particular," I paraphrased him, "but it reaches out to join awareness, like a grain of salt longs to join the brine."

"Very good," he said.

"So the Ground is aware?"

"Aye," he said.

"How do you know?"

"Do you wish to continue?"

My confidence had been disturbed by the last experience, and by the strangely insubstantial feeling of where we now were. But as I searched my mind, the compulsion to continue was still there. "I want to go on."

"Very well," he said. "Pay attention to thy breath."

This instruction was exactly what the teachers of the mind-body discipline of apathi had taught me, so I took the meditative posture and quickly stilled my mind. For a long time nothing happened, and I wanted to ask Dagget if I were doing it correctly, but I could no longer hear his breathing close by, and wasn't even sure he was there. I could have reached out to feel for him, but it would have meant breaking the pose and disobeying his instruction, so I focused again on my dova and tried to sink into it.

A feeling came to me, as of a vast whirlpool turning around and within me, both majestic and swift. I looked down into it, and saw the immensity of distance it plummeted, its spiral flow growing smaller and smaller till it was no larger than a keyhole. Then I was being drawn into it, and allowed myself to drop, spinning, deeper and deeper, till I was the size of an atom in a maelstrom of dizzying proportion.

At the very bottom of the vortex there was light, and my mind yearned for it after all this time in darkness. Yet I found it was not a light I could see by; it had no source and illuminated nothing, but filled me from within till I shone. It gave me such a feeling of joy and belonging that my spirits sang.

"Follow the wonder," said Dagget's voice close by. "Follow the awe."

There was awe—and reverence, too, for the immensity of what lay around me, and the light that animated me. I felt that I had merged with something immeasurable, and in it was everyone I knew and *everything I had experienced, as close as a hand-touch, all united in a joyful moment that would last forever. There was warmth, and fragrance, and love.*

"Keep together," Dagget said. "Do not let it fill you, or you will burst. Thou art a thing with a skin, an inside and an outside. Feel thy body-anchor."

Dagget's words brought me back to awareness of the breath in my lungs and the beating of my heart, the bag of flesh I occupied. I was back in the cave, cold and cramped and blind. I was back in my trivial, tiny existence after having felt completion and totality. A sharp grief of separation tore through me, and I gave a sob of loss, sitting there on the ground. Dagget stroked my shoulder and whispered comfort.

"I'm sorry," I said when I gained control of my emotions again. "It was overwhelming."

"Aye," he said, "some feel it so. To them, it is ever a danger that they will lose themselves and dissolve in the flow. It will be your task to resist."

"I don't want to resist," I said.

"Thou hast not lost the Ground," he said gently. "It is still here, around thee, at all times. All thou hast lost is awareness of it."

"How do I recapture it?"

"That," he said, "is a later lesson. For now, we must return."

I felt that an enormous time had passed, but when we returned to Torobe, people had barely noticed our absence. I returned to Hanna's house and slept for hours.

"Thou hast learned the first lesson," Dagget said when I went back to see him. "How to find thy way into the Ground."

I felt I had learned no such thing, and told him so. "Find my way? Without you, I could never return to where we were."

He answered patiently, "All thou dost need to know is what to shun, and what to seek."

I realized that the long journey through the cave was trivial in his mind; what mattered was what came after. Lowering my voice, I said, "You mean, avoid the thing I dread, and go toward the thing I long for? I would have done that anyway. It's just instinct."

"You would be surprised how many cannot follow their true instinct. Even you might find it harder to distinguish than it first seemed. There are no directions in the Ground—no up nor down, left nor right. There is only the good direction and the ill."

It sounded strangely moral when he said it that way. It had already occurred to me that if I had fit the experience into a different cultural construct, I would be talking about having touched God, and the devil. My experience was not new. Generations upon generations of humans must have sensed the Ground, but come back describing it in their own culture-bound ways. I was struck again by Dagget's pragmatism. He had taught me a moral compass through life, but spoke as if it were a mere problem in navigation.

"Thou hast also learned to preserve thyself from dissolution in the flow," he said. "It will take practice, but the first step is done."

I was still dissatisfied. For all I knew, my brain, starved for input and hallucinating on fumes, had created an elaborate illusion. I needed to know whether Dagget had experienced the same thing I did. "Did you have the impression of a whirlpool with light at the bottom?"

"Light?" he said, puzzled.

I realized there was an insurmountable linguistic barrier. Even if he had experienced light, he had no way to tell me.

But for that matter, how could I be sure that the experience I call "light" is what any of my sighted friends experience? Perhaps we are all going around using a single word for a collection of nonidentical experiences; how would we ever be the wiser?

I tried again. "There was a moment when I felt as if all the people I knew were there with me, and all the places I had been, and all the moments I had lived."

"Aye," he said, "that is so. In the Ground, all times are present at *once, and all places. It is not many places, it is one. And so all people who ever lived are also there, but not as separate beings. Separation is the illusion; in reality, we are all one, the same, together, manifestations of Awareness. In the Ground we cannot travel, because it is all one place. We cannot go back in time because it is all one moment, now. It is an eternal event, always happening."*

All I could say was, "When can I go back?"

"When do you wish to go back?" he said.

"Now," I said.

"Let us set out, then."

The second time was utterly unlike the first. I saw no whirlpool this time; rather, I followed the feeling of sublimity until I found myself in an immense place like a multifaceted, n-dimensional prism, at the intersection of a thousand planes, where each surface was the reflection of another world. It dwarfed me; in fact, I had no dimension myself. I felt sure that by turning sideways I could fit through a crack into another plane at right angles to all the ones I knew. If only I could align myself with the infinitely complex geometry of the place, I could slip into a reflection.

It was completely bewildering, and just as I was starting to feel panic at the sensory overload, I remembered Dagget's instruction that there were only two directions in the Ground. So I did the equivalent of closing my eyes: I ignored the visual imagery of planes and prisms, compelling as it was, and tried to navigate by my sense of emotion. It was like being in Torobe, finding my way without sight, but here I could sense the feel of home, the smell of memory, the snatch of a haunting song, the tug of love and hate. All of them were there, some more powerful than others. One "direction" called me with a thousand hearts of longing and desperation, another with a poignant sense of loss and regret, a third with urgent worry, a fourth with pinching resentment. I wanted to join them all, but as I turned my attention to the loudest, I felt a tug of familiarity and knew that Dagget wanted me back. I focused on the smell of pipe smoke I associated with him,

and the familiar wisdom he radiated, and soon I was sitting beside
him in the cave. He was holding my hand.

"Thou did forget thy body," he said to me.

"I'm sorry," I said, still elated and dizzy with the experience. "There
were so many people, so many places."

"Did thou feel the call of thy home?" he asked.

For once, his question did not quite hit the mark. I realized the
problem: the word "home." "I have had so many homes," I said.

This answer made him thoughtful. I realized that I had said some-
thing as incomprehensible to the grounded people of Torobe as if I
had spoken of prisms and planes. Then it occurred to me that per-
haps I was the one who had misunderstood. When he said "home,"
did he mean the assortment of places I had made my bed, or some-
thing deeper? Was there a place that was my true home?

"I think perhaps I have not found my home yet," I said.

"That may be," he said. "There are many habitudes, but only one
home."

A memory has come back to me, shaken loose by my experiences with
Dagget. When it first surfaced it was muffled, like a sound heard
through plugged ears. Then there was an abrupt clearing, like ears
popping, and it rushed into my consciousness, flashback-vivid. It must
be a memory the mentationists suppressed, because it is about Orem.

In it, my cheek rests against the gritty cement floor. The room is
hot, and the acrid smoke of a burning city hazes the air. I try to sit
up, and find my hands are tied behind me. My right elbow throbs,
and I remember the sickening pop the tendon made when they twisted
it behind me. My eyes are swollen and my throat is raw from tear gas.

I am in a cinderblock room with one small window high on the wall.
It is twilight, and the low, sooty clouds are lit with the reflection of the
fires. By the glow of the burning city I can see that the room has been
ransacked. Nothing is left but a built-in rope cot with a cornhusk

mattress, a broken mirror on one wall, and a dented mechanical typewriter lying in a corner.

A syncopated patter of gunfire nearby makes me recoil. My nerves are hypersensitive. Sitting cross-legged, I force myself to close my eyes and breathe evenly, to summon my dova. I repeat the apathi focus-phrases: All control is ultimately self-control. The world has no power over me if I have power over my mind. Gradually, the discipline forces back my panic, and my thoughts clarify.

My fear is probably exaggerated. Orem is prone to eruptions of violence, but they are rarely aimed against outsiders. The kithpacks hate each other far more than they hate us. The fact that I am not dead already proves that someone knows who I am and values the al-liance with Capella I can offer. There is every reason to be hopeful. I know the Oreman psyche, and that knowledge is my weapon.

A tickling behind my ear invades my detachment. Tiny worms like nematodes are the ever-present vermin of Orem, filling the ecological niche of insects. I have fought to keep them out of my clothes and hair ever since arriving here. This room is probably infested with them. I can feel them squirming against my scalp, but with my hands bound I cannot scratch. Breathing out, I try to detach myself from the itch and revulsion—not to deny it, but to acknowledge it and rise above.

Later, a gray dawn noses in the window. The gunfire has died down. The sound of voices outside my room breaks into the silence. I do not stir as they unbolt the door, but merely sit on the floor as if meditating.

There are two of them, both men. On their left temples is tattooed an open bird claw about to grasp the eyeball, a packmark I do not recognize. By their clothes they belong to one of the wild hillpacks. That means they will be superstitious, conservative, and militaristic. Possibly deferential to authority.

"Do you know who I am?" I ask coolly.

They ignore me. Not deferential, then. They are checking the room for invisible dangers. At last the older one, a man with yellowed teeth and a stubbled face, says, "Rise in respect for the Hunter of Men, Katarka."

My obedience is not quick enough, and the younger man sweeps out his machete and brings the flat of the blade down on my shoulders. It is exactly the same motion he would have made to sever my head. I stagger to my feet. Under my breastbone is a spot of quivering panic. I can no longer delude myself that I know what is going on. To these men, I am not an emissary of the Capellan Magisterium; I am a female body, anonymous and unimportant.

When the next two men enter the room, the first two kneel, each placing his forehead on one knee in a posture of obeisance. The second pair is as roughly dressed as the first, but have an air of mastery. One of them is a wiry, balding man who, without any obvious deformity, gives the impression of having been crumpled and broken. The other visitor stands in the shadows, so I cannot see him clearly.

With the guards still crouched on the floor, the twisted one comes forward to inspect me. When he catches me looking at him, he makes as if to strike me, and I drop my eyes. "This is the one who is kith to the king of the outworlders," he says.

"What is that on her forehead?" the man in the shadows says.

"A stone eye, Great Hunter," Twisted replies. "Only the outworld sleeks have them."

The other man mutters a warding charm.

"It is just a caste stone," I say. "It is inoperative outside my home world." Ordinarily, I do not explain, in order to keep people guessing. But now their fear is dangerous to me.

They pay no attention. They exchange some words in one of the badland country regional dialects. The Great Hunter Katarka calls his companion Scarinau. I have never heard either name, despite having kept track of the rival factions on Orem. Laocata, the kithmother I have dealt with, did not fear anyone from the badlands.

Scarinau turns back to me. "You will send a message to your

kith-king. You will tell him to send us weapons, many weapons, and supplies to make them work."

"I cannot do that," I say.

"Then you will die."

It is just a statement of fact: if I serve no purpose, I will be disposed of. Quickly, I say, "I would like to help you. I cannot get arms, but there are other things I can ask for."

"What things?"

Scarinau has a wily look. I realize that he might be ignorant and superstitious, but he is an opportunist. This is a man I can communicate with.

"Let me speak to my staff," I say.

Great Hunter Katarka comes forward from the shadows. He is a magnificent barbarian, younger than Scarinau, muscled and athletic. He says, "Your tame little man-slaves were disgusting creatures, so sapped of life force they tried to talk instead of resist. We put them out of their misery."

I cannot show the shock and grief I feel; he will see it as weakness. I must focus on the fact that I am alone now. There will be no help from home, and no Capellans working for my release on the planet. But I might still have Oreman allies. "Where is Laocata?" I ask.

"She cursed me, so I cut her tongue out," Katarka says. "Then she shook her fist at me, so I cut her hand off. Then she looked at me, so I put her eyes out. She was a pampered degenerate, not even fit to hunt."

Laocata was the most powerful kithmother I knew. If he is telling the truth, it will embroil the country in a bloody feud by her powerful kithpack—none of which seems to concern Katarka.

"What good are these outworlders?" he says to Scarinau.

"They have many riches, Hunter of Men."

"Their riches only corrupt. It is nobler to hunt the old way."

"Let me deal with her, then." Scarinau gives me a crooked leer.

On the whole, I would prefer to contend with Scarinau. But in some situations underlings are of little use. Katarka's ignorant savagery revolts me, but he is the one I need. I have to gamble, and do it quickly.

"Tell him the truth, Scarinau," I say softly.

"What?" Katarka says alertly.

"I don't know what she's talking about," Scarinau says.

"Yes, you do," I say.

I turn to Katarka as if we were standing in a council chamber. "Our satellites can make the name of Katarka echo around this world. It can echo in praise, or in infamy."

There is a perfect silence for several seconds. I can hear the blood rushing past my ears.

"Pull out that stone eye," Katarka orders.

The two soldiers rise to obey. The older one takes a tool like a pair of pliers from his belt.

"It won't come out," I say. "It's anchored to my skull."

"We'll send it to her kith-king," Katarka says. "It will be better than a finger or an ear. Everyone has fingers and ears. Only she has a third eye."

The younger soldier pushes me up against the wall, my arms still pinned behind me. I start to talk, to bargain, but he grips my jaw hard to keep my head immobile. I see the other man coming, the pliers gripped in his dirty hands, and I struggle, kicking out. The jaws of the pliers grate against the metal setting of the caste-stone. The first pull does not budge it. He presses my head back against the wall with the heel of his hand, and grips the pliers as if to pull a nail from wood. On his second tug, I feel unbearable pressure; then the metal roots break free of bone, the stem rips from my flesh, and he holds the device up, bloody and broken. A warm stream blinds me, and my legs give way.

Later, I wake in a fever-hot room. My skin feels pasty with the mix of sweat and dust on it, and my mouth is parched. The wound in my forehead has become infested with maggoty, squirming worms feeding on the dried blood and flesh. The sensation is maddening, but with my hands tied behind me there is nothing I can do about it.

When the guard comes in, I beg for water and a doctor. He brings the water in a dish, and I have to lap it up like a dog. Later, he brings the doctor—or rather, a streetcorner witch-doctor who makes no attempt to dress the wound, and thinks the word "antibiotic" is some sort of Capellan mockery. "It's infested with worms," I say, on the edge of delirious hysteria.

"Good worms," he says in a rough badlands accent. "Eat bad flesh, leave the good."

"What if they get inside my skull and start eating my brain?" I say.

"Think bad thoughts to keep them out," he suggests.

I would cry if I could spare the moisture.

After that, the universe contracts into a room-sized ball, and within that ball I am no longer a person, just a concentration of fever and thirst.

At one point the ghastly image of a face stares at me—reddened eyes, cracked lips, surmounted by a black and oozing wound. Frightened, I step back, only to realize that I have somehow crossed the room and am looking in the remains of the broken mirror the pillagers left on the wall. In my feverish state, I think they have made the mirror testify falsely, part of their wicked propaganda magic. They want to convince me that I am the person in that mirror.

Then one delirious night, I wake from a nightmare with the sensation that someone else is in my room. It is not one of my captors; I am sure of that, because I smell the cleansing smoke of sage. I feel a gentle touch on my forehead, and know it is the goddess Witassa who has come to my aid. She is standing there at my bedside, hacked by axes and still triumphant. The wound in my forehead then seems to glow with a sanctified heat. I whisper a prayer, the most heartfelt I have ever uttered. She does not answer, but I know she means me to turn suffering into strength.

The next morning my fever is better, and as a consequence I feel

ashamed at having broken down so badly as to have believed in one
of their gods. Aloud, I say, "I am Thora Lassiter, emissary of the Capellan Magisterium. I am Ral. They cannot make me into something
other than I am."

And yet, as the hot days wear on, my mind clogs with despondence,
and I know the solution to my situation lies not in clinging to my old
identity, but in embracing a new one.

When at last I hear voices at my door, I know who it will be: Scarinau, the twisted one.

He comes in, followed by the guard. He looks edgy. "Prepare yourself for the will of the Great Hunter Katarka," he says loudly. "He has
commanded me to rape you."

My head fills with a strange, lightheaded lucidity. I feel a breath
on the back of my neck, and know she is standing behind me. Tell
me what to do, I implore silently.

She answers, but in a language I do not know.

"You think I'm not serious?" he demands, his hand on his belt
buckle.

"I do," I say. "I am shameless."

There is an intake of breath from the guard. Scarinau's left hand
jerks as with a nervous tic. He wipes his mouth.

"She is lying," Scarinau sneers to the guard. "We will shame her
easily enough. Go on, strip off her clothes."

The guard hangs back, and Scarinau curses him. "She wears no
narakata," the guard whispers. Literally, it means "shame cover." It is
the undergarment women wrap around themselves, a strip of cotton
yards and yards long, like a mummy wrapping. It can take a quarter
of an hour to remove.

"How do you know that?" Scarinau demands. "Have you been con-
temptible with her?"

Instead of answering, the guard slinks forward, averting his eyes.
But when he unties my hands and reaches out to touch my shirt, I

slap him away. "I don't need your help," I say viciously. Or rather, she says it, not me.

In one motion I whip the knit shirt off over my head, leaving myself naked to the waist. It is so unexpected, the guard backs away, his eyes wide. Scarinau stands his ground, but he stares as if his eyes cannot leave my breasts. I wonder how many times either of them has seen a woman naked in daylight. I catch Scarinau's eye and say, "You will need the self-control of a great kithfather."

His eyes wander, and a muscle in his lean, stubbly cheek twitches. In a hard, unnecessarily loud voice he says, "I obey the Hunter of Men."

"Katarka fears you, Scarinau," I say softly. "Even I can see that. He sent you here so I would suck the life force from your body, and destroy you."

He turns to the guard. "Leave. I don't need protection."

The guard glances at me, then at Scarinau. This makes Scarinau furious, and he shouts, "Get out!" The guard leaves.

The man who has come to rape me crosses the room to listen at the door, clearly agitated. When assured that the guard has left, he stands indecisively for a moment. Then, without looking at me, he says, "Put your covering back on. I want to bargain."

The goddess laughs in the back of my brain.

He paces nervously till I am safely clothed again. "I am not a simple backwoods fellow like that one," he says. "I know much about your world. I have taken trouble to inform myself. Your men are addicts. They think of nothing but their own gratification, and that is how you rule them."

I neither confirm nor deny this. "You spoke of a bargain," the Capellan in me says.

"Yes." He begins chewing a broken thumbnail tensely.

"I will demand a price," I warn. "But if you do what I want, I will lie for you, and say that you have done Katarka's bidding."

"What do you want?"

My Capellan self wants to steer toward the narrow path of survival and escape. But the goddess wants me to plunge into the dark parts of their culture, and immerse myself in their minds. I can feel the wild heat of her body flowing up my spine.

"You want to escape," Scarinau says.

"No," the goddess says in my voice. "I want Katarka."

As my meaning sinks in, his eyes flick here and there, following chains of possibilities. "You think I am disloyal," he says. "I am not."

"You think Katarka is not equal to the challenge?" Witassa purrs with derision. "Then someone else should rule in his stead."

I can see his mind working. "I think I know a way to get the Hunter in the snare. It may be dangerous."

Witassa laughs scornfully.

He straightens as much as his caved-in body will allow. "I can do it. Katarka will be yours. The rest is up to you."

The recovered memory disturbed me so that I became preoccupied and moody. Hanna patiently waited to see if I wanted to talk, but I have not been able to tell her. It is not just the violence and degradation of the memory, or the unwelcome things it tells me about myself. This new version of events does not accord with the memories of Orem I had before. Up to now, I have believed I broke down and became a docile tool of my captors. But those memories are blurred and indistinct beside this one. Either this memory is a vivid delusion, or my previous memories were implanted. But why would the mentationists implant memories of a shameful surrender if it never happened? Could I have done something worse? But try as I may, I cannot pull up the rest of the memory.

At last I went to ask Dagget's advice.

"Ofttimes a wender will meet his or her own past," he said. "The Ground doth bestow self-knowledge as well as other-knowledge."

"Does that mean this is a true memory?"

"Only thou can answer that."

Waking, I have tried everything I know to recover more. To learn the truth, I think I will have to return to the Ground.

There has been a strange new turn of events. I first found out that Moth had returned by the banging and breathless chatter from the direction of Hanna's formerly peaceful kitchen. When I came over to find out what was going on, Moth greeted me with, "Thora! I have been to thy habitude, and met thy friends."

I thought at first she was joking, or telling an imaginative tale, but she soon convinced me otherwise. She knew the names of Sara, David, and Bakai. What was more, she had in her possession a head-net and a transmitter-recorder identical to the one I have been using to keep this diary. It could only have come from us. I was floored.

"Moth, how did you get there?" I said.

"I know not. I was in the songlands, searching for whatnuts, when something happened, and then I was on Escher."

Her tale was so similar to what had happened to me that I asked, "Were they surprised to see you?"

"Nay, they were expecting me," she said. "It is a habitude of wonders. Hanna, thou would not believe, but Thora's people are very clever and powerful in their own land. They possess a sense we have not—sight. Thora, why can thou not see like thy people?"

"I can, in my own home," I said. "I can't see here because there is no light."

I expected her to be confused, but instead she said knowingly, "Oh aye, Sara told me. Hanna, they have invented something called radiation. It is like unto tiny balls bouncing about. The balls are made by bulbs."

Hanna was mixing something in a bowl while listening. She said tolerantly, "Bulbs? Like yams?"

"Aye, I suppose, yams that give off seeds they call particles. When

the particles strike their eyes, they can feel them, and they make patterns. They tried to teach me, but it is very hard. When I go back I will master the skill and become a seer."

Moth's amazing tales were soon the talk of all Torobe. Many were skeptical, because I had gotten the reputation of being inoffensive but witless, and the idea of my coming from a race of godlike beings was more than they could swallow. But as the idea sank in, it occurred to more than one person that I might have been hiding my powers in order to lull them into trusting me. In a shorttime a village convocation was called to look into the matter.

They met in the Echo Sculpture, but this time rugs and pillows were spread for seating and to dampen the echoes. The Three presided at the center of a ring of witnesses. Their first step was to call on Moth to tell her story.

"Harken thou, Torobes!" Moth said dramatically, so that her voice echoed. She waited for silence to fall. "Harken, for I have been to a wondrous place."

She told the story in the manner of a discovery narrative where odd but simple natives turn out to have hidden powers. "Their habitude is made of boxes," Moth said. "They have boxes that slide, boxes that hinge, boxes that fold: they are never happy till they have made more boxes for themselves and everything about them. They sleep on boxes, and live in them, and teach them to do all manner of clever things. I brought one back to show thee. Here, this is a box they have taught to remember things. Anath-Not, tell it something."

"Nay, tell it something thyself," Anath-Not replied, her dignity affronted.

"Songta?"

"I would tell it thou art a lawless scamp," Songta responded.

Moth pressed a button and the recorder played back Songta's words in her own voice. Everyone laughed but Songta. "Thy little box is saucy," she said sourly.

Moth said, "Their boxes are their slaves which they make to sing, and heat their food, and talk to people far away. Their boxlore is deep and puissant."

"Thora Lassiter, is this true?" Songta demanded.

I hardly knew where to begin. I decided to allay any fears over Moth's demonstration. Preindustrial societies, I knew, were always suspicious of cameras because taking a person's image might steal his or her soul. In Torobe, a voice was the mark of individuality the way a face was elsewhere, so the fear might be the same. "Moth's box is harmless, elders," I said. "All it does is to record the sounds around it. It doesn't know what you are saying." We have a more powerful box for that, I thought, but did not say so. "Even so, I expect you could find it useful. You could record promises or contracts, or music, or listen to the voices of your loved ones even when they are gone."

This caused a stir of interest. Songta said, "Give me that box." We all heard Moth showing them how to operate it, and soon they were recording each other's voices and giggling a little self-consciously.

Finally, Anath-Not interrupted by scolding her colleagues, "For shame, you are like children! The box is clever, and learns its lesson fast, but if thou dost prate of twaddle, that is what it remembers."

"That is true," I said. "But you can make it forget, too."

"How?" Songta asked.

"I know not," Moth said.

I came forward and showed them how to erase. Anath-Not took the recorder firmly in hand and said, "Methinks it should be kept carefully by a person who will not waste its powers. From now on, only the wise shall touch it."

This caused some dissatisfaction, since everyone knew that Anath-Not's definition of "wise" was restricted to herself alone. So I said, "We have many such boxes. Perhaps in future you would like to trade for them."

"Thou would share thy boxpowers?" Songta said craftily.

I did not know what was on her mind, so I hesitated. Moth jumped in, "But I have not yet told thee the whole of their powers. I have not yet mentioned their eyes."

She then launched into an account that showed she had misunderstood sight as profoundly as technology. None of the benefits I would have mentioned—ability to find my way around or to read—seemed important to Moth. "Their eyes serve them to see the future," she said. "Sometimes they can see far into the future, but indistinctly, and sometimes only a short way, but clear. They can also see a person's thoughts and moods. The power of their eyes waxes and wanes, and when their sight is least mighty, they sleep. They can turn their eyes off and on at will. Their eyes are so mighty, they must live in boxes, or be vexed by knowing too much. I warrant they already know many things about Torobe."

"Elders, please," I interrupted. "Moth is exaggerating. It is true, our eyes are a great benefit to us. But we are different from you, not better. You have proved that sight is not necessary to be strong and independent. Look at all you have achieved: this village, these homes, your lives."

Rinka said softly, "And yet, thou hast hidden thy powers from us."

I felt annoyed at Moth. She had made us too dangerous and too alluring in their minds. I thought of the folktales where humans are able to enslave magical beings of frightening power. How temptingly similar this situation must seem to them. I tried my best not to seem evasive. "I have hidden nothing. I cannot see here, and you all know how helpless it makes me."

"Why can thou not see?" Songta asked.

To avoid getting into an explanation of electromagnetism, I said, "I don't have the proper box with me."

"So thy boxes give thee this power?"

"In some circumstances."

Moth broke in, "And if we had the proper box with a bulb inside, we also could see. They told me so. In fact, they promised to teach me."

Anath-Not said peremptorily, "This is improper. Such a gift should not go to an obdurate child like Moth, but to the great and wise."

"I am not a child!" Moth said indignantly.

I could only guess what my colleagues on Escher might have said to Moth, but I knew First Contact protocols. "We will do nothing without your permission," I said firmly. "My friends may have said something incautious to Moth because they were anxious to find me."

"Oh, aye," Moth said, "they want Thora back very badly. They asked me to lead them here."

"Did thou pledge to do it?" Anath-Not asked in alarm.

"Of course not. I told them I would ask you."

This gave the Three the decision whether to invite aliens to visit. Anath-Not was clearly against it, but Songta seemed willing to take the risk. "The Boxmasters may be mighty allies," she said. "They give us hope where yesterday we were sore perplexed."

"They may not consent to aid us," Rinka said.

Not a cough nor a shuffle came from the crowd. I realized that Rinka had made some sort of oblique demand, and everyone was listening for my reply. Not even sure what they wanted, I still did not want to let them down. I said, "I do not know if we can help you, but we will do everything in our power to try."

The riffle came when I was asleep. A sickening sensation roused me, as if I were rocking on the swell of a sea, but when I sat up, something like a wall of pressure hit me. My ears popped, my lungs lost all their air, and I had the feeling that the front of my body had passed through my back, then rebounded to its original place. It was not painful, but profoundly disturbing. I reached for the floor, but it seemed miles away, then so close each grain was a mountain. The world around me shivered, and my skin with it, like the surface of a lake. A rumbling sound of rockfall came from somewhere to my right, then silence.

I can't explain how unsettling it was. Something that has always been absolutely stable and predictable—the gridwork of space—seemed to have suffered a paroxysm, like a dimensional earthquake. As I tried to gather my wits, voices started to cry out as our neighbors checked with each other to make sure all was well. I called for Hanna, but she didn't answer, so I crawled on hands and knees, not trusting the floor to stay underneath me, until I reached the area where she slept. I heard frantic thumps and clattering, then Moth's voice saying, "Here he is, Hanna. Right at thy side." The baby then began to cry, and so did Hanna.

"Moth!" I cried out. "What happened?"

"'Twas but a riffle," she said, though her voice sounded less reassuring than her words. "Hanna thought the baby was gone. Ofttimes the little ones fare not well. Are thou all of a piece?"

"Yes," I said.

There was some sort of commotion in the village—footsteps, voices yelling, jangling chimes. Moth seized my hand. "Let's find what's afoot," she said.

She led me at far too fast a pace into the village center. A crowd had gathered, and people were talking in such a hubbub that I could not understand at first what had happened. Since they were crying out names and searching between two houses, I thought a building had collapsed. But when I asked Moth, she said, "Nay, it did not fall. It is gone."

"Gone?"

"Between the folds. Fawna's family lived there."

She sounded genuinely distressed, so I said, "I'm sorry."

The search continued for some time, and I found a place to stand out of the way, which seemed the most useful thing I could do. Hanna joined me after a while, carrying her baby. "Is he all right?" I asked.

"Oh, aye," she said. "I should not have doubted. He is Breel's son, after all."

After a while, the search was abandoned and everyone gathered round in silence. There was some weeping in the crowd. Then I heard Dagget's quiet voice, and there was instant silence.

"Mourn not," he said. "They did but sojourn with us a while, be-minded by our love. Now they have joined the Ground of all being."

In an anguished tone a woman said, "They may not yet be gone. They could be summoned back."

No one said anything. The same woman said, "Dagget-Min, can you not seek them on the other side?"

He did not reply; after a few moments Songta spoke instead. "We shall lose more than Fawna if we tarry. Our peril is now before us. This home of ours is no longer safe. The fold rain will soon be here, and we must seek haven in another habitude."

Sounds of protest and grief came from the crowd. I could scarcely believe that I had understood: was she proposing to leave their care-fully constructed home, so perfectly adapted to their needs? How would they ever find another such place, and how long would it take them to replicate this village?

My thoughts seemed to be widely shared, because arguments started up—some claiming it was not yet time, others that the omens were not certain. Songta said, "Peace, peace. I speak not of this shorttime. First the wenders must find another habitude willing to take us in."

Moth was suddenly at my side. "Thora, could we go to Escher?" she whispered.

I tried to dampen her hopes gently. "I don't think that would be practical, Moth. The ship isn't large enough for everyone. But we may be able to help you scout another place to live—an old lava tube or cave, perhaps. I wish I understood why you have to leave here."

"Because the fold rain cometh!"

"Is the fold rain like a riffle?"

"Like a great storm and conflagration of riffles! No one may sur-vive it. Is there no fold rain on Escher?"

"Not that I know."

Songta was speaking to the crowd. "Dagget will set out anon to seek another habitude. Have forbearance. Remember, our people have made pilgrimage before, in our mothers' mothers' time. We can do it again."

This was not the encouragement everyone needed. The crowd began to break up, disconsolate and unsettled. I heard Songta call out, "Is Thora Lassiter here?"

"Here, Songta," I said.

She came over to me and said, "If ever the Boxmasters wish to aid us, this is the time."

"I need to go with Dagget," I said. "He may be able to lead me to a place where I can contact my people."

"Nay," Dagget said, and I realized he was by Songta's side. "Thou'rt not ready. The ways I need to wend are too dangerous."

"My eyes will protect me," I said.

"Uh," he said, clearly unconvinced.

"Let me try."

"We shall think on it," Songta said.

But when I next went to their house to make my case, Dagget was already gone.

chapter ten

from the audio diary of thora lassiter:

Moth could not understand my frustration at Dagget's departure. "Why can thou not go back to Escher on thine own?" she asked.

Clearly, she thought our godlike powers had no limits. "They don't know where I am," I explained. "I can't tell them unless I can get to a place where the radiation can reach me. That's how we communicate. Moth, do you know how to get to a place where there is light?"

"Aye," she said as if I were demented. "I know how to get to Escher."

It occurred to me that she might have stumbled onto our planetary base camp, and gotten to the ship from there. "All right. Can you lead me there?"

"Of course. They will be right glad to see thee."

She was ready to set out then and there, but I insisted on telling Hanna, and getting some provisions for the journey. To my surprise, Hanna was unwilling to let me go. She sent Moth off on an errand so we could talk privately.

"Let not Moth lead thee astray," she said. "She is a skillful wender, but hath not the maturity to understand what she does. Breel taught her too young. I told him not to, but she was so eager he gave in. It is one reason Songta will not speak to him."

I didn't want to get in the middle of a family dispute, but if Moth truly knew her way to the surface, it seemed worth the risk. "Do you think she really knows how to get to Escher?"

"Dost thou believe she hath been there?"

"Yes."

"Then she knoweth the way. But that does not mean she can show thee safely, or go there herself without paying a price."

"What do you mean, price?"

Hanna hesitated, and I realized the question disturbed her. "The wending hath kept her unnaturally young," she said quietly. "It is my fault. Try as I may, I cannot bemind her as any other than the child I remember. When she returns, she falleth back into old ways."

I knew what she was talking about. I, too, had had the experience of being frozen in time in the minds of family. After a long absence, they still thought of me as the person who had left, and their belief had a frustrating influence on my own behavior. It was one reason I had never hesitated to leave again. It was that, or remain a person I no longer was. "It's a common problem," I said.

"Aye, but not this bad. We were once close in age."

This information surprised me, because I would have guessed them to be at least a decade apart, from their behavior. Perhaps, I thought, Moth had some developmental delay that Hanna blamed on herself. If she had not told me, I never would have guessed. Moth had seemed like a normal, even precocious, adolescent. But I had never seen her, so I could not guess her age. The news made me wary.

"Hanna, I'm sure it's nothing you have done. The same thing happens among my people, but we have cures for it. Maybe we can share them someday, after I get back. In the meantime, I will be careful."

"Thou art thine own woman," she said. "I cannot stop thee. But if thou wish to return, come to me."

I felt a surge of warmth toward her then, and reached out to hug her. "Thank you for everything," I said.

Moth and I set out armed with sticks and a backpack for some food. She led me through the village and on into the coldlands, just as Dagget had done. I said nothing as our path sloped downward, farther into the cave, but as we continued I finally asked Moth if she were sure this was the right way. "I have trod this path a thousand times," she said.

When we stopped by the shores of the underground lake to eat, I said, "I am sure Dagget led me this way."

"Good," she said. "If he hath led thee here, then no one can blame me for leading thee amiss, or prate of my youthful folly."

"Are you and Hanna really close in age?" I asked her.

"Not anymore," she said. "Hanna hath aged prematurely, from staying always in Torobe, where they spend their lives warding off the world."

"Well, it looks like the world is coming to Torobe now."

"Aye, that's true." She said it with regret, I thought.

"It's nice to have a place to come back to, isn't it?" I said.

"Aye," she said, and wouldn't reveal any more.

My conviction that we were on the path I had followed before became a certainty when I smelled the sulfuric fumes and felt the tug of apprehension. I made Moth stop. "Why have we come here?" I said. "This is not the way to the Escher. It's the way to the place Dagget calls the Ground."

"Aye," Moth said in a baffled tone. "The way to Escher is through the Ground. Dost thou know another way?"

A great many things that had not been making sense to me were swirling through my head. I had assumed that Dagget had brought me here to teach a spiritual tradition. In fact, I was sure he had. But Moth seemed to be speaking not of a psychic journey, but a physical one.

"You believe you can go to the Escher through the Ground?" I said carefully.

"Aye, and to the other habitudes. We call our cordwork of habitudes the tangle; 'tis like the cordwork of Torobe."

"Do you go in your mind, like a dream?" I pressed her.

"Nay, as I do stand here before thee," Moth said. "That is, if someone is there to bemind me."

I had thought I understood that word, as a synonym of "call to mind" or "think of." Now I realized it had another meaning. "Bemind you. What does that mean?"

"Why, conjure me through from the other side. Fill my bag. What else should I call it?"

"Humor me, Moth. What if there's no one in a habitude to bemind you?"

"I can still go there, but it is not the same. I can speak, but the sound is indistinct, as a whisper. If I touch a person, 'tis like the brush of gauze, or chill water. I can move things only as the wind does. Everything feels different."

"But if someone beminds you, are you physically there? In your body?"

"Aye, I told you that. If you know this not, how did you come here?"

"My people wend . . . well, another way. We don't use the Ground. These habitudes, the other places you go—are they nearby, or far?"

"They are all the same. There is no near or far in the Ground."

Dagget had told me that, but I had not taken it literally. "How do the people in the other habitudes know you?"

"From meeting other wenders. We have been visiting some of these places a longtime. Not all habitudes have people, and some have people shaped unlike us, and some have people who like us not, but *try to drive us out. There are places wenders have gone and never come back. We think the people there live in water or fire, or they breathe poison."*

A picture was forming in my mind of an alternative cosmography based not on the gridwork of space with its implacable light-speed limits, but of a chain of habitudes linked by aware minds through the medium of the timeless, spaceless Ground. If it were true, who knew where Torobe's wenders might have been—in this galaxy or others far away. If the only navigational limit were consciousness and not distance, they might have been to places we had never imagined reaching.

Or was Moth's tale all just superstition, akin to ancient fantasies of gods and immortals? "I need to see some of these habitudes," I said.

"Not just thine own?"

"I want to see that, too. But also others. Can you show me?"

"Of course," she said brightly, without any of the qualms Dagget had expressed.

I had to caution her that I was unskilled, and she might need to lead me. "I remember well," she said.

We entered the still place, and I settled into the familiar meditative posture. This time, the transitional experience was entirely auditory. I heard echoes around me, but not of any earthly sound. They were, I thought, echoes of the universe. Some were majestic oscillations that would take a century to complete, and some were the piccolo notes from the springing-into-being of subatomic particles. I was washed over by the tympanies of stars, the vibrato of space, all amplified by the impossible geometries around me. It was as if I were at the intersection of a thousand corridors—some wide, some narrow, some below, some overlapping one another.

I would have lingered, but I felt Moth's presence, tugging at me impatiently, and so I followed her. She led me through a boundary where I had the brief sensation that front and back were the same direction, and then I seemed to be standing on a beach of pregnant

globes, eggs bigger than a person, on the shore of a midnight-blue sea.
As I tried to move, my feet stirred the sand, and it made a twinkling
sound like a comet's tail. Beside me, Moth said a word that sounded
like an upside-down pyramid, its tip balanced on the palm of my hand.
I tried to answer, but the words crumbled into yellow dust. I drew near
one of the translucent eggs and saw inside a nest of golden, pickle-
flavored worms. I smelled a puff of cold, electric steam against my
neck and raised my eyes to the horizon, but it looked like glass pass-
ing across my skin, drawing blood.

I started to panic at the incomprehensibility of it all, and had to
close my eyes and flee backwards. For a moment everything was jum-
bled, a rain of sensations battering at me. Amid all the absurdities, I
felt that one direction was calling me strongly, smelling of sage. I con-
centrated on that haven of familiarity, and opened my eyes into an-
other memory of Orem.

The yellow light of the oil lamp cast dramatic shadows over the folds
of fabric covering the woman who stood over me. Her face was veiled.
I sat on my cot as she held the lamp to my face, studying me. I had
tied a strip of fabric around my forehead to cover the scar and hold
back my filthy hair, crawling with worms I had no comb to get out.
My shirt was stiff and crusty with old sweat. But I sat straight, think-
ing, They cannot make me into something other than I am.

"*I am Naorka,*" *she said at last.* "*Wife of the Great Hunter Katarka.*"

"*I am Thora Lassiter, emissary of the Capellan Magisterium.*"

"*I know what you are,*" *she said with a soft note of contempt.* "*You*
think you are fit to become my husband's abindo. That is what Scar-
inau says."

In the silence that followed, I could hear the buzzerbirds droning
outside. I did not know what was going on here. It might be that Scar-
inau had betrayed me.

"*Does that worry you?*" *I said.*

"No!" Her veil puffed out with the vehemence of the word. "You come from a decadent race. You may be able to enslave your own men, but my husband is greater than that. His discipline is like steel. He knows no such thing as self-gratification."

I knew what sort of marriage they had. He would never see or touch her. She would summon him to the women's compound on the nights when she was fertile. When he arrived she would be covered head to toe with a sheet that had one round hole in it, and he would do what he came for through that hole. There would always be an old woman in the room, to witness. It was the only decent way to be married, on Orem.

She reached deep into the folds of her shawls and drew out a weapon. I tensed, but she turned it around and offered me the handle. "I have brought this for you to use."

It was a drymen, a ceremonial bronze ax with a crescent-shaped blade. The lamplight glinted on the polished metal, and when I felt the edge, it was a razor-sharp inset of steel. I looked up at her, uncomprehending. "Why are you helping me?"

"He needs the power," she said intently. "There are so many doubters around him. Betrayers. They must know he can conquer even the most powerful force in the world, the madness of Witassa. That is why he must be tested. And when he has spurned you, and hacked your body apart, he will drink in your power, and Hers, and then nothing can stop him. He will rule the whole world."

The savagery in her voice was chilling, even in the heat of my cell.

"Has he ever had an abindo?" I asked.

Her head jerked, negative. "It is not easy to find worthy prey." She spat out the words.

Her shawls whispered as she turned to leave, but I stood up, still holding the ax. "And if he doesn't conquer me?"

She turned back, looking me up and down from behind her veil. There was a note of weird elation in her voice. "Then we will know he was not the man he said he was."

Half of her wanted me to win, I was sure of it. Perhaps half of every woman on Orem.

When she was gone, I felt as if some elemental force had blown from the room, leaving me weak and shaky. I fell back onto the bed, knowing I was the wrong person in the wrong place. My stomach felt queasy at the position I was in. Witassa had manipulated me to this point: there was no way out but through the scouring sandstorm of violence. The ax felt heavy in my lap, and I suddenly understood that it was not my weapon, but his. I was the one who was supposed to die by it.

A weak laugh escaped me. I was a diplomat, for heaven's sake. All my professional life I had been trained to negotiate, to seek compromise and reasonable solutions. And before that, I was a Vind, trained in apathi, all subtlety and indirection. What had these Oremen seen in me that made them think I was capable of something so alien as abindo? It was impossible: I did not have their killer instinct.

The night waited all around me. Even the buzzerbirds had fallen silent. "They cannot make me into something other than I am," I said aloud, but it sounded like a last weak protest. If I stayed what I was, I would probably die in this cell. The only way to get control back was to lose myself and become something else. Someone else.

I stood up, holding the ax out. "Witassa, Shameless One, come inhabit me," I prayed aloud. At first there was no answer, and my hand clenched around the handle, sweaty with fear. But I waited, and so suddenly I did not even notice the change, I was in motion.

I tore a strip of cloth from the mattress ticking and wrapped it twice around my waist, thrusting the ax handle through it. Then I went to the wall where I had hidden Scarinau's gift under a piece of broken plaster. It was a brittle spore casing from some native fungus, perfectly spherical and very light. I tucked it into my sash. Scarinau had instructed me how to use it: "Break it in a man's face so he inhales the spores, and it will paralyze him a little while."

Naorka had left the door ajar, and the guard was snoring, drunk.

From the angle of the moonlight I could tell that it was very late. Bare-
foot, I glided down the hall till the darkness hid me.

My prison was in what had once been Laocata's compound, so I
knew portions of it. It was like all Oreman compounds: grand and
opulent public spaces nested in warrens of little squalid rooms where
the kith lived. When I crossed a courtyard, I stopped a moment, seized
with sudden emotion at the sight of stars, my home, shining out of
the cool night air above the ovenlike mud-brick buildings. I had to
press my hand hard over my mouth as tears sprang into my eyes. The
outer gate was closed. Beyond it lay the city, where it would be easy
for me to lose myself in the mazy streets. As I wavered, Witassa's fierce
voice whispered for me to turn away. My way to freedom now was to
surrender my will to hers.

I knew the wing where the kithfathers' chambers had been, and
headed for it. The tunnel-like corridors of the sleeping warrens were
hot and breathless. I stopped on seeing a light ahead, around a bend,
and slid forward silently till I could glance around the corner. A ker-
osene lamp burned in a wall bracket beside a door. A guard was on
duty in the hall. His weapon—an automatic gun—leaned against the
wall. He crouched beside it, smoking a cigarette and listening to mu-
sic on a set of headphones. He would not be able to hear me approach.

I took the spore case from my sash and balanced on my toes to
make myself swift as a striking snake. Just then the soldier got up to
stretch his legs, and began to pace up and down. When I heard his
footsteps turn, I ducked out into the hall and rushed at his back. I hit
him at a run, knocking him to the floor and breaking the spore case
against his face. I had expected him to go limp, but instead his
muscles went rigid, like a seizure. Working fast while he was incapaci-
tated, I stripped off his belt to fasten his feet, then used the strap
from his bandolier to secure his arms. I gagged him with his own
bandana, then turned him over. He wore the face tattoo of Katarka's
bodyguards. I carefully gathered up the remains of the spore case;
half of it was still left, a cup dusted with black powder. I hoped there

was enough for my purpose. Leaving the guard trussed in the hallway, I crept to the door and opened it silently.

The Great Hunter slept with an oil lamp that gave off a dim glow. I had heard of this habit in soldiers, and knew it stemmed from a hypervigilant desire to wake oriented and ready to move. Softly, barely breathing, I came forward, the spore case cupped in my right hand, my left on the haft of my ax. He did not stir; the scuffle in the hall had not wakened him. I stood still a few seconds, knowing my timing now must be perfect. Then my hand snaked forward and clamped over his nose and mouth.

He reacted almost instantly, trying to twist away, but he had already taken a breath of the spores, and his muscles jerked convulsively, stiffening against his will. I seized one hand and lashed it fast to the bedpost with a strip from my sash, then lunged across the bed as his body arched and froze under me, and did the same with the other hand. "Assassin!" he whispered. He had meant it for a shout, to warn the guard outside, but his vocal cords were paralyzed and he could make no louder sound. I put my lips to his ear and whispered, "Yes, tonight you will die, Katarka."

Then I stepped back, my heart pounding, feeling a wild triumph. I understood the elation that makes wolves howl over their kill.

I turned up the bedside lamp to take a look at him. In the aftermath of action, my hands were as clumsy as my senses were acute, and I could barely make my fingers function. When the light flared, I saw my palms were covered with black spores, and I quickly wiped them on the bedsheet. Then I drew back the sheet to take a look at him. He had an extraordinary physique: lean, hard muscles under smooth brown skin. Without the spores, he could have overpowered me in a second. The thought gave me an intoxicating thrill of danger. I had expected to loathe him, and I did. But my power over him, and the beauty of his body, filled me with unnerving sensations.

His eyes were following me closely. I put one foot on the base of his bed and leaned my elbow on my raised knee, cradling the ax so

*he could see it. "I have been thinking: there is a lamp in the hallway.
I could pour the kerosene all over you, and set you afire. But maybe
the better way is just to hack you like a butchered pig." I swept up the
ax, and he flinched, from which I knew that his muscle control was
returning. Mine as well, but still my senses felt unnaturally acute.*

*His eyes on me were fierce. "Kill me if you must. At least I will die
without shame."*

*So then I knew what he really feared. I knelt at the head of the
bed, holding the ax blade to his throat. Feeling the edge, he fell very
still. "So you fear shame more than death? That is blasphemy to me,
Katarka. I can pour shame onto you like oil, and rub it into your skin
till you long for the flame to consume you. I could teach you shame
that would cut you open and close like a fist around your heart. And
the pleasure would be more than you have the courage to bear. You
are strong, Katarka, but not strong enough to know the holiest trans-
ports of shame."*

*I had no idea what was putting the words into my mouth. They
were swirling like smoke in my head. He was staring at me, transfixed.
"You are possessed," he whispered.*

*This was my chance to kill him, before his guards came, but in
this strange, wild mood it wasn't enough. I backed up, watching him
mockingly. "Great Hunter," I taunted, "do you dare to hunt what you
truly desire?"*

*I slipped out the door then. In the hall, the guard had worked the
gag from his mouth and now yelled at sight of me. I sprinted away,
but heard booted footsteps approaching and ducked into a dark side-
passage. The soldiers went first to Katarka's chamber, and I heard muffled exclamations from within. Then, Katarka's hoarse voice: "Which
way did she go?"*

"We will find her, Great Hunter."

*"No." There was a pause, and in that silence I knew he had taken
the goddess's bait. "I will find her. Give me that* rombala, *and don't
follow me."*

Through the maze of dark corridors I fled, luring him after me. I made for the assembly hall, the bastion of male power. I had not been allowed into it before; no woman ever had been. I knew I had found it when I saw the moonlight fall on the walls covered with dark racks of weapons, and a scuffed floor cluttered with low benches for the pack-mates to sit on. The smell of leather, oil, and tobacco smoke permeated everything. At one end was a screened-off alcove where the most powerful kithmothers might listen to the workings of war and state, but never speak or be seen. Even Laocata had rarely come to this sacred precinct of her male kin.

I walked barefoot across the board floor, profaning the sanctum. The very furniture seemed to shrink from me. Mockingly, I lay down and stretched out full length on the table where they set the ceremonial mace during deliberations. I did not move when I heard his step.

He stood in the doorway, taking in the sight of me with an expression of outrage and disbelief. "You blasphemous slut," he said. "You defile this place. Is nothing sacred to you?"

"Yes," I said. "Life and passion and madness are sacred to me."

Under his breath he said, "Witassa."

I stood to face him then. "You are being tested, Katarka," I said, the words coming unsummoned. "I have pierced a vein of rage that runs deep through this world: the rage of thousands of women who do not dare what I do, because they have something to lose. I am their vessel of revenge. I am all this world's women, and you are doomed before us."

"We shall see," he said. "Tonight I think you will die." He stepped forward, the image of controlled tension, and began to swing a weight on a cord, circling, building up momentum. This must be the rombala, his chosen weapon—a hunter's weapon. For an insane moment I stood mesmerized by the swinging stone. Then I turned and sprinted for the women's alcove. As I ducked behind the screen, I felt the stone whiz past my ear and hit the paneling with lethal force just where

my head had been a moment before. He cursed, and though every instinct told me to flee, I stopped to pick up the stone and cord.

He hesitated at the boundary of the women's domain; I knew his instincts were crying out that it was shameful for him to enter there. I knew it because shame was my weapon. There was a narrow spiral stair at the back of the alcove, and I took the steps two at a time. Behind me, I heard him tearing down the screen to expose the women's space to the rest of the room.

The steps led to a long gallery, the antithesis of the room below it. Through a long wall of windows, moonlight fell onto thickly carpeted floors. Looms and quilting frames were set out in conversational clusters, with mounds of pillows for seating. In this realm of softness and comfort, I knew, the women shed their narakatas and their secrecy, safe from male eyes.

At the end of the room, a door opened onto a broad stone balcony that overlooked the city. Out in the night air, I ducked behind a potted tree and readied my throwing-cord. Katarka emerged from the women's room at a dash, and I threw the stone. The cord wrapped around his legs and brought him down with stunning force on the pavement. I leaped onto his back, drawing the drymen from my sash. He pushed up onto hands and knees, trying to throw me off, but I clamped my legs around his stomach so that I was riding him like a horse. Giving a strangled oath, he rolled over, but I leaped away with an agility I did not possess, and as he was trying to rise, I swept the drymen down with all my strength.

A fierce, ululating cry broke from my throat as his blood spilled onto the stone floor. I hacked again, and again, and the head finally came free. I picked it up by the hair and carried it, dripping, to the edge of the balcony.

Time rippled, and I knew I was no longer in a memory, for the sun was rising, and now I saw all the rooftops lined with spectators. The huge square below me was filled with veiled women, packed so

*close that not a space was visible. When they saw me come to the bal-
cony, holding the severed head in one hand and the drymen in the
other, a wild sound of triumph emerged from them.*

*This was not how it had happened, I thought. But it was happen-
ing now. I was there, with sand-grit between my toes, but clothed in
a sheathlike dress, and my body was hacked with wounds I had never
received. The rising sun touched me, and my skin glowed like a copper
idol. The adoration of all those women below me was hotter than the
sun, rising like incense, reifying me in this goddess-guise. My voice
echoed out over the packed square: "Their shame is your weapon! Do
not let them bind you with it. My power is your birthright. Use it!"*

*The sound they made was savage, frightening. Some of them had
fallen to the ground; others were weeping or swaying in a frenzy. I
had to get away, or their need would bind me into a shape that was
not mine. I am Thora Lassiter, I thought, but the words had no meaning. All that had meaning was my own body, my breath, my center. I
concentrated on that, and felt myself falling backwards, dissolving into
the flow.*

▶   ▶   ▶

"This universe is too damn weird," Touli rumbled like an ava-
lanche.

"You ought to complain to the manufacturer," Ashok said.

"Ask for a refund," Sara suggested.

They were sitting in the *Escher*'s refectory over cups of coffee.
Touli had been studying the sensor data from the time of Sara's odd
experience and the breakdown of the wayport. The main evidence
of what had happened were some localized gravitational fluctua-
tions no one could explain. "Maybe it was a brane collision," Touli
mused.

"I've had those," Sara said.

"Not brain, *brane*—as in *mem*brane. Some of the cosmologists think that our universe is mapped on a three-dimensional surface called a brane, and there are other branes parallel to ours, but the only thing that can cross between them is gravity. If our brane got rumpled, it might intersect with one of the others in spots. But what that would look like, no one has ever worked out. Odd gravity might be a clue."

"Great," Sara said. "Our universe is bumping up against another one. Maybe they're mating. What are the odds that a spaceship will survive a brane collision?"

"Not too good. On the bright side, we might have some baby universes."

Gallows humor was just about the only response to their situation—that, or despair. Ashok had already told them in confidence how serious the wayport breakdown was. Without the quantum imbricator, the computer could not process signals into a reconstructable pattern. The *Escher* could still receive lightbeam codes, but they couldn't assemble anything. More worrying in the long run, they also couldn't disassemble anything and translate it into outbound signal. That meant no one could leave. Until the wayport was running, there was no way out.

"They can fix the wayport with paper clips and duct tape, can't they?" Sara said to Ashok.

Ashok stroked his Mephistopheles beard with a troubled frown. "What we need is a new quantum imbricator. We've been trying to figure out how to construct one from scratch. They're not exactly made of paper clips."

"Didn't we bring a spare?"

"There's another one in the wayport on the shuttle, but it's not powerful enough for long-range transmissions. Besides, we need that one to get to the planet."

When Sara went back to her quarters, it was hard to concentrate, so she turned off the lights and lay down on her bed to think. She had never been on an expedition cursed with such a collection of misfortunes. As she looked forward, it struck her that perhaps the time had come to start laying plans for a worst-case possibility—evacuation to the planet. No one here had signed up to be marooned on a primitive planet, and their survival skills might be rusty to non-existent, but at least there was breathable air and a native community to help. First Contact protocols or not, their situation now made it urgent to open relations with the natives in case it became necessary to ask for help.

Moth's absence was no longer funny; they needed her to guide them to Torobe. Sara tried to put herself in the mind of a teenage girl. She could not shake the feeling that Moth was close by, perhaps laughing at them all. Someday Sara would walk into the Embassy and there the girl would be, sitting on the couch munching a snack, acting as if she had never been gone, innocent and infuriating. Sara could picture it.

A sound from the common room made her glance to her bedroom door, and there, outlined against the dim light, was a figure she suddenly knew was Moth's, just as she had imagined.

Sara leaped from her bed and seized Moth by the shoulders, as if to keep her from disappearing again. "Moth! You came back!" she said.

"Aye," Moth said. "I have much to tell thee. Is Thora here?"

"Thora? No. How could she be?"

"She was with me. I fear she hath gone astray. I ought to go seek her."

Sara tightened her grip. "You're not going anywhere. Do you have any idea what trouble you've caused by disappearing like that? Where have you been?"

"I was in Torobe."

"Come on. I'm serious."

"Nay, so am I. I told them all about thee. They will be pleased to see thee, especially now that the fold rain cometh. We will need thy aid. Fawna's house fell through a fold, and Songta says we must leave Torobe. Thora was coming back here with me, but something hath gone amiss—"

"Stop," Sara cut her off. "What do you mean, you've been to Torobe?"

"I wended there through the Ground," Moth said. "Thora says thy people wend another way, but that is how I do it."

Sara drew Moth into the bedroom, ordered the lights on, and closed the door. She didn't know that the bedroom was any safer from prying eyes than the lounge, but she hoped Atlabatlow had had the decency to give her a little privacy. She led Moth to a chair, and sat down facing her.

"Moth, are you pulling my leg?" she said seriously.

"Nay, upon my honor."

"All right, I'll play along. Start by telling me how you got to Torobe."

Her explanation was muddled; she kept saying that she had been aided by something called the Ground—but whether that was an altered state of mind, a place, or an indescribable power was difficult to tell. Moth could not define it, only describe it experientially. She could say what it *felt* like, but not what it *was*. It was a series of sensations to her. She claimed to have gone many places through the Ground, but needed an accomplice in whatever place she wished to go, someone who would "bemind" her, or somehow bring her back into a normal state of consciousness.

Sara sat back, thinking. Was it possible that the Irisians, deprived of eyesight, had evolved a new ability that gave them access to some unsuspected aspect of reality? She thought of all the cortical acreage left fallow when their eyes had failed. Had that brainspace been repurposed?

"How long does it take you to get to Torobe through the Ground?" she asked.

"No time at all. There is no time there, for all times are the same."

Instantaneous travel? Capellan science had been seeking it for generations. They had even achieved it—for subatomic particles. But not for objects at a macroscopic scale. Sara was deeply skeptical that it could be achieved by a mere mental trick. All of Capellan science was founded on the principle that there was an unbreachable wall between the mental and the physical. The mind could not affect external reality—except on a quantum scale, where observation affected everything. Unless there were a mechanism to translate quantum effects into the macro world . . .

For a moment, Sara let her mind wander down that road, and she felt an almost sensual elation at the thought of owning such knowledge. A conduit outside space would erase all barriers of distance, all limits of light speed. She could go to Capella Two today, and be back on the *Escher* tomorrow. The rigid laws of time that kept all Wasters in exile would be repealed. They could join the human race again.

It was so seductive, her political instincts began vibrating with warning. The infocompany that was reported to own such a secret could hold the rest of humanity hostage. Even if the knowledge did not really exist, the mere rumor of it would make people act in ways Sara did not want to contemplate. Once the idea of instantaneous travel got out, there would be no stopping it. It would spread through the questship like contagion, and from there it would infect Epco's management back on Capella Two. There was no telling what might happen then. The thirst for knowledge was a kind of addiction that, like other addictions, made it easy for people to act in unethical ways. People could always justify questionable actions in the name of a greater good, and for Capellans no good was as great as knowledge.

"Moth, listen," Sara said. "This is important. You must not mention this to anyone else. Don't say that you have been to Torobe. Don't mention the Ground. We've got to keep this secret until I tell you it's all right. Okay?"

"Okay," she said, puzzled. "Why?"

Sara hesitated. "Let's just say there are some people here I don't trust."

When Sara pitched the idea of an expedition to Torobe at the next management meeting, she found she had an unexpected ally: Dagan Atlabatlow.

"The sooner we get the native off this ship, the better," he said. "There is no telling what information she has already had access to. She obviously has the ability to evade detection. Perhaps even to commit sabotage."

Sara restrained herself from accusing him of paranoid delusions, because at the moment his delusions were playing into her hands. But just as she thought everything was going her way, Atlabatlow announced that he wanted to lead the expedition to the planet himself.

"This is a First Contact," Sara protested. "If it isn't done properly by a trained exoethnologist, every penny Epco has invested in sending us here will go to waste."

"If it isn't done properly by a trained security professional, we may all die," Atlabatlow said.

Nelson Gavere looked as if he wanted to chew his manicured nails. "I will take the question under advisement," he said—by which Sara assumed he would be sending a panic-stricken message to Epco headquarters, asking for instructions.

When the answer came, it was a predictable bureaucratic solution: both Sara and Atlabatlow would be in charge. Sara would defer to Atlabatlow on logistics and security, and Atlabatlow would defer to Sara on relations with the natives; on everything else they would cooperate. "Oh, right, that's going to work," Sara muttered sarcastically as she left the meeting. Her only consolation was that Atlabatlow was equally disgruntled.

Because the wayport was out of commission, they could not get to the planet the easy way. Instead, the shuttle had to be brought back into orbit to ferry them down, at great expense in both fuel and wear to the equipment. The shuttle space was so limited that there would be no room for either the security detail Atlabatlow wanted or the scientific contingent Sara would have favored. But the physicists argued so loudly for more data that Touli was once again assigned to deploy sensors. Director Gavere decreed that Mr. Gibb would take up the last slot.

Moth was bemused and astonished by their elaborate preparations. "Thy manner of wending is toilsome," she said.

"We don't normally do it this way," Sara said. "Some of our equipment is broken."

Sara tried to quiz her about the location of Torobe, so they could bring down the shuttle close to their destination, but Moth could not give a single geographic clue. Mountains, valleys, distances, and directions were all unknown to her—or, rather, irrelevant. North and south, east and west meant nothing, since she had never seen the sun or stars.

"Think of the day when you came here," Sara coached. "Do you remember what you were doing?"

"Oh, aye, I was gathering whatnuts."

"Were you close to Torobe?"

"Nay, not very."

"Could you get back to Torobe from there?"

Apprehension crossed her face. "By songpath, you mean?"

"Well, through the forest."

Resolve replaced her irresolution. "I am as brave as any wender. I can do it. No problem." She was always picking up Capellan expressions.

To Moth, the crowning absurdity was the shuttle. When, on the day of their departure, she understood that they wanted her to get into it, she broke out laughing. "I knew thou did take pleasure in thy walls, but never did I think thou would bring them with thee! Marry, 'tis a crank and uncouth way to go. But I should have guessed thou would want to do thy wending in a box."

Sara and Moth sat side by side, with Touli opposite. Atlabatlow, a tense and silent presence in his black uniform, chose a seat in the back. Mr. Gibb was last to join them. He was dressed in jodhpurs, his recording headset under his arm like a fashion accessory. Once on board, he popped it on to take a recording of the interior, then turned to get a shot of Sara and Moth. "Moth, how does it feel to be going home?" he asked.

"All right," she said, sounding a little bored.

Moth's ennui disappeared as soon as the journey began. Sara watched her enjoy the jerk of decoupling from the hull, the alternate push of deceleration and drift of weightlessness, the roar of the atmosphere. By the time they landed, she was quite won over. "Would that I could show this box to everyone in Torobe!" she said enthusiastically.

This time Sara was prepared for the dazzle and the tangy smell when the air lock released them. They had landed in a wide clearing in shimmery woods that looked more botanical and less geometric than the anomaly they had called "forest" before. Downed trunks and dead vegetation, left by the previous landing of the shuttle, were turning dull ash-gray on the ground. Sara nudged the toppled shank of a pillar with her boot, and it collapsed into a brittle rubble.

Moth stood listening a while, then shook her head. "This place's voice is still. I know not rightly where I am."

"This is where you were gathering whatnuts when they found you," Sara prompted.

"Maybe," Moth said, "but I am turned about. Hush."

They all fell silent, watching her. She stood listening with great concentration, then moved cautiously twenty paces to her right. After listening a while in that spot, she walked forward another twenty paces and stood again.

"I have it now!" she said. "Torobe lies that way." She pointed southwest.

Atlabatlow motioned them all to assemble. "We'll go single file. Don't get distracted; keep an eye on the person in front of you at all times. Moth will go first, I will take the rear. Any questions?"

Mr. Gibb said, "Can you say something about how dangerous it is?"

He replied icily, "You have all had your safety briefing. Remember it."

Sara turned around to find Moth stripping off the flight suit they had given her. Underneath, she wore only Epco gym shorts and T-shirt. "What are you doing, Moth?" Sara protested. "You can't go into the forest that way."

"I cannot find my way all muffled up," she said.

Sara winced to see that her feet were bare again. "At least put something on your feet."

"Nay, I need my feet. They shall protect me. Now, not another word, nor a sound, or it will be very dangerous. I cannot do this if you give me not silence. Follow me exact."

She began moving toward the forest with an odd, high-stepping gait, bringing her toes down before her heels, so that she looked like a dancer. Mr. Gibb fell into place behind her, to record her performance, and Touli followed him, then Sara. Moth's graceful, bird-like steps took her forward with an even rhythm; she did not even pause when she passed into the scimitar jungle. Sara winced and almost called out a warning as Moth came within inches of amputating her patella on a razorlike leaf, but she gritted her teeth and obeyed the command of silence.

They all tried to obey, and step exactly where Moth stepped, but the rhythm of her movement was hard to pick up. She was humming or reciting to herself, and from time to time she would pause to give a kind of tuneless chorus. Then she would set off again, often in a different direction. The path she was following, if it was a path, staggered drunkenly around every point of the compass, skirting sharp groves, till Sara lost all sense of direction. When she glanced up to locate the sun, the sky above was crisscrossed with tiny, glinting threads floating on the air.

Sara came to a sudden halt. Her concentration had wavered for a second, and she was no longer certain of the path. Looking around, she had the disorienting sensation that nothing was cohering into a shape. She could see colors, edges, light, and shadow, but none of it made any sense. There were no trunks, no leaves, no near or far, just a jumble of light flowing into other jumbles of light. She dared not move, for fear the glints might cut. Just as panic was clutching her chest tight, she located something comprehensible: a shape, dark against the light, a human shape. She reached out toward it, unable to judge its distance.

"Magister Callicot?" It was Atlabatlow's voice. Suddenly, the shape became him. Sara drew back. "I lost the path," she said.

His eyes were unreadable beneath his dark goggles. He turned his back, and for an instant she thought he was going to leave. "Hold on to my belt," he said.

Sara didn't want to touch him. She had never touched him before. But he was the only landmark she could see; she had no choice. Slipping her fingers under his belt, she felt the heat of his body trapped there, the slight damp. As he moved away, she matched his steps, but tried to ignore the tactile proof that he had a body, and was therefore human.

They came across the others waiting in a clearing. They had not even noticed anyone was missing till they had stopped.

"Everyone check your emergency beacons," Atlabatlow said. "Activate them at the first sign that you have become separated."

They were all slightly winded. Mr. Gibb removed his headset and collapsed against a tree, panting. His jaunty silk scarf was soaked with sweat. "Can't we go a little slower?" he asked. "I'm not seeing anything but the ground in front of my feet. It's boring as hell."

But Moth said, "Nay, if we go slower the song will not scan aright."

"Is the song telling you where to go?" Sara asked her.

"Aye, it sings the notes of the orient bells," she said, then hummed a note. "That is next in the song, over yonder."

They were in the midst of a chime grove; as the wind passed through, the sound swelled up, first in one direction, then in another, like conversations in a crowded room. How Moth could distinguish a particular note from that fabric of noise was a mystery to Sara. But when she said so, Moth laughed. "The only noise that doth boggle me is what you all make. Zounds! The pack of you walk like a pile of stones a-thumping down a hill. 'Twould be much easier if you would take off your shoes."

It was just as well she could not see the blanched looks everyone gave.

"How much farther is Torobe?" Sara asked.

"About four verses, but they are not all the same length."

"How many verses have we come already?"

"Two and a bit."

The vow of silence was renewed as they continued on. The terrain became more hilly; now the forest was dominated by shaggy trees that put forth hairlike growths of long metallic wires, and by trees with enormous flat leaves that hung over their heads like silver platters. It was shadier, with less undergrowth. They stopped for lunch at the edge of a deep ravine with a stream running musically at the bottom.

Moth's names for the new flora were "whish trees" and "drum trees." "Touch not the whish tree," she warned, "it will give thee the prickles."

"We're not touching anything," Sara said, though in truth they were all a bit nicked in places where their concentration had failed. Moth seemed unscathed.

They dumped their packs and sat with their backs against them to eat—all but Atlabatlow, who moved away to be alone. "Friendly guy, isn't he?" Gibb muttered.

"Oh, he's just in hierarchy withdrawal," Sara said. "He's used to rigid relationships where his behavior is tightly defined."

"And here I thought he was just being rude," Gibb said.

When Moth had finished her lunch, she rose. "I must send a message from here," she announced, and walked over to the nearest chime tree. Her movements were more relaxed and confident here than on the questship. She picked up an old branch that seemed left there for the purpose, and began to strike the hanging leaves like a xylophone. On the slope of the next hill, another chime tree echoed the tune.

When she was done, Sara asked, "Will the chimes pass on your message?"

"Aye, all the way home, if anyone there is listening."

Atlabatlow had disappeared. Sara looked around for him, then exchanged a glance with Touli. Touli rose to search for him. When he returned a few minutes later, he whispered in Sara's ear, "He's doctoring his feet. Didn't want us to see that he had blisters."

"What did he expect, wearing military boots?" Sara said unsympathetically.

They had begun to think that the only Terran vegetation on Iris consisted of a ubiquitous ground layer of mosses, lichens, and other small vegetation, but as they climbed the hills, grasses, ferns, and bushes began to appear in amongst the Irisian trees. At last they came to the base of a sheer cliff from which they could look out across the glittering landscape. Touli set about assembling a satellite relay station. The rest of them tried to locate the spot where they had left the shuttle behind, but it was lost in the dazzle.

For some time they had been following a dirt track. Now Sara noticed a set of wind chimes hung from an upright pole as if to mark the spot. "Are we close?" she asked Moth.

"Aye. Here we leave the songlands. 'Tis downhill from here, and cooler."

As soon as Touli had finished testing the relay and Atlabatlow had talked to the ship, Moth led them toward the cliff. Between two shoulders of rock, a steep cleft led to a narrow opening, and they passed one by one into the cave.

Sara chastised herself for not having figured it out sooner: of *course* Torobe was in a cave. It explained everything: why they had been unable to detect it from orbit, why they could not pick up Thora's transmitter, perhaps even why Moth was blind. Everything echoed as the explorers removed their tinted goggles and searched their packs for flashlights. Atlabatlow was first to switch his on, and they all blinked at the display it made. They were in a large cavern with walls formed from some mirrorlike crystal that reflected the light and bounced it back and forth, so that there were a hundred light beams rather than just one, glinting from every angle. The floor was a talus heap of fallen blocks with reflective surfaces that broke up the light into a jewelline display.

"Hot damn!" Mr. Gibb said. "These visuals are incredible."

Moth was waiting impatiently, unable to understand what was delaying them. The path wound through the crystal debris, sloping gently downward into the earth. As they passed into other chambers, the sights changed. In one room the crystals were all tinted emerald; in another there were stalactites and rippled curtains made of opal and jade. They came to an underground cascade that fell into a cobalt-blue pool, and thereafter the path followed the stream. They had walked no more than half a mile when Sara noticed a warmer thread of air, bringing the smell of cooking. They came to a halt at a precipice on the edge of a lightless pit and shone their flashlights down over the edge.

There, lying in the perfect blackness beneath them, was Torobe.

chapter eleven

Torobe looked like a tangle of tripwires, or a web woven by a demented spider. Most of the streets, pathways, and living spaces were
defined by a cat's-cradle tangle of silver-gray cords stretched between
upright posts. There were no houses in the village, just campsites.
In a few places, it looked as if rooms were partitioned off with flimsy
screens or curtains, but they lacked roofs and walls.

The village lay at the base of a long flight of stone steps. As the
explorers' flashlights played over it, they heard a voice calling out
from below, "Hello! Hello! Who is it?"

Sara thought she recognized that voice. "Thora?" she yelled back.

"Yes. Is it Sara?"

"Yes. Are you all right?"

"Yes!"

"We'll be right there."

Now that they had inadvertently alerted the entire town to their presence, they descended the stairs into Torobe. Thora met them at the base of the cliff, looking pale and strained but so joyful that Sara gave her a warm hug. Moth said, "Thora! I thought thou was coming to *Escher*. I tried to bemind thee, but to no avail."

"Moth?" Thora stared at the girl as if seeing her for the first time. "I was . . . something happened. I got lost, but Hanna had told me to come to her if I needed to find my way back, so that is what I did."

A slight young woman with short hair and a pleasant, heart-shaped face was standing behind Thora, a sleeping baby slung in a pouch against her chest. Thora now drew her forward. "Sara, everyone, this is Hanna. She has been my host here. I owe her a great deal."

Sara held out a hand to shake, but then realized the young woman was blind, so touched her arm. Thora corrected her softly, "You greet a person by touching their face."

Remembering, Sara ran her hands down Hanna's cheeks, and allowed Hanna to touch hers. "We are all grateful to you," Sara said. "Thora is very dear to us."

"She hath pined for thee, too," said Hanna.

A curious crowd had gathered behind Hanna by now. Sara saw that they were making way for three old women dressed in finely woven gray tunics and pants, who were coming to investigate. Sara stepped forward and introduced herself to each of them.

"Mighty Boxmasters, we welcome thee," said the small, thickset woman named Songta-Min. "You come at a perilous time. But perhaps that is no accident." She paused as if waiting for confirmation or denial, but Sara had no idea what she was talking about, and so settled for a conventional expression of sympathy.

"We have heard many tales about thee," the elder named Anath-Not said. She had pure white hair and a noble, sculptured face that wore a strict and dour expression. "Which are true and which are fancies we could not tell. We never expected thee to come from the easebreath."

"They had to bring a great box with them," Moth piped up. "That is how they wend. Their box holds so many powers it was too big to bring close. We have spent a longtime coming here by songpath."

The elders seemed to be listening for Sara to deny this, but she didn't want to contradict Moth, and it was true, in a bizarre way. So she said, "Elders, we are travelers from a place called Capella Two. We have come a very long way to meet you, and to learn from your wisdom."

"Then come," said Rinka-Doon. She was a thin, birdlike woman who looked more conciliatory than the other two. "Let us welcome you."

The elders turned to lead the way. As Sara was about to follow, Atlabatlow was suddenly at her side. "It would be advisable to set up a base camp on the outskirts and reconnoiter before entering the village."

Sara said, "Go ahead, if you want to. My job is with these people."

"We can't get separated," he said.

"Then come with us," Sara answered, and turned to follow the elders.

Thora walked at Sara's side, staring in amazement at the ramshackle village. The street was paved in haphazard patches, as if people at different times had taken a notion to do it and then given up. The houses were delineated by racks strung with random pieces of laundry and matting. Nothing was straight or tidy, and everything man-made was a dingy gray color. The village looked chaotic, dilapidated, and dull.

"I've never seen this place before," Thora said. "It's always seemed so perfectly organized. How long have I been here?"

Sara calculated, then said, "Nine weeks. I'm sorry we didn't get here sooner. First we couldn't figure out where it was, and then the presence of natives complicated things a lot. We're lucky you have been a good ambassador."

"They thought I was an idiot, because I couldn't see."

For nine weeks she had been surviving without light. Sara glanced at her, and was struck again by the oddly fixed, inward-focused expression of her eyes. "That must have been horrible," Sara said.

"I learned a lot," Thora said.

Her tone implied more than she said. It struck Sara that Thora also might have heard folktales of instantaneous travel. "Listen, don't mention anything you've learned yet. We can do a debrief later."

They passed through the center of town toward a cliff face with an irregular opening at its base. Beyond it, they entered a large cavern whose floor was comfortably strewn with carpets. As they came in, a group of musicians began to play on drums, flutes, bells, and a type of small harp made from the wires of the whish tree. Quickly, the crowd took up the tune in a complex polyphonal harmony, apparently unrehearsed. As the music swelled all around, echoing pleasantly, they took seats in a field of downy pillows.

"I thought this place would be beautiful," Thora said, staring around her at the dull basalt walls.

When the music fell silent, the three old women proceeded to give long, formal recitals of their life histories. Sara listened to the trivial events of each woman's life, listed in numbing detail, and her mind wandered. Beyond the inner circle, the whole village seemed to be gathered, listening patiently in near-perfect silence. She studied them: strong-featured women with laughter-grooved faces; gentle old men, white and delicate. There was a distinct shortage of younger men.

When the life stories ended, there was a silence. Thora whispered, "They want you to give your story."

"Really?" Sara said, startled. "They won't understand—"

"I know. Just do it. It's polite."

So Sara stood and recited her résumé: universities, degrees, fellowships, jobs, publications, grants, and contracts. Everyone listened gravely, as if they were a job search committee weighing every word. When she had finished, her companions were obliged to do the same. As she listened, Sara realized how little she had known about them. She had based her impressions on snapshots—freeze-frame slices of the present, highly weighted toward appearance, mannerism, and dress. She listened carefully when Atlabatlow rose, hoping for some insight, but his account was terse and full of inscrutable military acronyms.

After the life histories, the food arrived in brimming kettles, and everyone helped themselves to stew and a mildly intoxicating beverage called quencher. When everyone was pleasantly relaxed, the old ladies steered the conversation to what was on their minds. "Thy people are great travelers and traders, so we hear," Songta said with studied casualness. "What sorts of things do you seek?"

"Information," Sara said. "Knowledge."

"Ah. We know not whether you would value ours."

"We do," Sara said confidently. "Almost all isolated cultures have unique traits we find valuable."

"Do thy people know aught of the fold rain?"

Sara paused, baffled. Thora said to her in an undertone, "It's a natural phenomenon, a kind of disturbance in the fabric of space. I told them we'd never encountered it."

"Actually, that may not be true," Sara said quietly. "We've been having some difficulties on the questship." Addressing Songta, she said, "Touli is our fold rain expert. He has come here to study it."

Touli, who was sitting behind Sara, leaned forward and whispered in her ear, "I'd like to hear what they know."

Sara said to Songta, "Perhaps if we pool our knowledge we can help one another. Is there a place where Touli could set up monitors to study fold rain?"

"What mean you by 'monitor'?"

Thora translated, "It's a kind of box."

"Ah."

"We would like to place it where we could catch fold rain falling," Sara said.

A new voice answered—a resonant man's voice, from the entrance to the cavern. "When the fold rain cometh, it cometh everywhere," he said. Sara swung her lamp to see who it was. A wiry, weatherbeaten man stood there. He had a life-worn face, deeply creased with lines of laughter and sorrow. Thora leaped from her seat and cried out, "Dagget!"

"Aye." He came forward, walking wearily. There was a rustle among the villagers to make way for him, usher him to a pillow, and press a bowl of stew into his hands. He accepted it all, but sat silent over his food, head bowed as if praying. There was a profound silence.

At last he straightened. "There is no escape from the fold rain," he said. "The only safe place is in another habitude. I have tried to find a refuge for us, but I have failed."

The silence that followed was full of dismay and disbelief. At last Rinka said gently, "Oh, surely not. Of all those we trade with, there must be one who would welcome us."

"Not all habitudes are fit for such as we to live in," Dagget said wearily. "They bemind us in ways that suit us not. In others, they let us come amongst them, but do not like us much. They regard us as devils and phantoms, and will pay us to go away. Some of our young wenders delight in the mischief they can wreak in such places. I did not bother to ask those to succor us. I asked only the friendliest, but none are willing to give us a place. They all have an excuse."

"Ungrateful churls," Anath-Not said indignantly. "After our wenders have been bringing them what they desire for years."

"Aye," Dagget said, "but we cannot force ourselves upon them. We are wenders, not warriors, and we cannot go where we have not good will."

Someone from the crowd spoke up: "The Boxmasters were sent

here to aid us! Ask them!" There was a murmur of assent from the crowd.

Sara shifted uncomfortably on her seat. "I'm not clear about what you need."

"We need to join thee in thy habitude," Rinka said.

"The *Escher* isn't big enough for all of you," Sara said.

"So they all say," Dagget said resignedly.

"No, really, it isn't big enough. And I'm not sure it would solve your problem anyway. When you say the fold rain comes *everywhere*, what do you mean?"

"Everywhere," Dagget said. "In the songlands, in the coldlands, above and below. There is no refuge."

Sara turned to Touli, speaking in an undertone. "Do you think it could be a planet-wide disturbance? Even system-wide?"

He gave a ponderous shrug. "Beats me. But remember, we could see there was something odd about this patch of space even from Capella Two. We assumed it was dark matter, but maybe this phenomenon mimics dark matter. Or maybe dark matter isn't matter at all. All we know is, the gravitometers show anomalies everywhere we look around this star. If the fold rain turned out to encompass the whole system, I wouldn't be surprised."

Thora interrupted in a whisper, "I'm sure it would be possible to find another planet to take these people in. The only question is whether we have time to evacuate them all."

"That's not the only question," Sara said, feeling grim. "The wayport is down. Even *we* can't get out. We were intending to ask these people if we could evacuate to the planet, if worse came to worst." She gave a humorless laugh. "I guess we didn't quite know what 'worst' meant."

They stared at each other, unable to think of what to say.

Thora was the first to break free of shock at their situation. "Between our knowledge and theirs, surely we can figure something out," she said. "I need to continue the studies I started here."

"You think they know something valuable?" Sara said.

"I'm sure of it. It's valuable, and dangerous. I just don't know how useful yet."

Sara didn't want her to reveal any more, so she said, "We'll talk about it later." She turned back to the Torobes, who had been waiting patiently as they conferred. "Elders, we would like to propose a trade."

"Ah," Songta said, as if this were now a situation she could understand. "What trade?"

"First let me ask, how many of you are there who need another habitude?"

This question caused quite a lot of discussion; it was clear they had not counted recently. At last they reached a consensus. "With the wenders, about half a thousand," Songta said.

There were not nearly that many here; clearly, many wenders were dispersed elsewhere. But Sara had feared it would be more. She continued, "We Boxmasters know many habitudes. In fact, we come from a coalition of habitudes called the Twenty Planets. There is plenty of space for you there, and people who would be pleased to have you as neighbors. The only problem will be getting you there. We will conduct more research on how to get you to a new planet, if that is truly what you want. In exchange, we want you to share your knowledge with us, just as you have been doing with Thora already."

This deal will never stand up in court, Sara thought to herself. If they were to discover something of value, Epco would never be able to defend ownership of intellectual property so irregularly obtained. But contractual niceties were the least of her worries just now.

The old ladies seemed a little suspicious at how easy the bargain was; they conferred amongst themselves till the crowd began to buzz with tension, then turned and said, "Very well, we are a generous people and you shall have your bargain."

The meeting broke up in a spirit of amity, and they were besieged with invitations to stay at people's houses. Sara would have accepted, but Atlabatlow was adamant that they had to stick together and establish a camp outside the village. But when he insisted that Thora come to stay with them, she utterly refused to consider it. "It would jeopardize my work to shun them now, after all they have done for me," she said. At last they reached a compromise; the rest of them would choose a campsite close to Hanna's house, where they could easily keep in touch.

Thora helped them choose a spot that was strategically located near running water and a hot spring. As soon as they had agreed, Atlabatlow decided to take Touli back to the cave mouth to set up a string of communication relays so they could be in touch with the ship at all times. In other circumstances, Sara would have cheerfully undertaken the domestic chores of setting up the camp, but since it was Atlabatlow, she bristled at the implication that she ought to do it while the men undertook important technical jobs. As she watched the colonel and Touli mounting the steps above the village, she said to Thora in a tight-clenched undertone, "That man makes me want to commit some sort of violence."

She wasn't prepared for Thora's reaction. Her face drained of color; she looked agitated, haunted. "What is it?" Sara said, concerned.

Thora's eyes were focused on something inside her head. At last she shook free and said in a strained voice, "Sara, you have to be careful. On Orem, there is a thing called an *abindo* relationship between a man and a woman. It is a hunter-prey relationship—violent, obsessive, sexually charged. It is forbidden, but key to their culture. It starts with a woman expressing antagonism or power."

Carefully, Sara said, "Are you telling me that he might interpret my standing up to him as some kind of . . . foreplay?" She could not have been more staggered.

"It's possible. He's not from Orem, but it's very embedded in their culture."

"Holy crap," was all Sara could say. To think that all this time he might have been reacting as if her defiance were a twisted attempt to seduce him—it was horrifying . . . and strangely interesting.

from the audio diary of thora lassiter:

I cannot get used to how completely light has altered my perceptions of Torobe. It is almost as if there were two different towns: the auditory and tactile one, and the visual one. The place I have known for nine weeks now is fading fast before the one re-created today by sight. The visual one seems so much more real to me.

At first it was hard even to relate what I saw to the village I knew. The layout of the streets and houses has snapped into focus, now that I can see it all at a glance. My mental maps of the spatial relationships were all wrong. And yet I wonder: why do I believe my eyes more than I believe my other senses? Why do I think I know the "real" Torobe now?

Just as light has transformed Torobe, my colleagues are quickly re-making it by their presence. Capellans everywhere have the reputation of being impatient and hurried, and now I can understand why. I have become accustomed to the measured, methodical pace of life here, where they simply cannot hurry safely. In Torobe, every task is done in a controlled way, conscious of where all tools are set down and what stage the job is at. My compatriots, by contrast, work in frenzied, chaotic spurts. There is constant noise coming from their camp—thumpings, beeps, radio static, conversations. They walk fast and talk fast. They have taken up more of the auditory space of the village than is strictly their share, making it impossible for anyone to ignore their presence. It seems like many more than four people have arrived.

At one point when the noise from the Capellan camp had died down—they must have been asleep—I overheard Hanna talking softly to someone who had missed their arrival. The story already had a mythic ring. "There are four of the Boxmasters," she explained. "One is wise and one is foolish, one is friendly and one is churlish. They all obey the woman. She is very mighty. They have promised to lead us away to a land where we will be reborn safe. First, we must pass their test."

All across Torobe, I have no doubt, people are fitting us into a story of their own devising, in order to make sense of us. Perhaps someday there will be an epic in which we all figure as magical visitors. If so, it will be no falser than the stories we tell of Torobe. Our stories will be scientific, or politically self-serving, or marketable back home. I wonder which version of Iris will dominate: Planet of the Blind? Dangerous Eden? Innocents in Peril? They are all false, because we brought them all with us. We look at the alien and see only ourselves.

The urgency of my work here has redoubled. I need to understand what I have found—that is, if I have found anything but delusion. I need to know: did I have an elaborate hallucination of Orem, or was I really there?

I took a lamp with me when I went to see Dagget. But even though I knew he could not tell, it felt like an invasion of his privacy to be watching him when he could not watch me, so I turned it off. It felt more familiar, more comfortable, without the distraction of sight.

I described what had happened when I attempted to reach the Escher with Moth. I did not tell him the details, just that I had felt and acted shockingly unlike myself. The memory still disturbed me; I was grateful for the privacy of the dark.

"What happened?" I said. "Was it a trick my mind played on me?"

He did not speak right away, and then it was not to answer directly. "There are wenders other than ourselves. I would have warned thee. We do not understand them all. Some loiter about certain habitudes waiting for other wenders to come nigh, as if they cannot take form without us. We shun such places. Did Moth take thee there?"

"No, it was a place—a habitude—I have been before. I felt I was being called there. As if I were needed."

"What sort of habitude is it?" he asked.

How to describe Orem to a blind man? All my impressions of it were of baking sunlight. "The place I know best lies in a desert, very hot and dry. It is a crowded city that smells of sewage, smoke, and spices. If you came by day, it would seem to be all men. The women live in compounds, hidden behind walls."

"I know it not," Dagget said. "You say you were called there?"

"By the women. That is what it felt like. The impression of being there was very vivid, very concrete, as if I were physically present."

"Aye, and so thou was," Dagget said, "if beminded by those who summoned thee."

"I don't understand how that works."

He gave a slight laugh. "Nor do I. Centuries of wisdom do not tell us."

"You said wenders could be beminded in 'ways that suit us not.' What did you mean?"

"What I said. It is another danger I would have taught thee. If they think us monsters, that is the shape we take."

"Or gods?" I said.

"That too."

I was sure that at the end I had not been Emissary Thora Lassiter. I had become the goddess Witassa, because that was who they had needed to see. I don't mean that in the psychological sense, that people mimic what their peer group expects. This had been no metaphor; Witassa had inhabited me, possessed me, and I had become her.

As I thought back to my original experience on Orem, trying to sort through the recovered memories, the false memories, and the memories blocked by my Capellan curators, I had an intuition that it had not been a case of psychotic delusion, but a much older thing: divine possession. Somehow, in the vulnerable state of mind induced by suffering and despair, I had been contacted by an entity other than myself. She had guided me, then inhabited me, and in return I had given *her a physical presence in the world of Orem. I had been her agent, her avatar, and now she and all her worshippers wanted me back.*

My Capellan self rebelled at the idea. It was so primitive, so superstitious. And yet, there were centuries of testimony from people with firsthand experience of contact with the supernatural—visionaries and saints . . . and lunatics. And yet, what is a lunatic but a person whose evidence we discount because it is at variance with the norm? Someone on the far end of the bell curve.

"Are you telling me that I cannot go to Orem except as the person they imagine me to be?" I said.

"We cannot go anywhere but in the guise our beminders give us. I would have warned thee not to venture where thou hast not left a fair and honest memory behind. To be true to one's self, one must be true to all others."

Once again, Dagget's teaching turned a moral precept into practical advice. It was almost as if common morality were woven into the rules of his cosmos.

"I understand now why you think maturity is so important to a wender," I said.

"Aye," he said with frustration in his voice. "These young folk who delight in knavish tricks make us unwelcome. Now we are in need, we shall all pay for it."

I was curious about the habitudes he visited, and asked him to describe them for me, but of course his experience of them was not visual, so I could not get the sort of detail I wanted. He knew the habitudes mainly as relationships with "people," though it seemed he did not use that word as we did, exclusively for humans. "They are oddly shaped," he said of the residents of one habitude, "with whiskers like snakes. But their hearts are good. They are quiet, honest folk." The implication that the wenders had discovered true alien worlds was intensely exciting. I could not recognize any of the Twenty Planets in his descriptions, but considering how vague and personal his experiences were, I also couldn't rule them out.

"How did you find these places?" I asked.

"Our forebears became acquainted with theirs. We have kept visiting these many years, bringing them rarities they desire in exchange for food and goods. They know us well by now."

"If you trade with them, you must be able to bring physical objects back and forth."

"Only what we can bemind," he said. "We must know a thing's true nature. Something we have used, or wrought, or tasted, or worn."

"Do you ever discover new habitudes?"

"We know of many, but they must discover us. If they know us not, and care not, we cannot go there."

That might explain a lack of contact with Twenty Planets worlds. Despite our many cultures, our educated classes share an overlay of scientific rationalism that discounts the reality of apparitions and spectres, as the wenders must appear to those who do not know them. But I might have an advantage over Torobe's wenders, for even after fifty-eight years there must still be people who remember me. On all the planets I have been to, I must have left traces of myself in the minds of those I have known. But do I want to let myself become whatever they thought of me? Not on Orem, clearly; what about elsewhere?

It is a question I might have to answer soon. If escape by the wayport remains cut off, the wenders' route might be the only alternative.

▶   ▶   ▶

It did not take long for Mr. Gibb to become dissatisfied with the undramatic life in Torobe. "All they do is sit around and make things," he grumbled. "That might be all right for the homey-crafty crowd, but there's no big audience appeal in it. I wish they hunted."

"Think more creatively," Sara said. "The Choristers have made a fortune selling music and cuisine, and Malvern crafts were all the rage for a while. There must be something here you can feature."

She soon regretted her advice. She was talking to Songta one morning when the old lady's granddaughters came rushing in asking for their jingle dresses. "Hath someone had a baby?" Songta asked in surprise.

"Nay, the Gibb is leading a ceremony," said Rillowa, the older one.

Sara could hear drumming from down the street. "I'd better check this out," she said.

When she reached the meeting-cave, she found a crowd assembled. A flock of young girls was at the center, sporting dresses fringed with broken bits of chime-leaf that glinted in Gibb's dazzling halogen lights. The dancers jingled and flashed at every move. Songta's granddaughters pushed past Sara like a pair of mobile suncatchers to join their friends. Mr. Gibb was at the center of the action, directing a group of musicians and trying to line up the girls into proper formation for dancing. Sara saw Rinka, usually the most reticent of the elders, standing on the sidelines listening and smiling at the proceedings. "What's going on?" Sara asked her.

"The Gibb is teaching the girls to be 'photogenic,'" Rinka said.

"This isn't something you normally do, then?"

She chuckled. "Nay, not this way."

"I'll put a stop to it," Sara said, starting forward. Rinka laid a hand on her arm.

"Nay, what's the harm? If this is what will interest thy people, and make them want to give us a home, then we are pleased to do it."

"Is that what Gibb told you?"

"Aye. Is it a falsehood, think you?"

No, Sara thought glumly. It was no falsehood. Gibb knew exactly what he was doing. A colorful ceremony involving nubile girls in pretty costumes would capture eyes back home. If such a custom did not exist, then why not invent it?

Never before had she seen an intact society, untouched by outside influence, start to manufacture pieces of cultural expression for export. The Torobes were cheerfully making themselves over to suit market demands. It had happened blindingly fast.

She returned to base camp feeling glum. "We've got to get out of here," she said to Touli. "We're polluting this culture beyond recognition. This is the most botched First Contact ever."

Sara knew she ought to concentrate on devising a proper research protocol, but the thought of their marooned spacecraft intervened whenever she sat down. As soon as she could, she seized a moment when the others were all occupied, and went in search of Thora. "Let's take a walk," she said.

They set out on a path that led deeper into the cave. It was well marked at first, but soon they left all trace of settlement behind and came to a shadowy labyrinth of boulders and old lava flows. The small pocket of light formed by their lamps seemed to contract as if compressed by the silence. Darkness followed behind them, until Sara felt enveloped by it. Fairly certain they were out of earshot, she stopped and said quietly, "Moth let slip some things I thought it was better not to spread around, and I need to know whether you've heard them, too. She seemed to be saying that the wenders know a way to get to other places without passing through intervening space. She claimed to be somehow teleporting herself between the *Escher* and Torobe."

Thora showed no disbelief; in fact, she was watching Sara intently. "Did you observe her doing it?" she asked.

"Not exactly. What I observed was that she was missing for a while, then returned with new information from Torobe."

"And I observed that she was missing from Torobe, then returned with a headnet recorder she could only have gotten on the *Escher*."

"Really? A headnet?"

"That, and a lot of news about all of you. This was some time ago, before you arrived."

The time when Moth had been missing from the ship, Sara thought. She let out a breath she hadn't realized she was holding. "So it's true."

Thora said, "Haven't you wondered how they survive in this cave? Where do they get their clothing, and tools, and grains? They claim to get it all through trade, from the profits of transporting small, valuable goods from habitude to habitude."

"You mean other cave-colonies like this one?"

Thora first shook her head, then corrected herself. "There may be some; I don't know. But if anyone were raising maize or smelting metal on Iris, surely we would have detected it."

Dropping her voice very low, Sara said, "You think they are traveling to other planets?"

Thora seemed reluctant to answer. She turned and shone her flashlight over the rocks behind them, as if to be sure that they were truly alone.

Sara guessed at what she was thinking. "Listen," she whispered, "if this is true, it's a fabulously valuable discovery. It would change everything. Epco will argue it's too valuable for a handful of pre-industrial natives to own, and cultural patrimony laws don't apply. I'd go even further. I think it's too valuable for *Epco* to own. It belongs to all of humanity."

Thora looked deeply troubled, and Sara felt a moment of misgiving about having voiced betrayal of their employer. But that was not what Thora was thinking. "I don't want the Torobes to be harmed," she said. "If the outside world starts thinking they have something valuable, they're going to get harmed, whether it is true or not."

"You think it might not be true?" Sara asked.

"I think it might not be simple. The first question is, why can they do it? Maybe blindness is necessary. Maybe this place is the key. I already know it's not an easy skill to learn. There are drawbacks and dangers to their method of travel, and limits to where they can go. Wending is a partnership between the traveler and a person at the destination, and both may need to have a knack. There is an entire body of traditional knowledge about it, precepts that warn about misuse. The thought of it being commercialized . . . it's not just abhorrent. It could be very dangerous."

"So . . . you think it's something the Magisterium ought to handle?" Sara said.

She wasn't prepared for the vehemence with which Thora said, "No! No, if you knew them as well as I do, you would not suggest that."

"Then what do we do?"

"Nothing yet," Thora said. She grasped Sara's arm tensely. "Give me time to find out more, Sara. Don't let it out. Please."

Sara made a motion to zipper her mouth. But she said, "We may be running out of time. If the Torobes know a way out . . ."

"I don't know if it's possible for us to use their method safely; probably not, or we would have discovered it long ago. But I need to find out."

Far back on the path to the village, a light was approaching. "Someone's following us," Sara said. "Better get back."

They had gone far enough into the cave that Sara was actually grateful to have a beacon to guide them back; without it, all directions seemed the same. It turned out to be Atlabatlow, of course; he gave Sara a gorgon stare as they met, but refrained from lecturing. Sara never got to use the impish retort she had prepared.

Atlabatlow and Touli had finished setting up a string of communication relays to the outside, and the monitors were sending a steady stream of readings back to the questship. "Anything interesting?" Sara asked Touli, but he shook his head.

"Not so far," he said. "Not even a fold shower, much less a rain."

They also had a radio link now, and Atlabatlow was constantly talking to his officers on the ship. Sara was busy with her own work and paid little attention to him till one day when she was washing her laundry in the hot spring, and his voice from just behind her back made her start. "Go fetch Lassiter," he said.

"Damn!" she said, turning around. "Don't sneak up on me that way." She took in his expression, hard and tense. "What is it?"

"There is an emergency on the ship. We need to get back."

She sat back on her heels. "What kind of emergency?"

"I can't tell."

She was about to say, *can't*, or *won't*? when she decided she would find out sooner if she didn't provoke him. Drying her hands on her coveralls, she rose slowly.

"Please hurry," he said, and set off to round up Gibb and Touli himself.

When they were all assembled, Atlabatlow said, "We are leaving immediately. Pack up everything you need to take back. Inform anyone here who needs to know. Leave the monitors in place. We will reassemble in fifteen minutes promptly."

Quietly, Thora said, "If you leave me a lamp and batteries, along with the radio, it will be all I need to continue my research."

"No," the colonel said in his command voice. "We cannot leave anyone here."

"My work is essential," Thora said. Sara could tell she was deeply alarmed, but her surface was unruffled.

"My orders are to ensure your safety, Emissary," Atlabatlow said. "I cannot leave you behind."

"Can you guarantee I will be safer on the ship?"

"I have control over the situation on the ship. Here, there is no control."

"Listen," Sara spoke up. "It's my job here to represent Epco's scientific mission. I say she stays."

The look Atlabatlow gave her was so ferocious she took an inadvertent step back, even though there was space between them. He

bit off his words one by one. "It is *my* job to keep you all alive. There is no mission if you are dead."

Sara quickly recovered her scrappiness. "I don't see anyone dying here," she said, "unlike on the ship."

"You are out of line," he snapped. "If I have to arrest you, I will."

"Oh, that will look good on Gibb's recording," she said sarcastically.

"Stop!" Thora intervened. "I will go." She turned to Sara, who was about to protest. "I can perform my next experiment from there. It will be all right. Just give me time to speak to Dagget."

In the end, Atlabatlow consented to give Thora some extra time, and Sara had to swallow the unsatisfying feeling that she had lost a round. She was forced to admit to herself that sparring with the colonel had become a kind of exhilarating, dangerous sport. The hint of sexual overtones only made it more interesting.

When word spread that they were leaving, a small crowd of villagers gathered to say farewell. They were less inconsolable than Sara had expected; in fact, they acted as if no one were going very far. "We are well pleased that we have friends in thy habitude now," Songta said. "Perhaps we can visit thee anon."

Sara had expected Moth to pester them to take her back, but after Thora had a private conversation with her, the girl said not a word. As the explorers hoisted their packs, the Torobes did not wave; they broke out in song. On the long climb up the steps to the cave passage, Sara trudged in time with the music.

After such a long time in dim lighting, they all fumbled for their dark goggles when they emerged into daylight. On taking in the scene, Sara discovered that Atlabatlow had ordered the shuttle to move closer to the cave mouth; it now waited in a clearing formed by its own landing just below the hill on which they stood. Glad not to have to retrace their long hike through the forest, they all hurried down to the vehicle and piled inside.

With Torobe behind them, Sara began to worry about what sort of emergency could have prompted Security to call them back so suddenly. All the while they strapped in and took off, Atlabatlow was carrying on a tense, low-toned conversation with someone, but he volunteered no information.

It was not until they were in orbit and approaching the quest-ship that they realized how profound the emergency was. "Oh my God," Sara said, her eyes on the monitor that showed the view ahead. The long spindle of the questship had been rearranged. Irregular appendages now jutted out from the spine, and the working areas of the ship, once evenly distributed, were now clumped at one end. It was impossible that the ship could still be functioning, that anyone inside it could still be alive.

chapter twelve

They returned to a different ship than they had left.

The interior layout had been thoroughly scrambled. Whole rooms had been relocated, rotated, or stretched into new shapes. Walls now intersected hallways, doors appeared in ceilings, areas that once had been adjacent were now separate. But strangest of all, the hull had not been breached and the life-support systems were rerouted but functioning—not well, but sufficiently well that no one had suffocated or frozen to death. The lights flickered and buzzed, but were mostly on.

As soon as the landing party disembarked from the shuttle, Atlabatlow left to take charge of his security team. Sara and Thora had no idea where their quarters were anymore, so they both went with Touli to find the Descriptive Sciences Department. In the halls, search teams were still patrolling for people who had been trapped in rooms that now lacked accessible doors; there were places where holes had been knocked in walls and ceilings to rescue people. They came across a large, arched doorway leading into the refectory, which had previously been accessible only through a closet. "Well, that's an improvement, at least," Sara said. When they glanced inside, they saw a posse of physicists camped around what seemed to be the only functioning coffeemaker. The scientists looked up from an intense argument when Sara, Touli, and Thora approached.

"What the hell happened here?" Sara said.

"You tell us," Magister Sarcodan replied. "And while you're doing that, you can tell us why we're not all dead."

Sara settled down at the table. "I take it you don't have an explanation."

"Hell, we don't even have a theory," Sarcodan said.

"It's a fascinating geometric puzzle, though," Emile Begoya said. "How such a complex shape as the questship could be refolded and yet not lose integrity."

"You said 'refolded'?" Sara said alertly.

"Yes. It's as if dimensionality itself underwent a reorganization, like an origami puzzle, and the *Escher* happened to be in the way. I take it you observed nothing similar on the planet?"

"No," Sara said, "but we heard a lot about folding. I think you may have been lucky this time. We'd better not count on it in future."

"I concur," Emile said. "In fact, I can't explain our survival this time."

"Consciousness," Thora said suddenly.

"I beg your pardon?"

"Have you considered the role consciousness may have played in keeping the ship intact? All the minds on board, convinced that they were in a ship that fit together as a whole, beminding it back into existence."

"You can join the physics mystics club," Sarcodan said. "But that doesn't explain how it happened before."

"Before?" Sara said. "You mean . . ."

"I mean before any of us arrived. Obviously, the ship was not designed the way we found it. There were no practical-joker architects playing tricks on us. The ship was refolded even before any minds were on board."

"There was an artificial intelligence," Thora pointed out. "The operating computer. Its machine consciousness may have been enough to maintain the ship's structural integrity. It had an understanding of the ship systems, because it was designed to monitor them."

"Sounds as plausible as anything I can think of," Touli muttered.

"Well, maybe if we all join hands and believe hard enough, we can wish a functioning wayport into existence," Sarcodan said sardonically.

"I take it there's no joy on that front?" Sara said.

Sarcodan shook his head. "Let's just say we hope you found some welcoming natives, because that's quickly becoming our only option."

The three from the landing party exchanged a look. Sara couldn't bear to break the news to them. She rose and said briskly, "Well, gotta go. Can anyone tell me where the clinic is now?"

Touli stayed behind with his colleagues; Sara and Thora plunged into the labyrinth again. With help from passing crewmates, they managed to find the Embassy and the clinic.

"Callicot! Lassiter! Welcome back to *Starship Calamity*," said David when he saw them.

"Hello, David," Sara said. "Apart from being stirred and shaken, how's it been going up here?"

"Oh, nothing much happening," he said. Then he became serious. "Actually, we were extraordinarily lucky. No one ended up with his legs growing out of his ears. Two people are still missing, and there were three amputations, but nothing fatal."

"Amputations?" Sara said queasily.

"Yes. Appendages cut off clean as a whistle, just like that poor bastard of a security guard when we first got here."

"You mean . . . the murder?"

"It wasn't a murder," David said. "No one did it; it was some localized outbreak of what we just experienced. The reason we couldn't find the head is that it's in some other dimension now."

Sara didn't feel relieved at this news, only more horrified. The fact that it had been a random natural phenomenon didn't make anyone less vulnerable. It just meant there was nothing they could do to lessen their chances of going the same way.

"We've got to get out of here," she said.

"I don't think you'd get much argument about that," David said, "but the news on the wayport isn't good. They've been trying to fabricate a new quantum imbricator, but apparently we don't have the topological superconducters."

"I have no idea what you just said," Sara said.

"It means everyone's begun banking on your news from the planet. Did you find any nice places?"

Sara shook her head gloomily. "The natives are just as desperate to get out as we are. They say a terrible natural disaster is coming that will make the planet uninhabitable. They call it fold rain."

David took in the implications of this news. "Well," he said. For once, he had nothing else to say.

Sara turned to Thora. "You said there was an experiment you wanted to do. What is it, are you going to try your hand at wending?"

Thora glanced mistrustfully at David, so Sara said, "He's all right. That's true, isn't it, David? You can keep a secret?" Thora still hesitated, so Sara said in a low tone, "Look, we need to know if it's possible for us to do what they do."

Reluctantly, as if forcing the words out, Thora said, "It is possible. I've done it. In fact, I even—no, let me tell you from the beginning."

She then described to them, in precise sensory detail, how Dagget had led her into the Ground. She did not try to explain it—just gave them the observational data, exactly as she had experienced it, finishing with the fact that she had briefly seen Orem. When she fell silent, David shifted restlessly. Sara looked at him.

"If someone came to me describing that kind of experience, my diagnosis would be TLE," he said. "Temporal lobe epilepsy. The classic symptoms are distorted perception of time, out-of-body experiences, sensory hallucinations, and overwhelming feelings of déjà vu, inspiration, or bliss."

Ironically, Thora said, "A disease. The mentationists on Capella would agree with you, only they called it psychosis."

"You mean this is what happened to you before?" Sara said.

"Not this precise experience. Something similar; only then I did not have a guide, but a kind of predator with me."

"So you don't believe it is a disease?"

"No. I think it is a natural perception we dismiss because it is so rare. In Torobe, it isn't rare; all the wenders experience it."

"There could be something on the planet inducing it," David said doggedly. "Sensory deprivation, for example. Their brains could be manufacturing an illusion of reality to replace the one they have lost. They have created an elaborate cultural construct to explain it. As a matter of fact, I could electrically stimulate your brain to produce the same experience."

"I could electrically stimulate *your* brain to create the sensation of sight. All I need to do is shine a light on something. That's what electromagnetism does, stimulates the brain to create a sensation. Yet you think that's real, and the other sensation is not. That is simply illogical." Thora was now speaking with controlled fervor. "The part of my brain that perceived the Ground evolved to sense an aspect of our environment less often encountered than light, but nonetheless real."

"All right, prove it."

Visibly forcing herself to be patient, Thora said, "I am hoping to do that. Or at least, I am hoping to prove the indirect effects of the Ground. Proving its existence is a little like trying to prove the existence of beauty. You have to experience it yourself." She paused thoughtfully. "I wish you could. There was such a strong feeling of authority, authenticity—no, not just that, *insight,* as if I were perceiving something more real than everyday reality. Almost like revelation, like finally figuring it all out."

"Limbic system involvement," David said.

"Yes," she said. "Precisely. As if it were coming from that vast volume of the interior brain that is inaccessible to conscious thought. All we're normally aware of is what the thin layer of cortex on the surface tells us; the majority of the brain makes itself known only through intuition, emotion, and the subconscious. I'm saying we need to expand our definition of evidence to include that."

"What about Moth's headnet?" Sara interrupted impatiently. "That's pretty concrete evidence."

"What headnet?" David said.

"Remember when Moth disappeared, and we turned the ship upside down looking for her? Thora says she was in Torobe then, and brought one of our headnet recorders to show everyone."

"Did you see the headnet?" David asked Thora.

"No, of course not. It was dark. I felt it."

"Well then, if Moth really did transport a headnet to Torobe, and it wasn't just some sleight-of-hand, all I'm saying is she didn't do it by using her mind. Prove me wrong if you can. I hope you do. But until then, I'm still hoping they fix the wayport."

Thora seemed preoccupied when they left the clinic and went to the Embassy. They found the suite of rooms relatively untouched by spatial distortion. Sara watched Thora pace, eyes on the floor, hands kneading each other nervously. She looked a little mad.

"I knew I would face opposition here," Thora said.

"*I* believe you," Sara said. "Or at least, I want to, but for a reason David wouldn't accept. Every culture we've ever encountered has held common beliefs that scientists scoff at—spirit possession, ghosts, spells, mind reading, out-of-body travel, that sort of stuff. I've always wondered why those ideas seem so plausible that virtually every society but ours believes in them, and continues to believe in them because they just seem intuitively *right*. I like the idea that those people aren't just superstitious and deluded—that they're dimly perceiving something that's not fully accessible to our senses."

"But they may be explaining it wrong," Thora said, her eyes fixed on Sara. "Spells, ghosts—those are simplistic, inexact explanations. The Torobes' explanation may be no more right. That's why we need to continue the research. It's why I came up here."

"What do you want to do?" Sara said. "Can I help?"

Thora looked around, as if seeing the room for the first time. "Is this where Moth stayed when she was up here?"

"Yes."

"Then this is the place she would come back to. I told her to try as soon as we had time to return. We need to bemind her. Or rather, one of us needs to bemind her, while the other observes, so we can prove it objectively."

Sara was tired and would have put it off, but Thora was now filled with a kind of manic energy. She positioned a chair where Sara could sit and see the whole room, then dimmed the lights a little and settled on the floor in a posture of meditation.

The room grew very quiet. Sara could hear the whoosh of the ventilation, and random clicks and creaks of the questship structure. She was not accustomed to sitting still without anything to occupy her mind, and first grew impatient, then inattentive as her mind wandered. She kept having to pull her mind back so as not to miss anything. But there was nothing to miss. Eventually an itch started on her back, then a cramp in her leg. She kept glancing at the clock, wondering how long this experiment would take.

At last Thora sighed and opened her eyes. "This is not working," she said.

Sara yawned. "Right. I need a break."

"You beminded her before, didn't you?"

"I don't know. I suppose I must have."

"It might work better if you tried to bemind her, and I observed."

"Not before I get some coffee."

Sara left to stretch her legs and fetch something from the refectory. When she got back, Thora was sound asleep on the couch. Sara didn't disturb her, just stood sipping coffee and wondering what to believe. Here, surrounded by the bulkheads built by rationality, Thora's theory seemed so much less plausible than in the earthy, whispering darkness of Torobe. But if it were true . . .

Sara could feel the thrill of power right down to her fingertips. Something humanity had been seeking for centuries might be within her grasp, hiding in the scrambled mind of this woman sleeping on her couch, and in a handful of blind villagers below. For once in her life, Sara might be at the center of a momentous discovery, at the fulcrum where everything would change. If Thora were right, the fundamental geometry of space would be repealed. It would erase the barriers that had kept humankind imprisoned in their little patch of space, and open up the galaxies to exploration.

How ironic that the breakthrough wasn't information at all—not something that could be published, trademarked, or copyrighted. It was a skill. A rare skill that, so far, only the mad and the blind had been able to acquire.

She turned off the lights and went into her bedroom, and was soon asleep herself.

The next two days were filled with a series of repeat experiments, all similar failures. They tried to bemind Moth with their roles reversed, and with conditions changed. Thora repeatedly attempted to touch the Ground herself, without any success. At first she seemed grimly determined, then desperate, then despondent. With every failure, Sara's doubts grew, and she felt a little foolish for continuing.

"There must be a localized spatial phenomenon on the planet," Thora finally said. "We always went to a specific place to touch the Ground. I thought I might be able to do it from here, but I was wrong. The place is more important than I realized."

On the third morning, Sara was wakened by the sound of voices out in the common room. She listened vaguely at first, still half asleep. Then she realized what she was hearing, and was instantly wide awake. One of the voices was Moth's.

Moth looked exactly as she had when they left her in Torobe— wearing the same Epco shorts and shirt, the same bare feet, the same expression of smug conspiracy. At sight of her, all Sara's doubts evaporated and she cried out, "You did it, Thora! You beminded her!"

"Not deliberately," Thora said, looking troubled. "I dreamed of her."

"Aye, that was me touching thee from without," Moth said.

"Then I became half awake, and it was as if she were standing close to me. The sense of her presence was quite vivid. Then I woke up, and she was actually there."

"Did you see her . . . materialize?"

"No, I was asleep, and the room was dark." Thora sounded frustrated. "We still haven't observed it happening. Someone could argue that she followed us and sneaked onto the shuttle while we weren't watching. We can't prove what we've done."

"What *have* we done?" Sara said. They looked at each other, unable to answer.

"We need more evidence," Thora said.

Moth was quite willing to collaborate with them. This time they set up a camera so they would have unimpeachable evidence, as well as two witnesses. When all was ready, they told Moth to return to Torobe.

She did not settle down to meditate, as Thora had done. Instead, she stood in the middle of the room, poised on the balls of her feet, as if trying to pick up a rhythm, like a child about to step in on a jump rope. At last she took a small, dancing step forward, then stumbled, tried to regain her balance, and turned around, as if confused.

"What happened?" she said, looking disoriented.

"Nothing happened," Sara said.

"I missed it!" Moth was clearly disturbed and embarrassed. "I have not failed so for years, not since the first time I tried."

"Well, try again," Thora said.

But nothing worked. They tried it a variety of ways: with just Sara observing, just Thora, and just the camera. At last Moth became so upset by her repeated failures she burst out, "You are thwarting me! You are interfering!" Then she stormed off into her bedroom and slammed the door.

Sara silently switched off the camera and looked at Thora. "Do you suppose she really did stow away on the shuttle?"

Thora looked thoughtful. "She wended to Torobe from here before, true?"

"So she claimed."

"Then maybe we *are* preventing her, just by observing. Maybe it's a phenomenon that can't happen if someone is watching, like particles on a subatomic scale. We can't observe an electron shell in an atom, because the electrons exist in all the possible positions simultaneously until they are observed, and then the effect collapses. That doesn't mean it didn't exist before."

"So you think that we also could exist in more than one place simultaneously? But physicists have been looking for an effect like that for centuries."

"Maybe that's the problem," Thora said. "They're *looking*. Maybe it can't be observed, because if you observe, you prevent it. Maybe sight actually obscures reality, and that's why removing it makes it easier to perceive the Ground." She seemed intense, keyed up, a little obsessed. There were dark circles under her eyes.

Frustrated, Sara said, "If that's true, then wending isn't going to get us out of here. We're still trapped. None of us grew up blind, and if *you* can't do it again, with all your practice and skill, there's no hope for the rest of us."

Thora's voice dropped very low. "I haven't given up, and the rest of you shouldn't either. If I could just get back into the Ground, as I did before, perhaps I could find someone on Capella to bemind me. Then I could get a replacement imbricator for the wayport and return."

A twinge of hope nudged Sara's optimism awake again. "So what do we do?"

"I'll have to go back to Torobe," Thora said. "I can't do it from here. Maybe it's because there is a thin spot there, where dimensions overlap and space is fluid. Or maybe it's because I've seen the *Escher*, and I am too convinced of its spatial reality. Regardless, I have to take the shuttle back down."

Sara shook her head. "Colonel Atlabatlow will never allow that, even if we tell him the truth. The scientists might support us if only we had some evidence."

"How can we have evidence? It's a subjective phenomenon. But that doesn't mean it's not real. Pain exists, and it is subjective. Consciousness exists, but we can't prove it. We only know it's real because we experience it."

Sara thought of trying to convince Sarcodan or Prem with an argument like that—to support doing something impossible by an improbable method whose existence they couldn't prove. The thought was so discouraging, she got up to knock softly on Moth's door. "Moth, come out," she said. "You're our only evidence." Moth didn't answer, so she said, "Let's have some popcorn."

There was still no answer. With a sudden misgiving, Sara opened the door.

Moth was gone.

Every time Sara saw Touli in the refectory, he looked more gloomy than the day before.

The astrophysicists had been busy mapping the gravitational anomalies in the space around them, in order to predict the outbreaks of instability. "You're not going to like this," he said when she asked him what was up.

"You mean it gets worse?" she said.

He nodded. "The unstable spots are all around us. Local space is simply peppered with them. In fact, there's a huge cluster just ahead, in the path of the planet we're orbiting. We're trying to calculate when we're going to pass through it."

"Are we talking hours, or months from now?" Sara asked cautiously.

He just shrugged and left Sara to imagine the worst.

When the answer came, it spread like panic. They had two weeks, give or take a day.

Just when they needed strong leadership most, the Director seemed to have vanished. Penny Sutton was intercepting all attempts to speak with him. "He is very busy dealing with the situation," she said. But what he was doing, no one knew. What he wasn't doing was far more obvious. He wasn't making decisions or coordinating any efforts to solve their problem.

"Maybe he's using one of his innovative management techniques," David said to Sara. "Cleverly bonding us by giving us a common enemy to criticize."

"You sure don't have an irony deficiency, David," Sara said.

Sara decided it was time to play her Magisterium card. She marched into the Director's antechamber and asked to see him.

Penny Sutton appeared instead, wearing an iron-gray skirt-suit that made her look like a gunmetal fireplug. "Director Gavere can't be interrupted," she said. "He is—"

"I know. Dealing with the situation," Sara said. "Well, I can help him there. I have a solution, but it's for his ears only."

Sutton hesitated a moment, then said, "Write me a report and I will give it to him."

"I said, for his ears only."

"I *am* his ears," Sutton said. "If I didn't screen his appointments, he would be overwhelmed with complaints about offices being re-arranged." She made it sound like a minor inconvenience. As it would have been, if offices hadn't been rearranged upside down on the other side of the ship.

Sara took a stab at what she thought motivated Penny Sutton. "Listen, I'm not interested in taking credit for saving us," she said. "I can make him a hero if he'll just listen."

Her face was stony, but at last she said, "I'll see if he is free."

When Sara entered the Director's office she was surprised to see how he dominated the space—until she realized the room had been distorted so that ceiling and walls converged to create a false per-spective that made him look larger than he was. As he walked over to greet her, he shrank back down to size.

"Magister Callicot, so wonderful to see you again," he said, grasp-ing her hand as if they were old friends. His tailored suit and silk shirt were still perfect, but his hand was sweaty and his face a little flushed. "How is your work going? Are you getting all the coopera-tion you need?"

"Yes, I'm fine, thanks. But I—"

"It is so difficult, so difficult." His chiseled face took on an ex-pression of concern. "Getting people to accept new ideas. They re-sist, you know."

"Yes, as a matter of fact, that's why—"

"Trans-methodism gives us all the resources we need to solve the most challenging problem, if only the buy-in factor were what it ought to be. It's the perfect matrix for cross-platform, acumen-based strategic alliances. We are all stakeholders here, that's what people should recognize."

"Um, yes. I need you to authorize something. Thora Lassiter and I have to take the shuttle down to the planet. We think we have a solution."

"The planet? Risky place, so I've heard. Safety is Epco's number one priority."

"Yes, but remember what they say: high risk, high reward."

For a moment he seemed paralyzed, caught in a slogan clash. "Well, write up a proposal," he said. "I'll have my people do a risk-benefit analysis."

That was precisely what Sara didn't want. "This is your chance to take a decisive stand," she said. "Seize the moment. Show the hesitators how it's done."

"Yes, true. Write me that proposal. I'll be looking for it. We'll run it past the department heads, and Security, and then you'll see decisiveness in action. Thanks so much for stopping in. My door is always open."

It was useless to continue; Nelson Gavere was a void where a man should have been. As she was about to leave, he spoke again. She turned; he had retreated to the distorted end of the room so as to appear seven feet tall. "Great minds," he said, "on a great mission. That's what makes us . . . great."

She gave him an ironic thumbs-up and left.

It was not Sarcodan, but the mouselike Sandhya Prem who finally took action. The news spread by word of mouth through the professional staff. Prem had called a meeting with one agenda item: to share solutions.

They gathered in a large room newly created by the fusing of a former recreation hall and laundry, both difficult to use now because the floor was tilted at five degrees. Prem ran the meeting briskly, first briefing everyone about the lack of progress on the wayport, the discouraging news from the planet, and what the physicists were calling the "paradox cluster" ahead. She then called on each department in succession to present proposals for a solution. Most of the ideas centered on ways of fixing the wayport. Some of the more theoretical physicists were working on an idea for a "stability field" to keep local space pasted together. But the simplest suggestion was to start up the engines and leave.

Sara listened as the engineers debated the challenges of reviving engines shut down 120 years before, when the ship had entered orbit and sent back its original message. The scientists argued about whether there was enough fuel, whether enough acceleration could be achieved, and even whether there was another destination reachable within their lifetimes. At last Sara stood up and said, "Excuse me, but there are five hundred people on the planet we've promised to help if we can. Shouldn't our solution include them?"

Scientists, she learned, had the same priorities as other human beings: self first, others second. No one wanted to propose sacrificing the Torobes, but it was clear that saving them had not entered anyone's calculations. At least Sara's question deflected the conversation back to fixing the wayport rather than abandoning the planet. But even with a functioning wayport, evacuating five hundred refugees in two weeks presented serious logistical challenges.

"Maybe we shouldn't have made any promises," an electronic technician finally said.

Sara was about to protest that the moral responsibility would still exist, when Sri Paul Niyama stood up to represent the Corroborative Sciences Department. "Excuse me," he said with his usual gentle earnestness, "I believe my department has something to offer." Assorted rationalists rolled their eyes, but he continued unperturbed, "Paraclete Btiri was seeking guidance about why our expedition has been cursed, and the meaning of Iris came to him in a dream. He wishes you to know that the planet was put here as a metaphor, a test, a lesson. The natives are central to its meaning: blind but wise, unseeing but insightful. We are meant to learn that sight is an illusion. It blinds us to the true reality. We place too much faith in the visible world, and not enough in the invisible. To find a solution, we must be more like the natives: search our hearts, not our heads. Thank you."

He sat down. Sara looked at Thora, intrigued by how Sri Paul's message echoed hers. But instead of looking affirmed, Thora looked deeply frustrated, even a little angry.

"Thank you, Sri Paul," Sandhya Prem said. "Would anyone else like to comment?" Reminded that there was one other department they hadn't heard from, she turned to Thora. "Emissary Lassiter? Does the Intuitive Sciences Department wish to offer any proposals?"

Slowly, Thora stood. "Paraclete Btiri offers us poetry, which gives us hope, but not actionable information. Only rigorous research will solve this problem. Even if the Paraclete is right, being right is not enough. We have to know *why* we are right."

There were smiles all around the room. Thora continued, "I was in the midst of some very promising research when I was forced to come back here. I find that I need to return to the planet to continue it. I request your support." She sat down again.

"What sort of research?" Prem asked. "Anything related to our current problem?"

"Possibly," Thora said. "I can't promise yet."

"All right," Prem said, then turned to the rest of the room. "We need to form some task forces to pursue our best ideas . . ."

Soon everyone was caucusing together, forming teams. Thora and Sara sat alone, and no one approached them.

"Why didn't you tell them?" Sara whispered.

"Sri Paul sabotaged me," Thora said.

"But he was right, in his way."

Thora looked at her fixedly. "The right conclusion, the wrong methodology. If I had tried to make my case after that, I would have been classified with the religious zealots." Abruptly, she rose to leave.

Mystified, Sara followed her to the door. "But your methodology is—"

Thora stopped, confronting her. "The same as Btiri's? No. He is religious, I am a scientist, but that's a trivial difference. The real divide is between muddy and rigorous thinking."

She left then, and Sara did not follow her. Unlike Thora, Sara was not accustomed to being left out, so she scanned the room to find some group to join. But they were all talking technical fixes, and she could add nothing to their conversations. As she left the room, her feet turned by a kind of magnetism toward the object of her thoughts, the shuttle bay.

The dock was located at the very rear of the ship's spindle, nestled in among the silent engines that would soon be blazing again if the technicians had their way. When she entered, the shuttle loomed over her, filling most of the cavernous space, secured to the floor by clamps in the low gravity. A lone maintenance worker had his head in one of the wheel wells. He was tethered to the craft by a web.

"Hey," Sara hailed him, not knowing his name. "Is it ready to fly?"

The man peered out at her. "Why, do they need it?" he asked.

"Soon," Sara promised. "Say, how hard is it to operate this thing?" She could hardly believe what she was thinking.

"No idea," the man said.

She let go of the wall and made a leap that carried her in a high arc toward the cockpit, but before she got there, something wrapped around her ankle and jerked her back. She looked down to find she was being reeled in like a fish on a line by one of Atlabatlow's uniformed guards. Two of them flanked the door she had entered through. She shook her foot furiously, but the line held fast. When they had gotten her back through the door, they detached it and fell in on either side of her.

"Come with us, please," said the taller one.

"Where?" she demanded.

"Just come."

They led her back into the complex of offices where Security had its headquarters. She glimpsed a room where a woman sat watching a bank of monitors showing camera feeds from all over the ship, including the scientists still in their meeting. The guards took her into a small room that held only two chairs and a table. It looked like an interrogation room. When they left, she immediately tried the door. It was locked.

She waited half an hour, building up a head of steam, before Atlabatlow finally entered. He was back in a spotless uniform. He laid a folder on the table and said, "Please, have a seat, Magister. I must warn you this conversation is being recorded."

So it *was* an interrogation. She said, "Nice to see you, too, Colonel."

He sat down, so she did, too. They stared at each other across the table.

"What did you think you were going to do, hijack the shuttle?" he said.

She felt a little foolish, so she said, "Thora and I want to go back to the planet."

"I know." When she frowned, he added, "It is my duty to know what is going on."

"Then you may have noticed this expedition is going to hell. I'm trying to save it. Listen, I know we haven't always gotten along—"

He interrupted, "I need to know who you are working for."

At last, some honesty. She decided not to insult his intelligence by claiming to work for Epco, but she was damned if she was going to show her cards first. Instead, she said, "Funny. I was going to ask you the same thing."

His eyelids half lowered, making him look secretive and a little snakelike. She noticed for the first time how black his eyes were.

"I know you're not working for Epco—or not just them," she went on. "All I know is, it's someone who wants Thora Lassiter out of the way. Who is it? Someone on Orem?"

His jaw clenched. She realized she'd hit a nerve. In a reasonable tone, she said, "Whatever she did on Orem, it's not worth bringing the vendetta—"

"This has nothing to do with Orem!" he said, his anger just under the surface.

"Then what?"

"You tell me."

She glanced at the surveillance camera. Atlabatlow took the hint. He removed a device from his pocket and made an adjustment. "We are private now," he said. "I can assure you that I am not working for anyone who wishes harm to Emissary Lassiter. I am here to protect her against an agent they knew would be on board." He skewered her with his gaze. "They knew about the agent because the party who wishes her harm approached me first, making the same stupid, ethnocentric mistake you just made—thinking I was not a Capellan first and foremost, that I would have some sort of racial tie to that barbarous planet where she was captured and attacked."

"But if you're not working for Orem, who—"

"I was born on Capella Two," he said, his fury building as he spoke. "I have a graduate degree from UIC. Orem never entered my mind till the day it came into the news, when those savages kidnapped her, one of *our* diplomats. I was as angry as any Capellan— no, angrier, because suddenly I wasn't just another person, I was one of *them*. I was suspect everywhere, because of my looks and my parents. Do you know what it's like to have people think they know what you are, just by looking at you?

"I am working for the Magisterium. I *volunteered* for this assignment, to come to this godforsaken planet, just to prove who I really was. And you're still assigning me an identity I abhor."

Sara was struck dumb—not only from finding out what was actually on his mind, but from realizing how shallow her own assumptions had been. She knew she ought to apologize, but it came hard—and then he didn't give her a chance.

"So now," he said, once more under control, "I will ask you again—who are you working for? Bear in mind that I already know."

For a moment she didn't understand, and then it became obvious. "You think I'm the agent. The one they hired after you turned them down." He said nothing, just waited for her confession. She broke out laughing. "Oh, what a piss-poor operation they would be, to hire *me*! No, I'm here doing a favor for a friend—a mentor, really—Delegate Gossup. He asked me to look after her; they're related somehow. I thought *you* were the one conspiring against her." She shook her head, still not quite convinced of his innocence. "If we're on the same side, why the hell didn't they tell us?"

His face showed he didn't really believe her either, but her question didn't puzzle him. "You know something," she said. "Why they might have set us up at cross-purposes."

He paused as if considering whether to answer, but finally said, "The conspiracy is all within the Magisterium, and Lassiter is not the real target—Delegate Gossup is. By sabotaging her, they are hoping to force him to intervene, which would reveal some secrets that could lead to his ruin. He may not have completely trusted either of us."

"And so right he was," Sara said. "Why did you act so damned suspiciously? Always shadowing us, watching us, trying to intimidate."

"I was protecting her," he said, "from you. The moment you came here you were worming your way into her confidence, with your checkered past and your false show of unsophistication."

She was flattered, at least, that he thought it was false.

"You were constantly trying to provoke me, and undermine my authority. Every time something adverse happened, you were there. The one thing I was unable to connect you with was the murder of her bodyguard."

"He was her guard?" Sara said, surprised.

"Of course. I know now that all her misadventures were the result of natural forces, not conspiracy. But now you are trying to engineer it so she will return to danger."

"As if she isn't in danger already! Colonel, we've got to do a reset. I'm sorry for my assumptions, but whatever happened in the past, it doesn't matter now. Nothing matters but getting back alive. Thora Lassiter may be our best hope of going home again. Given a year, the scientists might come up with a fix, but we don't have a year; we've got two weeks. We've got to help her."

"I am aware of her theories," he said. "She doesn't have much scientific support."

"She can't produce the evidence if she can't do the experiment. That's all she's asking for. And the experiment could save our sorry skins."

He still looked suspicious—or maybe that was just his normal expression, she couldn't tell. "You are convinced that going back to the planet is what she needs to do?" he said.

"It's not what I say, it's what she says."

He came to a decision. "Tell her I can authorize a shuttle mission for her and a single companion of my choosing. It cannot be you."

Now it was Sara who felt a twinge of suspicion. She looked him in the eye. "Swear to me that you're not a threat to her."

"I swear," he said.

She held out a hand. "Truce?"

He looked at her hand as if it were a cobra, but finally shook it.

chapter thirteen

from the audio diary of thora lassiter:

I am going back to Torobe.

When Sara told me the news, she confided how she had mistak-enly suspected Colonel Atlabatlow of foul play. I said automatically, "You were beminding him wrong." She laughed and said it was a good metaphor. But now that I think about it, I wonder if it is a metaphor at all. We bemind people all the time—making assumptions, creat-ing illusory roles for them—and it alters their reality. They start to become what we expect them to be, just like the "forest" of Iris did when we "discovered" it. In a sense, we have beminded a whole planet here. It is a credit to Colonel Atlabatlow that he was able to resist reinvention and demand his own reality. Even I looked at him and saw only the reflection of my own past. I must think about this more when I have time.

Right now, I have no time. We have less than two weeks before colliding with the paradox cluster. There were many preparations to make for my experiment. First, I spent some time on the pepci, sending messages to Capella Two. One was to my friends in the refugee relocation program, requesting asylum for five hundred blind villagers who need to stay together in a place where they can be independent of outside assistance, however well-meaning. The response was good-natured but a bit daunted: "You don't like to send us easy problems, do you?" I told them to be grateful it wasn't five thousand.

The second message was harder. I am forced to rely on my father now, despite all that has gone on between us. It would have been easier to explain my request verbally, but I didn't want to face him, so I sent it by text. It was a strange message, and I pray he will not dismiss it as lunacy. After explaining our desperate situation, I said, "Think of me at night, when you are alone or meditating. If you dream of me, imagine I am trying to contact you. Close your eyes and visualize me. Believe that I am there." Then, as if that were not odd enough, I told him to have a certain piece of equipment on hand. The wayport technician gave me the specifications of the quantum imbricator they need, and I attached them.

My greatest uncertainty is about transporting such a complex object through the Ground. I made the technician show it to me, and explain it in detail, so that I can visualize it and understand its essence. I held it in my hand with my eyes closed. It is small, and shaped like a seahorse, with a ribbed central section that contains a processor powerful enough to assemble every molecule in a human body in the proper order. I asked the technician if I could take it with me to show Dagget, but he was unwilling to risk sending it to the planet, even broken as it is.

The shuttle was ready to depart, and my companion-guard was waiting, but I had one last thing to arrange. I said to Sara, "Listen *for me at night, and in solitude. Be prepared for me to come." She understood, and hugged me in her warm, demonstrative way.*

And now I return to darkness. I know I must, because it was the weeks I spent learning to sense the world without light that primed me to touch the Ground. I need to reenter that transformed reality.

It was a normal shuttle flight until we had descended to about fifteen thousand feet, and I was busy dictating into my diary, when I heard a curse of disbelief from the pilot, and looked up to the monitor that showed what he saw. The ground below us was the same sea of glitter I had seen before; then I noticed the disturbance. A field of distortion was sweeping across the land toward us, as if a powerful lens were passing through the air. In its wake, everything was disrupted. On the plains, it left behind a linear path of shining rubble—an outcropping like crumpled tinfoil, jumbled cubes of polished metal. In the hills where it had passed, brown rock now showed, as if relocated from far underground to the surface. The pilot banked and accelerated to avoid the phenomenon, but as it passed, a gravity shift pulled us sideways with a sickening sensation of dropping.

"Keep away!" the copilot shouted, and I was tossed roughly to one side, then almost lifted from my seat. Then, suddenly, everything was quiet, and we were flying as normal. But the place where we had intended to land, the entrance to the cavern of Torobe, was no longer visible. I could hear the pilot asking the ship for coordinates as he brought the shuttle to a hover over the spot where we should have landed. It was unrecognizable. I was not even sure that what I saw below was solid ground. Occasionally, a complex surface below us would pop out of existence, like a bubble bursting, and return to a simpler configuration.

We returned to the questship shaken and anxious. This time the *Escher* had escaped. They had witnessed the phenomenon—we automatically called it fold rain, though it had looked more like a fold *tornado—and even gathered some useful data. The sensors Touli had left in Torobe had transmitted readings right up to the end, then fallen silent.*

I was frantic with worry about my friends in Torobe. I could not stop thinking about Hanna and her baby, Moth, Dagget, and even the pompous old ladies. If the village had been in the path of the fold rain, all of them had surely perished. As I returned to the Embassy, my thoughts became insistent, and I had an irrational premonition that Moth would be waiting in her room. She was not there, of course. So I turned off the lights, closed my eyes, and waited.

Almost as soon as my jangled thoughts cleared, I felt a sensation that I was not alone. It was similar to seeing a flash of movement from the corner of your eye that disappears when you look, or feeling a tickle on your skin when nothing is touching it. I did not look, but the thought of Moth came to me, so I visualized her standing there just as I had last seen her, all adolescent bravado and moodiness. The sensation became ever more vivid, and presently I heard someone move.

"Moth?" I said, my eyes still closed.

"Aye," she answered. "Thora, I beseech thee, come to our aid. We are sore afflicted."

I rose and turned on the lights. She was there, but her expression was more serious than I had ever seen before; in fact, she was desperate. "Moth, what happened?" I said.

"The fold rain came," she said. "Torobe is no more."

"No more?" I said. "What do you mean? How did you escape?"

"The world is topsy-turvy," she said. "Houses, paths, people—all are jumbled and upturned. We cannot find each other. The town is gone."

"But the people? Are they all right?"

"I know not how many are left. Hanna is all right, and her babe, for we were holding fast to one another. Please, can we come to Escher? It is our only hope."

I took her hand. "Moth, I was trying to return to Torobe when the

fold rain struck. We can't land the shuttle anymore; there is no way
to get to you."

Impatiently, she said, "We need not thy box! Just permit me to bemind Hanna, and she will bemind her friends, and they will bemind
all they know, and soon we will all be here."

My mind was racing. Five hundred refugees, on a ship built for
half that and already fully staffed. Could it be done? What choice
did we have?

"I need to speak with someone in authority," I said. "Wait—no,
come with me." I took her hand and headed out into the hall.

I did not bother with any pretense of going to the Director's office.
I headed straight for the real leader of our expedition now, Dagan
Atlabatlow.

He was in a meeting, but I pulled rank and demanded to inter-
rupt him. He came out looking grave and said, "Emissary, what can
I do for you?"

I pulled Moth forward. "Moth has come to let us know that Torobe was directly in the path of the fold rain, and they are in need of
emergency assistance. They have made a request for humanitarian
aid. They wish to evacuate temporarily to the Escher until we can
resettle them in another place."

I had chosen my words carefully. If Atlabatlow had been captain
of a ship, he would have been bound by interplanetary law to render
assistance. Of course, he was nothing of the kind, but I was gambling
that he would rise above his station.

He gestured us into the nearest office and ordered its occupant out.
"You saw the situation down there," he said. "We can't reach them
anymore."

"They will get here on their own," I said, "the same way Moth did.
Don't ask me to explain; it sounds mad even to me. What they need
from us is a space to assemble, where they can be isolated from the
rest of the ship. No observers, no surveillance cameras, no light. We
must completely ignore them, even the ship's AI."

"How many?" he said.

"We're not sure. The upper limit would be five hundred."

"Five—! We can't feed them, or fit them in. It would overwhelm our sanitary systems, our water, our medical . . . And the wayport—"

"They would leave the same way they came, unobserved."

His face was stern. "You realize, don't you, that you are asking me to endanger the lives of everyone on board? The people whose safety is my primary responsibility?"

"It is temporary," I said.

"How temporary?"

I didn't dare let him know I hadn't the faintest idea. I was going on faith that we would be able to improvise something. "Give me four days," I said with serene, but false, confidence.

He looked grim. "I can give you two," he said. "That meeting you just took me out of—the scientists have revised their estimate of when we will encounter the area of spatial instability. Now they think we will hit it in three days."

Has there ever been an expedition so cursed? "Can we get the engines started in time?" I asked.

"That's what we were discussing. Five hundred refugees do not simplify the situation."

"Colonel, if anyone can handle it, you can," I said with confidence. I was deliberately beminding him as the hero we need. I knew I would not be the only one.

His lips were pressed together into a tense line. "We'll have to clear half the residential rings of the ship," he said. "I'll get Lieutenant Devaux on it. You will have to be in charge of refugees."

"I am afraid I will need to delegate that to Sara Callicot. I am hoping to be gone for a while." He shot me a glance like a man too overloaded with emergencies to even consider what I had just said.

Lieutenant Devaux turned out to be a very junior officer, but he embraced his new assignment with the earnestness of someone eager to succeed. Once he had worked out which areas would be easiest to isolate, he showed me the plan and I immediately approved it, impressing on him the need to work swiftly. Moth was getting frantic at all the delays, so I led her to a vacant room and left her alone with instructions to start beminding people at once. Then I went back to the Embassy to consider my next step.

Moth's description of the Torobes' daisy-chain method of transport gave me an idea. Moth can wend from here, and I cannot, but she cannot reach the Twenty Planets because no one there can bemind her. Somehow, she needs to piggyback me into the Ground, and I need to carry her on from there. I need to ride her consciousness over the threshold that is standing in my way.

There is a way that may work, but it is unethical. Even Sara would disapprove, though she is Balavati and they think all rules exist to be broken. I cannot implicate her, but I need her help. So I will have to deceive her.

I told Sara that I had to become blind again, and would need her help. She readily agreed. She was very good at it. I blindfolded myself, and she spun me around, then led me on such a circuitous path that I was soon disoriented. She brought me to a place where the gravity was less than usual, my only clue as to where I was on the ship, then she went to fetch Moth. When they returned, I said to Sara, "You are sure there are no cameras here? No light?"

"No cameras," she said. "There will be no light as soon as I leave."

"Now forget about us," I instructed her. "Don't check on us. I will come to you. If this works, I will not come in the usual way."

She left. I grasped Moth's hand. "Is Hanna safe on board?" I asked.

"Aye," she said. "Breel, too, and the babe. They are seeking the others."

She sounded very serious and adult. Gravely, I said, "It all depends on you now, Moth. I will need your help to touch the Ground. When we did it before, down in the still place outside Torobe, I could do it myself, but not here."

"It is easier for everyone there," she said. "It was our great treasure, and we have lost it."

She seemed about to cry, so I said, "Who knows, there may be other places like it. But that's for later. Now we must save my people and yours. I want to link to you by headnet. It will allow me to share what you—" I almost said "see," since that is what headnets normally do, but I corrected myself—"feel and hear and experience. I won't know your thoughts or memories, just your sensory perceptions. My people would say it is wrong for me to ask you this, so I need you to consent."

"Of course," she said. "Why would it be wrong?"

"It's an invasion of privacy."

"Huh," she said, mystified at our inhibitions. "Thy privacy is of no account to me. Let us proceed."

I draped one headnet over her hair, and then another over my own, linked to hers through a recorder. They are designed to prevent mind-sharing, but nearly every college student learns to disable the safe-guards, and I had already done so.

When I switched it on, I did not experience the usual disorienting moment of double vision, but there was a far subtler feeling of double existence. I was standing both where I was and where she was, feel-ing her on my left and myself on my right. I needed to erase as much as possible of my own consciousness, and inhabit only hers. I used a meditation technique, but instead of concentrating on my own dova, I sought out hers.

She had no extra senses; I was certain of that now. But she did have a heightened sensitivity to echoes, air currents, and temperature, which her visual cortex assembled into a kind of picture of the room around us. I had experienced something similar in the Echo Sculp-ture, when I had "seen" the shape of the cavern through music. To her, everyday life was like that concert. She could tell, as I could not, *that the room we were in was square and boxlike, with some irregular shapes along the wall, possibly storage shelves.*

When I said "go ahead," I was pleased to hear the voice coming from outside my body.

Her attention switched, and I now became aware of a kind of subliminal noise—a fizzing, vibrating sensation of everywhere-energy. It was inside me, around me, but infinitesimally small and quiet. I saw that I would have to dive down into it, turning my outside in. She was listening for something—a rhythm, I realized, then heard it, like waves, but not waves on a surface, like water; that was something she had never seen. They were dimensionless waves of something she interpreted as sound. Like a surfer, she waited for a moment in the pattern, and then dived, and I dived with her.

I was dissolving in a sea of immanence, losing particularity. I remembered Dagget's warning to stay aware of my body—but which body, mine or hers? As I struggled to differentiate, she pushed me away, and the connection was severed. I could feel myself again, but far away. Around me was a fog of prickling particles with beacons of consciousness forming condensations in it. I could clearly sense an urgent call from Orem. They wanted me, yearned for me, and I wanted to go back to them, but not now. I was seeking a quieter call—more intimate, more familiar, more conflicted. It would be a call full of guilt and grief, disappointment and longing. Searching, I found myself mirrored in half a dozen other minds that were thinking of me. I was surprised that I had left a trace in so many lives. But the one I wanted was not there. Could he have ignored my instructions, failed me once again? I cursed my cowardice for not having spoken to him.

I called out with all my energy, and then he was there, close to me, but confused. He had been asleep, I realized. Now I was his dream. I touched him to wake him up, to make me real. His consciousness clarified, focused, and with it I condensed as well, out of that fog of potential existence, into a particular time, a particular place.

The room was dark. He sat up in bed. "Thora?" he said softly, barely a whisper.

"Père," I said.

He turned on a light, and I realized he had beminded me without the blindfold. In fact, I could see in the mirror beside his dressing stand that he had beminded me younger and better-looking than I really am—his image of the ideal daughter, not me. I felt a stab of irritation that he did not know me better. But then, he never had.

"Are you really here, or am I dreaming?" he asked.

"I am really here. And you are dreaming."

"How are you?" he said.

I was grateful that he asked. "I am good," I said. "No longer mad. In fact, I think I never was."

He was silent with disagreement. "You are in trouble again."

"Yes."

"I am sorry I have done nothing. I could not. Circumstances—"

"I understand," I said. "The Great Design must be maintained."

The Great Design of the Vind Expatria, that centuries-long strategy for the betterment of humankind, did not include my existence. I had been an accident, a violation. It was why he had not acknowledged me. And now he never could acknowledge me, after what they had had to cover up.

He heard bitterness in my tone, even though it was not there. "It was not that," he said. "Your name has been in the news recently. Because of the new events on Orem."

"What has happened on Orem?" I asked.

"You haven't heard? A movement of women has risen up, rebelled. It is a religious revival that the men have been afraid to put down. The women invoke your name. They say you came in the guise of a goddess and commanded them."

"So I did," I said, knowing he would think me mad.

"I am glad this is a dream," he said.

"Did you get my message?"

"Yes. It was very odd, but I obeyed. The item you wanted is there, by the mirror."

I went to pick it up. The imbricator looked exactly as I expected, but my own false face in the mirror did not. My reflection was his expectations made real, the ones I had always rejected. I sensed that if I were to stay in this guise, as he had re-created me, I would come to be ever more the perfect china-figurine daughter he wanted, and not the cracked and stained one I was. The thought of living such a falsehood was unbearable. I had to get away.

"Thank you," I said. "Now you may return to sleep. This has merely been a dream."

"And yet," he said, "I think when I wake the imbricator will be gone."

I smiled. Accustomed to enigma, he turned off the light and lay down again. I waited for his breathing to become even, then listened within me for the waves of the vacuum sea. When they lifted me I fell backward into them.

Returning was much easier than going, as I had found before. I searched for that bright, irrepressible consciousness that was Sara Callicot, tugging at it till she did my bidding. As I felt myself emerging into darkness, I concentrated on the imbricator in my hand—its power, its hidden complexity, its purpose. I hoped my beminding would be enough.

I was wearing the blindfold again. I tore it off and ordered the lights on. Sara blinked in surprise. "Where is a mirror?" I demanded. She is not a vain person, and didn't have one, but there was one in the adjoining bathroom. I was back in my old shape, my real one. I was so grateful that I embraced Sara for knowing me as I am. She was very startled.

"How much time has passed?" I asked.

"A day," she said.

It had seemed mere moments to me. We had no time to waste now. I showed her what was in my hand.

"What's that?" she said.

"A quantum imbricator. For the wayport."

"I'll get it to them," she said, taking it.

While she was gone I checked my messages for a response from the refugee relocation program. They were still negotiating with potential sponsors. It was taking too long; the Torobes couldn't wait anymore. I had to think of something else.

When Sara returned, I asked, "How many refugees do we have?"

"I don't know," she said. "You told us not to disturb them, so we haven't. Lieutenant Devaux is obeying your orders to the letter. He is nothing if not conscientious."

"Good," I said, "but now I need to speak to them. Has Moth returned?"

"Not here."

I put the blindfold back on, and Sara led me to the area set aside for refugees. There was a guard posted to keep out the curious, but she immediately let me in.

Refugee camps are squalid and depressing places no matter where they are. This one was no exception, but it was also pitch-black and very crowded. The smell was already foul, since none of them had ever seen a toilet and did not know how they worked; they had been improvising by using the bathtubs. Only recently had they discovered that faucets yielded water. Devaux had provided dry ration bars, but the Torobes had not intuited that the stacks of sealed boxes contained other sealed boxes that contained food. Children were crying from hunger within reach of them.

Despite all of it, the Torobes were stoic and cheerful, making the best of their situation, grateful to be back together again. They crowded around me, asking questions, which I answered as best I could.

They were unable to tell me if everyone was accounted for, since each family was in charge of assembling its own members. A few wenders were still absent but presumed safe. Still, it seemed that the great majority of the village had survived, just as we had on the Escher.

It was added evidence for my theory that consciousness interacted with the fold rain.

I finally found where Hanna and her family were camped, and for the first time met Breel, the baby's father. I could not see him, of course, but his quiet, aphoristic manner of speaking reminded me sharply of his father, Dagget.

"Is Dagget here?" I asked.

"Nay," Breel said, "he left again to seek another habitude. Since our friends failed us, he is trying our enemies."

"Will he be able to find you?"

"Oh, aye. Wherever Songta is, there will he come."

My estimation of Songta went up, to think that she was the one who had been beminding him all these years. He would not be the man he was without her. It was one of those mysterious marriages where the partners co-create one another.

I asked Hanna if Moth were here, but she denied it. I became a little worried, not just for Moth, but for how I was going to return to the Ground without her. For it was clear that I needed to return, and soon.

When I left the camp, Lieutenant Devaux was outside, waiting for orders. I relayed to him some of the more pressing needs inside.

"Baby diapers?" he said, flummoxed. "I don't think we have any in stock."

"Improvise," I told him.

Once again, Sara led me blindfolded to the place where Moth and I had felt the Ground. I was growing as tired as if a day or more had indeed passed, but I could not stop; nervous energy would have to sustain me.

Sara paused before leaving me this time, and said, "So it's true. The instantaneous travel. That imbricator—"

"Will it work?"

"They're testing it right now. Did you get it from Capella?"

"As far as I could tell."

She hesitated, and I wished I could see her face. "What do you intend to do with the knowledge?" she asked.

"Save the Torobes," I answered.

"That's all?"

"I haven't thought beyond that."

As soon as Sara left and I stilled my mind, I felt a strong premonition that Moth was nearby. Did she want me to bemind her? No, I realized, she wanted to bemind me from the other side, to lead me through like a spirit familiar. I surrendered to her, and felt myself pulled like silk through a keyhole.

Once again the void was spangled with points of consciousness, numerous as stars, but I paid heed only to those where I saw my own reflection. I knew now why there were so many; people in the Twenty Planets had been hearing my name again, because of Orem, and those who had known me were thinking of me. I searched, and finally found one I wanted, someone capable of beminding me and trustworthy enough to do it well. I touched her, knowing she would feel it as a ghostly presence, hoping she would think of me.

As in a vision, I saw a dimly lit room, quiet except for the trickle of water and the flutelike call of a griever bird from the garden outside. An ancient woman was meditating on a mat before me. I never would have recognized her face, she had changed so much, but I knew who she was. "Bdiwa?" I said softly. Bdiwa Ral, the cousin who had taught me the discipline of apathi.

She opened her eyes slowly, and did not seem surprised to see me. "Thora," she said. "I felt there was something I needed to do for you."

I knelt before her and took her hand, as I had done when I was young. I felt a deep love for this tiny, frail woman, and sorrow for all the grief I must have given her. "I am glad you are still alive," I said.

"We are a long-lived family," she said. She had always included me, in defiance of the guardians of the lineage. She touched my cheek. "I knew that you would shake them up," she said, and I saw the humor still shining in her eyes.

She moved to rise, and I helped her to her feet. She barely came to my shoulder, though once she had been taller than I. She walked slowly across the room and shoved aside the sliding screen between us and the garden. The sun was setting, and streaks of caramel light lay on the lawn, between the shadows of the huge old trees. It was a beautiful estate, with the cared-for look that only land that has been loved takes on.

"It is just the same," I said.

She turned to look at me. "Why have you come?" She never questioned that I was there.

"I need your help." I explained it all then—the refugees, their special needs, the danger they were in, the precious knowledge they carried. I had not even finished before she was nodding her assent.

"Of course," she said. "What good is a place like this, if it can't help those in need?"

I put my arms around her, something I never would have dared to do when I was young. She laughed. "Your nkida has less power over you than before," she said.

"If so, it is because of these people of Torobe," I said.

At my request she showed me to a private room, then left to speak with the estate manager. I settled down in silence and concentrated on Moth until she stood beside me. I took her to meet my cousin.

"You are about the same age Thora was when she first came to live with me," Bdiwa said to her. This surprised me a little, but when I looked at Moth she did seem older than before. Then I realized that I had beminded her that way.

We spoke for some time of arrangements and needs, but soon we had to break off. "I will return," I told Bdiwa, "but now I need to go fetch my friends. Moth has to stay here." I turned to Moth. "I will tell Hanna to seek you out, all right?" She agreed, looking slightly homesick, but resolute. Just as I must have looked, all those years ago.

I took Moth back to the private room that would soon be filling with guests, and there I left her. This time I did not seek out Sara's *consciousness-point, but went straight to Hanna, who beminded me as faithfully as she had done once before. I told her the news that there was a new home waiting for them. It would be unlike their old home, I warned, and require some adjustments, but the neighbors would be friendly and there would be no fold rain. The news spread quickly through the crowd of refugees.*

Before Hanna left, I told her that if I did not come to her in her new home within a day, she should tell Moth to come help me through. Still, I am hopeful that this time I can manage to touch the Ground on my own, for I have some other business to transact. This time when I enter that strange state of nowhere-being, I am not going to ignore the call from Orem. I am going to return there, and tell them to have courage in their own power.

When I attempt to go, I will leave this diary behind on the Escher. *If someone should find it, you will know where I have gone. I have a new purpose now, with the people of Torobe. I intend to stay with them, and learn from them, and help them ease into their new life. I will try to protect them from the outside world. Good-bye to all my friends on the* Escher. *Do not be concerned for me. I will be all right.*

▶   ▶   ▶

When the news went out that the wayport was working again, the time was almost too short for celebration. There was only a day and a half left, and the engines were not yet working. Security established a first-come, first-served sign-up system for transport back, and soon the wayport was running around the clock. One of the first to leave was Nelson Gavere, ostensibly to deliver important reports to Epco management.

Sara decided to wait along with the engineers, die-hard astrophysicists, and other essential personnel. Eight hours before the evacuation deadline, she broke the seal into the refugee center to see if there was anyone who would need to go by wayport. The area was soiled and littered, but deserted. How many people might have been there, she could not guess. None, for all she could prove. It could all be a giant hoax perpetrated by one insane Vind.

She went to report to Atlabatlow that the refugee problem was solved. As she walked the familiar halls, the ship already seemed deserted. It was odd how homelike the *Escher* had come to seem in such a short time, and odder that she could actually regret leaving it.

Even the security forces were thinning out, she found when she reached their headquarters. No one stopped her from going straight to Atlabatlow's office and leaning against the doorframe. She found him frowning at a screen that showed the evacuation list. When she reported her news, he nodded tensely. "Emissary Lassiter? Where is she?"

Sara held up the small recorder she had found, left in a prominent spot in the refugee center. "If you believe her diary, she's already on Vindahar. At any rate, she's not here."

"Gone?" he said sharply. "Again?"

Sara shrugged. "She's a hard person to keep nailed down."

"We'll search for her. You need to evacuate," he said. "I am putting your name on the list." He consulted his screen. "Be at the wayport at 10:15:05."

"What about you?" Sara asked. "Are you going down with the ship?"

"No one is going down," he said. "If you see your physicist friends, tell them to consult their tablets for their mandatory departure times. Their request to stay is denied."

Sara shook her head at the fanatical devotion to knowledge that must have motivated that request. "What about the engines?" she said. "Can we save the ship, at least?"

"The automated system will start the engines the moment everyone is out. Whether that will save the ship or blow it up, I can't say. That's not my responsibility."

Sara was silent for a few beats, and at last he looked up to see what she wanted. "Colonel," she said, "we were lucky to have you, in the end."

She couldn't interpret the expression on his face. It wasn't a smile, but it wasn't a frown either.

She had some time before her appointment with the wayport, and there was no packing to do because no baggage was allowed, so she went to see David. He was alone in the clinic, tidying up as if for the next doctor to arrive.

"Ready to see Capella Two again?" she asked.

He gave a shrug that expressed more than the usual world-weariness. She realized that he was actually reluctant to leave.

"There's not much for me to go back to," he said at last. "I don't know whether my employers will think I'm a genius or a fool."

From the way he said "employers," Sara realized that he wasn't speaking of Epco. A revelation struck her, and she said, "David— *you* were the enemy agent? You were the one sent to sabotage Lassiter?"

He didn't answer at first. But when he looked at her, he saw that pretense was futile. "To sabotage the whole expedition, if I could," he said.

"Mission accomplished," she said sourly.

"I barely had to lift a finger," David said. "All I did was stop her meds, and all hell broke loose. For a while there, I thought I was a genius. But now I'm not so sure. I just have this funny premonition that somehow, the expedition might succeed in spite of all that went wrong."

Sara thought about that as she walked through empty halls to her rendezvous with the wayport. She had learned to trust premonitions in her time here. But a lot was still riding on what Thora Lassiter decided to do with her discovery—whether she would conceal it to protect the Torobes, or reveal it for the good of all humanity.

In a few minutes—and fifty-eight years—Sara would find out one way or another. She would either arrive back to a Capella that would remember the Iris Expedition as a historic failure, or a Capella transformed by the knowledge that Thora had brought back. Would she open her eyes next onto a world where there were not Twenty Planets, but a thousand?

"It'll be interesting," she said to herself as the technician waved her into the translation chamber.